the
effects
of
light

the effects of light

miranda
beverly-whittemore

WARNER BOOKS

NEW YORK   BOSTON

The Craftsman's Handbook "Il libro dell'arte," by Cennino d'Andrea Cennini, translated by Daniel V. Thompson, Jr. New York: Dover Publications, Inc. © 1960
Upon Julia's Clothes by Robert Herrick in *The New Oxford Book of English Verse 1250–1950*, edited by Helen Gardner. Oxford: Oxford University Press © 1972

Warner Books

Time Warner Book Group
1271 Avenue of the Americas, New York, NY 10020
Visit our Web site at www.twbookmark.com.

Printed in the United States of America

First Printing: February 2005
10 9 8 7 6 5 4 3 2 1

Library of Congress Cataloging-in-Publication Data
Beverly-Whittemore, Miranda
     The effects of light / Miranda Beverly-Whittemore.
        p. cm.
     ISBN 0-446-53329-7
     1. Women college teachers—Fiction. 2. Photography of the nude—Fiction.
3. Photographers' models—Fiction. 4. Motherless families—Fiction. 5.
Women photographers—Fiction. 6. Loss (Psychology)—Fiction. 7.
Women—Oregon—Fiction. 8. Sisters—Fiction. 9. Oregon—Fiction. I. Title.
     PS3602.E845E34 2005
        813'.6—dc22
                                                               2004001647

Book design by Giorgetta Bell McRee

For Mama and Kai,
gat poots in all they do

And so Adam, recognizing the error which he had committed, after being so royally endowed by God as the source, beginning, and father of us all, realized theoretically that some means of living by labor had to be found. And so he started with the spade, and Eve, with spinning . . . [Man pursued many occupations, and one is] known as painting, which calls for imagination, and skill of hand, in order to discover things not seen, hiding themselves under the shadow of natural objects, and to fix them with the hand, presenting to plain sight what does not actually exist.

—Cennino d'Andrea Cennini
Il libro dell'arte
(*The Craftsman's Handbook*)

the
effects
of
light

proof

two girls lie languid on the floor of a room streaming with light. There's a window seat beyond them, but it holds no pillows. On the floor, underneath the girls, is a thick rug. You can tell that the rug is comfortable, infinitely more comfortable than the hard wood of the window seat, so it makes sense that the girls are there on the floor.

Both girls lie with their heads to the right, and their bodies stretch long and lean across the photograph. The far girl is lying on her stomach, her head up and angled toward you, her weight supported on her elbows. Her long hair, full of late-afternoon sunlight, spills onto her naked back. Light kisses down her spine to her bottom, then over the backs of her knees and up her legs into the swivel of her toes. Sunshine glosses her.

The older, longer girl lies across the front of the frame on her back. Her eyes are closed, her right hand splayed across her chest, her left hand spread open on the floor beside her. She's dressed in a diaphanous gown, glowing in the sunlight. She's coltish and long in her legs in ways she's never been since, and her stomach is a small swell of warmth. You can see that her toenails—peeking out from the bottom of her gown—are painted a dark color.

The younger girl has something in her hands, something the older girl isn't aware of. It looks like a picture frame, what the younger one is cherishing, but you can't make out the picture; it isn't facing you.

The older girl doesn't seem to mind. On her face is the placid warmth of an afternoon nap. She basks, trusting.

chapter one

i step out of the car into dust. Just one step and my flip-flopped foot is brown with sweat and air and the dust all around us. Off the vinyl, my knee backs are sticky and help me pretend there's wind here. Only for a minute, though, and then they dry. Myla steps out too and she slams the front door and scowls at me. She goes to help Ruth. She thinks I should be helping too. Instead I roll up the window slowly and hope they unload before I'm done. Myla says she knows my tricks and she's right. Even now, even with trees above us, the sun feels like a huge quilt pressing on my head. Like the stuff that goes in quilts, the insulation, the waffle part. Hot, like you can't breathe as deep as you want. Smothering.

Myla slams the hatch shut. I can tell it's her without even looking because it's her kind of slam: a little angry, but mostly bored and bossy and knowing what's about to come. She wants credit and thinks that no matter how hard she tries, she won't get it. She helps and I stand here. Then Ruth's voice comes, bright bells

across the hot hot day: "Pru, come carry." I close my
door softly and walk around to the back of the car. Myla
already has one of the coolers that Ruth has rigged up
for carrying film. Myla's also trying to put the backpack
on when Ruth says, "There's no way you can carry the
backpack like that while we're hiking. Give it to Pru."
So Myla puts it on my back and I smile at her over my
shoulder. Ruth says, "Keys?" and Myla holds up her
right hand and jingles them in the air. "Okay," says
Ruth. "Good to go." And she hoists the tripod onto one
shoulder and takes off, out of the parking area and into
the grass. The dust billows up, brown coughing air, and
we walk into it. Myla goes last. She pushes me into
place in front of her.

The river air cools us when we walk, but I still feel
hot all over until we stop for a drink. Then I get shiv-
ery. I move out on the rock to the break in the trees. I
lie in the sun and it warms me. Myla comes and sits
next to me and sloshes the canteen in the air. She's
whistling, quiet, humming too, and then Ruth says, "I
know we've been to this part of the river a million
times, but I want to take you guys in a little farther, if
you're up for a bit of a hike. It's only about half a mile."
She's making her voice sound excited so we'll get excited, even though it means carrying everything for a
lot longer. "Oh, come on," she says. "I'm hoping to
work on this one ravine; you guys are going to die when
you see it." She looks at us, squinting her eyes. "What
you're doing right now is beautiful, but there's no way
I can get it in this light. Remember where your feet and
hands are, and maybe we can redo it later on." Without

looking, I can hear her getting the heavy tripod ready for lifting up and balancing on her shoulder.

Myla rolls her eyes. She says quietly, "Like we were sitting this way so she'd want to take a picture." I know what she's saying, and I also know she's right and a little bit wrong. I did come lie on the rock because I was cold, but also because I wanted Ruth to see. Not just because she'd want to take my picture but because she'd see Myla and me together, two girls basking, and think, "I've got to capture that." Then she'd take pictures of Myla and me together, and Myla would still want them. And things would feel the same again.

We catch up with Ruth and she tells us a joke about Kissinger and Nixon and Kennedy on the *Titanic*. I don't get all of it but I like the part where Kissinger says, "Women and children first," and Nixon says, "Fuck the women and children," and Kennedy says, "Do you think we have time?" Myla and I giggle and everything feels laughing and loose. But then Ruth says, half-joking, because she knows our dad swears all the time, "Don't tell David I said that," and Myla says, fast, "God, Ruth, we're not little kids anymore. Pru's ten. I'm fifteen. Remember? I think we can handle a little swearing," and the dark shadow comes back. Then we turn a corner and climb up a big boulder and see out over this perfect place of green and water and smooth rocks. Ruth laughs and says, "Well, maybe it's more of a lagoon than a ravine. What's the difference? Myla, you always seem to know that kind of thing."

"I do not," says Myla, still grumpy. Ruth's already setting up the tripod and stretching the black accordion-paper part of the camera. She gestures me over and opens the backpack, pulling out the delicate lens and unwrapping it softly. She touches my shoulder and says to both of us, "Just put the stuff up there, on the bank. Make sure none of it gets wet." Myla mutters, "We know," and I nudge her foot. She gives me a look but I know she's not as mad as she seems.

Now's the part that always feels strange because who knows when or what will start the shoot. It's like the three of us do a dance around one another, and either Myla or I will react to something in a way that makes Ruth stop and say, "Hold still." But sometimes the things I think will make her excited don't work and instead we'll just eat sandwiches and not take pictures at all. But today I lean over to look at a tiny swimming frog and Ruth says, "Pru, hold it. Myla, can I have the reflector?" and they're both already into place, Ruth grabbing her dark-cloth and shrouding it over her shoulders and her camera like they have secrets, and Myla shaking the reflector into a big round circle of white that gleams into my eye and makes me want to blink. Myla already knows it's too much so she stands back, moves the white to a different angle, and shimmers my ankle a little bit but not much more. Ruth grabs the cooler and pulls out a film holder, focuses the camera, slides the holder into the back of the camera, and checks the shutter. She pulls out the slide, leaving the film inside the camera, and says, "Look here, but just with your eyes," and then cllllick goes the shutter and Ruth says, "One more. This time no clothes." So I memorize my feet in their certain way on the rocks and my hands pressing on my knees and where my hair slides down my cheek and then I stand up and take off my dress and throw Ruth that and my underpants. They get wet when I step through them out of the water, but they'll dry. I get back in place, even though it'll never be exactly right, and look back down in the water. The tiny frog has swum away. Ruth says, "Head down a little," and she's looking through the camera again, the eye of it all the way open. Then she focuses, takes another holder, pushes it in, pulls out the slide, and says, "One-two-three," and clllllick it's taken. Ruth stands up and squints her eyes. That's the sign to let me stand up, and she turns to Myla and says, "Now you. There, where Pru is. And Pru-y, you back there on that rock."

Myla walks up and she's already naked and takes my place and I can see she's proud, proud to be noticed. Ruth says, "Crouch, Myla. Beautiful. Lovely hands," and I take my place back on the boulder and lean my body into the sun. "Arms out, Pru," Ruth calls. And out my arms grow into the air. And Ruth says something funny, something I can't hear but I know it's a joke be-cause it makes Myla giggle. And then Ruth calls, "Beautiful, girls. Beautiful." The sun is on me and I smile. What an easy day to make pictures. I want to stay and stay like this, with Myla in front and me in the sun, me out of focus and happy. Ruth calls out instruc-tions, and for each picture I lower my head, or lift up my arms, or turn to one side or the other. Myla stays the same in front of me, even her back seeming full of joy. And everything is cool and warm at once.

A LATE-APRIL BREEZE SHIVERED across the lake as Kate Scott and Samuel Blake walked at the edge of the water, almost holding hands. These words repeated themselves over and over in Kate's mind as she and Samuel walked beside each other, really almost holding hands. The brisk air had driven most of the students into the warmth of early supper in the dining hall, so not holding hands for reasons of discretion seemed hardly necessary. Samuel wanted to touch her, she could feel it, and though being wanted was not altogether new, what was exciting was the part of the experience that *was* new: Kate's wanting to touch him. Just a graze of his finger and she'd be undone. She wanted to laugh at herself. This was so unusual. What was she thinking?

Samuel had arrived at the college in early September, fresh from a doctoral program in American cultural studies. Because he was new and good-looking, he stood out at the president's reception for incoming faculty. Both Kate and her colleague and best friend, Mark Rios, had designated Samuel Blake as the most likely candidate for the role of new friend and/or lover. Samuel didn't swing Mark's direction—the mention of an ex-girlfriend had cleared up whatever mystery there might have been—so Mark kissed Kate's hand, bowing, admitting defeat. "We lose all the good ones to your side," he said, and Samuel blushed at Mark's teasing. As the evening cooled, Kate, Mark, and Samuel talked and talked on the president's lawn, forgetting the earlier innuendo about who might sleep with whom, the other faculty milling about, and the impending school year, and Kate's body grew warm. It was more than the wine. She recognized within her a small burst of joy; she was relaxing in the company of others.

That had been early in the school year, when it was customary to be full of hope about everything: class enrollments, committee work, departmental politics. By late September the first cool days served as a reminder that time was racing, that no matter how hard Kate worked, she'd never be able to read all the papers as thoroughly as she wanted, to advise all her students as closely as they deserved, to complete as much of her own research as she'd planned. Mark and Samuel and a number of other young hires had launched a Thursday-night tradition informally dubbed "Beer 'n' Pool," but try as she might, Kate was always too busy to attend. For the first time at the college, she felt herself resenting the work she'd made for herself, work she'd previously embraced. When she'd arrived five years before, very few students had shown interest in medieval literature; now she knew she had only herself to blame for being so overcommitted. Students liked her even though she worked them hard; they flocked to her courses and jammed her office hours, eager to speak with the resident expert on valor and courtly love.

As for the role courtly love played in her own life, Kate kept intending to fall in love when she had enough time and met the right man. Until that happened, her friendship with Mark Rios was just about perfect. He was gay, so their relationship had none of the complications of sex, and yet she still had someone to change overhead lightbulbs for her and tell her if she needed a haircut and tease her about not changing the toilet-paper roll. In return, she offered unconditional encouragement for his research and played a mean game of Scrabble. Over the last half-decade they'd established a pattern of passing October breaks in New York City, winter breaks in Mark's modest off-campus house, and Augusts on a lake in New Hampshire. They discussed their childhoods rarely and only in passing; Mark's Catholic family in Maryland had felt betrayed by the revelation of his sexual preference, and Kate referred to her background only in vague terms. She told Mark that her father, an attorney, had died years before, and she had no living family. The past was a subject they never touched, and as far as Kate was concerned, she couldn't have asked for more.

But then there was the panic. One cloudy afternoon in November, Kate opened her mailbox and found a thick cream envelope sporting an unknown return address. Inside was a letter from a lawyer named Marcus Berger. He'd enclosed several flight coupons and referred to them in precise language, urging her to come home. She'd been found. Of course she didn't mention anything to Mark, she couldn't, she simply shoved the envelope into the bottom drawer of her desk as soon as she made it safely back to her apartment. She promised herself she'd throw the letter away, but as the days passed, she found herself unable to touch it long enough to get rid of it. She tried to ignore its dark tug on her mind, the way it kept her awake at night, the horror she felt about keeping secrets from Mark. She told herself that as long as the past was closed, there were no secrets and no problems.

She felt guilty about her silence and knew she'd feel better if she put aside her work for one night and showed up for Beer 'n' Pool, if only for Mark's sake. He'd asked her, somewhat defensively, what was so wrong with Samuel, and Kate knew Mark was irritated by what he saw as her pickiness. The truth was, she could feel herself being tugged toward Samuel Blake, could feel herself springing to life when he waved at her from across the library. She even knew she was dressing for him on Monday and Wednesday mornings, when they passed each other on the path behind the student center, striding to their respective classes. She tried to keep her expectations simple; she'd go to the next Beer 'n' Pool, sit next to Mark, chat with Samuel, and remind herself that life didn't come in huge, sweeping, irreversible strokes. This life, the life she'd chosen, could be simple. She'd just break down her attraction to Samuel into easy, digestible pieces.

But by the time Kate made it to the pool hall in mid-December, Samuel was on the cusp of what would become a highly visible romance with Natalie Cormier, the petite French professor who was obviously a fan of both beer and pool. Kate found herself chatting with a few members of the chemistry department, idly watching Samuel as he held back Natalie's long hair so she could take a particularly difficult shot. It was just as well. Samuel and Natalie left early, and on the walk home, Kate had no problem telling Mark, "I mean, Samuel's a great guy, and yeah, he's attractive, but that's not everything. He's happy with Natalie, and I'm happy for them. Obviously nothing's going to happen between us. So that's that." She didn't know whether to take Mark's silence for agreement, but she more than half agreed with herself, and besides, there was always work to consume her.

And so the snow and sleet and freezing rain came and went. At the end of February, Mark walked into her apartment, beaming, his arms spread wide. "They broke up!" he declared, and Kate couldn't help but notice two rather alarming things: first, she knew exactly who Mark was talking about, and second, she was happy. Mark urged her to call Samuel: "You know, the whole 'cry on my shoulder' thing, and before long, he's crying on your . . ." But it wasn't until the tight buds of early spring had set up residence on every branch that Kate really saw Samuel Blake again.

It was eight A.M. on a Saturday, and Kate and Mark were sitting in their usual spot in the deserted student dining hall. This was the only time all week they dared venture into this student space, but they risked it for the free coffee and good omelets. Besides, early on Saturday mornings, it may as well have been their private quarters; most students didn't show until well after noon. On this particular morning, Kate glanced up from the conversation to see Samuel Blake striding toward her, smiling, his eyes bright. She looked at Mark, who turned and waved, gesturing Samuel over. Then, to Kate's amazement, Mark stood and, lifting his plate from the table, said, "Oh my, will you look at this. I need a waffle. Right now." He left the table, nodding to Samuel as they passed each other. Kate could have killed Mark, but smiled at Samuel as he pulled up a chair. She tried to ignore her own wild pulse.

"Good morning," Samuel said softly, setting his tray

down. Some of his coffee had spilled, leaving a cloudy puddle around the base of the cup.

"Good morning," replied Kate, unsure exactly what to say next. She'd had no rehearsal for this.

"I've been trying to get up earlier on the weekends. The time just keeps slipping away from me. Mark said you guys had this standing date. I hope I'm not intruding—"

"Oh, not at all," said Kate, a little too loudly. She wanted to seem more carefree. "We just eat omelets and talk. Nothing top-secret."

"Okay. So to fit in, I've got to be able to eat omelets and to talk." He grinned, pointing to his plate. "Step one accomplished. What about step two? What do we talk about?"

The real answer was "We gossip." Kate imagined these words coming out of her mouth and felt shallow, so instead she said, "Our research," although this was a stretch. Most Saturday mornings, she and Mark could barely muster the energy for a couple of grunts. She was glad Mark wasn't there to call her a show-off.

Samuel shook his head. "Oh no. I've made friends with the smart kids! The smart kids who actually have careers!"

"Hardly," laughed Kate. "We discuss our failed research, our rejection letters from press after press, all the convincing reasons not to argue what we're arguing—"

"And what are you arguing?" asked Samuel, taking a swig of his coffee. His eyes were zinging into her, blue and sharp.

"Oh, well, I'm not sure yet, actually." She cleared

her throat. She remembered now just what she'd enjoyed so much about Samuel all those months earlier on the president's lawn: his forthrightness. When he had a question, he asked it. He wasn't particularly cocky either, a trait that usually went hand in hand with forthrightness, especially in young male academics. His clarity had caught her off guard. She felt he could see right into her, into her brain, and she was willing to give him access. She changed the subject. "And we talk about our classes—"

"Please don't dumb down the conversation on my account!" Samuel teased. "I swear I'll try to keep up." He held his coffee cup in the curve of his hand, looking down at it, swirling it around. When he looked up, his eyes were serious again. "Really, Kate. I'd love to know. What are you researching?"

"Mary and the color blue. There have always been miraculous sightings of the Virgin Mary, always. While I was writing my dissertation on Mallory, I ran across a number of medieval accounts of such visions, but the timing was all wrong for me. So I made some photocopies about this tiny German village where all these men, descendants of this one family line, keep spotting her. Or rather, she keeps appearing to them. She's been visiting them for millennia."

For an instant after Samuel posed his question, before the words rushed from her mouth almost on their own, Kate had wondered how she'd answer. Revealing her thoughts about Mary felt a bit like speaking about her family, something she couldn't let herself do. The subject was intensely personal, powerfully irrational, and didn't necessarily follow the neat paths of academic inquiry. But Samuel's honesty, his avid stare, had made the words surge out of her. She'd just started blurting about Mary instead of responding the way she usually did with colleagues. Usually she tried to sound both dazzlingly erudite and breezily witty. Now, here, she may have just made a fool of herself. So much passion over something so potentially boring: medieval research!

But then she looked up. Samuel was smiling at her. He didn't say anything. He was waiting, waiting for her to continue. So she smiled back, letting her mind sink into the delicious conundrum of Mary's blue robes. This time she spoke more slowly. "You see, I believe that even *paintings* of Mary count as sightings. Because sight is the sense that experiences two-dimensional art, and sight is the sense with which these men report witnessing her. Both paintings and visions point to an imagined, altered reality."

Samuel nodded. "Wow."

"I know, I know. And get this: everyone, to a person, who sights her reports the piercing, blinding blue of Mary's robes. Blue like gold. English doesn't have a word for that kind of blue. Azure? Lapis lazuli? A brilliant, blinding blue. Nothing like the blue we encounter in our daily lives."

Samuel was leaning forward in his seat. "Mark told me you were smart."

Kate blushed. "Not *that* smart. I haven't exactly got an argument yet. That's my next task. I do have a title: 'Mary's Blue.' I just need to find a damn argument already." She felt herself deflating a little. She needed her full mind to do this work, and somehow, with

Samuel in front of her, she couldn't gather her whole brain together. She felt lost in ideas.

But Samuel shook his head, smiling. "That's interesting. I'd love to talk to you about this some more. See, I've been thinking a lot about the relationship between art and life, about how art informs our lives and doesn't simply reflect the way we live. Wasn't it Plato who said— Ah, Mark! Come sit!" Samuel gestured a smiling Mark back to the table.

Kate Scott, Samuel Blake, and Mark Rios sat together for two hours, as sunlight moved across the walls, and coffee cooled, and the first students to brave the day began to show their sleep-filled faces. Outside the dining hall, before they parted on the path, Samuel asked Kate if she'd be interested in coming to one or two of his lectures. Maybe she'd even consider guest-lecturing on her own idea sometime. Kate said she wasn't sure, and Samuel put his warm hand on her arm and said, "Just come, then. Come and see what you think."

As Samuel walked away, Kate could feel Mark thrilling beside her. All he said was "I guess you've met your match. Doesn't even ask you out. Invites you to a lecture."

And so her courtship with Samuel began. They spoke about ideas: hers, his, those of the great minds of literature and history. They kissed, and they hiked together on Saturday afternoons, and Kate spent less time alone with books about the Virgin Mary. Soon Kate and Samuel were having easy, good sex and spending nearly every night wound around each other in Samuel's queen-size bed. Kate could feel, as spring swelled, a rush of good feeling inside herself, a new hope, a loosening. It was as if she were unpacking her vital organs out of a deep freeze. She found herself unable to remember the last full day she'd spent in the library. She surprised even herself when she asked the seminar she taught if they'd be up for holding class outside, under the blossoming cherry tree, on the first bright day of spring. Meanwhile, Kate visited Samuel's lectures and listened as his voice lilted up to her in the back of the lecture hall. Being pulled into Samuel's world made her body warm. She pretended she was visiting a different life. Samuel Blake kept the reality of Marcus Berger's letter, lingering in Kate's desk drawer, at bay.

A late April breeze shivered across the lake as Kate Scott and Samuel Blake walked at the edge of the water, almost holding hands, on an evening that would surely end in lovemaking. Not just sex but lovemaking, something new. Kate knew that what she wanted now from this man was lovemaking, and yet some dark glimmer in the back of her mind told her she wasn't prepared, wasn't worthy of what could come. Maybe giving her whole self to the act of sex would be crossing an irreversible, invisible line. She'd have to reveal truths she hadn't shared even with Mark, revisit a past she'd hidden from herself.

She pulled her attention to what Samuel was saying about his stepmother's intrusion into the family. Samuel and his brother had been brutal. "I can't believe she endured us," he said.

"She obviously loved your father, Samuel."

He stopped walking. "Why do you always call me Samuel?"

She laughed and started walking again, forcing him to catch up. "That's your name, isn't it?"

"Technically, yes. But you've heard people; they call me Sam all the time."

"Yes, but Samuel has a ring to it. Samuel is beautiful to say, to hold on your tongue." She felt herself smiling at the literal interpretation of her words.

Samuel laughed. "I've never heard it put that way. I like it when you call me Samuel." He put his arm around her, making a warm bubble around their two bodies. "I just don't think I've ever heard someone so determined to say my name before."

"I suppose names just matter a lot to me. They're powerful."

They walked in silence, the crunch of gravel under their shoes, until Samuel's voice filled the air. "And what about you?"

"My name? Oh, very boring. Just Kate Scott. Kate short for Katharine. With two A's." She almost added, "Because I liked that spelling," then caught herself. People didn't name themselves.

Samuel stopped walking and turned to face her. "You're beautiful," he said, brushing her hair off her shoulder, and it was this simple clarity, this truth he could share with her, that made Kate want him in her bed.

They were in Kate's bedroom now and they were kissing. He was still wearing his tweed jacket, and the rough of it was harsh through her blouse. It smelled of him, tinged with a trace of cinnamon and rain, and it made a soft scratching sound between them as they kissed. The kissing was soft and familiar. She knew his tongue already, the warm hush of his mouth as it opened on her lips, the bright smoothness of his teeth.

Samuel looked up and laughed. "I feel like a kid again. In a dorm room with a beautiful girl. About to do something."

"Standard issue," she joked, knowing he felt the shift too, felt the knowledge that this time their sex would feed more than just their bodies. Not just because she'd finally invited him to spend the night at her place; they both knew it was more. Kate gestured grandly around her small dorm apartment. "I figured I was a perfect fit for a house fellow. I'm schoolmarmish, able to make really good brownies for study breaks, and I'm not someone who needs a lot of sleep."

"That's really why you live here?"

"Well." His hands were warm on her back. "I like the students. It sounds strange, but I like the noises they make. Their racket keeps me from feeling lonely." Samuel nodded. Kate was surprised at her honesty with this man, and further surprised that her liking the noises made sense to him. Everyone else, including Mark, thought she was insane for wanting to live in the middle of a dorm, surrounded on all sides by eighteen-year-olds.

Now Samuel was walking to the head of the bed. He pointed to the poster hanging above it and looked closely, blinking in the shadows of the room.

"Mark brought it back to me from a conference in New Orleans," Kate said. "He said it reminded him of me." The poster was a photograph of an African statue, a female nude outlined from the side. She was curved, with hips and breasts and thighs and wide arms. Kate found herself considering the poster from Samuel's point of view, and of course the woman looked nothing like her. But she'd known what Mark had meant when he'd given it to her. He'd meant that this woman was brave and alone, fierce in the world. Kate had so appreciated what it said about Mark's understanding of her that she'd framed the poster and kept it over her bed so she could sleep under it every night. The woman was a dream, an aspiration. She heard herself say: "It's funny, you know? Because he was right. I look at it, and it helps me remember not just who I want to be but who I am. How to be."

Samuel smiled at her and said, "Do you mind if I do something strange without explaining myself?"

She looked at the bed and said, "Well, it depends on how strange it is."

For the first time she saw Samuel flash with embarrassment. "No no no oh God no!" He laughed. "I should watch how I phrase things. No, I just mean about her," and he pointed at the poster.

"Sure."

He shrugged his jacket off his shoulders, then brought it in front of him, opening it with both hands as he leaned over the bed to reach to the top of the poster. He tucked his jacket over the top of the frame, draping and shrouding the African woman.

"Don't I even get to ask?" she managed after a moment.

"Come to my lecture tomorrow and all will be explained," he said as he reached toward her. "You know where it is. Evans 206. Two P.M." He pulled her onto the bed, and from that moment on, there would only ever be a *before* and an *after*.

THE FIRST TIME I EVER KNOW what a picture is is when Myla shows me a picture of our mom. She tells me stories about Mom and how she flies and looks in our window at night and makes sure we won't die or injure our persons. But this time Myla reaches up to the picture on the piano and puts the frame on the ground and opens up the back and pulls out just the plain photo and says, "Pru. You know what this picture means?" and of course I don't know. So I say no and she says, "It means Mom was real once. Only three years ago, before the car accident, she was here. You were just a newborn," she says, "but I was five years old and I remember her. And this picture remembers her. It means she was real. It means she lived on this earth." Then she points to this poster we have in our living room. "And that painting means the painter was real. Monet, the guy who painted that picture? He saw those lily pads on his pond and in his head and wanted to make them real, so he painted them. But they weren't art before that." Then she holds up the picture of our mom. I want to kiss it, but Myla says I'll have to wait until it's back under glass before I do that. "You'll ruin it," she says. "You have to realize it's precious. Once this picture goes away, then she's gone. Then the proof of her is missing." Even though I'm so little that I don't even know what "proof" means,

I know what she's saying is serious. Proof is a good thing to have. And pictures can give it.

ON THE PHONE THE NEXT DAY, Kate gave Mark the usual update, stopping short, as always, before providing the salacious details he craved. She also held back on the way things had changed, about the newness she and Samuel had made together. Even explaining about the jacket, about the way Samuel had placed it over the poster, sounded silly. She didn't know how to tell Mark that she knew it was an important thing to do, even if she didn't know what it meant, or why Samuel had done it.

"So, coffee? This afternoon?"

"I can't," said Kate. She could practically hear Mark's eye roll over the phone.

"Another Professor Blake lecture, I presume?" he said, unable to hide his hurt.

"Yeah."

"Yeah." Mark paused. "I should have made you guys sign a contract promising that once you started doing whatever it is you're doing, it wouldn't disrupt my normal schedule. I mean, I have needs too."

"How about dinner?"

"You sure you don't have plans with the Professor of Love?"

"I'm sure. I'll come over. We'll reinstate movie night. I promise."

Kate hung up and got off the bed, where she'd been sitting since Samuel had gone. Growing aware of the time, she went into the bathroom and brushed her hair in front of the mirror, examining her face. More than once Mark had commented on her natural aversion to mirrors, to the fact that the only one hanging in her apartment was here, built in to the cabinet. She hid the real reason for such omission: her face was a shock to her each time she saw it. It was a shock because it was *her*, the *her* that was the carryover from everything else. And yes, it was beautiful. There was no denying it. Her body had changed with age; she'd become curved, and her hair had been long and short and long and short in the interim, but her wide eyes, the scooped bridge of her nose, her lips that pinked when she bit them, the freckles dappling her cheeks, all that was the same. When she thought about her looks, it seemed strange that no one ever recognized her; apparently people were willing to believe what they were told before they'd trust their own eyes.

She opened the cabinet and traded her reflection for a collection of lotions and creams. She'd cut her finger-nails, and that would give her just about enough time to make it to Evans 206 by 1:55.

Inside Evans, her heels clipped down the echoing hallway and made her sound adult. They sounded au-thoritative, the way she thought she must look from the outside. Kate Scott Kate Scott Kate Scott, they beat out.

The lecture hall was old-fashioned, a relic from the early days when the college had devoted itself to nur-turing the young minds of aristocratic women. Kate had taken to entering at the back, so she could look down on the heads of all the students as they settled in. They clapped down the wooden chairs before they sat, oblivious at first to Samuel's presence at the head of the room, where he was waiting for their eyes. The room buzzed with sound and movement: the swish and scratch of jackets being stuffed under chairs, the crackle of gum being unwrapped, the pock of pens being uncapped, the unzipping of bags, the thump of books on the terraced floor.

Samuel flipped off the lights, and simultaneously a projector burst bright light against a screen at the front of the room. In the first of Samuel's lectures Kate had attended, she'd noted with jealousy the presence of a teaching assistant. Not only did TAs diminish the paper-grading load, they also undertook such mundanities as the turning on of projectors, a task Kate always had to figure out on her own. She'd suffered through more than one embarrassing disaster with in-class slide shows.

Kate could make out Samuel's sharp shadow cast on the screen, and as he walked toward the class, his shadow grew larger and less distinct. Then he sat. She found an aisle seat in the top row and sat as well, glad for the darkness. The whir of the projector contributed to the warmth and safety of the room. She looked to her left and watched the spotlight growing from the booth, swirling with dust and whiteness, then distilling itself against the screen.

When he began speaking, Samuel's voice sounded different from the way it had the night before; it was ten times more formal now, but it still bore a trace of genuine kindness that she knew she rarely revealed

when she was teaching. He gave off an air of trustwor-
thiness. That was when she realized the obvious:
Samuel was like her father. He was like David. She was
having more and more moments like this, moments
when her past was on the tip of her tongue. She didn't
know what to do with this swelling past. For now she'd
try to quell it and listen, for she was Kate Scott, and
Kate Scott had been invited to attend this lecture. With
a great surge of concentration, she leaned forward.

"We're going to be doing something slightly different today, rewind a couple of millennia. Trust me that
this will all hook in to what we've been talking about,
even if it seems off the mark at first. Oh, and though
she wasn't able to be here today, I'd like to thank Professor Frasar from the art-history department for helping me put together this presentation. It's a little out of
my time frame, if you know what I mean." A couple of
girls twittered from the front row; Kate had watched
them gushing over Samuel in the last few months. She
knew they must discuss Professor Blake over meals: his
forearms, how he adjusted his glasses, the way he
tossed his jacket over the back of his chair. She blushed
when she thought about the jacket and the last time
she'd been near it.

"So." Samuel pressed a button and an image clicked
into place. A drawing of a settlement from above, as if
reconstructed by an anthropologist. "Ancient Greece,
about the third century B.C. Give or take. Let's look at
some of the images, the sculpture from that time, and I
want each of you to think about what these images
might do to people looking at them." Samuel was silent
for a while as he clicked through fifteen slides of nude

sculpture, mostly of women standing. Kate could count ten or twelve seconds between each slide, and caught herself in the rhythm of the counting. When he got to the last one, he said, "Okay, someone get the lights," and as the fluorescents came on, everyone groaned at the brightness. "Sorry about that, folks." As the room rustled into activity, Samuel caught Kate's eye and smiled. Then he handed out a pile of images. "These are the photocopied versions of what we just saw up there, but I wanted to give you a better perspective on how powerful that work is in its full glory. Does anyone want to start us off?"

A boy in front whom Kate had taken to calling the Dream Student raised his hand. "I guess what I'd notice first is how sensual those images are." Samuel had no idea how good he had it.

Samuel smiled. "Okay, good. Sensual how?"

"Well, it's not like they turned me on or anything"—general laughter erupted—"but I can tell that they might have had that power. To the Greeks."

"The point here," said Samuel, "is that those images do something to us even now, right? We recognize them as powerful even though they're just carved from marble. But what about them makes them powerful?"

A girl on the left spoke without raising her hand. "They're naked."

"So?"

"So. The naked body is powerful."

"Just to look at?"

"I don't know. I guess so."

Samuel walked over toward the girl. "Go on. I think you're on to something." Then he turned to the rest of the lecture hall. "Why is nakedness inherently power-ful? Why does looking at a picture of someone naked do things to us?"

Another boy raised his hand. "I think it's more com-plicated than that. I think these sculptures stand for more than just plain naked bodies, because someone chose to carve them. The sculptor wouldn't have ex-pended the effort if the statues didn't have a deeper meaning."

Over the past two months, Kate had been consis-tently impressed by how engaged these students were. With the exception of her one 300-level course, her lec-tures were routinely filled with drowsy, unprepared teenagers who were enticed by the idea of courtly love but didn't want to deal with the difficulty of Middle English. She smiled to herself when she realized the sharp, focused intensity of today's class might have something to do with the naked ladies Samuel had cho-sen to project. He had great instincts for luring stu-dents in, getting them excited about potentially boring subjects by dangling something tantalizing in front of their noses. Kate knew she lacked such salesmanship; certainly no such interest had accompanied her stu-dents' discussion of *The Friar's Tale*. Her yearly lecture on the Wife of Bath always assured one interesting dis-cussion, but even that was nothing like this.

She could tell that Samuel was getting excited. His ideas filled him up, literally, like helium inflating a bal-loon. Suddenly he seemed lighter than them all, mov-ing his arms in large circles of thought, nodding with comedic intensity. Even his feet seemed to barely graze the ground. He continued, "Okay, well, here's

the cool part. The ancient Greeks would use image—
and not just sculpture like this, but also paintings—to
aid them in certain things, especially conception. They
believed that if you looked at a picture while engaged
in the sexual act—or even if the picture was looking
down on you while you and your husband or wife were
making love—the picture would instill in the new life
the picture's virtues. They'd hang pictures of beautiful,
nubile bodies over their beds not because, in a modern
sense, those pictures 'turned them on'—this wasn't
Playboy—but because they believed those pictures
were so powerful that making love under them would
create a new life and endow that new life with attri-
butes like beauty, truth, and virtue."

Samuel looked up at Kate and smiled. She blushed
in the sharp recognition of his gaze. He'd asked her
here to tell her something important. He'd covered
that woman in her bedroom because he'd known they
were about to do something powerful, and he'd wanted
to keep a baby from her bed. Frenzy coursed into her.
She flushed with possibility, with knowing she'd been
right last night, that things *had* changed. Here was a
man who understood something about the power of the
face and body in a way she hadn't heard anyone speak
of it in a long time. She was filled with an urge so strong
that she wanted to stand up, tell the students, "No
more class today." To push a disbelieving Samuel out
of the room, into the hallway, and confide all her secrets. The lecture continued, but Kate didn't listen,
just watched Samuel's soft hands move through the air.

She smiled at him from her distraction, from her
knowledge that he was the one. She would unburden

herself to him. He said to the class, "Not long ago, I was talking with a colleague. We were discussing the role that the unseen but beautifully imagined has on our consciousness. Like the Virgin Mary's beautiful blue robes that appear in so many medieval paintings. Like the sculptures I just showed you." Kate felt herself relaxing, joyful.

Samuel continued, "A painter paints something and makes it real to the beholder. But what happens in photography, when an image is captured on film? We are a culture savvy in visual interpretation. We look at a photograph and know that more or less, what we're seeing is what actually happened. And that leads the imagination all over the place.

"This is why pornography works. When you look at porn, you know that somewhere, some woman actually posed for those pictures, knowing it would turn on her viewers." There were titters, but Samuel went on. "This is the power and allure of the photograph: it's personal. You look at a picture of that woman and know she's chosen to share her body with you. This doesn't even have to be about porn. How many times have you looked at a picture of a celebrity and believed it reveals something about them? The photograph is a supposed depiction of the real."

Samuel cleared his throat, obviously waiting for the giggles to die down. When he had the room's attention, it was as if the air were taut, expectant. Kate wondered what he had up his sleeve next. "If you've looked at your syllabus, you'll realize that our next series of readings concerns the Ruth Handel photographs. You may be too young to remember this controversy, but you

were alive when it happened. It's an extremely important episode to consider as we continue our discussion
on art in America. How many of you have heard of
these pictures and the surrounding controversy? Good.
Those of you who've been complaining about the rele-
vance of all that theory I've been making you read,
well, here it is. This is popular culture; a *Vanity Fair* article mentioned the case just last May. The Ruth Handel photographs were some of the first to draw a line in
the sand between so-called defenders of the Constitution and so-called defenders of children's causes. You
may remember that the photographs in question were
nudes of two girls given the pseudonyms May and
Rose. One of those girls is dead. Ask yourself: is she
dead because of Handel's photographs?

"This is a course in cultural studies. I promised you
an exploration into the role that culture plays in deter-
mining our personal, moral, and social responses to art.
In light of that, let's think about the Handel case in
terms of the devastating effects of child pornography.
Can nudity ever be innocent? Yes, of course it can. But
what about the nudity of children in a culture that au-
tomatically associates nudity with sexual availability?
What kind of people are we if we allow ourselves to forget what our culture expects of us? Those little girls
had a father. Those photographs were taken by a
woman who called herself a friend of the family. We
have to ask: What is pornography? What is art? Can
they ever be the same thing? Is the issue of intention
even relevant? Does it matter when tragedy strikes?
One hesitates to place blame on these adults, and yet

where else can it lie? The tragedy and media blitz that ensued . . ."

Kate willed her legs to stand. All around her, the students were rapt, and Samuel, arrogant, compelling, sure of himself, talked on. But Kate couldn't listen to him anymore. She got out of there and kept walking. When he looked up, she'd be gone.

chapter two

the first day in the studio with Ruth I'm still a little kid, only three years old. I'm so little I haven't even ever seen a big camera until this day. Myla keeps looking at David like she's tattling when I want to touch things like the paintbrushes or the heavy black paper boxes that fill up Ruth's bookshelves. Myla doesn't touch anything. She holds David's hand and talks to Ruth. I don't want to talk. I don't want holding still.

Then Ruth comes over and says she wants to take our picture. David comes over too and says, "Remember how I told you about the beautiful photographs Ruth's taken of all those horses?" and I nod like I know what he's talking about, but I don't remember at all. Then Myla and I go sit in a place that's all white with umbrellas and a sheet that comes from the ceiling and spreads all out on the floor. I'm wearing my red shoes, the ones with the holes on top that I can squeeze my fingers in. The white around us makes me blink, and sun comes in the windows and patters our arms.

Myla is holding my hand and squeezes my fingers

hard. "Don't move." She grips me, and then I see outside myself and realize I'm tapping my knees back and forth. I can even imagine how I'll look if I hold still and smile. So I stop and I smile. David comes over and moves the hair out of my eyes. Myla pulls the ribbon tighter and straightens the bottom of my dress and then she stands up again and holds my hand.

Ruth says, "Prudence, did you know my kind of camera only sees things upside down?"

"Really?" asks Myla. I don't understand. I let Myla talk for me.

"My camera is like your eye, except while your eye has one extra step built in, to turn pictures back to right side up, my camera doesn't do that."

"Does it have a name?" I ask.

"No," says Ruth, "but you two can name it if you like." All this time Ruth is bustling outside the whiteness, on the other side of the camera, carrying things back and forth. David is sitting on a stool watching us. "Okay," says Ruth, "I think I'm ready. Now, you guys can hold hands if you like, but you don't have to. You don't even have to smile, as far as I'm concerned. Today we'll just spend time letting you get to know the camera and how you want to seem in front of it. We'll worry how the pictures look later on."

David says, "Thanks for doing this, Ruth."

She smiles. "Play the innocent all you want, David. Pretend you didn't strong-arm me out of depression by promising artistic renaissance." She stops. "But you're right. I think Sarah would want them." It's strange to hear our mother's name in Ruth's mouth. I want to hear more. I look at Myla but she doesn't look at me or even blink. Then Ruth says, "Okay now, Myla, just relax your face. Good." Ruth presses a button and light bursts around us. It sounds loud and looks loud too. She moves us around and around each other for what feels like a whole day, bursting the light on us and clicking the eye in front of her. But it's fun. Myla laughs and David laughs and Ruth laughs.

Even then I know it's a beginning.

SOMEONE WAS POUNDING on the door and the sound wasn't going away. It would stop for a few minutes or so and then the pounding would begin again. Kate heard a voice, but she didn't want to listen, and she pulled the pillow farther over her head. She was a scary kind of hungover; even her feet flipped in a nausea accompanied by a sucking feeling of sickened hunger that made her head spin. She wanted to sleep more, to sleep, only sleep, but the pounding would begin again any second.

She heard the syllables of her name being called: "Kay-ate. Kath-ar-ine. Open up. Kay-ate." The name seemed to belong to someone else, even though it was Mark's voice calling it. She could hear that he was angry. She wondered if there were students gathered outside, hungry to see if Professor Scott had suffered a hysterical breakdown. She smiled in spite of herself. As liberal and coeducational as they strove to make themselves, these former women's colleges couldn't get away from hysteria, its inextricable gender, its derivation from the Greek word for "womb." She raised her eyebrows and tried to make out shapes in the ceiling shadows. That diagnosis wasn't too far off. "Insane" didn't even begin to describe her. Soon she'd have to tell them.

She tried sitting up. The room swayed with her slightest motion, but she had to stop that pounding. She'd have to walk, and it seemed impossible. But she forced herself to stand, to move through the quaking in her hands, knees, and toes. And thinking about those parts of herself made her hum "Head, Shoulders, Knees, and Toes." By the end of the first chorus, she was standing at the closet and had already tied her robe.

She stopped by the bathroom to vomit on her way to the door. It felt good, actually. As a girl she'd always fought against vomiting, even when she had the flu and everyone told her she'd feel better afterward. But now she relished feeling something, anything, even if what she felt was a lurching stab inside. She rinsed her mouth out at the sink and didn't lift her eyes to meet Kate Scott's face in the mirror.

Mark was still out there. He was back to calling her name. "Kate. Kate. Let me in. If you're in there, let. Me. In. Kay-ate." Then pound. Pound. Pound. She opened the door midpound, and he was stunned for a split second; then she saw rage paint itself over every inch of him. "You're drunk."

"No." She backed up to let him in. Walking backward threw her off balance again, and she gripped the door. "Not exactly. Hungover."

"Drunk," he said as he pushed inside, and she didn't know if he was addressing her or identifying her state.

"What can I do for you?" she asked, trying to smile

to keep the room from swimming. She closed the door and gripped the handle, then leaned her head against the wood, resting, before turning around to look at Mark.

"We had dinner plans," he clipped.

"Let's go," she said.

"Last night. It's the afternoon. You missed your class."

"Oh." It was hard to stand. She slid down the doorway and sat propped up against it, her legs sprawling into the room. Then she said, "You should have called."

"I tried to call. The phone rang for hours." Kate vaguely remembered unplugging the phone the day before, in the early hours of drinking. Mark continued, "Then I came over. I knocked. I used my keys but couldn't get in because you'd put up the chain. I threw rocks at your window." He was looking angrier and angrier by the minute. "You'd put the chain up, so I knew you had to be in here. But then this morning I thought maybe someone had gotten in here with you. I made sure your car was still parked in its space. Samuel said the last time he saw you was at his lecture. We were going to call the police. Do you have any idea—"

"I'm sorry," she said with as much emotion as she could muster. All she could remember was the bottle, standing in the middle of the room with Marcus Berger's letter in one hand and the bottle in the other, and something soft playing on the CD player.

"Fuck you," he said. "Don't you dare say you're sorry to me." He started to move toward the door, but she was blocking it, and she wasn't going to budge. He stopped in front of her, crossing his arms. "So you just got drunk." He sounded let down.

"I'm sorry I didn't do something more exciting, like getting abducted or raped or—"

"Why, Kate, why? Why do you *do* this to yourself?"

Kate shook her head, looking at the floor. "I don't know."

"You're going to have to do better than that. For my sake. God, look at you. You're disgusting."

Kate nodded. "I know."

"Don't say you know. Don't let me talk to you that way. Fight back."

"I can't," she said.

Mark was quiet for a while, and she could feel his eyes boring into her. She could feel him discarding question after question, but he didn't say anything.

"Don't you think it's weird that I never talk about my past?" Kate found herself speaking, not even knowing where the words were coming from. She was surprised at how calm she felt. "Don't you think it's weird that I never ask about your family? That we're just existing *now*, that there's no past or future—"

"Speak for yourself," said Mark, his voice gentler. "I've got a future with a gorgeous astronaut. Oh, come on, you can smile. I swear I won't tell anyone." He sighed, and Kate could see his anger leaving him. "I don't know what you mean. I don't know what I'm supposed to do."

Kate didn't know what to tell him. "I'm your best friend, and I've never asked you your father's name."

"My father's a jerk."

"That's not the point. I should have asked. We

should ask each other. We should just ask, and then we should tell each other the truth. We should talk about our pasts and tell each other everything we know, everything we remember."

Mark squatted in front of her, and it wasn't until he touched her face that she realized he was wiping tears away. "What happened?" he asked, and it was soft.

"Nothing."

"That's a lie."

He was right. Lying was normal to her. She didn't know how to tell the truth. She didn't even know what the truth was. She was afraid of it, afraid that all around her, every other person had one real story about their origin and destination. She knew she craved this and she also knew she'd have no idea what to do with such a vision of herself. All she wanted to do was run; she didn't want to have to think anymore. She also knew that even if she could come up with a clear sense of where she'd come from, there'd be no way to explain it to Mark. There was just too much. Too many words. Sobs overtook her.

Mark sat down on the floor next to her, bringing his arm around her back so she could lean on his shoulder. "Was it Samuel?" he asked.

Of course it was and it wasn't. Samuel, and what he believed, and what he'd said, and what she'd hoped about him, well, all of that was unthinkable. All Kate could do was cry.

"We'll figure it out," said Mark. "You know I'd do anything for you, don't you? Rob banks and convenience stores? Enter a life of crime? I'll even be angry at Samuel if that's what it takes." Kate decided to let

Mark have that. To let him believe it was as simple as all that, that her heart was that easy to break, and that Mark would have the power to fix it. Soon enough he'd find out otherwise. She burrowed her head into Mark's shoulder and let him hug her, gently, let him remind her she was herself. She knew, even as she closed her eyes and settled into sleeping, that she was planning something he wouldn't understand.

MYLA AND I CALL DAVID AT his office at the college. She lets me hold the receiver and talk into the talking part even though it's so heavy in my hand. She tells me what to say when David picks up the phone.

"We don't like Leslie," she whispers. So I say it too and then David speaks back.

"You two need to stop worrying about Leslie and start taking care of yourselves."

Myla has her head pushed hard against my ear so she can hear everything he says. "Stop pushing," I tell her and then she pinches me in the arm and whispers, "He doesn't know I'm here. Just repeat what I say." So I nod yes. Then she whispers, "How can you know how great she's supposed to be if you're never home for dinner anyway?" so I say the same and then David is quiet.

"Listen, Pru, I know that Myla's right there, so can you just hand the phone over to her?" I try, but Myla moves away from the phone like we're pretending it's poison. She points to it over and over and mouths, "TALK," with wide eyes, so I put the phone back up to my ear. I can't think of anything to say, though, so I just breathe. "Pru?" David says.

"Mhmmm," I say.

"Hang up the phone and tell Myla we can talk about this when I get home."

Myla breathes on my other ear and whispers, "Ask him when he'll be home and make it sound like you're little and helpless." I stick my tongue out at her, but I still do it.

I make my voice a tiny bit sad. I say, "But Daddy, when will you be home?"

And then he says something that makes Myla mad. "Tell her the daddy trick doesn't work on me. Tell her that you're only four and she shouldn't use you like this. I'm hanging up now. Don't call me back—I have student conferences all afternoon. Love you, Pru." And then the phone is blank from sound. It makes an empty note in my ear.

Myla glares at me, but she can't think of anything mean to say. I want to tell her that I like Leslie, that she smells like patchouli and grown-up-girl things like shampoo and lotion and new clothes. Myla hates Leslie for one reason only: Leslie isn't David. She makes up other reasons sometimes: that Leslie probably wouldn't know what to do if one of us broke an arm, that Leslie sometimes smells like she's been smoking and what kind of example is that, that Leslie obviously doesn't care about our nutritional health because who do I know who makes chicken cutlets *and* mac and cheese for dinner and doesn't even include a vegetable?

Now Myla goes outside to ride her bike around the block. I don't even have a two-wheeler with training

wheels yet, and my tricycle isn't fast enough to catch
her. She doesn't have to tell me I'm not allowed to
come. Instead I go sit with Leslie. She's on the porch
reading a magazine. On hot days like this, she makes
iced tea from a yellow round can and she braids my
hair. We sing all the verses we can remember from
"The Twelve Days of Christmas." She gives me her
bracelet made out of hemp. Myla passes us every five
minutes and glares at us from her bike seat until she's
out of sight again. Eventually she gets bored and comes
and has iced tea too. And then things feel good again. I
know Leslie will go somewhere sometime, away from
me, and I won't know her anymore, and probably
someone else who smells like her and likes the same
things will sit on this porch and be the same kind of
person to me. For some reason, that makes me feel
happy. Because even when things change, they'll be
the same for us, for Myla and me. We'll both of us be
floating, together, with different people holding us to
the ground by our ankles. The air around us will feel
fine. We'll remind each other who we are.

KATE SCOTT ENTERED HER small room in the basement
of the library knowing it would be the last time. In her
five years here, this room with its one lamp and sturdy
old desk—so heavy she'd never been able to move it
against any of the four walls—had been the only home
of which she'd been sure. On weekend mornings, soon
after the first librarian propped open the set of doors to
signal a new day of studying, Kate would clip through

the halls, seeking the quiet. She'd move swiftly past the girls whispering by the copiers, the boy spreading out his papers on a long oak table. Until recently, the research had opened up a sharp clean force inside her that kept her happier than anything else. Heading like an arrow toward this room, Kate would shed her demands on herself, knowing that soon the room around her would lend strength to her brain. She'd grip her key and her hands would warm in anticipation of the clicked lock. Finally inside, she'd descend into the safe depths of analytical thought. Her retreat.

She couldn't help imagining the room literally carved out of the earth, constructed with the spines of books, held up internally by thought itself. She'd lock her door and her brain would at last let go, loosen itself within the cell's cool silence. In this room she didn't need a name or a body or food or conversation. Before Samuel, she'd relied solely on her thoughts, believing they were all she needed. Each weekend they blossomed and made the cold walls pulse with color and sound and ideas. Then, at the end of every day, she'd pack up her books and papers and pens. She'd pack up her mind, cramming in everything she'd discovered, in much the same way she might command a sleeping bag back into its sack. Every time this seemed to be an impossible task, but until Samuel, she'd always managed to do it.

She looked around the room in which she'd found divine comfort. The medievalist was medieval. She knew she'd chosen to study men like Theodorus and Tundal not simply because she admired their minds, but because she admired their lives. These men lived in monkish simplicity, their minds burning with a life their bodies didn't share. But now, looking around the room where she'd spent so many blissful solitary hours, she knew the similarities between the monks and her were more superficial than she'd believed. Those men had been able to leave behind the world, and had delved into their work because of a steadfast and unwavering belief in God. But Kate believed in nothing but the act of work itself, and that had gotten her into trouble. Because it had been easy to stray from this work, easy to be distracted by the likes of Samuel Blake. Medieval monks were rewarded with ecstatic visions, and she had nothing of the sort.

Now that she knew what she was planning, the room felt different, smelled different. The walls were cool, but this time they were nothing more than walls. She wanted to leave the room empty so that no one would expect anything of it. She wanted it still to be hers, and the only way to do that would be to leave it with nothing of hers in it, nothing for anyone to interrogate. Only Mark knew that this room was truly her home. When they came to pick it apart, he wouldn't be surprised to learn she'd thoroughly emptied it.

She didn't let herself think about Samuel, or what he'd believe once she'd gone away. He'd lost the privilege of claiming any real estate in her mind. She'd told herself this over and over again, ever since she'd heard Ruth Handel's name pass over his lips. Samuel Blake was unthinkable.

And then Kate, standing for the last time in her cool dark basement room, realized that perhaps Samuel was unthinkable simply because she had no one to help her think. Perhaps it was the familiar woody smell of wet spring earth moistening outside the basement walls that made Kate long in a deep, gaping way for what she'd been wanting all along: her father's brain. David would have been able to explain Samuel's ignorance and unintentional cruelty in words that she could understand. For a moment she imagined how extraordinary it would be to speak to David right then. He'd been the first person to teach her how to think, yet somewhere along the way, she'd lost him. Lost the thoughts he'd given her. Knowing this, Kate remembered why she loved this room. She let her mind cast back.

David had a room like this in his library too. She remembered the girl students smiling at her when he led her down through the carrels and the stacks. She thought she had to be so quiet; someone must have told her that the library was not a place to make noise or laugh or even crack a smile. So even while David nodded to students and spoke to a passing colleague, she kept her eyes turned as far down as she could and watched her quiet feet passing over tile. This must have been when her mother was alive, because Kate was so small she had to look up to the door handle, and because there was no shadow of worry at the back of her thinking. David was popping in to get something he'd left in his room. She'd probably been strapped onto his bicycle, and he knew he couldn't leave her outside.

Tiny streams of light cobbled down over his desk. She knew it was a desk only because she saw the shape of it, but every part of the tiny room was filled with paper and envelopes and folders and books. It smelled smart. It smelled of thinking and being full of words that made your body grow strong. The light folded over the edges of all of David's grown-up things, of all the things she knew really mattered to him, and it made her long to stay there all afternoon. She wanted to have the words to say to her father, "Sit down and let me watch you work. That's all I want today, to watch." But she knew this was strange. She knew she couldn't even read yet. She knew she wanted these reams smoothing underneath her fingers, she wanted the tree roots curled outside David's window to part the light for her, she wanted to stand inside the smell of these papers and understand what the smell meant. Words. She wanted them to love her.

Sometime then David must have closed the door. They must have strapped themselves back onto his bicycle and left the library behind them. She realized now, standing in her own emptied room, that some people must look at such a memory and think, "That's when I knew what I wanted to do." For her, it was bigger. That was when she knew who she was, her very being defined by the swell of her own mind. Strapped behind her father, hurtling across campus on a spring morning, her hand must have waved through the air, over and over, a physical chant of the promise her life would be. She was the luckiest person alive. She knew the world and it welcomed her.

chapter three

kate was early to her gate, and unlike the man sitting kitty corner to her, she didn't feel like sleeping. She didn't feel like reading either; every time she looked at a book, she recognized the enormity of what she'd just done. She'd left the semester with three full weeks to go, simply walked out on her classes. She hadn't told anyone she was going, didn't even leave a cat for someone to feed. Just left. She would lose her job. Guilt and terror tugged in her when she realized she'd fled her carefully constructed life; at the same time, it made her want to whoop with liberation.

In her bag was a ticket she'd bought with the flight coupons Marcus Berger had sent. The moment she'd heard Samuel utter Ruth's name, she'd felt herself flooding with shock; when she'd heard *what* he said, she was sick with panic. In the past, getting drunk had provided some solace when she'd felt such terror. After each episode, she'd been provided with concrete worries—was she a drunk? did she need help?—and those concrete worries would successfully distract her from thinking about ancient history.

There was a bustle over by the check-in desk, as men and women in brightly colored uniforms smiled at each approaching passenger. How simple all their movements were. The three clerks joked, tilting their heads from side to side, printing out tickets, assisting every distressed and needy flier. They belonged to each other, and what she felt was envy. Who would have predicted that one day she'd be sitting in an airport longing to be a gate attendant so she could feel she was part of something that mattered?

She had twenty-five minutes before boarding, time enough to worry whether she'd done the right thing, specifically in terms of Mark. She'd contemplated asking him to come with her, to leave school behind, to join her in her quest, but she hadn't known where to begin. He didn't even know who she was. She wanted to simply skip to Portland, to see him there, where everything began. See him as herself, and then he would understand.

Instead of offering him an explanation, she'd simply left. She hadn't even said goodbye, and she knew this would hurt him. So she took the two letters out of her bag to read them once again. She'd mail them on the other side, in the other airport, so Mark could have a postmark that would prove she'd gone where she said she'd gone. Maybe that would put his mind at ease.

Samuel—

Did you have any idea who I really am? If you did, if what we shared was just part of some sick game you were playing, then you aren't even worth wasting these words on. If you didn't, then my God, you are the stunningly common combination of intellectual snob and weak scholar. I thought I admired your ideas, but now I can see they're based not on research or on reason but on whim and theoretical notions of how people "are." How's this: instead of expounding on other people's lives, try getting one of your own. Climb down from your ivory tower, and you'll find it's a lot less cut-and-dried for the rest of us.

She put the letter back in its envelope and back into her bag, then turned to the tender letter, the one she'd tried to make as uncowardly as possible.

Dear Mark,

My name is not Kate Scott. My name is Myla Rose Wolfe. I am the elder sister of the Ruth Handel girls, and if you don't understand what that means, ask Samuel. I'm sure he'll be pleased to explain his version of the whole story.

I was eighteen when my family died: my sister and my father, within months of each other. I had two choices: die myself or change who I was. I can't explain it any better than that—I know, me, at a loss for words—but that's the best I can do. I transferred schools and forced my way through academia. I changed my name along the way to the most innocuous, unremarkable one I could find.

I've realized recently that this plan isn't going to work anymore. I'm broken. Until I figure out how I'm broken, I can't be a friend to anyone. So I'm going home, Mark. To Portland, Oregon.

I'm sorry for the mess I've made. I hope you can for-
give all my lying. You're all the family I have. That
doesn't mean you owe me anything; I just wanted you
to know.
  Don't worry.

Love,

Myla

They were calling Myla's row as she folded the letter
into thirds, stuck it back into the envelope for the last
time, and licked the flap shut. She was crying, but the
tears were caused by the simplest thing. She'd written
her name. Her real name. Myla. And now she was going
home.

WE SING PAUL SIMON WITH David, we sing Odetta, the
Supremes, Gilbert and Sullivan, Ella Fitzgerald, and
Louis Armstrong. We sing songs people think I
shouldn't know. David pops the needle down on each
record and Myla knows all the words. She knows all the
harmonies, and she and David teach me to sing the
straight tune, the regular part, so she can make chords
and play with each song. I never get to sing harmony,
except when Myla is at soccer or we've dropped her off
at a friend's and it's just me and David in the car, then
he lets me sing harmony. Then he says, "Pru, you take
it!" and the first thing out of my mouth is singing.
  Bedtime is best, though. Usually we'll put on a

record and dance around the house, washing dishes and sweeping up the floor in the kitchen when it's covered with onion paper and potato peels and pieces of zucchini. I have a little red broom that my mother had when she was a little girl. We keep it in the closet next to the fridge. The record will be on loud, and it will already be nine or nine-thirty even and then David will look at us and say, "It's nine? Why didn't you girls remind me about bed?" and that makes us laugh. He picks me up and helps me put the broom away. Even he knows the bedtime comment is a joke, even he knows all the pretend he makes about being a dad kind of man is silly. He's a dad in all the ways that matter, even if they're not about bedtime.

Then we bundle ourselves upstairs. We take a bath or we just brush our teeth and take our time peeing. Myla always wants us to take as much time as we can before he pokes his head in and says, "You two, B-E-D. Bed. Now." Then we know we've got to scramble into bed if we want a story.

We have a real girl's room. It's the one piece of the house where everything looks the same. All blue and matching, with stars and moons. Myla tells me it's the room our mother made for her. When I was small, this made me feel left out because it seemed our mother hadn't made anything for just me. But then Myla explained I was too little to ever be just me when our mother knew me. When our mother died, I was just a baby. I was still a piece of her. And then after our mother died, I became a piece of Myla, because Myla knew I was still too small to be a whole thing on my own. So sharing Myla's room is Myla sharing a part of our mom with me. I guess I understand that, but it's still hard sometimes to be four and three quarters and not have anything all to myself that I can keep a secret from Myla.

David comes in and sits on the edge of our bed. He tucks the sheets around us and always pretends he's going to leave us there in the dark. But after he says good night, one of us says, "Tell us another one." So he'll breathe quiet and sometimes he'll pretend he doesn't want to tell us. But he always does. And then the stories paint our room for sleeping.

"Once upon a time, there were two friends who decided to live and work together in a yellow house in Arles, France. Their names were Vincent and Paul. Vincent wasn't a very happy man, but he was thrilled when Paul agreed to move into the vacation house for nine weeks in the fall of 1888. They'd work side by side, stretching the boundaries of the work they'd done before this. The work these men did was—"

"Painting!" says Myla. Each night one of us gets to say this, because each night David makes the stories about people who make pictures.

"Exactly," says David, and smiles at us for knowing the answer. "The work these men did was painting. Each day they took long walks in the countryside surrounding Arles, and one evening they noticed a vineyard after a rainfall, radiant with color: reds, yellows, purples. They decided to give themselves an assignment: each would create a painting based on his memory of that vineyard in that exact moment when they'd walked by.

"We can only imagine what it must have been like

for them, working in the same house, using their memories and imaginations to make that vineyard real. Perhaps the next morning Vincent happened by Paul's
studio to find Paul already laying a base coat, already
entranced in what he was about to create. Perhaps that
afternoon, an idea came to Vincent, and he too began to
work in earnest.

"Vincent and Paul became engrossed in their pictures, and worked from the moment the first light appeared, until just after night had fallen. They probably
even forgot to eat. At last came the day when they were
both finished, when they'd show each other what
they'd created. I imagine they did it in the morning,
when the light was warm and soft and at an angle. They
flipped their paintings around at the same moment, released them into the world simultaneously. Then Vincent saw what Paul had painted, and Paul saw what
Vincent had painted.

"Paul had painted the vineyard in the background.
In the front of the picture, the foreground, was a girl,
crying. She was so very sad that it was nearly unbearable for Vincent to look at. Paul had called his painting
Grape Harvest at Arles: Human Misery. The painting was
dark. There was none of the joy that Vincent had seen
on the day he walked by the vineyard.

"Vincent's painting, on the other hand, depicted
women tending the field, working with their hands to
gather fruit. Sunlight bathed the workers. Vincent
called his painting *The Red Vineyard*. The painting was
bright. There was none of the sadness that Paul had
seen on the day he walked by the vineyard.

"And that, for me, is the best part of this story: both

men painted what they sensed. Neither painted what his eyes saw; instead, the paintings were guided by artistic vision. And because both of their minds saw the world so differently, both painted entirely different works of art. That's what made them great painters. That element of listening to their artistic selves is what makes both of their bodies of work compelling, even invigorating, today."

David stops talking and our three breathings fill the room. Then he says, "Does anyone want to guess who these men were?"

Myla whispers in my ear, "Pru-y, you know the first one, don't you? Think. What last name goes well with Vincent?" So in my head I go over some last names I might have heard with Vincent, and then all of a sudden I know, just like Vincent knew his picture.

"Van Gogh," I say.

And David says, "Good." But we can't remember the second one and he says, "You've probably heard less about him, so I'll tell you. It's Gauguin. Paul Gauguin. Tomorrow I'll show you some of his work. But now it's time for bed."

Then I ask, "What happened after that, after the paintings were made?"

"Well," says David, "it becomes a sad story. Paul Gauguin moved soon after, and Vincent van Gogh went crazy. He died. But we have his pictures to remember the way he saw the world when he was happy and working." David leans over and kisses us on the cheeks. Then, like always, he lies down on the floor next to our bed and holds my hand. "Just a little nap,"

he says. He'll be downstairs flipping through papers all
night. For now he's just for us.

ON THE AIRPLANE, SOARING above the Midwest, Myla's
brain quickened with dreams. She was too tired to keep
them at bay any longer, and settled into an unusually
delicious sleep underneath a blue flannel blanket, her
head tucked against the body of the plane. The first
dream was warm and gentle. All she knew was that
there was someone else beside her, pressing against her,
keeping her safe. There was orange light all around
them, and though she couldn't see the other person's
face, she knew he was a friend, knew he'd touch her
and soothe her and keep her from loneliness.

The seatbelt light dinged Myla back into semicon-
sciousness as a flight attendant's voice warned of coming turbulence. Myla tried to will herself back to the
place she'd been, to the soft body of the unknown
other, but she took a wrong turn. She was asleep again,
but this time the territory was much more familiar. She
clenched her stomach in her sleep, as always.

She was near the ocean. It was in front of her. She
could hear the tide moving up and down the shoreline,
and she was running toward it, sure she'd be able to
reach it at any moment. She ran because in front of
her, just out of sight, just out of reach, were Pru and
David. There was always one sand dune between her
and them, and she could catch pieces of their voices, of
their laughter, lilting back over the sand as she
sprinted to catch up. She knew they'd have to stop

soon, because the ocean was just up ahead, just out of sight. It was only a question of catching up. Then she realized darkness was falling, that soon she wouldn't be able to rely on their footprints to guide her. So she called their names. She stopped at the top of the next dune and called to them, her hands around her mouth, listening for a response. And then, somehow, she just knew: they were gone. They'd left her. They'd simply disappeared. She started to panic. She told herself that all she needed to do was get to the ocean and she'd find them. But when she listened for the ocean, it too was gone. There was nothing to run toward. There was nothing to want. All around her there was only sand, miles and miles of sand, and the darkness was coming fast.

AT THE END OF THE SEMESTERS, David invites his classes over for dinner. It's a nice thing he does for them, without their parents near them, and Myla and I are in charge of putting out the food on the tables and making sure each bowl has a serving spoon. It's called a potluck, but sometimes David calls it a groaning board because the table is like a board that's groaning with all the heavy food.

This time it's spring. We set up the table inside, but everyone takes their paper plates and napkins and goes and sits in the backyard. The students smell our rose-bushes and sit in the folding chairs that Myla and I put into circles before they came over.

The class is big, all freshmen. I get confused by what

order the years go in, but "freshman" is easy to remember. I memorized the name of this class because
Myla taught me how to sound it out, off David's syllabus, the one that's been sitting by our telephone all
year. This is the Freshman 101–102 Survey of Art History, and the students have been together all year so
they're probably all friends. David invites all the other
teachers who helped him to come too, so Mr. Chang
brings his son, Frankie, to hang out with Myla and me.
Frankie's all right, but he wants to hold his dad's hand
the whole time. So I walk around and watch the students' eyes, see the way they look at me and want to be
my friend. Other teachers come, all the boring men
who have offices on David's hall. And then a lady with
funny hair and Ruth too.

I don't even notice that Myla is alone with Ruth and
talking to her until one of the girl students says to me,
"It must be cool to grow up on campus."

I say, "Well, we don't live on campus, you know."

And she nods and says, "I mean, hanging out on
campus. Getting to know all the profs." She pops a potato chip into her mouth and points at Ruth and Myla
standing by the roses. "Getting to know them like
they're real people." Then her friend comes up and
doesn't really know how to talk to kids. So I leave
them. I go to Ruth and Myla's conversation.

When I get there, they stop talking. Myla smiles at
me like she and I aren't the same right now. Ruth says,
"Hi, Prudence."

"You can call me Pru," I say.

"Hi, Pru," she says. "We were just talking about
those pictures I took of you two." The pictures seem so

long ago that it takes me time to put myself back in that day.

Myla says, "You know, Prudence, the pictures in Ruth's studio?" I glare at her. She shouldn't call me Prudence. I can tell she's only using the word "studio" to show off.

"I know," I say. I put my hand on a rose leaf and wait to see if the edges will slice.

"Well," says Ruth, "I don't know how you'd feel about this, and I need to talk to your dad about it, but I was thinking, if you guys want to, we could take more pictures sometime." She pauses. "You see, for a long time I've been taking pictures of horses! Imagine that!"

"Horses are beautiful," I say.

Ruth looks at me. "Yes, they are." She smiles. "But honestly, I'd also like to take pictures of you."

"Cool," says Myla.

"Yeah," I say, "that would be fun, right?"

"Well," Ruth says, "we'll have to see. With you two, I'd like to do a mix of portraiture and more figurative work—I'm sorry, I must be talking over your heads a little—"

But Myla is fast. "We know what those words mean," she says. "Our dad uses those words all the time. 'Portraiture'—that's your portrait. 'Figurative'—that's more about the body." And Myla takes my hand and holds it hard. She looks at me and smiles. "Let us know, Ruth," she says, almost like a mom. "We'd love to work with you sometime." And then David calls us in for cake.

proof

two girls stand side by side. The older one is taller, and her frame fills the right side of the photograph. Her shoulders are square to the camera, her chin level, her eyes piercing. Her hair is pulled back, but messily, and loose strands frame her face. She's wearing a sundress, and the strap over her left shoulder has slipped, so it rests loosely around her forearm. The other strap, on her other shoulder, is taut.

The younger girl is shorter, but it's obvious she doesn't want to be. Her neck and chin are stretching into the air, and she's managing a sort of smile in the midst of all that pushing. Her hands rest on her hips, giving her further purchase with which to extend up into air. She's nude with the exception of a pair of white cotton underpants. She is also soaking wet. Her hair, loose and dripping, sends rivulets of water down her stomach. Each water bullet leaves a pathway behind it, a traced history of its travel down her. Her clavicle and navel bud with wetness. Her underwear is nearly transparent, showing the vague outline of her lower belly and her pubis. In milky patches, the underwear sticks to the contours of her skin.

You notice the obvious juxtapositions: older to younger, taller to shorter, dry to wet, dressed to naked. And then you look up. Above the younger girl's head is sky, and in the midst of it, the outline of an unplanned bird, caught in midflight. It soars above her, in that space she cannot yet reach but is desperate to achieve. You see it, but she does not.

chapter four

the sky was clear around Myla's plane as it swooped over the southeastern slice of Washington State. Oregon spread out and out on her left. Only a few clouds ranged over the dry grassy spread of land. Everything was brilliant from above, a sun-bright afternoon of straw-colored land stretching into more straightness. And then, just when the grasses seemed to have pledged a monotonous eternal ownership of the land, touches of green began to show, so slowly that at first they seemed imaginary. As the land came closer and closer, green gave way to lush, dark wetness.

Then Myla realized she hadn't been looking straight out the window, only down. Because when her eyes met with the outside, she caught Mount Hood out her window, gleaming and snow-covered. So close was the airplane to the mountain's point that Myla believed she could touch it; in fact, it seemed as if only the window was keeping her from forcing her arm into the atmosphere and raking her fingers down the mountain's white face. The sun gleaming off it made her want to sneeze.

She craned her neck to look down and caught a glimpse of the blue band of the Columbia ribboning against the blanket of green. Things were getting closer and closer every minute. The Columbia curled and waved and caught sharp points of light that made squinting the only way to see. Soon she caught the gleam of Multnomah Falls, a little wave to her of white in the now nearly black darkness of Pacific rainforest. She had to keep her hand over her mouth as they skipped over Crown Point. She could even make out the little visitors' center. It was too far away to make out people.

As the plane continued to descend, she noticed the highway, then the cars. Far off, she made out Portland. Sinking into the Portland afternoon, she could already anticipate the warm, moist air springing around her once she was outside. She wasn't even here on the plane, she thought. She was there, down below, waiting for her body to join her. She knew now that she hadn't ever been anywhere else. Her mind had been here all along. If only her body could be convinced. If only her body were willing.

EVEN THOUGH EMMA IS ONLY two and a half and I'm five and a half, Emma's my best friend. If sisters were allowed to be best friends, then maybe I'd say Myla was, but sisters don't count, and it's easier to be friends with someone three years younger than you than with someone five years older. Especially when the older person is Myla. I think Emma is my best friend because I've known her since she was a baby, and that means we can trust each other. Also, I can boss her around the way Myla bosses me.

Emma's favorite game to play is Dogs, and we play it under the rhododendron bush in my front yard. If we're over at her house, we make a fort in her room, under the old crib where she doesn't sleep anymore. She's always the baby dog, and she's also in charge of making some of the stuffed animals talk. I'm the mother dog and I take care of all of them.

One time Myla comes up to the rhododendron bush. I can tell she's watching us, but I pretend to ignore her. Finally she says, "Emma's only two, you know. You can't expect her to do everything in the game."

Emma starts barking at her, and it's funny because Myla doesn't pay attention to how smart Emma is. Emma just keeps barking until Myla rolls her eyes and goes and sits down next to the babysitter, Leslie. Myla's bored, I can tell, and bossing us seems like fun. But Emma doesn't let her win, like I sometimes do, and I like that. Emma guards our house, just like a dog would, just like I'd tell her to if she didn't know how. We might be three years apart, but we fit. And secretly I wonder if Myla's kind of jealous. There just weren't as many kids around when she was little like us.

Another time when I'm over at Emma's house, we decide that we should make Emma look more like a dog. So I take markers and put a nose and whiskers on her face.

Then Myla comes upstairs. As soon as she sees

Emma, she says, "You two are going to be in big trouble. Jane is going to freak out when she sees what you did to Emma."

But then when Jane comes upstairs, she just laughs. I can see that Myla is crossing her arms in the corner of the room and watching to see us get it, but Jane's not really that mad. She says to me, "You're so artistic, Pru. Look at our little puppy. But next time, why don't you draw on paper instead?"

Then Jane picks up Emma and holds her on her hip, and Emma nuzzles like a real puppy into Jane's neck. I watch them and I want something, but it isn't Myla and it isn't Jane and it isn't Ruth or even David. I know it's silly to think I want my mother—because I barely met her anyway, so how can I remember what she felt like—but I think that might be it. I miss her, and she was barely there in the first place. Missing her makes a hollow place inside, one I can't ever reach by myself.

MYLA'S RENTAL CAR WAS SHINY, red, and small. The woman behind the counter asked if she needed any maps, and Myla hesitated, then said no. It had been thirteen years, but she knew exactly how to get around. The air around her jumped with possibility.

First of all, things smelled better than they did back east. Walking to her car, she could almost taste the wet in the air, the way she might hear a beehive buzzing with sound. That was the way the earth smelled, full and busy. There was no rain in the sky now, but it was always lurking, as clouds swifted over the airport, moving from the ocean inland, over Myla and over the city. She'd forgotten how quickly the weather changed here; hail one minute, brilliant sunshine the next. Or this. Quick-moving clouds.

The trees planted in the median of the parking lot were newly, scandalously green, a green that seemed plastic. But here they were, leaf buds fluorescent in their greenness. She pinched a new green curl between her fingers, and the moist rankled her taste buds as she unlocked the car door.

Once she was on the road, it was easy to hurtle toward the city, easy to see the metaphor of moving toward one's future. She listened to the hum of tires as she turned from one highway to the next, moving into the center of what was once her life. She'd left the East Coast as Kate Scott, but she was here as Myla Wolfe. She felt the three thousand miles between her and the Kate Scott she'd left behind growing larger and larger with each inch she covered. She was moving toward hope, and the journey was quick.

Myla couldn't stop the cry, the stab of wonder, when the road curled up a small hill, then evened out so it paralleled the Willamette River, with Portland laid out just on the other side. The buildings were beautiful and wet and glistening. This city was more alive than she'd imagined. It was smaller too, and she unrolled her window and let the fresh spring wind whip in to wet her hair and lips and hands. A stream of cool water jetted up from her tires, rooting up the damp left in the macadam by an early-morning rainstorm. She was suspended on the bridge now, driving toward the city, crossing the river. She relished this second, and it was the first honest thing she'd relished in an uncountably long time. It was delicious, this moment, a perfection. Going and not yet there. Things were getting bigger, but she wanted to hold on to *now*, on to this moment of plans, possibilities, unexplored ideas. Now there was a goal. She was driving into this place, she was pushing into it, she would bore into it, find what she'd buried, and carry it out into day.

WORKING WITH RUTH IS WORK, there's no question about that. Even when we're over at her house just to have dinner or pick up an article David wants to read, being with Ruth is still a working thing. But it's funny too, because in the beginning we just hang out. First Myla asks Ruth about her boyfriends. I think it's boring, but Myla always asks questions like: "So how old were you when you met John?" And then that starts it off. The two of them in the kitchen brushing each other's hair, and talking about dates and kissing and holding hands. I usually color in the living room, where I can sit on my knees at the coffee table and be far away from their talking.

The good part is that sometimes Ruth talks about making pictures. She shows us things. Like when she let us look at the ground glass on the back of the eight-by-ten camera, where the pictures show up upside down. I saw the pictures right away, all clear. An upside-down chair and an upside-down Myla sitting in the chair. When Myla looked—after stomping around all rude because she wanted a turn—at first she couldn't see anything because she was looking *through* the glass, not *at* it. Ruth had to get under the dark-cloth with her and show her how to see. And when she finally saw me in the ground glass, she acted like it was no big deal. I knew she was mad because she needed help to see and I didn't. But what I wanted was to be like Ruth, who told us that even though it's supposed to be easier to make a good picture if everything is upside down because then you just see lines and shapes and colors, she can't do that anymore. She's been looking at the ground glass for so long that everything on it is turned right side up.

When it's a shoot, it's hard work but it's fun. Myla calls Ruth "The Queen of Inspiration" because that's what Ruth becomes. We'll be there in the afternoon, sitting and painting, drinking tea, listening to Mozart's *Requiem.* Then all of a sudden Ruth's eyes work a different way. She'll be looking at my arm one minute, and I'll know she's thinking it's just my arm, and then the next minute I can see her looking at the shape of it, how it moves, what muscles in it work what way. And then she says something like, "Pru. There. Don't move." And she goes and gets a camera, sometimes the thirty-five-millimeter, or if the light is right, it'll be the eight-by-ten. Then it's like her mind has power over her whole body, and she won't get tired. She'll work until there's no more film. She'll work until there's no more light. She'll work until Myla or I finally open our mouths and say we're hungry or bored.

I like it. I like sitting there before the shoot, telling jokes. I like it when David leaves us there so he can get some work done. Ruth lets us eat whatever we want, even if it's chocolate at eight in the morning. She says it's her job to spoil us. But she doesn't spoil us either. Because she opens us up to how big her work is, to how tired it can make you, to how good it feels to have it and the missing of it when she has to put it away for the night.

After the afternoons, she'll make us big pasta dinners with pesto and garlic bread. David comes back from the college and has a glass of merlot. They talk and talk until Myla and I crawl out to the living room and lie on Ruth's pillows on the floor. And then the next thing I know, David is heaving me onto his shoulder and saying, "School tomorrow." And then I watch Ruth over his shoulder as he carries me to the car. School tomorrow means five days until the next time we come, and sometimes that seems forever.

chapter five

myla believed that if she didn't go directly to the source, she'd find herself floating. At least someone had called her here, and even though she'd never met him, and didn't know for certain what he held for her, she knew this lawyer, this Marcus Berger, was the place to start. So she placed a call and was surprised when Marcus Berger answered the phone, surprised at his straining vocal quality, so like a teenage boy's, surprised at his lack of surprise when she announced she was in town. He suggested she come immediately.

The office was in a neighborhood Myla had always remembered as poised on the cusp of being cool—cool, that is, in the eyes of daughters of college professors and the girl students who took care of them. So it wasn't such a surprise when, searching in vain for free parking, she witnessed flocks of yuppies with their strollers and cell phones herding through store after store. Stores with Italian names and designer dresses, stores with thirty-five-dollar candles in the windows, stores selling angular, uncomfortable-looking shoes ("Two pairs for

$99!," although Myla did have to remind herself that this was considered cheap these days). Was it inappropriate to feel old at the age of thirty-one? The drive up and down Northwest Twenty-third was slow. None of the pedestrians seemed to know what a crosswalk was, so she read the names of the shops: Urbino Home, Slang Bette, Mama Ro's. Like a poem.

She found a side street with parking, a minor miracle, and backed into a space. On the opposite side of the street, nestled between two ostentatious Victorian houses patinaed with color like well-manicured toenails, she saw what looked like a halfway house. Stretching around the two monstrosities were large, white, disinfected porches, porches that disregarded dirt and the outdoors in general. The halfway house, on the other hand, was small and dark, and Myla imagined it was filled with flora and fauna. It was tropical in its promise. Two old men in flannel shirts smoked on the stoop.

Up until this moment, she hadn't really allowed herself to contemplate the reason Marcus Berger had contacted her; or perhaps more precisely, she hadn't let herself imagine the identity of his client. But now Myla realized that all along she'd assumed the client was Ruth. As far as Myla knew, no one had seen or heard from Ruth Handel in thirteen years. But now, here, it was thrilling to imagine that Ruth had orchestrated this. That she was the "unnamed client" who'd provided the flight coupons and summoned Myla to this meeting. It would mean she was alive. That she'd survived. It would mean Myla would get to see her.

Still, if Ruth were to present herself alive, there'd be

all sorts of problems. Issues needing to be addressed, conversations. If Ruth were sitting upstairs . . .

Myla opened the car door then and let the Portland of her childhood rush in to greet her. It still seeped. The glorious rain, a permanent wet that thoroughly soaked into hedges and tires and sidewalk cracks, was strangely surreptitious: when she leaned down to press her hand against the sidewalk, her palm came up dry. And yet moss edged every asphalt and concrete crack, tingeing the world with green. This was seepage. It was an old wet, deeper than the surface. It made you moist inside your heart, made your insides warm as rotting, mottled wood.

It started to drizzle, and she looked up and saw tiny bits of wet gleaming down on her. She felt them pattering on her hand, weightless, translucent. It could rain here for days, and you'd never feel the wet as something distinct from the whole vast dampness of the world. You were never that separated from the ground and its constant pull on sky. The sky spilled and made it all—the ground, the city, the people— deeper and greener with each passing day. She felt like a little girl again.

All that wet outside her made her realize she was intensely thirsty, longing for a long draw of water down her throat. She hoped the building would have a drinking fountain. She focused on her thirst—an easy need to meet—to avoid thinking about Ruth.

Marcus Berger's office was on the third floor. He buzzed her in from the street and was waiting outside his office door when she walked up the stairs. She shook his hand and soon realized there was no drinking fountain and no Ruth. Upon Myla's request for something drinkable, Berger brought his guest a cup of lukewarm water from the men's bathroom. This left something to be desired. They settled into chairs side by side and angled toward each other. She'd expected him to be sitting behind a desk, and she was glad she'd spoken to him on the phone; otherwise the shock of his youth might have been laughable. She liked him immediately, though she wasn't about to admit it.

With no sign of Ruth, Myla felt bitter, disappointed. She hadn't let herself admit how much she'd been hoping to see Ruth again. Meanwhile, Berger crossed his legs. "If you wouldn't mind, let me explain myself. My client has hired me to transfer into your hands certain items that are rightfully yours, legally yours. My client wishes to remain anonymous, so I'll be unable to answer any questions about who or where he or she is." Myla felt a stab of sadness; perhaps Ruth simply didn't want to see her. She nodded for Berger to continue.

"In any case, my client has instructed me to transfer one item in person if at all possible—*my* person, I mean," he added with a nervous smile. "Which is why, of course, I asked you to come all this way. I myself am not privy to the contents of the envelope. It's been sealed for just about thirteen years." He stood and walked to a file cabinet, pulled out a file folder with a manila envelope inside, and brought the envelope back to her. He kept the folder for himself. The envelope was heavy with paper, and she could feel the metal spine of a spiral notebook inside.

"Now, before you open it," he continued, "I've been asked to read you this letter: 'I've been holding this for you. Your father asked me to wait until you were ready. Each day passes more quickly than the last, but that doesn't mean our past gets any further away from us. Which is all to say: I don't know if you're ready, but I do know it's time. Thirteen years have passed. Extend yourself. Perhaps you'll get some answers.'" Berger looked up and smiled. "So. Any questions?"

So many. Did this mean Ruth was alive? The note didn't necessarily sound like Ruth, but what did that mean, anyway? Myla hungered for thousands of answers, but she couldn't frame a single question. Suddenly the immensity of what she faced hit her. She was exhilarated and also exhausted: in one instant she'd left behind everything that had kept her safe for years and had headed straight back into the unknown. Was she ready for this? Obviously Ruth, or whoever was orchestrating this—it could be someone else, she reminded herself—thought she was. "Extend yourself," the letter said. She'd left the East Coast precisely because she needed to learn how to stretch beyond herself, and this letter read her mind. This made her want to touch it. "Can I see that?" Her hand reached for the paper.

"No, I'm afraid not." He drew back. "One of my client's conditions."

Myla could see through the paper that the note had been written by hand, with black ink. Berger noticed her glance and placed the paper quickly back into the file folder in his hand.

"So this is it? Whatever's in this envelope?" She fingered the package, her heart sinking a bit. Not heavy enough. Bound. Not what it could have been.

Berger shook his head. "The client's condition is that I may read you this letter"—he tapped the folder—"and you can draw any conclusions you want from that. But unfortunately, *I* am unable to answer that question."

In the midst of all this frustration, Myla knew the plan had worked. She was here, wasn't she? And she was tantalized. She was itching to know what was in the envelope, even if it wasn't what she'd initially hoped for. Her palms were greedy for it. She asked Berger to read the letter again. He read it twice.

She asked him, "Must I open this now?"

"You can open the envelope whenever you want to. It's just in my charge to make sure you have it in your possession. After that, you can do whatever you'd like with it." He smiled at her, obviously relieved that he could do something she wanted.

"Well, thanks." She stood. "Until we meet again?"

He shook her hand. "Let's be in touch."

The light outside was brighter than she'd remembered. Her hands trembled against the envelope. She was distracted by the world outside, by being swept up into a movement, like a Mozart piano concerto that would guide her, ineffably, toward beauty and completion. It was a feeling she hadn't experienced since walking these streets with Pru on one side and David and Ruth on the other. The envelope made a smooth bundle under her fingers. She was hugging it, she noticed, all the way to the car.

SOMETIMES I LIE IN BED ON Saturday mornings and I watch the sun play on the ceiling, through the shadows of the branches. And it's funny when you lie like that because all sorts of thoughts come into your head, and you're not exactly asleep but you're not exactly awake either. Those are the moments I think about my mother.

Her name is Sarah, but I wouldn't call her that if she were alive. I think I'd call her Mama, because I like that better than Mommy, which is too baby. I'm five, not a baby. And I like it better than Mom, because Mom isn't soft. "Mama," I'd say, "let's go for a walk," and she'd probably take me on one. I'd hold her hand and it would be soft. And Myla would still be asleep in bed and David would be grading his papers and there'd be this whole good feeling around our house, like the smell of bread when it's baking.

She's dead, though, and I don't even remember her. I was two months old when another car crashed into hers. She was driving back from her writing group. Myla showed me the road once, but I got it all mixed up in my head, and the next time I asked her where it was, she got mad at me. The truth is, it really isn't so bad. Myla told me once that she could still see our mother's face and that made it even worse, remembering what you couldn't have. I think she might be right. On Saturday mornings, I wish for someone I never had. But then we all wake up and suddenly there's a plan, and then my family does something together. That makes me forget all about the hollow piece inside me.

The truth is, I may not have a mother who is more than a picture, but I know I have a family. David and Myla—they're related to me, they're what people ask about when they say, "How's your sister?" or "What time is your dad picking you up?" But one day David sits me down and tells me I'm lucky because I have more family than just the people I was born to.

There's Ruth. She's nothing like a mother and she's nothing like a big sister. But that's nice because she's a third thing. She's an artist. By being that, she helps us as much as mothers who do dishes, or fathers who fix the gutter, help keep a family going. She lives in a different house, but we can always come over, anytime we want. She said so.

Then there are Emma and Jane and Steve. They live in a different house too, but not the one Ruth lives in. Emma's my best friend but she's like my sister. And Jane's like a mom, and even though she's not my mom, I let her put me in the bathtub and I let her tell me when I'm being rude and I let her tickle me until I have to pee. Steve's like a dad, but he's not my dad. He's also David's best friend, and they sit in the living room and talk for hours about pictures and ideas. Sometimes Emma and I fold them hats out of newspaper and make them wear them when they talk.

We have dinner at Emma and Jane and Steve's every single Friday night, when it's raining, and when it's heat-wave hot, and when there's snow on the ground. You could say I look forward to it, but that's a dumb way to say it. The thing about family is that you aren't supposed to look forward to them; they aren't supposed to make you excited the way a big surprise would. That would mean you don't know them very well. When David and Myla and I go over there on Friday nights, we know we belong. We can take whatever we want out of the fridge and we can wash the dishes in the sink. Emma and Jane and Steve expect us there, and when we drive up, we don't even have to knock.

I'm lucky. I'm my family and their family and Ruth's family too. And each lets me belong.

MYLA DROVE TO THE COLLEGE. Her body led her even as her mind wondered if everything was happening too fast. She hadn't been here even a day. Was she ready for what this collision with the past could do?

But then she saw the stately Georgian buildings, peeking out from behind the trees. The lawns, green-felt heavens for the college dogs playing Frisbee with their owners. The library, a stone tribute to Gothic architecture. She could dissect each spot, remember it, and in doing so, make the going back manageable. She was walking into a past time, but she was braced, and so it didn't tilt her. If anything, being on campus called up more immediate feelings of guilt about leaving Mark and the other college three thousand miles behind. Mark was probably sick with worry. She'd sent both letters Express Mail from the post office, to get them out of her hands, to get them to their destinations quickly so Samuel would know she wanted nothing to do with him, and so Mark would know, finally, who she was. As far as she was concerned, after a cross-country flight with the letters in her bag, they couldn't get back to their designated recipients fast enough. Those slim envelopes weighed too much for her, the information in them too much to handle alone. She couldn't bear to

think of Samuel. She felt ashamed for running away
from Mark. The sooner he got his letter, the closer he'd
be to understanding what had happened, and the closer
she'd be to getting him back. For in all this new
strangeness, she wanted to call Mark. She needed him
to root her in the world. She dreaded their coming conversation—he'd be justified in feeling terribly hurt—
but that didn't keep her from longing for his presence.
Especially now that this mysterious envelope was waiting like a patient but needy child in her passenger seat.

The grass here at the college glowed nearly neon.
David had always advised, "Don't roll around on that
grass. Full of chemicals," and so, naturally, she'd rolled
down each hill on campus when he wasn't looking.
Even pulled grass stems out of the ground and chewed
on their sweet white ends.

Now she turned off the idling car in the turnaround
and reached for the envelope beside her. It slid across
the seat, under her hand, and she gathered up its
weight and guessed at all the possibilities. A diary?
Whose? The envelope flap looked fused to the envelope, sealed, as Berger had explained, for just around
thirteen years. The truth was, there was no proof of its
being sealed that long, but she chose to believe Berger
and found herself wondering whether David had
breathed the air inside it, whether he'd sealed it in
there before his heart attack, then given it to Ruth.
Why Ruth would have a diary of David's was a mystery
Myla couldn't dare consider.

Myla held the envelope up to the light and made out
the clear shape of a spiral notebook, which she'd gathered anyway simply from feeling with academic fin-

gers. The researcher in her implored her to wait longer, to see what else she could discover from the primary source of the envelope itself, but curiosity was killing her. So she opened it.

Old air pocked out into her face. She pushed away her impulse toward sentimentality and reached into the envelope, curving open the top to see inside. She latched her fingers over the rim of the notebook and pulled it out to her, into the light. It was red, obviously well loved, with scratches and bends and dents in the cardboard cover. Thinner than it should be, which meant pages had been torn out. Nothing written on either cover. She had to open it, had to see what waited inside. She slipped her nail under the front cover and flipped it open.

There was blank space for most of the page. Then, written in the middle, in small brown letters, the word *Lines*. It was unmistakably her father's handwriting. Myla caught her breath and turned the page.

Blank space, but this time three words in the middle. Linked by lines: *Lines—Thought—Time.*

Next page, those same words in the middle, surrounded by one circle, and then branching out from that circle, more lines to more words, making a sun of language: *Industrial Revolution—death of the imagination—Vermeer—Jesus in the frescoes—elimination of self—van Gogh's paint globs—photography as realism—*the burst of words stopped Myla. She was trying to make out what this was. It looked like brainstorming, the kind she'd been taught in fifth-grade history, complete with thought bubbles on the blackboard. There was no question David had written page after page, but why

on earth would Ruth have had this? And if this notebook had, as Marcus Berger claimed, been sealed thirteen years ago, that would have been just around the
time Ruth went missing. It hurt Myla's brain too much
to think about. She flipped through the rest of the
book, turning page after page of circles upon circles,
words upon words, until she reached a section that
seemed to be all about photography.

Technical terms abounded here, words like *aperture*
and *foreshortening*. Written in the middle of the page
was *Camera Obscura*, and branching out from it were the
words *invention of the real—Vermeer—Dutch masters,
etc.—photography and realism*. She flipped to the surrounding pages, but this was the only one about photography. Myla was surprised it held no mention of
Ruth's photographs.

Myla sighed, looking at her father's handwriting. She
wanted to know what it all meant. She wanted to know
now.

MYLA AND I MAKE UP A GAME. It starts simple enough—
I run to the table and touch it, then jump on the couch
before Myla catches me. But she doesn't catch me with
her body; she catches me with words. First we play that
Myla has to say a rhyme like "Peter Piper" or "She sells
seashells." She has to say the rhyme really fast, and
meanwhile I'm running. I try to get to the couch before
Myla finishes the rhyme. Her words race my legs.

When I get too fast at touching the table, Myla says
we have to make the running distance farther, and even

though I know she's mad because I keep winning, I let
her change the rules because it does get a little boring
to win over and over again. So this time I have to run
around the couch once, then touch the table, then sit
down. Pretty soon she's saying the rhymes so fast that
her words start to beat my legs. She decides we should
go outside and make the rhododendron bush and the
big tree the distance to run between. Also, she has a
new idea about the words. No more rhymes, she says.
"You're five and three quarters, Pru. You should really
be practicing your reading on a daily basis." And she
goes to the two-book dictionary with the tiny doll-size
words in it and the magnifying glass. She gets the book
with the end of the alphabet. She says it'll have all the
hard X and Y words.

The night is cool and smells like grass. In another
week we'll have to put on sweaters. But for now we can
run in the same clothes we threw on that morning. It's
a day when you never even bother with shoes.

First it's my turn to run. I go hold on to the smooth
rhododendron leaves, and Myla puts her hand up in the
air. When she drops it, I run hard to the tree bark,
scratch my face against it. Then she drops her hand
again and I run back into the night, toward where I
think the bush might be. She squints with the magnifying glass as she sits in the light from the porch and
tells into the night one definition for each round. One
word and its meanings for each time her hand goes
down into the night to send me out into it.

We know it's a stupid game. We know that we have
to play this in the dark because the other kids in the
neighborhood want to ride bikes and play Horse in the

basketball hoops their dads hung on their garage doors. We'd never do this in the day when someone could catch us. But this night smells so sweet, like you could run in it forever and your legs would never get tired. You'd never even get cold. Myla's voice matches the air, and even when we know the game is over and we're tired of it, even when I come sit next to her, she keeps reading. She flips the book, points to a word, reads it. The meanings don't mean anything to us. They only make marks in the air, *obovoid* and *obrize* and *obrotund* flouncing themselves into the air above us and disappearing into the blue-dark sky.

Then Myla says, "Ooooh, here's one. This one's dirty, Pru." Her voice gets secret, as if David might be listening to us, even though we know he hasn't looked up from his desk all day. She says, "I'll read the word and you sound it out after me. Put your finger under the word to help you." She takes my pointer finger and puts it under the word, but my hand jabs a shadow over everything. She moves my hand away. "Forget it," she says. "*Pretend* your finger's under it. Okay, ready to read?" I nod yes. So we begin.

"*Obscene*," says Myla. So I say it after her. Then she points to the tiny words after it, in cursive and with all kinds of marks and numbers. "Don't worry about that stuff," she says. "It's just there to tell you where the word came from. No one pays attention to the origins anyway. Okay. Here's the fun part. Now you get to see everything it means. Read the number."

I read, "*One*."

"Good. *Offensive* . . ." She points to me.

I read, ". . . *to the* . . ."

"*. . . senses . . .*"

"*. . . or to taste or . . .*"

"*. . . refinement; disgusting, repulsive, filthy, foul, abom-inable, loathsome. Now somewhat 'arch.'* I don't know what 'arch' means." And when Myla says all these words, she puts on her lady-in-waiting voice, fancy.

Then I read, "*Two.*"

She looks at me. "I think these words are too hard for you, Pru. How about I just read them and you follow along with your eyes?" She knows I don't want this. She knows I want to read them too. "Fine," she says. And then quieter she says, "We'll be out here all night," but she lets us keep reading. "Where were we?"

"Two," I tell her.

"Right. *Offensive . . .*"

"*. . . to . . .*"

"*. . . modesty or decency; expressing . . .*"

"*. . . or . . .*"

"*. . . suggesting unchaste or lustful ideas: impure, indecent, lewd. Obscene parts, privy parts.*" Myla is giggling. She whispers, "You know, private parts, Pru?" and I get what she's saying, and I understand why it should be funny, but it doesn't make me want to laugh. I turn the page and go to definition number three.

I say, "*Three.*" Myla's still laughing, so I look at the first part of the first word and see that I can read it. "*Ill,*" I read.

"Good," says Myla. "Like when you're sick."

"I know," I say, "I'm not stupid." But I can't read the second part of the word no matter how hard I look at it. Finally I have to look at Myla so she'll help me.

"*Ill-omened*," she says, "*inauspicious*. That means like a bad sign, like something that shouldn't be the way it is." She shrugs. "I don't know, I can't explain. Inauspicious just means what it means, you know?"

But that's not why I'm looking at her the way I am. I'm trying to work my mind around all the meanings. Why would a word that's only about people's bodies and their private parts also be about spirits and omens and bad signs? Like if you have a body and it does the things it's made to do, then the future can only be bad?.

Myla folds the dictionary under her arm. She's bored and already wondering if there's anything good on TV. So I can't say these thoughts to her. But I know something new is in me, a question, a wondering, a thought.

chapter six

the thrill of discovery at the college had worn off. Now Myla was flopped on the bed she'd rented in the downtown Hilton. She'd placed David's notebook squarely on the bedside table an hour before and was still staring at it. She'd flipped through the notebook over and over, but as time passed, no hidden knowledge had revealed itself. In fact, looking at page after page had merely confirmed that her father had written down hundreds of words and connected them with lines. She didn't understand the connections, didn't know why *van Gogh* was linked with *perspective*, couldn't fathom what *Jesus* had to do with *Vermeer*.

Myla groaned. She was frustrated. Frustrated if this was all there was left. Frustrated that she'd never learn who'd given it to her. Had David set this up himself, years ago, knowing he was sick? She knew there'd been a book, what they'd all called The Book, The Masterpiece, the one he pounded onto paper every night, words flying from his hands into his typewriter. Back then she'd found him grown up and messy. She'd been irritated by the slabs of paper scattered all around the house. But now she was concerned for him, and concerned for herself. She looked at the options methodically. There were two.

The first went something like this: the notebook had nothing to do with The Book. This possibility left her with nothing. There'd been no sign of a manuscript, no notes, no acknowledgment of anything book-related in the house when she'd ransacked it after his death. She realized now that she'd come back here because, at some level, she'd allowed herself to believe Berger knew something about this final piece. Of course she'd wanted Ruth, but more than that, she'd wanted her father's voice. As the years had passed, no matter how hard she'd pretended otherwise, she'd longed for her father's words and mind. If this notebook had nothing to do with The Book, that meant there was likely nothing left of it in the world.

But there was a second, equally frightening option. What if this notebook *did* have to do with The Book or, worse yet, was all there was left of it? That meant she, Myla Rose Wolfe, was the only link between David's mind and the world. And then: what if she simply couldn't decode her father's message? If she were unable to do so, that would mean she'd completely lost what she once had of her father's mind. She'd be at an ending point practically before she began.

What to do? There were two people who'd welcome her into their home, who might well have some answers. She told herself she hadn't contacted them already because she didn't want to bother them, but her silence owed itself to more than that. She felt a certain shame. Thirteen years. She'd kept herself away from them for thirteen years. Emma must be twenty-three. For a long time Myla had held firmly on to strings of residual anger, but over time, another sentiment had replaced the rage. Simply put, she was embarrassed. Deeply. And she wanted to sort that out before she saw any of them. Especially sweet little Em.

Myla wanted to be able to talk to Mark about all this, to express her fear that she'd lost the pathway of her father's thinking, to mention her shame at not having contacted Steve and Jane and Emma, to describe the spongy, lung-filling air of Portland. She wanted, even believed she needed, Mark to help her navigate through this new lexicon, offering alternatives, nodding conspiratorially, challenging her with questions, as if he'd always known about these worries and this world. But she knew Mark had been Kate Scott's partner in crime in a world he'd recognized. Perhaps the revelation that she was someone else, that she'd hidden her "real" past, had lied to him, would mean he wouldn't, couldn't, know her anymore. In any case, she couldn't call him yet, since her letter had been sent only this afternoon, and he wouldn't be checking his mailbox until after tomorrow's classes. She'd call him later, when he was informed, and then she'd just have to see what happened next.

And now, without a phone call to make, or any discernible answers in David's notebook, Myla closed her eyes. She accepted, grudgingly, that there was nothing else to do but sleep, and dreams came fast.

She knew Pru was waiting. They were in the forest and Myla was feeling brave. She knew all she had to do was find Pru. At first this seemed possible, even likely. She could hear Pru crying, crying the way she'd cried when she was new and their mother had still been alive, and she sounded close. But soon the whimpering began to move farther and farther away. Myla started to run, moving fast, pushing through the ever thickening brambles, but she was having a hard time breathing. The air was filling with the smell of pine, and what had started as subtle and sweet, a hint of forest in the air, soon turned pungent, sickening. It was asthma in her chest, this air, like rocks heavying her lungs, and even though she tried to run faster, she knew she'd have to stop running soon.

That was the worst part of this dream. She'd had it for years, and the worst part, even beyond hearing her baby sister's cries, or the discomfort of the air, or the smell that made her want to retch, was the moment when she had to decide to stop. Then she'd know it was over. Then she'd lose Pru's sound, lose any sense of where she was standing. She'd be alone. The air would clear. And then she'd wake up.

JANE IS GOING ON ERRANDS SO she drops Emma over to play with us. The new babysitter is here and David isn't coming home for another two hours. After Jane leaves, Emma and I start playing Dogs, but then we see Myla running fast down the driveway. We follow her and see that Ruth just pulled up.

"Hi guys," says Ruth, and it's like there's a sparkle in

the air because it's so much fun that she just came over without calling first.

Myla asks her, "Can't you stay? David's coming home at six, and you could send home the stinky babysitter. Please? Anyway, no one else in sixth grade needs someone to take care of them. I'm eleven, Ruth. It's embarrassing. It's these babies who need someone to watch them."

Ruth gets out of the car. She says, "That's beside the point," and smiles at us. She never treats me like being six years old is a bad thing. Then she looks at Emma. "What do you think?" she asks her.

"Stay and play," says Emma.

So that's what Ruth does. We take her film coolers and the camera out of the car so they can stay safe in the house. The new babysitter rides her bike away and then we sit on the front porch and eat fruit pops. Myla tells us a story about this goofball, Pete, in her class, and when she talks she stands up and acts it out for us. She makes me stand up and I pretend to be her and she pretends to be Pete and makes monkey noises and then Emma gets to be the teacher writing on the chalkboard and then turning around really slow to glare in Pete's direction. It makes Ruth laugh so we act it out again, but it isn't as funny the second time.

Then we're kind of bored. Myla asks Ruth where she was coming from, and Ruth tells us she was at a horse barn taking some more pictures of horses and their riders. "Racehorse riders are called jockeys," she says, and I like that word because it makes me think of jumping. Ruth promises she'll take us to the stables sometime.

Then Myla asks, "Did you use up all your film?"

"As a matter of fact, I didn't," says Ruth, and I can see what Myla's thinking.

"Yeah!" I say. "Let's take pictures!"

Ruth looks at Emma. "I don't know. Do you think you'd be up for it, Em?"

"Okay," says Emma. I can see that she's nervous but also excited. I hold her hand.

Myla steps close to us and puts her arm around our shoulders. "You can take pictures of the three sisters."

We go to the backyard and stand underneath the big tree that makes tiny pink flowers. We start off with just pictures of Myla and me, and then Emma wants to be in the pictures so badly. So Ruth invites her in, and we laugh and get excited every time Ruth takes a picture. We've discovered that in the pictures we can pretend anything, and pretending Emma's our sister is a great thing to imagine.

MYLA LEFT THE HOTEL AND pierced through the Portland day. She'd woken up angry, but she wasn't sure why. Part of it was that Mark wasn't answering. She'd tried at nine, after awakening from her night of dark dreams. She'd left three messages for him at his office and home, then had called back his answering machine, leaving another message that she was staying at the Hilton, mentioning her room number again. It wasn't his fault. He obviously couldn't talk to her, and she cursed herself for not being more honest with him when they were face-to-face.

In the back of her mind lurked the realization that Mark's silence wasn't the sole cause of her anger. Granted, she wanted to speak to him, but she'd walked away knowing he wouldn't understand what she'd done, and that her explanation would be even more puzzling. She found herself sitting on a bench in the middle of the Park Blocks, in front of the art museum, trying to pinpoint the exact source of her frustration.

She was afraid. She was afraid of what was to come. Initially she'd been liberated, leaving Kate Scott behind, but now she missed Kate Scott's ability to plan. Myla hadn't any idea of what to do next. A part of her had believed that just by returning to Portland and breathing the air, she would get back in touch with what she'd been hungering for: an explanation of her past, a clear road to the future. This would come to her like a revelation, honed in the manner of her father's beautifully polished mind. Hadn't she believed that if only she could remember his way of thinking, she'd be able to put Samuel Blake into perspective? Shouldn't the discovery of David's notebook give her a clear task, one to help her reclaim his life at its most hopeful? Didn't this notebook give her purpose in Portland, as well as a sensible reason for having left behind her other life?

But David's notebook didn't make any sense. This morning, as soon as Myla's eyes opened, she'd felt for the notebook, hoping that with new light would come new perspective. And yet once again all she could see was words linked by lines. In place of those lines, she knew her father had a million brilliant ideas, but these connections were invisible to the naked eye. And yet they were the only link. They were the only thing left representing the workings of her father's mind.

Myla looked above her, up at the trees. Today there was sun, and the newness of it in usually rainy Portland made her smile. She closed her eyes. She tried to be satisfied with just being alone and quiet, tried to quell the rush of her own mind. Letting her body relax, with the trees interwoven like locked lace above her, and the sun filtering onto her arms and face, she tried to summon a simple memory of her father. She couldn't read his mind about the notebook, but she could remember the things he'd shared with her. What would he have said to her just at this moment? She closed her eyes and imagined him sitting beside her. Then she remembered him in her darkened bedroom, his hand holding hers, telling her about her mother helping her learn to read.

This was one of David's favorite Myla stories, one he told her whenever she felt sad or unsure of herself. She made herself remember the clear way David had told it many times before.

When Myla was tiny, two years old, she'd wanted to read, just like her parents. So Sarah had said to David, "Why not?" She didn't want to push Myla, but this was, after all, Myla's initiative. Sarah took a red marker and sheets of paper and labeled the main objects in the house: chair, table, bed, window. That way, when Myla saw these things in her daily life, she also saw their names. Sarah felt this was an organic progression; if Myla wanted to learn to read words on her own, she could. In the evenings Sarah would gather Myla onto her lap and open up all sorts of books and read aloud, her fingers passing under the words as her voice touched each one.

When David told this story, Myla loved hearing the way he talked about her mother. She could hear how much her father had loved her mother. He'd smile as if Sarah were still alive. What Myla didn't like about the story was the part about herself. Because yes, one day, with a new book open in front of her, she'd started reading aloud, following her mother's finger as it skipped along the page. Sarah tried a different book to make sure Myla hadn't just memorized the story, and was thrilled when she discovered that two-year-old Myla had started to read on her own. "Listen to you! You can read!" Sarah said proudly.

Here came the part that the older Myla hated hearing David recount. She didn't like what she'd done next, for it sounded too precocious, too wise, too precious. According to David, little Myla had taken the book off her lap, hurled it across the room, and cried, "I don't want to read! I don't want to!" When asked why, she'd said, "You never told me that when you read, there's only one story in every book." Only one story in every book! When David related this anecdote, he wasn't bragging about having a daughter who'd been able to read at the age of two. No, he treasured this memory because he was thrilled to have a child wise enough to recognize something so profound as the tyranny of the text. He told Myla she'd been right. Right to decide she wasn't going to learn to read for another two years, because she'd known she wasn't ready yet to lose the big picture.

Myla smiled to herself as she sat in the park. For the

first time in all the hundreds of times she'd heard this story, she understood why her father had loved telling it. As a teenager, she'd rolled her eyes, embarrassed by his determination to prove how well he'd always understood her, based simply on this dumb story about her brattiness. But now she saw, and it lifted her mind. This perspective was one she and David shared. He too was not willing to lose the big picture. He too was angered by the rules of text and time. That's why he loved art, because there were no words to boss him around, nothing to insist on a single meaning. There was image, there was form, and it spilled forth thought and spurred one toward new ideas.

Myla could feel her mind swelling with memory, and she knew if she were ever to understand her father or his notebook, or maybe even herself, she needed more. She needed to remember what it felt like to rise up over a page and see things in patterns. To let go of the direct line of argument, to embrace complication. To let her mind be more like her father's. She looked up to the sun, glad for its warmth, and knew what she had to do. She wouldn't be able to do it alone. No, she had to surround herself with what her father had chosen to surround himself. She had to ask for help. And she knew exactly where to start.

WE'RE OVER AT RUTH'S HOUSE and we're coloring in the back room when we hear the doorbell ring. We think it might be David, done with his student conferences early, so Myla races me down the hallway toward the living room. I'm saying, "Not fair, not fair," because it isn't; she got a head start and I had to go all the way around the table before I could even start running. But then she freezes and puts her finger up to her mouth and tells me to be quiet. At first I don't know what she's doing and I think it's funny, but then I hear the angry voice and I know it's not a joke.

We tiptoe up to where we can peek in between the cracks in the door, and we watch them talking. We can't see who it is because Ruth's back is in the way, blocking the doorway. But then Ruth says, "I'd like it if you would come inside."

Then she backs up, and we see that Jane's there at the door. She's really angry, angry like I've only seen her get once with Emma when she ran into the street after a soccer ball. I'm glad Jane doesn't get angry at me like that; maybe there are some nice things about having a dead mother.

Then Jane comes inside but you can tell she doesn't want to. "Where are the girls?" she asks, and Myla squeezes my hand hard so it's like I lose all the blood in it.

"Do you want to see them?" asks Ruth, and I can tell she's surprised.

Jane looks at her like she's an idiot. "No. I just want to make sure they won't hear us."

Ruth yells over her shoulder, "Myla? Pru?" and we breathe as quiet as we can and are glad for the darkness of the hallway. After a minute, Ruth turns back. "They can't hear a thing."

Jane says, "Emma told me you took pictures of her the other day."

Ruth says, "Yes, I did. I was over at the house and the girls—"

Jane says, "You had no right to do that."

"Oh, come on, Jane, it was four or five pictures. The girls wanted to play with the camera—"

"I may not be a photographer, Ruth, but I know that the camera is not a toy. It's an incredible invasion of privacy. You're lucky we know you, that we aren't the kind of people who'll press charges—"

"Whoa," says Ruth. "Press charges? I took a couple of pictures of your daughter. I had no idea you wouldn't like that. In the future, I'll make sure she doesn't wander in front of the camera, but other than that—"

"Listen to me carefully," says Jane, talking slow now, like this is the angriest moment she has. "I'll say this once. You can take pictures of whatever you like. It's a free country. David lets you use his daughters—"

"*Use* his daughters?!"

"—in any kind of pictures you want to take, but Steve and I, that's right, *both* of us, disagree with the kind of pictures you're taking."

"Ohhhhhhh," says Ruth, like she's just figured something out and it's satisfying. "That's what this is about."

"Let me finish," says Jane, and her voice is getting angrier with every word. "Those girls have been isolated enough as it is. A dead mother, a workaholic for a father, no real routine. And then their extraordinary intelligence—"

Ruth almost laughs. "You make their precocity sound like a disease."

"Certainly not," says Jane. "The girls are extraordinarily gifted, and that's wonderful. But it separates them. It makes them different. The last thing they need is something else excluding them from their peers."

Ruth says, "I have no idea what you're talking about."

"Then think, Ruth. Pictures of them? And naked pictures at that?"

"*That's* what this is about? David showed you some of the pictures? Well, sure, some of the photographs are nude. But there are tons of them that aren't. Besides, that's how the girls live. They have no idea that people like you think they should cover up every time—"

"You know nothing about people like me," says Jane. "And that's not the point. The point is that before you take a picture, you have to think about it. Before you take a photograph of anything, use your brain. Emma's too little to know what she wants, and if you ask my opinion, so are Myla and Pru, but it's been made clear to me that's none of my damn business."

Before I know it, Myla is letting go of my hand and walking into the bright room. I want her to come back, but not because I'm afraid they'll know we were hiding. I want her to come back because I'm scared without her. I don't like how anger makes Ruth and Jane different, and I don't like that their anger is all because of us.

They turn and see Myla and she speaks to Jane. "We *are* old enough. Eleven and six. Old enough to make decisions for ourselves. And even if we weren't, it doesn't matter what you think, because you aren't our mother." Then Myla calls my name and makes me come out and stand beside her. "Right, Pru?" she asks, but I'm too scared to say anything with all of them looking at me.

Then Ruth says, "Go back to the other room. I don't want you here for this."

But Myla says, "No." She says, "You know what, Ruth? You can't tell us what to do either. You aren't our mother either." And I can tell Myla's angry, I can feel it making her arm strong and tight against me, and she looks like a grown-up the way she's trying to scare Jane and Ruth.

Jane sighs then. She turns and walks out of the house, fast, without even saying goodbye. Ruth walks to the door, watches Jane get in her car and drive off, then closes the door to the outside and turns the lock. She walks right past us, like we aren't even there. We can hear her walking into her bedroom and the door slamming shut behind her.

Myla puts her arm around me, and we stand like that for a long time, listening.

proof

this image is of one girl only: the older one, as you have come to recognize her. She stands waist-deep in a lake. Trees rise behind her, on the far side of the water. In the distance, a pine forest stretches out, and nearer, split trunks are the sharp remnants of a lightning strike.

The girl holds her arms out, palms spread down, fingers splayed like the legs of water bugs. It looks as if her hands are resting on the top of the lake, arched upon the meniscus. Water traces its way around her hips and belly and the very beginnings of her pubic hair.

In all of this, the lake around her is still. Not a trace of wind. Not a ripple. Not even from her breathing. Her eyes are closed. It is as if someone has placed her from above.

chapter seven

Myla knew she should probably call first, but she was ready to act. She found her way to their house so easily. She just drove up Malden, and when she pulled up in front of the large bungalow with the sagging porch, she wasn't surprised that no one was home, for it was the middle of the afternoon. She parked her car on the street, strode up the walkway, and sat down on the front steps to wait.

Myla knew exactly the last time she'd been here. It had been the night before she went for good. She was eighteen and angry, and she'd had something to drink, but instead of the alcohol quelling her rage, it had compressed it, made it a bullet ready to burst from her. Her illogic had led her to believe that there was no one to blame except the two people who were left. She'd come back here to this house to pick up her things so she could pack her car.

Emma, thank goodness, had been at a slumber party, since Jane and Steve had been trying to keep their daughter's life as normal as they could. The couple came home after Myla had already packed, surprising her on the front porch as she was leaving, bags in hand. She'd denied their entreaties for her to come inside. She'd pointed her finger at both of them and said, "Don't you dare come near me. Don't you dare." They'd begged her to come in. She'd stayed outside and continued on. "You know whose fault this is? It's yours. All of yours. You were the fucking adults."

Myla's words from that night rang in her ears, turned them red against her skull. She could still taste a trace of that raw rage, even though she knew things were infinitely more complicated than that. But perhaps the core feeling was true. Righteous. So many people—strangers around the country, reading their local paper and watching the news—would have agreed with her at the time. Blame was everywhere, blanketing everything.

Now Myla pushed that past away. She clasped the notebook in her bag and moved her feet back and forth between the step beneath her and the step below that. An orange cat came around the stairway and purred against her, nudging its head under her hand until she consented to pat him. It was a new cat, but just its presence served as an anchor, tethering their old house to domesticity. They'd always had at least one cat, and she traced in her mind the lineage of the three she'd known in her years here. She introduced herself to the fourth.

A few cars passed, but none was theirs, none even looked like a car she knew they might own. They'd owned a station wagon when she knew them. Then a gust of wind made her shiver, and she suddenly wondered what she was doing here. What was she hoping to accomplish? She almost stood to leave, and then a blue station wagon pulled into the driveway. The window reflected light at such an angle that Myla couldn't make out who was driving. She panicked for a moment. Maybe she'd become unrecognizable. Maybe they'd moved.

The door slammed, and she heard the back opening, heard bags being piled out. Then the slam again, and steps on the sidewalk. It was a woman. It was Jane. Myla stood, then sat again, then half-stood, so that when Jane came around the corner, Myla realized she must look like some ridiculous dancer caught in mid-move. She saw Jane look up to her face, take her in, realize who she was. Myla didn't know what to expect, but Jane dropped her groceries and sang, "Myla Myla Myla," almost like a chant. Myla hadn't known it would make her cry to see Jane like this, to walk to her and hug her, to remember the soft way her long hair—now graying—teased her arm. "Myla Myla Myla," Jane kept saying. "Myla Myla Myla."

Then they broke apart, slowly, softly. Myla picked up the groceries from either side of Jane, and Jane asked, without even trying to wipe the tears from her cheeks, "Where on earth did you come from?"

Myla had to admit it made her happy to see her very existence create joy in the heart of someone else's day. But she also played it cool: "I'm in town for a little bit."

"My God. Look at you!" Jane clapped her hands. "Steve will be overjoyed. It's . . . it's astonishing to see you. You're all right, right? You're all here?" Myla felt

Jane's eyes surveying her, the concerned eyes of a mother.

Myla nodded. "Ten fingers, ten toes. Still got 'em."

Jane reached out and touched her arm. "Let's go inside." Jane unlocked the door and Myla walked into the living room. It was smelling the past to enter here—the deep ash of the fireplace, the ancient earthiness of the carpeting. Had she been blindfolded, she would have known exactly where she was, simply from the taste of the air. Dust clung to the sun coming in the windows. Things were slow; it was like being underwater.

Jane took the groceries from Myla and jaunted straight back to the kitchen, leaving Myla standing at the door. She had the presence of mind to pull the screen door shut behind her, the tiny voice in the back of her mind reminding, "Keep the cat out." Then Jane came back in the room and clasped her hands. "Myla. Myla." It was a surprise, Myla realized, for Jane to be the first person to use her name after all the years of being called Kate. It was right to have *Myla* uttered here.

Jane ushered Myla to a spot on the couch, piling newspapers and magazines on the floor to clear a space. Myla smiled and looked around the unchanged room. "I hope this is okay."

"What?"

"Coming here. Like this."

"Are you kidding?" Jane looked incredulous. "This is a miracle to us. I've called Steve. He's on his way. He and I . . ." Jane looked at her again with those mother eyes. "He and I think about you every day. We aren't religious people, you know, but we do the closest thing we can to praying." Then she smiled self-consciously. "Oh, but it doesn't need to be as dramatic as all that. I'm sure your life is just excellent." She looked down at her hands, which kept fluttering in her lap, and Myla wanted to tell Jane it was fine for the older woman to touch her, fine for her to use her mother's hands as she longed to use them. But instead there was a whistling from the kitchen. Jane stood up. "I put some water on to boil. I'll make us tea."

So Myla followed Jane into the kitchen, and Jane poured piping-hot water into two handmade mugs. "Here's my latest attempt at something artistic." Jane smiled somewhat apologetically as she handed one to Myla. "The problem is, I'm not really that good. But they hold water, and that's got to count for something."

Myla knew Jane's movements so well that it was as if she'd been in this kitchen every day for the last decade. Jane would give two tugs on her tea bag, then walk to the utensil drawer to the right of the sink, extract a spoon, tease the tea bag onto the spoon, wind the string until it squeezed out all the juice, then unwind the string as she walked to the garbage and deposited the tea bag. Then there was the honey procedure: half a spoonful of honey, centrifuged expertly so that there'd be a taste of sweetness throughout. Myla looked hopelessly down at her cup of tea, now turning a deep brown from neglect. She wouldn't even try to put in honey: she'd end up with a glob of stickiness at the bottom that would make her feel hopeless. She wished she were young enough to ask Jane for assistance. But now Jane was moving toward her, seeing a fully formed adult, and trying, truly trying, to treat her like one. Myla could tell it was difficult and was amazed by Jane's restraint. So Myla volunteered information: about being a professor of medieval English and about her research on Mary's blue robes, which— she realized with a flash of surprise as she was explaining it to Jane's open face—she hadn't thought about since she'd been in Portland.

And then Jane told Myla about their lives. "Steve's no longer at the university." Myla nodded. She wouldn't have been surprised to hear Jane say something like, "It was too difficult for him to be there after everything that happened," but instead Jane smiled and said, "He'll recount his renunciation of the laws of mathematics to anyone who's willing to listen. Consider yourself warned. Having left behind the glamorous life of a math professor, he's fallen in love with recycling. He takes the discards from one company and figures out what another company can do with them. Unused pieces of plastic, that kind of thing. He really loves it. And I'm still teaching eighth grade. The year's almost at an end, and the kids have been pretty tough, but I still do it. It's what I do." Myla knew she was working toward something, but wasn't going to say it without knowing that Myla wanted to know.

"And Emma?"

Jane's face broke into a smile even as her eyes welled with tears. "Em's doing well. She's celebrating two years of sobriety. She's living in San Francisco with her wonderful boyfriend—they graduated from Berkeley last year."

"Oh God," said Myla, shocked by this new reality. "Two years of sobriety? Is she—"

"It's all right," said Jane, wiping the tears from her eyes. "Emma's doing really well now. She's just fine." Jane obviously didn't want to talk about this part of Emma's past. But she added, "She'll be so happy to know you're here. She'd love to see you." Jane had decided to let Emma speak for herself.

Myla flashed with knowing that there was no reason to assume only *her* life had been shattered by Pru's death. In the intervening years, Myla had occasionally revisited her treatment of Jane and Steve with great regret, but even in those moments of remorse, Emma had remained a perpetually sunny ten-year-old in Myla's mind. Of course, now she saw her desire to believe that Emma would be just fine had been selfish and unrealistic. Myla tried to push away the wave of grief that surged up when she thought of what Emma had obviously endured since she'd seen her last.

Jane finally took Myla's hand and squeezed it, bringing Myla back to her present self. Jane looked Myla in the eye. She said, "We miss you, Myla. We think about you every day. We do." And Myla knew she was telling the truth.

IT'S VERY HOT ONE DAY, SO I'm sitting in my underpants in Ruth's backyard. I want to go home to get our wading pool so we can fill it up with water and I can lie in it, but Ruth says that will take too much time. She already has the camera outside, and she says she doesn't want to carry all the equipment in and lock up the house and drive us home. But I tell her it's so hot that I don't want to take pictures. Myla rolls her eyes because she's afraid that means Ruth won't take pictures of her either. But Ruth says, "Okay." And then, all of a sudden, she looks excited. She goes into the garage and comes back with a sprinkler and takes it all the way down to the bottom of the yard, away from the camera, and screws it into the hose. And when she turns it on, cold water sprays out all over me, like rain. And then I run in it again and again, until I'm cool all over.

After a while, I'm bored, and I come over to where Ruth is taking pictures of Myla sitting on a towel. Ruth is saying to Myla, "And then Agostino Tassi, a good friend of Artemisia's father, Orazio, rapes Artemisia—"

"Shh," says Myla. "Don't say that."

"What?" asks Ruth.

"Don't say that word."

I know they're talking about me, but I pretend I'm not even listening. Then Myla says to me, like she knows everything, "Ruth was just telling me about this painter, Artemisia Gentileschi. She lived in the seventeenth century. Her father was a painter too, and then one of his friends *hurt* her. Right, Ruth?"

Ruth says, "Sorry about that, kiddo. You two are so grown up that I forget sometimes."

"That's okay," says Myla, like she owns the situation. "You should just be careful. Even though you don't have any kids of your own, you still have to be responsible."

I'm sick of them acting all bossy to each other, so I say, "That's what I want to be when I grow up."

Ruth asks, "What, Pru?"

I tell them again. "That's what I want to be. A painter. I'm going to be a painter."

Myla giggles. "Well, everyone wants to be *something* when they're six. Kids want to be astronauts and archaeologists and doctors all the time, but you know, Pru-y, it's hard to actually be those things."

Then Ruth looks serious at Myla and I can tell she's the grown-up again. She says, "Pru, you'll be an incredible painter. What kind of paintings do you think you'll do?"

This is something I haven't thought about, but now that Ruth's listening, I don't want Myla to take it all away. So without knowing what I mean, I say, "I want to work in large formats."

"That sounds great," Ruth says, smiling. "Maybe we'll do a show together someday, with my photographs of you, and your paintings."

"What will we call the show?" I ask.

"What do you mean?"

"It has to have a good name, so people will be interested in coming to see it."

"Well," she says, "I don't know. What do you guys think?"

I think about it for a minute. My idea comes to me like a shape, without words. So I have to put words on it and I don't know how. "We could name it after what we call this."

Myla giggles again. "I have no idea what that means," she says.

But Ruth says, "Can you explain it to us?"

"Like this," I say. "What do you call this? What do

you call us when you're doing this? Like I know we have names, but that's not what I mean. What do you call us?"

Ruth nods. "Well, most photographers would call you subjects or models—"

"Call us models!" says Myla, but I shake my head.

"That doesn't describe it," I say.

"Remember that first day I took a photograph of you guys? In my studio? Remember how I told you you could name my camera? And you never did. Well, how about you name this instead? How about *you* name what you are."

So I stop and I think. And then the shape inside me finds its words. And before I know it, the words are outside me. "Camera girls," I say. "We're your camera girls."

Ruth says, "Lovely."

Myla says, "Boring. Let's go run in the sprinkler."

But Ruth says, "Wait. Side by side, just like that." And we know what's coming. So we hold still and relax our faces, and I'm happy because I have my idea, and Myla's happy because she has her picture. Ruth slides the film into the back of the camera, and we take one photograph. One photograph to remember that I'll be a painter—to remember we have a name. A name for what we are.

STEVE BOUNDED IN THE DOOR, and Myla felt the shock of realizing he looked old in a way that David never would have. David would have remained tall and lean.

He was the kind of man who would have been able to wear the same pair of pants into his old age. But Steve, though not elderly yet, had changed. He had a belly now that pressed hard against her when she hugged him. And he had turned gray, whereas David's hair, thick and brown, would have stayed that way for a long, long time. Steve hugged her again, and kissed the top of her head. She could feel Jane watching them. "Jane and I hope you'll be staying," he said. His first words to her in years.

"Oh, thanks, I've actually got a hotel room—"

"Nonsense," he said. "You're staying with us. I can't believe you didn't come by before this. How long've you been here?"

"Only a day," she apologized.

"Well, there's nothing we can do about last night, but you're damn well staying here now." Myla nodded, bent to him. Now that she was here, it seemed the only option.

Steve ushered them into the kitchen, and Myla remembered this about them, that the kitchen was where this family did their familying. Their kitchen was bigger than their living room, tucked into the back of their bungalow. They settled down in chairs around the table while Jane started moving around. Myla knew Jane was beginning dinner. It was exciting to witness such motivation over something so routine. She watched as Jane opened the fridge and emerged with vegetables and chicken breasts. She checked with Myla that she wasn't a vegetarian, and Steve smiled with relief when she shook her head.

"Well, thank God for that," he said. "You kids always

loved my special sauce. How about I grill this weekend?" The question hung like darkness in the air as
Myla watched Jane's back flinch at "you kids." Myla
wanted to stand up and put her hand on Jane's shoulder, to tell her not to worry, that she could hear these
things, but Myla didn't move.

"That would be great," said Myla, smiling.

Steve leaned back in his chair. "You're looking
good."

Myla looked down at herself, cased out her grown-up
body. Her arms seemed too long, so she folded them
against her. "Yes. I've been fine."

"See, that's the problem, Myles. You haven't been
good. You've been fine."

She opened her mouth to justify the habitualness of
the phrase, but Steve put up his hand. She'd forgotten
how hard it was to argue against him. "Where've you
been?" he asked. Myla could see that Jane was focusing
her whole attention on the chopping of the knife against
the wooden board. Jane wasn't going to interfere, and
each chop seemed to resound with her determination.

"I'm sorry." Myla looked down at her folded, too-
long arms.

"Don't apologize, Myla. Just tell me what happened."

She waited for a way to explain it. She'd rehearsed
this conversation for over a dozen years, and it had always started with her proudly standing up for her decisions, glancing Steve's questions off her shiny shell of
self-confidence. In her imagination, the conversation
hadn't gone like this. "I changed my name."

Steve nodded. "Well, we figured that much out." He
turned to Jane. "Didn't we?"

Jane was turning on the stove. "We looked for you. When we heard you'd left college, Steve was certain you'd transferred somewhere else."

"I knew you wouldn't give up on your smarts," he said.

Myla nodded. "Well, you were right. I've been telling Jane, I teach medieval English. I'm trying to write a book. I guess that isn't much of a shock."

Steve laughed. "Well, we weren't hungry for a shock. We just wanted you to come home." He reached across the table and freed one of her hands. "Now that you're home, you can explain it all to us."

Now Jane came forward, and Myla could see that she was speaking to Steve, directing him, even though she was looking at Myla. "You must be wiped. I'm whipping dinner up, and then you can relax." She knew Jane was giving Steve her assessment of the situation: Myla would be here for a while, so Steve should stop pestering her.

Steve took the hint. "You've always known you have a home here, Myles." He stood and pecked Jane on the cheek. "I'm going to go freshen up," he said.

Once they sat down and ate, Steve didn't ask any more big questions. The windows in the dining room were open, so in drifted the late-spring sounds of kids biking home from the park, of people barbecuing on their back porches. Jane related all of Myla's news to Steve. He listened politely to Jane's rendition, then asked Myla some questions about her research. She obliged. The candles became the only light, flickering against the walls. Then it was nighttime, and Steve told stories about his Dumpster-diving adventures for the recycling firm, Jane talked about her students and their literature projects, and Myla saw the evening from outside. From outside, this gathering would not look unusual. Someone would see a family, and after all, this *was* family, and not just anyone's. This was *her* family. They wanted to be this for her. The solidarity was foreign, yes, but it gave her back her name. Jane and Steve said "Myla." They said "Myles." She liked this. She liked it all the way to bed.

RUTH CALLS US ONE SATURDAY and says, "Guess what, guys, I've got a show!" There's a gallery downtown interested in her photographs. She says they're interested in everything: the first portraits of horses and jockeys she took when she was living in Kentucky, and the ones she's taken since she's lived in Oregon, and now the photographs of Myla and me. "My camera girls," she says to me when I'm on the phone.

Myla takes the phone from my ear and asks, "Does everyone at the gallery wear black and talk like the Beats?" Then she laughs at whatever Ruth says back. I don't hear it. But then Myla puts the phone to David's ear and says to him, "Ruth wants us in the show, David."

David's face is all listening. He keeps the phone by his ear and smiles down at me. He says, "Wow, Ruthie. I'll talk to them, see what they say. Great. And Ruth? Congratulations! You've hit the big time! Okay, bye now." Then he looks at us. "Well, it looks as if your mugs might end up in Ruth's show. How about that?"

Myla sticks out her tongue. "Don't call them mugs." Her nose wrinkles up. "Call them countenances, call them visages." Then she giggles.

"So what do you think, Pru? Do you think it would be okay to have your picture hanging in a gallery?"

"Like a van Gogh portrait, Pru-y, think of it!" Myla says, and twirls toward the fridge like a prima ballerina.

David says, "Ruth said you guys can look at the ones she's thinking of proposing to the gallery, and I guess the gallery'll make the final decision. But she also said"—and here he reaches out his arms and pulls me onto his lap—"that you don't have to have your picture on any wall if you don't want it there. And Prudence, she means that. I know her. If you don't want your face on the wall, it doesn't have to be there."

I know I want it hanging there, and that scares me a little. What is it in me that wants people to see my face? But then I realize—it's the part of me that's been working with Ruth for what feels like forever, the three of us, a team of artists. So it's not exactly that I want my picture on the wall, and it's not exactly that I don't want it there. It's that I don't want to know that having a picture on the wall is what makes it real. I want the *moment* to be real. I don't want the picture to fall into anyone else's life but my own. But I know I'll say yes. Myla twirls around the sun-bright kitchen and winds me into the yes I know I'll give.

chapter eight

When Myla woke up, Steve was sitting at the foot of her bed. "Good morning," he whispered. She wondered why he was whispering if she was already awake; she heard the soft hushing sound of the shower.

"Good morning," she managed as she pulled herself up into sitting.

"I'm on my way to work," he said by way of explanation. "But I wanted to make sure you'd be okay." He glanced over his shoulder, and Myla realized he'd be in trouble with Jane if she saw him in here bugging her.

"Oh, I'll be fine."

"There's a spare key in the second plant to the left of the door," he said. He hesitated. "You won't leave, will you?"

The question stuck her like a needle. She shook her head. "No. I promise."

"Good." He was still looking at her, and she knew he didn't entirely believe her.

"Look," she said as she climbed from bed and crawled over to her bag. She'd waited to show him the notebook because she hadn't wanted him to think the only reason she'd come was to pick his brain. But now that he wanted assurance that she'd be staying, this notebook was the closest thing to a guarantee she could give. She pushed it into his hand, and he opened it.

"David's handwriting," he said.

"Yes. Some lawyer called me and gave me this, insisting it was my inheritance." She looked at Steve and saw the question before he asked it. "It's full of notes."

He nodded. "Do you want me to take a look at this?"

It was like shorthand, talking to Steve. "If you can. I tried to understand it, but it was too far out of my league."

"Okay. Just keep in mind that I'm no art historian. Most days I just nodded like an idiot while he spouted theory." The shower turned off. Steve looked over his shoulder again and shrugged. "Have a great day. I've got a light day at work, so I'll get a chance to look at this—I'll let you know what I can by tonight."

Myla heard Steve pattering down the stairs, then heard the bathroom door opening as Jane emerged from the steam. It was clockwork, this world, and comforting. How strange to find safety here, when safety was what she'd been looking for everywhere else. A nagging concern flared at the back of her mind: maybe this wasn't real safety, maybe this was just a convenient kind of laziness. She knew that no matter how much she wished to rest, now wouldn't be the time for it. Things would inevitably get harder.

For one thing, here was a day alone with nothing organized. This was the very thing she'd avoided for the last thirteen years: a day off, with no research, no classes, no notebook. A day with nothing but her own mind. There was room in her for pondering—time for remembering.

And like that, a memory came rushing in. A conversation with Ruth. They'd been inside; it was raining. Just the two of them. Myla felt her mind swerve away from thinking about Pru. This was a day between her and Ruth.

Ruth, tall and lovely. Slowly, Myla let herself remember the woman she hadn't seen for over a decade. Saw each detail just for a moment, before the glimmer of memory moved away. Ruth had been beautiful. Myla had treasured sitting behind her and brushing her thick black mane that thickened with each passage of the bristles. On nights when Ruth was gussying herself up for one of her infamous dates, she always let Myla select nail colors from the drawer devoted solely to beautification, and while Ruth showered and plucked and powdered and dabbed, Myla would scrunch up in the corner and paint each of her own toenails a different color. After her showers, Ruth would slather lavender-scented lotion all over her body. Then she'd carefully choose a pair of earrings from the hundreds hanging on the wall, asking Myla's advice. And finally, before she left the bathroom, she'd always dab a tiny bead of rose oil on each wrist. To this day Myla was always distracted when a woman walked into a room smelling of rose oil.

In this specific memory, Myla must have been twelve, because it was just before Ruth's first gallery show. On this day the rain had cozied them up with a pot of tea and a package of gingersnaps, and they were talking about Myla's school. They were by the window in Ruth's front room. Myla remembered the distracted feeling of speaking and watching as rain streamed over the pane. The speaking and the streaming kept each other going, and she remembered knowing with certainty that if the rain stopped, her words would have to stop too. She was telling Ruth about the Robert Herrick poem her seventh-grade teacher had made them read, "Upon Julia's Clothes." Ruth was impressed. Myla had it memorized.

> "Whenas in silks my Julia goes,
> Then, then, methinks, how sweetly flows
> That liquefaction of her clothes!
>
> Next, when I cast mine eyes and see
> That brave vibration each way free,
> —O how that glittering taketh me!"

"Myla, that's lovely. What does it mean?"

"Well, he loves Julia. And it's pretty simple; he's watching her walk in her silken clothes. But it's more than that, I think. It feels like you can hear her walking, doesn't it? She's so beautiful, and he loves watching her dress move over her. Because under that, she's naked. And he wants to *be* the clothes." Myla looked up at Ruth, and Ruth was frowning. "Or. Something. I don't know. That's just my opinion."

"No, no, it's fascinating. I was just thinking how smart you are."

Myla wished Ruth would stop frowning. "I'm not

that smart. It's just David or something. It rubbed off on us."

"And your mom too. She was a poet and a painter. Sarah was a talent."

"I guess." Myla didn't want to talk about her with Ruth. It felt funny. It felt like telling someone a secret when you knew you shouldn't. "Anyway." Myla felt strange. She shouldn't have recited the poem. She felt like a show-off, as if she and Ruth had been standing on the same side of a river and the poem had pushed her to the other side. So that now, looking at Ruth across the table, they seemed miles apart.

But then Ruth spoke. "Myla, you and your dad have so much to say about everything. It's amazing. It makes me wish I was like that too. But I just see things. I see them, and I live in a time when the camera's been invented, so I take pictures. But I don't have a mind like yours. I've never thought about a poem."

"Sure you have. I bet you read poems in school."

Ruth waved her arm in the air. "Sure, but I'm talking about something different. How did you hear that poem and know what it means?"

"I don't know." Myla didn't. "I just know what it means. You must feel that way about something."

"Pictures. That's it." The rain got harder. Myla pulled the blanket tighter around her shoulders. Ruth went on, "Okay, my pictures may be a little like poems. They may have metaphors. Only simpler."

Ruth turned from the window where she'd been watching the sky growing darker. She looked right at Myla then. "Let's say I want to take a picture that shows how you, Myla, have all these thoughts inside you, all this inner life. You're a fascinating child with profound ideas. Maybe you do something with your body, like stretching out your arms. That can represent you reaching for your dreams, or something like that. Or—here's an example—you know that sister picture I took of you and Pru last summer? Out in the back-yard—the one where you're in the sundress and Pru's dripping wet? It wasn't until I printed it that I saw the story, and it's not even your story or her story. It's a nar-rative all its own. And it's very simple. There's this older girl who is tall and dry and clean, and then there's this younger girl who is wet and wild and messy. And the younger girl desperately wants to be as big as her sister is, and is reaching so high to prove that she's as old. Above her, in the space that her head can't fill, there happens to be a bird. And that bird is a metaphor for all that soaring she'll do when she finally grows up. But it also makes the viewer long for childhood just as she's longing for adulthood, long for that simple place in the past where a bird stood for significant things, like the future, or hope, or ambition. For that time in their lives when simple objects were simultaneously them-selves and metaphors."

Ruth shrugged. "See how simpleminded it is on my end? It feels so reductive. Most of what I know about my work comes long afterward, when I can see the pic-tures that work and notice trends between them." She laughed and brought her hands together. "I must be boring you. Really, trust me. I am not smart the way you are, the way David is." Then she thought for a minute. "It's just frustrating to me sometimes, that the creation of the photographs is so haphazard. That I never know if a picture is going to be good until I see it."

Myla thought. She asked, "What do you want the pictures to say?"

Ruth smiled at her, and that smile brought them back together. "You always know the right question to ask. Just like your dad. But it's a hard one." Ruth shook her head. "I don't want them to be overtly political. But I want people to see that you girls have a glorious life. That you're beautiful because you've been taught to think for yourselves, to trust yourselves. To trust your bodies."

Myla nodded. "I think that's what they say too."

"Good," said Ruth, pouring more tea. "Now let's just hope the bigwigs in the art world think that!"

Ruth's saying that reminded Myla that the photographs were going to become public. That her life with Pru was going to be seen as something of an example, something for people to envy. If Ruth had asked whether she wanted that, she would have said yes a hundred times. It was a strange feeling, to hope you might soon be famous. It made her glad to be in here, in the warm, instead of outside, in the sloshy gray day.

WE WEAR NEW LONG DRESSES to the opening. Mine is white with tiny pink flowers, and Myla's is blue and yellow. David took us to Nordstrom himself and let us pick them out. He usually never takes us shopping; mostly we go with Jane and Emma, and he gives us a fold of money and says, "Don't spend it all in one place!" But

when he took us to Nordstrom, we knew he was doing
something special. That's why we picked out the nicest
dresses we could find.

We drive slowly by the gallery because we're looking
for parking. Myla's in the front seat and she keeps
pointing out possible places to park but there are always fire hydrants or driveways. Then she gets mad
and says, "We're going to miss it if we don't hurry."
David puts up his hand and says, "Honey, I'm doing
the best I can." So we circle around again and I watch
them up in the front seat. Their bodies are little fighting shoulders and heads, getting harder and harder the
longer it takes. Myla keeps sighing and exasperating
until David says, "Okay, girls, why don't I just drop you
off and I'll come in when I find parking?" I don't want
to leave him, but Myla knows I'll say that so she turns
around and glares. I unsnap my seatbelt.

David drives away, and Myla and I walk to the cross-
walk and wait for the light. Myla is a bird now, fluttery
and looking at all the people crowding the gallery entrance. I think it looks kind of boring because there are
only grown-ups going in. Maybe Emma will come and
I can show her around, but then I remember the fight
between Jane and Ruth. I hope Emma can come anyway.

When we get close to the glass doors, all I can see are
people with wineglasses, and Ruth was right, they're all
dressed in black. Myla pushes hard against the door,
and the door handle jangles a bell, and the people
standing by it turn and look at us. Myla ignores them
and strains to see Ruth, moving us into the swish of

legs. But I turn around and can see them pointing at us, mouthing.

Then Myla's found Ruth, and Ruth comes and hugs us. She hands us each a cookie from the refreshment table and says, "Come look at the show, you guys." A couple of men she was talking to turn and walk away.

The first picture is of an old man's back, moving away. He has a coat on, but you can see the tiny hairs on his neck, like little tree trunks close up. Then there are five pictures of horses: two showing just the horses' heads, three whole horses with their jockeys standing next to them. These are in color, and big on the wall. They make me feel almost like the horses are in the gallery with us. They look like velvet and chocolate at the same time, and I bet touching the pictures would feel good.

David comes in and catches up with us. We keep moving around the gallery; there are pictures of horse faces, and ears, even one of a hoof. Then we come to the pictures of us. The first picture is of Myla lying down, and in it her backbone is like the curve of a road. One picture is of the two of us standing side by side, from last summer, and I'm next to Myla's shoulder. It's a sister picture, and when I look at it, I remember how good it felt to run in the sprinkler that day when the sun was burning down. And the next picture is from last summer too, taken in our living room, near the window seat. We are lying on the floor, because it's cooler and the rug is soft under us, and I'm looking at the picture of my mother. I can remember the sun hitting my back and the way it made things feel sharper and softer at the same time. And then there's a picture of us in our dresses the first day we posed for Ruth. That one's funny; when I look at it, I can see I was only three years old, but when I remember it, I think about myself being big, even though it was almost four whole years ago.

It is a strange thing to see myself on the wall. All these people looking at us makes me see myself a new way. I see that the pictures are pretty, that they're pretty because I'm pretty, and that makes me feel like a show-off. People gather around us but sort of far away, and someone asks Ruth to introduce us. So she uses the names we've talked about, our middle names, the names we are in the pictures. "This is Rose," she says, pointing to Myla. "And May." The people shake our hands. They think they know us.

WHEN JANE CAME HOME, Myla was finally sitting again. She'd been on overdrive since morning, anxious that this tangle of memories might be too much for her, hungry to hear Steve's estimation of David's notebook. So she'd cleaned Jane and Steve's home, realizing only halfway through that they might think it odd to find her mopping their floors, doing their laundry, scrubbing down the kitchen sink.

The other thing that had set off her restlessness was the round of calls she'd made to Mark, again with no answer. She was beginning to worry about him. She'd tried once before bed last night, then called the hotel to pass on her forwarding number and address. After waking up this morning, she'd tried Mark again, then driven into town to pick up her things. The front desk insisted there'd been no calls. So she'd frenzied away the afternoon immersed in housework, trying to keep her mind safe from concern about Mark and memories of her past.

Jane laughed when she came in the door and saw the vacuum cleaner uncloseted. "I was wondering how you were planning to entertain yourself."

"I hope it's okay," said Myla. "It's not as if your house was dirty or anything."

Jane touched her arm. "Steve told you this home is your home. You can do whatever you want here. Besides," she continued, once again pulling their conversation into the kitchen, where she put the water on to boil, "it's in your blood. I can remember your father coming over one summer afternoon when Steve was away doing some research. You should have seen David, the way he fixed the back porch light and trimmed the hedge. It was how he took care of us, and you and Pru were such help to me. You, I remember, helped me fold all of Emma's baby clothes one particular afternoon."

The memories pressing in on Myla formed a question in her mind, one she didn't know she had. But she knew that if she didn't start asking questions, she wouldn't start getting answers. So she said, "Jane, did Pru and I stay with you right after our mother died?"

Jane didn't skip a beat. "I can't believe you remember that! You were both such itty-bitty things. Yes, in fact, you did. For nearly two months." She touched Myla's arm. "Your father was devastated when Sarah died. He wanted to be able to take care of you two, but Pru was only a couple of months old at the time. And you were five, so you still needed a significant amount of parenting. Not to mention that your father refused to take a leave of absence. So Steve and I took you for a while. It was a pleasure."

As Jane spoke, bits of that tiny childhood were forming themselves in Myla's mind: the way the guest room had been arranged for them, the sound of Pru crying in the night and Jane coming in to soothe them both with a lullaby, Steve letting her ride around on his back on the living room floor.

Jane must have taken Myla's silence for sadness, because she said, "As soon as your father was living on a normal schedule again—sleeping, eating, showering— we put you girls right back in his arms. He once told me it was the greatest gift we could have given him: the knowledge that his girls were safe and happy, without his having to worry if he'd make any mistakes. That was his biggest fear, that he wouldn't know how to take care of you two."

"I'm impressed," said Myla. "You and Steve just moved us in with you. And you were young, right?"

"Early thirties. Your age."

"Exactly," said Myla. "I'd have no idea what to do if a newborn landed in my lap."

Jane laughed. "Well, Steve had been around for your babyhood, and I'd been a big sister. So we both knew how to change a diaper. But you're right. It was pretty brave, now that I think about it. If you want to know the truth, I think that time with you guys sealed it for Steve and me. It made us realize we wanted to be together in the long term. That we wanted a baby of our own." The kettle shrieked, and Jane asked, "Tea?"

"Thanks," said Myla, and watched Jane's ritual unfolding all over again. This time Myla left her mug next to Jane's and watched as Jane prepared both of their teacups the same way, almost unconscious that she was doing it twice.

"I called Emma last night," said Jane as she wound the tea bags meticulously. "She was thrilled to hear you're here, that you're all in one piece. She wants me to give you a butterfly kiss for her." Jane laughed. "I don't even know what that is."

Myla did. Myla remembered awakening to Pru on one side and Emma on the other, fluttering their eyelashes against her cheeks, giggling when she'd open her own eyes into frustration and the day. "It's simple. You blink your eyes against someone, like this," Myla said, and she lifted Jane's hand and blinked against it. "They used to wake me up like that all the time."

The doorbell rang, cutting into the soft quiet of their conversation. Jane handed Myla the spoon she'd been using to stir the tea. "Keep stirring," she said. "Just a few more seconds."

Myla heard the front door opening, heard Jane talking. There was surprise in her voice, but Myla didn't register it until Jane appeared at the doorway. "Myla," she said, smiling, "there's someone here for you. A friend? From the college?"

"Who?"

"He didn't say. He said he flew all the way from New York to see you." And then Myla knew why Mark hadn't been returning her calls. He'd come to her. She moved past Jane, into the living room, exultant. He'd read her letter and come here, for her, to work this out.

She found herself running the last three steps to the front door, but when she got closer, she stopped dead.

It wasn't Mark outside. It was Samuel.

AT FIRST, AT SCHOOL, MYLA says she thinks people might recognize us. But they don't. I tell her I knew they wouldn't. She says, "Well, maybe they won't recognize you in your baby school, but eighth-graders pass me in the hall all the time. Someone's bound to say something." But I can tell they don't. Pretty soon she drops it.

Then one night we're lying in bed. I'm warm and floating into sleep, and then Myla moves the bed by sitting up on one elbow and tilting me into awake. She pokes me. "Pru," she whispers.

"I hear you," I say, and pull my eyes open to look at her in the dark.

"Don't you think it's weird that people can look at us whenever they want?"

"What do you mean?" I ask. I'm tired. "I want to go to sleep."

"Okay, okay, in a minute. But think about it, Pru. Did you see those pictures in the gallery? They're for sale. Someone who doesn't know us can buy us and put us on the wall."

"I know." I can't think of anything else to say. "But it's just like snapshots, isn't it? Or—"

"No," she says, and the force of her voice shakes me. "It's *nothing* like snapshots. Snapshots are just for your family or your friends or the people who come to your birthday party. Ruth's pictures are for everybody."

So I sit up. I say, "Well, do you not want them up there? I mean, I bet you could talk to Ruth and she wouldn't put them on sale. Or if you didn't want her to show them, she wouldn't."

"No, it's nothing like that. The thing is—don't you think it's cool? It's cool to be up there like that. People look at us and imagine what we're thinking. We're like these mysteries."

"Like mystery books?" I don't get it.

"Not like mystery books, Pru. I mean like mysterious. People can see that we're thinking or talking, but they don't know what we're thinking or talking about." Then she stops and listens to hear if it's David's footsteps on the stairs or just the wind outside. Nothing moves while we listen. Finally she whispers, "But you're right about the book part. I mean, it's almost like our pictures are books that people want to read. It feels good. It feels like every time someone looks at one of those pictures, I can feel it in here." She touches her chest.

I lie back down. I can't think of anything to say. I've thought about it that way, but I've never heard it in words. And hearing it in words makes it seem scary to me. It makes Myla happy, but it starts to make me sad. Then Myla leaves me. I can hear her breathing trail her into sleep, and I don't catch her in time. When I touch her arm and say her name, she mumbles and turns on her side. I try to go to sleep, but her breathing keeps me awake. It turns into a chant in me with the last words Myla spoke: "Feel it in here, feel it in here, feel it in here." And then I am sleeping.

chapter nine

What are you doing here?" Myla had no control over her voice. She was shocked; reality swerved. Samuel Blake, here at this house? She couldn't name her emotion.

Samuel smiled, small. "I'm here to see you."

"To see me."

"Yes."

"I don't know what that means." She tried to figure out what to say next. She wanted to sit down, to ask where Mark was, to sort out how Samuel Blake could possibly be here and what she was supposed to do with him, but sitting down would mean she was weak. She stepped onto the porch and let the screen door slam behind her. She crossed her arms, gathering herself. "What are you doing here?"

Samuel raked his fingers through his hair. "I know I upset you. I didn't know I'd upset you until I got your letter, and by then I could tell you were more than upset. I still didn't know why, though, and you didn't sign your letter, so . . ." He cleared his throat. "So I called Mark, and he'd just gotten your letter, and then he explained who you were." Myla tried to keep herself from noticing how nervous Samuel was. She looked at him, and he continued. "I know you think I was playing some kind of game with you, that I knew who you were. Rather, who you *are*. But I didn't. I had absolutely no idea you're Myla Rose Wolfe. And I want you to know that."

"Okay." She didn't know what else to say.

"Okay."

Then a surge of anger shot up through her as she remembered the last things she'd heard Samuel speak: words disparaging her father, words blaming Ruth's photographs for Pru's death. She felt her voice turn clipped, cold, as she reached for the door handle. "Well, you've seen me. So I guess that's it. You can leave."

"Could you hear me out?" Myla didn't move her hand from the door, but she didn't move away from Samuel either. "I flew all the way across the country. Surely that counts for something?"

"I didn't know there was a point system." Myla felt herself wanting to argue with Samuel, to engage with him, but she realized that the less she argued, the sooner he'd leave. That *was* what she wanted, wasn't it? She looked at him and said, "Okay."

"I can't believe it. I really can't." Myla watched Samuel's mouth spread into a slow smile. "You just— it's amazing that you're really Myla Rose Wolfe. It's so strange. In a good way, of course. So strange that I've looked at those photographs a hundred times and never even once recognized you. Maybe I intuited something—"

"Hold on." She felt herself growing strong. "Just be-cause I'm in some photographs that you happen to think you know a lot about doesn't mean you know *anything* about me. I'm not who I was when you and I were involved. I'm not Kate Scott. You don't know me." She pulled the screen door open and placed one foot inside the house. "Please leave me alone."

"You disagreed with what I said about your family and the photographs, didn't you? In my lecture? That's why you're so angry at me."

"I'm not anything at you. I'm not talking about this anymore."

"Wait, Myla." His voice hooked her, suddenly sure of itself. He'd said her name. She waited. The house before her was dark, cool. And behind her, where Samuel stood, it was bright. She turned her head and listened. "You think I said horrible things about your family. You don't even know what to do with the things I said. And what I said was even more confusing be-cause we were really falling for each other. I mean, at least I was falling for you. I really was. I don't care what your name is or what it was."

Myla turned her body so she could see Samuel's face. She leaned against the door frame, propping open the screen door with her foot. She was tired. "What does it matter? That was a week ago. I had a different name. I had a different life."

"Maybe it doesn't all have to disappear."

"It didn't disappear, Samuel. I left it. I left you. Re-member?"

"Because of what I said."

"Okay, yes. You insulted my dead father, accusing

him of parental irresponsibility and who knows what else. For all I know, you truly believe that Ruth Handel was a pornographer and that she and my father were trafficking dirty pictures of his daughters. Hell, you probably think my coming all the way across the country simply proves your point: I was a traumatized girl who's become a traumatized woman. And you probably think you're going to save me. Well, I don't need a prince. I just need time."

"Would it help if I apologized?"

"It wouldn't even help if you took it back. Because I know it's what you believe. You were honest in your classroom. You believe what you said. And I can't be with someone who thinks . . ." Myla straightened her shoulders and looked Samuel squarely in the eye. She planned to break him. "The thought of being with you sickens me."

"That's why I'm here," Samuel said.

"What?" Myla was shocked to see Samuel looking so triumphant. "You're here because you sicken me? That's the most pathetic—"

"Not that," he said. "Jesus, Myla, I have a backbone. No, no, just listen. I'll tell you why I'm here. Please? Just give me one minute of your time, and then I'll leave you alone." She nodded for him to continue. "You've more or less been in hiding for your entire adult life, right?" he asked.

"I haven't been in hiding—"

"Whatever you want to call it. No one's known who you really are."

"Okay. Yeah. So?"

He nodded. "And now you've disappeared in a very

dramatic way from a very respected college. Mark's going to have to tell the authorities everything he knows, if only because the college turned your departure into a missing-persons case. And then, pretty soon, the press'll get wind of it—remember that piece in *Vanity Fair*?—and someone will figure out where you're living, and some asshole with a tape recorder will find you. And then you'll have to answer for your family. I know it's not fair, but it's bound to happen. And I'm going to help you."

"Help me?" Myla was stunned, mainly because she realized Samuel had a good point. She'd planned Kate Scott's life down to the last detail, except she hadn't been discreet about her disappearance. She'd simply left, and he was right: if there was anyone interested in finding the current whereabouts of Myla Rose Wolfe, it would be easy.

Samuel continued, "The people who'll buy an article about the Ruth Handel case won't buy it because they're bad or just ignorant. They'll buy it because they're *concerned*; a little girl died, as far as they know, because of naked pictures. And they want to know how her sister's faring. And when it's put that way, I think you'd realize why someone like me would be curious. Why someone like me might wonder just exactly how a man could still be a good father and allow naked pictures of his children to be taken."

Myla groaned. She tightened her grip on the door and said, "Leave, Samuel."

Jane came up from inside the house and placed her hand on Myla's shoulder, making her jump. "Is every-

thing all right?" Jane asked, trying to sound intimi-
dating.

"Yes. We're fine. This is Samuel. Sorry for the noise,
Jane. We're just figuring something out. But Samuel's
leaving in a minute, aren't you?"

"Nice to officially meet you," said Samuel, reaching
inside the screen door for Jane's hand.

"You flew all the way from New York just to see
Myla?" Jane asked, repeating what he'd already told
her.

"Yeah," said Samuel.

"Wow," said Jane, arching one eyebrow at Myla as
she went back inside the house.

Samuel spoke fluidly now, rapidly, looking Myla
straight in the eye. "You said in your letter that I had to
climb out of the ivory tower and look at how others live.
You called me a weak scholar, saying I knew nothing of
what I spoke. And maybe you're right. Maybe I've
made my own version of a story out of a slim number of
events. But I'm everyone out there. I'm the person you
need to think about. If your father really was a good
man, and if you really believe those photographs are
not only innocent but important in their own right,
then you're going to have to convince me of it. Because
if you don't convince me, someone else, someone from
the media, will be knocking on your door next week,
and they sure as hell won't care if they tear you limb
from limb. They won't have held you while you slept,
they won't give a damn if it breaks your heart. Rest assured, they'll drag your father's name through the mud,
and they'll dishonor your sister's memory. And I can't

let that happen. For one simple reason: because I like you. I'm here to see you, and I'm here to help."

The world was spinning again. Myla needed a glass of water. "I can't do this," she said. She stepped inside and let the screen door go, separating her from Samuel. As she turned and strode into the darkness, retreating into the cool, she heard the door yawn closed, then the clip of the latch behind her. Her eyes adjusted, and she saw Jane standing in front of her.

"So you're going to let him leave?" Jane's voice was low, whispering.

"What am I supposed to do? I didn't ask him to come. I don't know what he wants."

"He wants to help you, Myla. He wants to talk to you."

"But what if I don't want his help? I never asked for it. I don't need him, Jane." Myla felt herself hovering on the brink of a decision, but she didn't know how to make it: either trust him, believe he wanted to help her, and let him stay, or listen to those things he'd said in his lecture hall and ask him to leave because of them.

Jane put her hands on both of Myla's shoulders. She said, "It's not my practice to nose into other people's business. But Emma would do something. Emma would tell me I have to do something." Jane walked around Myla to the screen door and pushed it open. Myla heard Jane's footsteps on the porch and then the low mumble of talking. Myla listened as an indiscernible conversation passed, and after a minute—a long, long minute—Jane pulled the door open again.

She walked to Myla and placed her hand on the small of her back.

"He's staying for dinner. I told him it's up to you what happens next, but this is my house, and I want to be hospitable. A man who's flown across the country deserves at least one meal before turning around again." She leaned in to Myla. "I'm making lemonade. Go talk to him. I told him you don't want to talk about anything serious. But he's sitting on the porch swing. He just wants to know you're okay."

Jane headed toward the kitchen, leaving Myla alone in the living room. Myla knew Jane was right: no matter what Samuel's beliefs, it took a lot of *something* to fly across the country after a woman you barely knew. She turned around, squinting into the light of the day. And then she went toward it. Toward Samuel.

EVERYBODY HAS AN OPINION about the pictures. Ruth makes them. Jane hates them. Emma wants to be in them. Myla uses them to show off. Everyone has an opinion. Everyone but me.

And David too. I like to be in the pictures, and I know David likes that. So one afternoon when Myla's over at someone's house, and there's no babysitter, and David has a cold, I decide to ask him. But I don't ask him what he thinks. I ask him why Jane gets so mad.

David's sitting on the green couch in the sunlight with a box of Kleenex and a pile of student papers. I keep refilling his glass of orange juice that's crusty around the top. I just ask him. I say, "Why does Jane hate the pictures so much?"

David looks surprised, moves the papers off his lap. "What makes you say that, Prudence?" He uses my whole name when he's being serious.

He and I both know that Jane hates the pictures. What I don't know is why. What I also don't know is this other thing. So I ask him another question. "Does Jane hate Ruth?"

That makes him stand up and go across the room and pull a big heavy book off the bottom shelf. He dusts it with his sleeve. This is one thing I love about David. He is always answering questions about one thing with examples from something else. Sure enough, he opens up the book, sits beside me, and spreads it across our laps so it smushes my legs.

"Look at this," he says.

I look.

"What do you see?" he asks.

It's a picture. A photograph. An old brown photograph. And even though I know it's the ocean and the sky, it doesn't really look like the ocean and the sky. Black rocks are at the bottom, black clouds are at the top, the water and the air are in the middle.

"The ocean," I tell him.

"And how do you know it's the ocean?" David asks.

"Because," I say.

"Does it look like the ocean?" he asks me.

"Not really," I say.

"Why not?"

It's all so obvious, and I wonder what this has to do with Jane. "Because."

"Let me help you think about this," David says. "You see the ocean because you *know* it's the ocean. You know it's supposed to be the ocean because you see a boat there, in the middle. But what if you didn't know about boats? What if you'd never seen the ocean before? What you'd see—what it looks like—is a wall of water and air.

"This photograph is called *The Great Wave,* and a French photographer named Gustave Le Gray took it in 1856. What we know is that the ocean stretches far out. But that's what we know with our brains, from experience. If we forget our brains, we see a wall. Our eyes see a wall because our eyes are dumb, with no experience of their own."

I hear what he's saying, and I stare hard at the picture. It's a new kind of idea, because you just think, "The ocean's the ocean." So I stare at it and try to see a wall. But my experience keeps me from seeing it. I can only see it stretching out. And then, just in a flash, I see what he means. It *is* a wall. And then it's gone.

After I try to see the wall again, I start to get bored. I wonder what this has to do with Jane hating Ruth. And almost as if he reads my mind, David says, "Trust me. I'm talking about Jane here and how she sees the pictures of you and Myla. Because, Prudence, we *learn* how to see. Our brains teach our eyes how to see the world. First we learn how to see the world, and then we learn how to see pictures of the world. Representations. And we get so smart and so fast and so good at it that we don't even realize we have opinions about what we're seeing that have nothing to do with what we actually see.

"When I look at this picture, I can see both a wall and a stretch of sea. And when Jane looks at a picture of you, she sees a wonderful, beautiful, sweet, seven-year-old girl whom she loves. But she can also imagine the way a stranger might see the picture. And she tries to imagine what a stranger might think. So she doesn't hate the picture. She doesn't hate Ruth. She may not even hate the stranger. But she's scared."

I ask him, "Then why aren't we scared?"

"The answer is simple. The pictures are good and beautiful. They are pictures of you and Myla living your lives, growing up. And the taking of the photographs has become an important part of who you are, of part of that growing up. I wouldn't take that away from you for a million dollars, unless *you* didn't want to be a part of them anymore."

He stops talking for a minute. "Just having you be in the photographs has helped you learn that you're in charge of your own bodies. That you are in charge of your own minds. Jane loves you so much that she wants to protect you. I love you so much that I want to protect you, and I think letting you form opinions from your own experience is the best way to do that. So we disagree. But to tell you the truth, I like that Jane loves you so much. I like that Jane makes us think about all this. I bet you do too."

I nod. He's right, I do like that about Jane. I think about it then, for a long time. David lets me think. His answer isn't an answer so much as another bunch of questions. David's opinion about the pictures is to let me form my own opinion. He closes the book and kisses the top of my head. I have to think about it. He knows I do. So I get him a fresh glass of orange juice so he can correct his papers, and I go out to ride my bike.

CONVERSING WITH SAMUEL went better than Myla had anticipated. Once she sat down beside him on the porch swing, talking was easy. Perhaps it was the comfort of watching Jane's back as she weeded in the front yard, close enough for reassurance and far enough for privacy. Or perhaps it was Samuel's mention of Mark's name, which dredged up in Myla a deep missing that made her feel honest, that relaxed her into the giving of herself. "Mark's fine," said Samuel. "He's just worried about you." Conversation drifted to innocuous subjects—the coming baseball season, recently published fiction, movies they'd seen—and Myla realized that she did know *some* of Samuel, even if she didn't know, or didn't want to know, all of him.

When Steve got home that evening, Jane stopped her weeding, walking to the side of the house, obviously giving him some kind of explanation and instruction to be discreet. Jane's sudden stride brought Myla and Samuel out of the hollow of their conversation. Around them, they saw the evening light low and red, and Myla realized she was hungry. Time had flown. Then Steve walked around the corner of the house, up the front steps, and right over to Samuel. He stuck out his hand and chuckled. "Myla's told us absolutely nothing about you."

Jane arrived behind him, shaking her head. "Pay no

attention to anything he says." Myla was surprised to catch a glimmer of flirtation in Jane's exasperation.

"Well, Samuel, is it? The sooner Samuel learns that I'm constantly putting my foot in my mouth, the better off he'll be. Everyone thinks I'm an idiot." Steve chuckled again. "Isn't that right, Jane?"

Jane tossed her hair over her shoulder, creating her own wind tunnel. "I've often been impressed by the depths of idiocy you're capable of reaching." Myla saw the force of their love, something she'd never much considered. Steve stepped forward and grabbed Jane's hand, danced her around the front porch. They were alone in that dancing space together, wonderful to watch, until Steve got winded and leaned against the door frame.

"Not as spry as I used to be." He pointed to Samuel's suitcase, sitting in the middle of the front walk. "You better bring that inside or everyone'll think Jane's finally leaving me." He wheezed, then pulled the squeaky screen door open. "Well, aren't you all coming inside? It's nearly dark. And I'm hungry."

Soon Myla found herself in the kitchen with Jane, preparing dinner as the men sat in the living room, drinking beer and watching a basketball game. Myla had met a lot of academic women disgusted by such gender division, and she'd always publicly agreed with them, acknowledging that all their careers existed only because their mothers had fought for liberation from apron strings. She'd openly criticized girls her own age who'd given up promising careers for families. But during each of these conversations, she'd had to keep a secret to herself: despite all the political, moral, economic reasons to deplore "women's work," she loved it. She loved being in that kitchen with Jane, being ordered around by a recipe-savvy woman. The onions sizzled with lightning intensity. Myla watched Jane's dexterity with the wooden spoon, ached to be able to arrange a plate so beautifully. She remembered past moments with Jane, moments when it was just Jane's body she'd watch, when Jane would let go of words and simply move. Now that Myla was herself a woman, she realized she still longed for this ease.

She remembered witnessing this quality in Ruth too, in the moment just before Ruth would crouch behind the camera, gathering the dark-cloth to her shoulders. Her eyes would look different. She'd use words, but they weren't conversation, they were words from another part of her body, words to service her eyes: "Shift left. Eyes here. Blink. Now." It had seemed such an easy way to be, such a comfortable solution. Myla wondered if she'd lost all capacity to practice such grace.

That night they ate well and sat at the table long after they'd finished devouring everything on it. Steve and Samuel seemed to have hit it off famously. It helped Myla to watch the younger man befriend her father's closest friend. Myla imagined her father with such a man, imagined how David would have handled Samuel's sudden appearance. She forced herself to believe that he would have been as jovial as this other father figure, but had to admit to herself that David, always caught up in his mind, probably would have been oblivious. He'd demonstrated none of the formalities of manliness that Steve had. It was good to consider David this way, realistically, without the tragedy of life washing over all her memories. And remembering her father like this made the reality of his notebook all the more compelling. She wanted to know what Steve had figured out.

As they contemplated dessert, Steve leaned back in his chair and undid the top button of his pants. Myla saw her chance, saw the possibility to ask. But she knew she'd have to divulge the few truths she had about her father's notebook to Samuel, to a man who only days before had defamed her father to a roomful of people. She looked at Samuel as he leaned his elbows on the table, asking Jane about her curriculum, and realized that telling him about David's notebook was a chance she'd have to take if she were going to get to know Steve's mind right now. At this moment, waiting any longer for a private audience with him seemed excruciating. Besides, Samuel had been on his best behavior all afternoon. So Myla led the conversation in her own direction, hooking in the details of Marcus Berger and the mysterious envelope, catching Samuel's eye, willing him through her honesty to understand that her father, a brilliant scholar, was to be taken seriously. "And that leads us to Steve, who's been looking at the notebook and interpreting—"

Steve grunted. "I was afraid of this."

"Have you looked at it yet?" Myla asked.

"Of course I've looked at it," he said, a wave of darkness passing across his face.

"So what does it mean?" She couldn't help asking the most basic question.

"I'm afraid you have a rather high estimation of my mental abilities, Myla. To assume I—"

"Okay, okay," said Myla. "Be humble if you must." She turned back to Samuel. "He's much more of an intellectual than he gives himself credit for. Am I right, Jane?" Jane nodded, smiling. "Tell us, Steve," said Myla. "Tell us what you figured out."

Steve shook his head. "See, here it is, Myla, I don't want you to get your hopes up about all this—"

"Just tell me," said Myla. "I *know* you understand my father's brain. I know you've picked something up, even just one tiny thing, and that thing's going to help us."

But Steve rumbled, "No no no. I will not let this go on. No misplaced reverence."

"It isn't misplaced, Steve. It's the truth. I came to you. I came here for your help because I knew you'd be the only person who could help me. The only person in the world." Myla put her hand on Steve's, but he didn't reciprocate the touch. Suddenly Myla read him, understood what he'd been trying to say; it was almost as though his frustration was pumping into her through her fingers. Then he spoke.

"The truth, Myles, is that I have no idea what the hell your father's talking about. Not a clue." To himself, he muttered, "Dammit." Then he looked down the table and bellowed at Jane. "Impossible to try to get a point across in this family when everyone keeps talking over you. I've been trying to tell you that I looked at the notebook—spent hours with it, in fact—and I'm no closer to understanding it than I was in the first place. So much for my intellectual abilities."

Jane spoke first. "There's no reason to raise your

voice. No one's expecting anything of you except your opinion. Right, Myla?"

Myla could feel her face warming. She could feel tears burning her eyes. She nodded her head and managed, "Of course not," even though she knew that what she'd been expecting was answers. She'd expected Steve to tell her what the hell the notebook meant. And now she was alone again, alone with her father's indiscernible thoughts and no one to help her interpret them.

Steve understood. "I'm sorry," he said after a while. "I told you, I'm a math guy. I loved your dad like a brother, and I was good at nodding along whenever he'd posit one of his theories, but even then I wasn't privy to his mind." He pulled his napkin from his lap and folded it on the table. Then he pushed back his chair and stood. He looked for a minute as if he had something to say, then he shook his head. He gathered the dishes from the table and walked to the kitchen.

Myla put her head in her hands. She wished she could help her physical response, her sickened disappointment, if only to spare Steve's feelings. But she needed a moment to gather herself before she could go to him and absolve him of his responsibility.

Samuel leaned toward her across the table. "You said the notebook was full of words, like brainstorming?"

Myla had all but forgotten Samuel's presence. She glimpsed him through her fingers, realizing she'd let him in on something dangerous. She'd proved his point for him: not only would he believe her father was a bad man, he'd also think him an indecipherable scholar. Myla couldn't speak. She nodded.

"Could I see it?" he asked.

Jane cleared her throat. "I'll get it from Steve," she said, excusing herself from the table, while Myla hid herself from everyone's eyes. He was in this far. He might as well rip her father's notebook apart as well.

Fifteen minutes later, they were all gathered on the couch in the living room. Samuel had called them to him, and now he was flipping through the notebook with rapid excitement. "Your father was doing some pretty sophisticated thinking about response theory. I'm almost sure of it."

"Response theory?" Jane asked.

"See, I've been forcing David Freedberg's *The Power of Images* down my students' throats, which, as we all know, doesn't guarantee that I know anything about his thesis. But his basic assumption is that image alone exerts enormous power over the human psyche. Even if we're not aware of the mechanism." Samuel paused, then looked at Myla and smiled. "Myla sat in on one of the lectures when we were talking about this idea. Basically, it posits that certain physical responses, uncontrollable by the mind, are unleashed when humans see certain things depicted."

"Okay." Steve smirked. "And in plain English?"

Samuel smiled. "This isn't a revolutionary theory; in fact, people have believed it since the first man drew a painting on a cave wall. Here's an example: we know that when people eat off a yellow plate, they eat faster and they eat more. The conclusion we draw is—"

Jane spoke. "That yellow does something to human brains to make them think they're hungry."

"Right. Now, the thing is that even in the last ten years" —here Samuel hesitated—"since David's death, scientists have been hooking people up to electrodes and seeing what part of the brain responds to yellow. But it looks to me like there isn't much science in his notes. The words he's written down: *Jesus in the frescoes*, oh, and *Vermeer* over here, well, they seem to be highlighting an artistic point of view. Maybe he's trying to get at specific ways in art that response theory works."

Myla was nodding. "Welcome to Myla's Childhood 101: An Overview of David Wolfe's Scintillating Bedtime Stories." Everyone laughed at the touch of sarcasm in her voice, and Myla felt herself flush with possibility. She put her hand on Steve's shoulder.

Samuel was eager to continue. "So it seems your father was suggesting that just looking at a picture can make people believe or act in specific ways that they'd never consciously admit."

Steve turned to Myla, patting the hand she'd placed on him. "Nabbed a good one, I see. One who can help you in your research."

"In *my* research?" said Myla. "I thought this was *our* project."

Steve shook his head. "Some help I've been. Okay, yes, I'll get you into the library—the woman at the front desk owes me a favor, and no, Jane, not that kind of favor—but after that, you're on your own. Except that you've got Samuel here."

Samuel coughed.

"Samuel," Steve beamed, "you should know, before you tackle this project, the exact pedigree of the brain you'll be trying to unearth. Myla's dad loved art. It was the guiding philosophy of his life. David believed art was the most powerful force on earth. He once told me that image was the closest we could get to God." This surprised Myla. She'd never once heard David mention God. Steve continued, "So I guess the good news here, if we choose to trust this Samuel person, is that the notebook may be the precursor to a bigger enterprise. Does that seem in the realm of possibility?"

"Sure," said Samuel. "Are we looking for something bigger?"

"My father may have written a book," explained Myla. "We all expected to find it somewhere among his things, but it never emerged."

Steve continued Myla's thought. "Perhaps this notebook encodes a shorthand for bigger ideas filed away somewhere. Imagine that each word is a tab on a file folder. Each word calls up a whole file of ideas that David held in his head. So what we've got to do is figure out what those files consisted of."

But Myla wanted more. "What about the diagrams in the notebook? The brainstorming that it looks like he's doing?"

Samuel was all professor: "They read to me like different ways of getting at the same question. The problem is, I don't know what that question is, so it's hard to figure out how David's trying to answer it."

Steve was getting excited too. "Here's the deal, though: no one thought about art the way your father did. According to Samuel, the notebook gives us hints about what David's connecting to what. And maybe, probably, those things are so unusual that we'll detect a pattern. And perhaps within that pattern, we'll find ourselves an argument." He touched Myla on the arm. "Your father was a professor, sure, and there were lots of things about him that made him good at that—diligence, love of the job, intelligence. But there was something else in him, something huge, that made it fun to hear him talk about art. Art was his breath.

"One day—I'll never forget—I came home from school and you guys were over at the house. It was the mid-eighties, so you girls must have been about fifteen and ten. You were upstairs with Emma. Jane came and met me at the front door, looking white as a sheet, and said, 'I think you'd better go outside.' I found David on the back porch with a glass of lemonade. And he looked devastated. I'd seen him looking like that only once before. When your mother died.

"I'm scared, so I pull up a chair. I ask what's happened, and he looks at me and says, 'Didn't you hear? Didn't you hear the news?' I shake my head no and prepare for the worst. He says, 'Rembrandt's *Danaë*. Some man in Russia attacked her. With a knife. With acid.'

"It was a painting, Myla. A painting. And you'd have thought that someone he loved had died. I admired him for that personal love. Nothing mathematic ever made me feel that way."

It was delicious to hear Steve speak about her father like this, especially after seeing him so devastated, so distant, earlier in the evening. "That's the kind of man your father was," he went on. "He was extraordinary. And it's too bad you have only me to tell you that. Because you're a hell of a lot more like him than you think."

Myla was whirling with possibility, watching Steve believe again in David's words. She was shocked by Samuel's presence, amazed by his sudden insertion into the very heart of her family. Amazed that he'd helped. She was elated, rising, in the promise of what he was offering: an interpretation of the notebook that had, on first glance, been full of foreign concepts.

But she felt the need to tell Steve and Jane one more thing. "We'd stopped talking, you know. At the end." She paused. "David and I." Myla looked up, and all eyes were on her. "I was so angry, so angry. And of course I thought both of us were doomed to live forever." Her eyes were dry.

"Sweetheart, your dad understood. Trust me." Steve spoke with authority. "I'm a dad. Silence is hard, but it's still a kind of speech. And now you have this." Steve touched the notebook. "He's still talking."

I ASK EMMA, "REMEMBER how I used to paint you?"

She looks up from her drawing. "No," she says.

"How I used to paint your face."

That makes her laugh. She asks me, "What would you paint?"

"Oh, dog faces, or rabbit faces. I used face paint after I got in trouble once for using markers."

That makes Emma laugh more. Then I say, "So I've been thinking. We were little kids then, and we did one kind of painting. But now I'm eight. I want to try a new kind of painting. I used to paint you, but now I want to *paint* you."

She tries to figure out the riddle, and then I see her understand. "Oooooh," she says. "You want to paint some pictures of me."

"Exactly," I say. "Artists need practice, and it's important to study the figure."

She asks me, "How do you know all that stuff?"

I tell her, "I don't know. I just do. Anyway. Would you be my model? You'll have to hold still for long periods."

She nods.

And then I say, "And would you mind keeping it a secret?"

She nods, but she asks me why.

I have to think about exactly the right way to explain. "Everyone around us knows more about art than we do. So maybe if we do pictures by ourselves, we'll get to be the experts for once."

The next day I try to paint her with watercolors, but the paper gets too soggy and the colors run into each other. Her face and her hair turn into one big brown blob and I don't even get to the rest of her body.

It's frustrating, because I had such a clear picture in my mind about what the painting would look like. And I can't do it. Emma's patient but I'm not. After a couple of tries, I tell her thank you and give her a piece of chocolate left over from Halloween.

"Don't worry," she tells me, "I bet this is how a lot of artists start out."

proof

the younger girl is older now, but you recognize her. Long legs, long hair, but no hips yet, no breasts. She's nude, and she stands on the far edge of a small lake. On either side of her, pine stumps stud the ground, and you imagine splinters knifing through her bare feet as she climbed to her spot. Perhaps her shoes are hidden somewhere, behind a stump. Or perhaps she swam, but no, her hair is dry, so she must have walked from here, where the camera is, all the way around the lip of the lake, wading some of the way. Now she is far.

Her white body stands out against the dark lines of trees behind her. Her hands are open, solid; she spreads them wide, as if she is blessing the day. Her eyes are closed. A smile plays on her face, and it suggests to you that she knows something special, a secret. The sky behind her, beyond the forest, is open, painted with the whisper of clouds.

At the back of the picture, you see a dark smudge. At first you think it must be a mistake, but when you look closely, you make out looming clouds, a storm moving in. She doesn't see it. It will come from behind her. From your vantage point, nothing acknowledges the wind about to whip up, the air that will fill with wet. And yet you know it is coming.

How will she get back?

chapter ten

myla came down the stairs with bedding in her arms. Through the open window, cool darkness filtered into the living room. Samuel was sitting on the couch with his hands folded in his lap. He looked up when he saw her descending. "I was wondering what happened to you guys," he said as he glanced at her armload.

"The linen closet's a mess," she said.

"Oh." Samuel stood, confusion on his face. "Well, I just wanted to say good night before I headed out—"

"These are for you," said Myla as she handed him the bedding.

Samuel took the blankets and sheets from her arms, but was looking at her face, shaking his head. "I'm going to find a hotel. I don't think I—"

"You don't know these people. You eat dinner at their house, you have to sleep here. Their rules, not mine." She tried to keep the warmth from her voice as she said: "They think we're friends."

Samuel raised an eyebrow. "And are we?"

Myla sat down on the couch. "You helped me out

tonight. You helped us all out. And honestly, I was surprised. I didn't expect you to show up on my doorstep claiming you could help and then actually be able to help me. So that counts for something."

"On the other hand . . ." Samuel began for her.

"There is no other hand. A week ago I thought we were friends. This morning I thought we were enemies. Now you're here. Now I don't know what we are."

"Fair enough," said Samuel.

"And just how long are you planning on staying, anyway?" Myla caught herself. "That sounded ruder than I meant it. I just mean, how did you leave the college before the semester ended?"

Samuel smiled. "You're not the only one who can just pick up and leave dramatically. No, I'm glad you asked. Two words: 'family emergency.' I've got to call in and let them know how my 'grandmother' is faring." Myla felt a set of worried questions about to spill out, but Samuel spoke before she could voice them. "No pressure," he said. "No expectations. It was my chance and I took it. I won't regret that, no matter what happens."

"Okay. So." Myla stood as a pulse of exhaustion shivered up her body. She scanned the pile of bedding now pressed against Samuel's chest. "Will you be warm enough?"

Samuel laughed. "It's May. You've handed me, like, ten blankets. I think I'll be fine."

"Okay," said Myla.

"Okay," said Samuel. Myla turned and walked to the

stairs, but Samuel's voice stopped her. "I want to apologize."

"For what?"

"For what I said in my lecture. I wish I could take it back."

Myla put her hand on the banister. It was smooth and cool. She closed her eyes and waited for the right words. "I learned a long time ago that no one can be responsible for anyone else's beliefs. You believe what you believe. You know what you know. The best any of us can do is to examine our own prejudices, our own assumptions, and correct ourselves when we're wrong." She smiled at him, then looked up the staircase. She was weary. She put one foot on the next step.

"Sleep well," Samuel said, after a moment. Myla climbed the carpeted stairs one at a time, into the light of the upstairs hallway.

Now Myla was lying in bed, and she could feel herself drifting, heavy, into sleep. She imagined Samuel curled almost directly beneath her, one floor down, and in her drowsiness, she remembered his breath, warm and frequent on her back. She remembered it, and it comforted her. She knew she'd dream.

She was in a dark room, alone. There was a television on the opposite wall, and though it provided both blinking light and image, no sound emerged. She knew, from entering this dream before, that she had no control over the volume. She stepped forward until the television came into focus, and watched what she knew would be showing. It was an interview, an interview that had never happened except in Myla's nightmares.

Pru sat in an armrested chair, wearing a collared dress with a white cardigan. Her feet barely reached the edge of the cushion. She was tiny, unable to span the distance to the floor.

Myla kept stepping closer and closer to the screen, trying to read Pru's lips. The camera was now focused in close-up on her head; it switched quickly to the woman interviewing her, coiffed and red-faced. Myla knew the interviewer was starting to ask questions Pru wouldn't know how to answer, and in her mind, Myla tried to send Pru messages: "Say you don't know. Say you don't want to answer that. Say they should ask Ruth."

Even though Myla knew she had no power in this dream, no way to communicate anything to her sister, she still tried and tried, tried so hard it hurt her brain. She could see Pru shifting uncomfortably; she read her little sister's body language loud and clear. There was nothing to be done but watch. That was when Myla would start to panic, would cough and punch. She'd yell at the television, try to get Pru to hear her. Meanwhile, the smell of pine would fill her lungs, taking away her air. She'd scream herself awake.

This time the end was different. The end was cut short. Instead of awakening in a room alone, having tried everything she could, she felt her mind being pulled back into her body. Someone was shaking her before she even started fighting hard. Someone was calling her back.

Myla opened her eyes and Samuel was over her. "It's a dream," he said. "A nightmare. Wake up. It's over."

She was confused. How was Samuel here, in her

bedroom? She sat up in bed and noticed a shadow at the door.

Samuel turned and said, "She's awake now."

Myla heard Jane's croaky nighttime voice: "Do you need anything?"

Myla couldn't remember how to speak. Samuel said over his shoulder, "Go back to sleep. I'll get her whatever she wants."

Jane yawned. "Good night." Her shadow faded down the hallway, and her bedroom door shut.

"God," said Myla, coming into herself. "I must have been making a lot of noise."

"Yeah," said Samuel. "You were screaming." He touched her hair. "Are you okay?" he asked, then took his hand away, as if aware that his touch might alarm her.

"Oh, sure," said Myla. "I'm sorry I woke you guys up. I have these dreams sometimes. And they're always pretty dark. But it's gotten to a place where I can control them." She shrugged. "Or at least I thought I could."

"You never once woke me when—" Samuel caught himself. "How do the students react?"

Myla laughed, embarrassed. "Everyone makes such crazy sounds in the dorm that a little screaming doesn't show up on the radar." Then she asked, "How's the couch?"

"Comfortable." He stood up. "I guess I'll be going. Unless you need something."

"No."

Myla lay back and listened to Samuel's thuds down the stairs. As she closed her eyes, she realized her face was warm, but not from her nightmare. It was Samuel's mention of the many nights they'd spent together. It was the sweet memory those words held of all the hours she'd slept in his bed, when his body had kept her from her terrors. And now he was below her, one floor below. She listened for him, but he was back in bed. The house was quiet. She slept.

PRETTY SOON I FORGET ABOUT the pictures. It gets cold, but at first it's beautiful—yellow leaves make our street round with fake sunlight. Walking home from school is walking through a tunnel of gold. Even when it's raining, which is all the time. Then the leaves paste themselves on the streets and make trenches of brown for every step I take. This lasts for months. I have to wear boots big enough to reach my knees. We lean the boots, green and heavy, upside down over the heating vent every night before I go to sleep. In the morning the soft flannel in them is burning hot. Burning hot all the way to school.

Myla decides she wants her own room. She says my things get in her way, and she kicks them when she yells down the stairs at David. "I'm a teenager now. Thirteen? Doesn't that mean anything to you? None of the rest of my friends have to share a bed with an eight-year-old!" She says she needs her privacy, and when we're alone, she mouths "Sorry." But she isn't, not really, and I don't blame her. I don't understand her enough to blame her. I want to be with her, but she doesn't want to be near me. So I let her move.

David lets me have a bunk bed, even though it's only me who sleeps in my room. I tell him I want to sleep in a place where you have to use a ladder to get up, and he says that sounds like a pretty good reason. When we go to pick it out, Myla tries out the beds with me and tells me she's jealous because David never let her get a brand-new bed when she was eight. I pick out a shiny red one, with metal bars and legs. You can even take the bottom bunk out and make a desk space underneath it. Myla says that when I'm older, that kind of study space will be invaluable.

Then Myla moves down the hall to the guest room. That's what we call it, but it's never been a place for guests. More like David's boxes, and even boxes of our mother's books. David says he'll move them down to the basement, but Myla likes them there. She acts like she doesn't care but I know her better. I think David does too. He moves them into a corner and puts a sheet over them.

The first night without her is silent. I don't get scared, but that's the closest feeling I know to what it's like. It makes no sense to me that her breath is gone. It makes no sense that she wants to sleep down the hall, when I'm so close. So I get out of bed and peek out my doorway. The hall is dark, and her door is closed. Light slices out from under her door. I squat down on the floor and wait. I wait for the light to turn out, and it takes a long time. When it does, when the faint click comes from her room, I know it's time. I go back to my bed, fumble my feet over the cold steps of the ladder, and go up into the darkness. I climb into bed and wait for it to warm up. Only *my* heat now. Only *my* breath.

SAMUEL SNEAKED A CUP OF coffee into the library by holding it inside his briefcase. Myla watched him carefully balancing the bag as he walked through the building's entrance. Sipping coffee in a library seemed an extravagance, one she'd never considered. She admired the way he persevered, risking spillage and burns, not to mention the possibility of scolding librarians, just because he loved coffee. She wondered if she needed any single thing that strongly.

Steve escorted them to a wide oak table where they spread out their notebooks. He placed David's notebook squarely in the middle, patting it as he set it down. Myla felt a wave of fear that leaving it out on the table risked theft, but she knew this was paranoid. This notebook was her treasure, but to anyone else, it was nothing special. Steve showed them around, giving a mini-tour of the reference desk and the stacks and the reserve room. In the time since she'd last been here, the whole place had been renovated; things seemed slightly dislocated, though familiar.

Steve reminded them that he was doing the best he could, "But keep in mind, I'm no professor emeritus in art history. Hell, I was never emeritus in mathematics either, but who's counting?" He suggested they start by looking at something concrete. So when they headed off into the stacks and returned with armfuls of large books, he rumbled around, examining each, then thrust one heavy tome into Myla's arms and took one for himself. He let Samuel choose his own. Steve flipped through her book, pointed to a chapter, and said, "Start here." His finger jabbed the page. They settled opposite each other, Steve smiling from finally being able to help her. They read in silence.

The book Steve had given Myla was about Rembrandt. At first Myla had no idea why he had chosen Rembrandt specifically—as far as she knew, none of the brainstorming circles in the notebook had anything to do with the Dutch painter. And the chapter Steve had given her was relatively mundane, a re-creation of Rembrandt's married life to Saskia van Uylenburgh and analyses of some of the Saskia paintings: *Saskia Wearing a Veil*, *Saskia Laughing*. Then numerous speculations about whether Saskia was in fact the subject of two of Rembrandt's paintings, both portraits of Flora, the goddess of spring. Myla felt her mind turning off, felt it asking, "Who cares which painting is based on her? If he loved her, wouldn't they all be?" This had always been her problem with the study of art: she never understood how people could spend hours interpreting the tiniest turn of a finger or the direction of the eyes. When she looked at representations of Mary, she hardly looked at the robes themselves; she looked *through* them to the meaning *behind* them. What did azure mean to medieval painters imagining Mary? Why was she clothed in velvet? Myla was never satisfied by simply looking at the pictures. She wanted context. She wanted something bigger.

Then, just as she felt her resistance pushing her over into frustration, she flipped the page and fell into such exhilaration, it caught her breath. Steve looked up from his reading, and she smiled until he settled down again.

For here was the author's explanation of the attack on the *Danaë*.

In Leningrad, on June 15, 1985, a Lithuanian man had walked into the Rembrandt gallery in the Hermitage. The *Danaë* was the first painting in the gallery, and the man walked to her, stabbed her in the groin, punctured her a second time, and then threw sulfuric acid on her face, torso, and legs. The guards didn't reach her in time to intervene, and even if they had, they wouldn't have known what to do, because they hadn't been trained for such an attack. Who wants to murder paintings?

No one knew why the man had attacked that particular painting. Some argued that it was simply because the *Danaë* was the first Rembrandt in the gallery, the most accessible, that he'd been out to damage anything. Some argued that it was because the *Danaë* was the most expensive painting in the room. The attacker himself claimed it was out of nationalist protest.

But the book Myla read posited that it was none of these things. Rather, it theorized that the man had attacked the painting because of its pure sensuality: the display of Danaë's recumbent nakedness, the slide of her breasts into her wide belly into the chalice of her hips, the fact that her crotch was at the very mathematically calculable center of the painting. What could be more of a taunt to a religious zealot?

Danaë was nude. She reclined on the bed. She had been imprisoned by her father, Acrisius, the king of the Argives, because of a prophecy that his grandson, Danaë's son, would murder him. So Acrisius locked his daughter in a tall, unreachable tower. Jupiter, formidable, tricky Jupiter, found his way through the walls of the tower and impregnated Danaë in a golden shower of sunlight. And here she lay in Rembrandt's eye, washed golden in the light of Jupiter's lust. She bore Jupiter a child because he had shone upon her. And then, thousands of years later, a man painted her story, and hundreds of years after that, another man came and cut her with a knife.

Myla scribbled down a few notes, thinking about how David would have spoken to her about Rembrandt. He would have reminded Myla the child that Rembrandt and his art had given Danaë life, but Myla the adult knew things were more complicated. The painter may have given Danaë life, but he'd also failed to protect her. He'd put her out there, left her subject to someone's knife.

She lifted her eyes, watching Samuel as he read. His words from the lecture hall echoed in her head, filling her with doubt. If exploring this notebook meant having to think about things like this, about all their lost chances, was such exploration truly worth it? Pondering these issues meant taking David down from the shelf, studying him. And that meant picking him apart, examining him critically, doubting him, judging his limitations. Perhaps that would be too hard. She closed the book. She needed space for thinking. She needed to move.

MY BIRTHDAY COMES AT THE start of school, when Oregon isn't at all like Oregon but is dry, dry, dry, hot, hot,

hot. You can wear shorts to school, play soccer on bristly grass instead of mud, but just as soon as you get used to these things, just as you begin to think about a Halloween costume that doesn't need a sweater under it, everything changes. The wind blasts and the sky starts pouring. But my birthday is still summer, and David suggests we all drive up the gorge and have a picnic by Multnomah Falls. Then we make a list of all the people we want to invite.

When we're driving to the store for food, David says, "Pru, all sorts of people are coming for your birthday, and I'm wondering if I could bring a friend."

"Sure," I say, and I think that's the end.

But Myla perks up from the backseat. "Who's the friend?"

David coughs. "A colleague, actually. An adjunct in anthro. She's—"

"I knew it!" says Myla. "I knew it was a girl."

David glances in the rearview mirror. "Oh, really? How'd you know that?"

"Because if she wasn't your girlfriend, you wouldn't have made such a big deal about it. You would have just introduced them when they showed up." I can't tell if Myla is speaking fact or finding fault. She sounds angry but excited too.

I shrug. "Sounds fine to me."

Everyone meets at our house early. Jane and Steve and Emma get there first, and when they see we aren't ready, Jane teases David, "I thought you said we'd take off at nine."

"I guess our household's working on relative time these days," he says.

Steve laughs and says, "Gee, David, we have no idea what that's like," and he nods his head toward Emma. Then Myla comes down from the house, yawning. She hasn't brushed her hair.

"Happy birthday, Pru," she says, and slips her hand around my waist while she kisses Jane.

"What's this?" asks Jane. "I thought you wanted to wear your new dress."

"I don't know," says Myla. "I don't really feel like going." She lets it drop like a heavy rock into our lake of conversation. She doesn't look at David. She doesn't look at me.

Jane smiles at me and says, "Well, that's nonsense," and puts her hand on Myla's back and steers her toward the house. Emma runs to me and grabs my hand and pulls me out of the gloom Myla has left behind. We're not interested in playing Dogs anymore, so we sit under the rhododendron bush and plan turning it into our fort. Then Ruth pokes her head in. "Happy birthday, kiddo. I can't believe you're nine. Where'd my little girl go?" I kiss her on the cheek and she says she thinks everyone's ready to go. But then she says, "I see the new anthro lady just arrived," and when she says "lady" I can see that she has opinions.

Myla will come, but only if Ruth rides in our car. I want to ride with Emma, but that might hurt Ruth's feelings, and Myla's glaring at me not to leave her alone with the grown-ups. So Jane and Steve and Emma follow us in their car, and in our car, the backseat is me, then Myla, then Ruth. That's because in the front seat is David and his friend, Helaine.

She's quiet. She looks out the windshield, not out the side window. It's like a pole runs straight up through her neck and keeps her head extra straight. Ruth, Myla, and I decide not to pay attention to her. Instead, we sing most of the way, and the windows are rolled down too much to listen to a word either Helaine or David is saying.

Pretty soon we're out of the city, and trees blur past us. We start the narrow twist and turn up through the rocks, and the sun dapples down on us, green through the trees. I roll my window down as far as it can go and stick my hand out to ride it on the wind. The wind hits my eyes so hard that I almost have to close them to see.

Then one more turn, and we pop out of the top of the trees and onto Crown Point. Myla jumps out and gets David, pulls him away from the car to the lookout. We ask Helaine if she wants to come too, but she says, "Thank you, no," and she turns her head a little and smiles with a closed mouth. "My back," she says. "Once I'm in the car, I'm in." So Ruth and I get out and wave to Jane and Steve sitting in the car next to us. Emma gets out of her car and comes with us.

"Should we wait with her?" I ask Ruth.

"Who? Jane?"

"No," I say. "Helaine."

Ruth snorts. "I'm sure she'll be fine." She grabs my hand and pulls me out to the lookout.

Up here, the Columbia is like a big blue and gold scarf. It moves like silk flicking in the wind, and the boats below are tiny buttons. Across the river lies Washington, green and hilled. Up here, falling feels like it would be simple, beautiful, easy.

Then Ruth starts singing "Roll On, Columbia," and Myla and Emma join in. I don't know the verse, only the chorus part, and on our walk back to the car, David explains all about the WPA and Woody Guthrie.

When we get to Multnomah Falls, we grab bags and blankets from the back. We can't see the falls yet from the road, so we have to walk a little bit. And then before we see it, it's the sound that makes us know it's there, like quiet thunder. Everything smells like moss before I see the sheet of white.

"Food first?" asks David, and we all say yes, so he heads us down to the grassy part below the falls. We spread out with grapes and olives and cheese and bread and we eat. Then everyone pretends there's nothing more to do, and Myla gets sneaky and pulls me away to play behind a big rock. Emma keeps spying over a boulder at us and then running back to the picnic. I know when I get back there'll be cake, but I get sneaky too and play along.

Myla and I sit down on a log. "Do you like your birthday so far?" she asks.

"Well, it's not really my birthday," I remind her. "Not until Tuesday."

"I know, I know," she says, "but I mean, do you like your party?"

"Yeah, I guess." Then we're quiet.

"Do you wish Mom was here?" The question's like a match in a dark room.

"I guess so," I say. "Yeah. I wish she was here."

"Me too," says Myla, and she pats her hand on my back.

Later, after cake, after presents, we go up to the bridge that stretches across the bottom part of the falls. The air is wet in my lungs, and the hand railing is slick and soft. I hold on tight and look down at the water slipping and slamming below us. David comes up behind me and puts his hands over mine.

"Happy birthday, Pru."

Then Myla comes up beside us. "David," she says, "Pru and I are riding home in Jane's car."

"Okay," he says.

"So just be sure you don't forget Ruth, okay? 'Cause she won't be with us."

"Fine, good," he says, and leans down to point out something across the river.

"Be sure Ruth goes with you. Just be sure."

"Yes, Myla, understood! I won't forget!" he says. And then Myla stomps off. David goes to talk to Helaine, and Ruth goes to comfort Myla, and Jane and Emma are on the other side of the bridge, looking up at the water. Steve comes and stands next to me. He doesn't say anything, just stands beside me and looks, like he wants me to know things are okay.

We stay up here, on the slick stone bridge, facing the river, and try to make out shapes: our car, the place where our blanket was, and the tiny dots of people looking up at us and pointing, like we are more important because of the waterfall behind us, like because of it, they want to imagine being in our lives.

chapter eleven

Samuel and Myla wound up the road she'd traveled innumerable times. She was aching for what was to come: the rush of water in her ears, the dampness in her lungs, the force and size of a river as it ended in air. "We're going to Multnomah Falls," she said, and Samuel nodded, although she knew he had no idea what that was.

As they crossed the Sandy River, passing the metal dragon someone had welded—"Very seventies," Samuel remarked—and wended their way through the town of Corbett, Myla was caught in her mind. There was plenty to contend with already: Jane and Steve's expectations, Samuel's sudden presence, David's notebook needing translation. Compared to all this, a mess of student papers was nothing. Were she at the college with Mark, life would be easy. Gossip exchanged, a shared muffin, an eye roll or two about their enormous course loads. Nothing this big.

Now the car broke into farmland, riding the spine of the ridge. Myla knew soon enough they'd see the change in altitude. Samuel gazed out the windows at the light and architecture and sky and trees. He tapped his hand against his knee, and Myla couldn't tell if that revealed nervousness or an ingrained habit. She didn't know him well enough to know such things, and the absurdity of their current situation—alone in a car together, halfway across the world, with perhaps nothing to say to each other—made her smile.

"What?" asked Samuel.

"Oh, nothing. I was just hoping Steve's enthusiasm hasn't been too much for you. He can be a bit overwhelming when he likes something. And he sure likes you."

"No, not at all. He's great. He and Jane seem very vibrant. Young, I mean."

Though Samuel hadn't asked for anything to be explained, Myla said, "They were my father's closest friends. They were integral in raising me." She paused, then chose to say her sister's name. "Integral in raising Pru and me. But before coming back this time, I hadn't spoken to them in thirteen years. Since I left home."

"Oh," said Samuel. "Wow." Then silence. It was funny, because Myla expected this silence between them to become more and more uncomfortable as it went on, but it didn't. Instead the silence softened gently, taking into account the sounds and smells of the car, the light breeze skipping in through the crack from Samuel's rolled-down window, the sun illuminating the deciduous trees that lined the roadbed. As she drove, Myla watched the new leaves in the sunlight, made out their tiny shapes above her. It seemed at this moment that she hadn't noticed leaves in a very long time; that in her life as Kate Scott, the tops of trees had been swaddled only in a vague, undefined green. Kate Scott could not live here. There were too many trees to be accounted for.

At first Myla hadn't known why she wanted to bring Samuel to Multnomah Falls. It was an intensely personal gesture, although of course he would have no way of knowing that. But following her instincts was the only thing she could do, and so they'd buckled into the car and backed out of the driveway. Now, with the knowledge that the Columbia would come into view below them in just a few miles, she gripped the steering wheel and understood. She was being David. Samuel was being her.

When she was a child, whenever David had been puzzling over something—Myla wondered now if those "somethings" had been related to The Book—he'd load her and Pru into the car and say, "Let's drive." Though he'd never mention their destination, Pru and Myla always knew where they were headed. They'd drive up the Columbia River Highway, elbow their way around Crown Point, then head straight to Multnomah Falls. At the falls, there'd always be a quick stroll up to the bridge, after which, depending on the season, there'd be ice cream at the outdoor stand or French-onion gratinée served at a heavy wood table in front of the restaurant's giant fireplace. The gratinée had always seemed terribly exotic to Myla, even before she was old enough to make out the word as foreign.

Now, as Myla drove, she laughed at herself. Here she was, years later, sitting exactly where David had sat, heading out to the country to allow her brain some breathing room. And Samuel sat beside her, her hostage, just as she, as a child, had been David's. She'd spent many hours sitting in the passenger seat, idly wondering what was on David's mind. And now Samuel was doing just the same thing with her.

"First stop," she said as they pulled up at the lookout point. Myla eased her door open, unbuckled her seatbelt, and walked to the edge. Below her, the Columbia swelled and tossed, and her hair was rumpled in the wind. Her arms liked the reminder of life on them, and she felt Samuel's cool shadow velvet her back.

"My God," he said. "This is gorgeous."

Myla nodded and smiled. Words seemed unnecessary. They might as well have left them behind in Portland. Samuel walked the rim of the lookout point, squinting down at the bright tossing waters. Myla watched a barge passing patiently below. It was simple up here, above life. The sound of a distant engine made her notice a plane flying above, made her remember her own place in the air only a few days before.

Back in the car, before starting it, Myla let words emerge from her, slow and easy. "I'd like your help. And you're welcome to stay as long as you want. But I can't offer myself. I don't have my self to offer."

Samuel nodded after a time. Myla tried to create a new sentence, to explain further, but everything she thought was too complicated to put into words. The sound of her voice in this car would be too loud. And having said what she needed to say, she felt an odd sense of elation. It felt good to be so honest, to let silence take back over, to be able to locate what she needed. It gave her hope that she might someday have a self to give.

After pulling out of the lookout point, they started down the ridge. Myla hesitated at Crown Point, then sloped the car down the mossy old highway. It was slower this way, much slower than passage on the swift new road below that paralleled the Columbia and flashed with cars and semi trucks. But this was the way Myla knew, the way to Multnomah Falls. This was the way she'd traveled with her family, and it seemed important to know that Samuel would like it. It was beautiful. It was green.

ALL OF A SUDDEN FOURTH grade is over and at last it's summer again. It pounces on us and makes us hot. Even though David is out of school, he still spends every day at the college. Myla goes to camp and hates it. I spend most days with Jane and Emma.

They take me to the pool and I learn breaststroke, the crawl, and the beginnings of the butterfly. But I miss Myla. She's only gone for three weeks, but it feels like forever. She writes me letters—most of which I don't get until she's already back—talking about all the stupid songs they have to sing and all the stupid boys in her group and how bad the food is. I know some of those things are true and some of those things she's just saying.

One day before Myla gets back, Ruth comes over and tells the girl taking care of me to take the rest of the afternoon off. So we sit on the front porch and eat plums and Ruth says, "I haven't gotten any great pictures of you for a while. So I'm thinking—how would you like to come up to Elk Lake with me sometime in July?"

"What's Elk Lake?"

"There's a cabin up there that's been in my family for a while. It's in the woods. If I didn't have more responsible relatives, it'd be rotten and crumbled by now. But I'd like to go there and make pictures, and I'd like it if you'd come—you and Myla."

"Sure," I say. "That'd be cool."

"We could make s'mores, and Myla could teach us camp songs—"

"She hates camp songs."

"Okay, well, I could teach you a camp song or two, and we could go swimming and canoeing—"

"What about David?" I ask.

"Well," she says, "David's welcome, of course. But I think he might have stuff to do here, like work." Ruth looks away.

"It's okay," I tell her. "You don't have to keep it a secret. He probably wants to be alone with Helaine, right?"

Ruth sighs. "We can't pull anything over on you, can we?" She smiles. "He probably does. But do me a favor, okay, Pru-y?"

So I say yes.

"Try not to be hard on him about it. Let him have the time." I nod. I want to tell her that I'm not the one who'll be hard on him. But I don't need to. She knows.

*   *   *

The drive down to Bend, the town where we'll spend one night with Ruth's uncle before going to the cabin, is long and hot. Myla and I take turns sitting in the front seat, and she gets mad when the times don't match up. But Ruth tells her there're no whiny teenagers allowed in her car, so Myla pouts until we turn on the radio and she forgets to be mad.

The air turns to hot desert around us once we're over the mountain. All of a sudden there are fewer trees and there are deep canyons that run beside the road. We cross more canyons on bridges, canyons so deep that you can only see the flash of water at the bottom of them for just a second. The sky gets wider. The sun swoops over everything.

We eat at a truck stop that has a pay phone at every table. We try to call David, but he isn't home so Ruth lets us order milkshakes *and* ice cream to make up for it. Then we drive to her uncle's house and let ourselves in. It's dark and smells like dust and old newspapers.

The next morning I don't even wake up until I open my eyes and I'm already in the car, speeding past sky and trees and rocks. When I sit up, Ruth smiles and reaches back to squeeze my knee. "Hey, kiddo. Want a Danish?" She passes one back. Pretty soon Myla wakes up too and climbs back over the seat and lies down with her head in my lap. She kisses my knees.

The car sounds change when we move onto the gravel. We crunch along, and dust crowds the air behind us. We follow the road until the lake is bright and glistening before us. Ruth laughs and claps her hands. "I always forget how gorgeous it is," she says. And so we start our week.

MYLA HAD THE LIBRARY TO herself. Steve was at work. Jane was at work. Samuel had been dressed, sitting on the couch, by the time Myla came downstairs. Bus map in hand, he'd said, "I'm planning to spend the day adventuring. Jane gave me some suggestions." She noticed a guide to Portland with a couple of marked-up Post-its on the cover. "So I'll see you later," he said as he walked out the door. She'd been left to the lonely house, and her anxieties had begun to swirl around her. She'd been sensible enough to grab her bag and get out of there.

Myla looked up from the oak table where she was sitting, surrounded on two sides by curlicued iron bookcases. She distracted her mind with the architecture, its elegant simplicity, all the while trying to get her brain back to David. The best part about the space, apart from the privacy, was the full-length window that abutted the table and let light pour in. It was an old window, contemporary with the library, and the glass rippled toward the bottom of the panes. Glass was a liquid that moved so slowly that it spanned centuries, all the time looking like it wasn't moving at all. That was why centuries-old windows like this were thicker at the bottom than the top. David had told Myla this when she was young.

His notebook lay like a flat hand against the desktop. Her own hands curved around the book spread before her, tracing words, marking whole passages, framing paragraphs, her fingers their own busy, autonomous people. She'd always looked at her fingers and invented personalities for them: her right ring finger looked sad, her left pointer was the leader of the group, her left pinky lagged behind like a child. She didn't particularly like how her hands looked except that they resembled David's. They were what he'd given her, and every time she looked at them, they summoned his memory.

He'd also left her this notebook, but she was feeling more and more that her hard thinking, her busy page-turning, her own notes in crisp black ink, were amounting to nothing. What had been planned as a blissful undertaking, a joyful reunion, was turning out to be less than positive. She hated to admit it, but without Samuel's guidance or Steve's company, Myla couldn't decipher any of David's notes. It would have been easier if they'd been in Greek, because then at least she could have checked out a dictionary. This was too hard, trying to determine the significance of each circled word, and beyond that, imagining all the different ideas, images, and theories that word would have signaled in David's mind.

She was searching her memory for traces of these ideas. She felt sure he must have explained some of this to her, and she cursed her teenage disinterest. She flipped open the notebook, hoping it would jog something, anything. They were just words: *paint globs— vanishing point—renditions of the real—Freud.*

She refocused. She looked at David's handwriting, at the words *Camera Obscura*, relaxed in them, and listened to her mind. She remembered what David had told her years before.

They'd been walking home from the college, Myla pushing her bike, David walking with two bags full of papers. She'd met him after school, and he was delivering one of his mini-lectures on European painting. She must have been about ten, which didn't stop him from believing she should know everything there was to know about art. She'd been vaguing out, kicking along a stone, tossing him the occasional "uh-huh" to make him believe she was listening, when she found herself actually pulled in by something. He was in the middle of a sentence when she said, "Wait, say that again."

"Say what again?"

"The part about the big debate."

"Oh. Well, there have been recent rumblings in the art-history world, because some believe that Vermeer may have used the camera obscura as a tool in the creation of his paintings. It's not a new assertion, but every once in a while my colleagues like to get up in arms over allegations that Vermeer 'cheated,' tracing the camera obscura's projection—"

Once again, he'd lost her. "Wait. What's a camera obscura?"

"Oh, it's a simple mechanism, the first kind of camera we ever had, long before film was invented. See, someone realized that if you make a tiny hole in one side of a perfectly dark box, and you make things very bright outside the box, you get a projection on the opposite wall, inside of the box. You see whatever is outside. Upside down, of course. Exactly the way your eye works. Exactly the way Ruth's camera works. Your brain turns the image right side up again. Ruth does it with her printing."

"But how do they think Vermeer used it?"

"Well, now, that's up to some debate. My money's on the guy who thinks that Vermeer set up a camera obscura right at the painting's viewpoint, and then projected the image onto the back wall. There's all sorts of evidence too; the paintings are blurry in some places, hinting at the image being 'out of focus,' which never happens with the naked eye. And there's a whole geometric study of the paintings as well. I'm not so interested in the hows of it as in the glorious idea of this painter using a camera as a tool. As if time could be captured." David paused, reflecting, then shook his head. "The point these dissenters don't understand is that regardless of whether Vermeer did or didn't use a camera obscura—which actually means 'dark chamber' in Latin, in case you were interested—"

"I'm not—"

"Well, the point is, Vermeer still had to do the painting itself. Even after the tracing, he had, at some point, to take the canvas down and turn it right side up and make the traced world look real. Fill it with life. That's where the talent lies. So I think we should be celebrating Vermeer's entrepreneurial spirit. Not to mention the precedent this sets for photography. If someone could prove that this were the case, it would show, once and for all, that the concept behind photography, the depiction of the real, has been around much longer than people thought—"

And he was off again. Myla remembered him walking ahead of her, oblivious to her falling behind. She'd been interested. Something had thrilled her to think that all those years ago, people had done exactly what she did with Ruth, holding still so they could be recorded. Recorded as she *was*. Recorded as she saw *herself*. Maybe that was how Vermeer's subjects had felt too. It truly proved her work with Ruth was art, and important.

Now Myla sat and tried to piece these ideas together. She could sense David's ideas circling high above her, just out of reach, but that was even more frustrating than when she'd felt nothing pulling her at all. He seemed to be thinking about realism, or about how art depicted life. Every way she tried to put it in her mind, it felt trite, already examined. Maybe her father had just been a good man without good ideas.

She wished so much more for him. She was angry that this was all he'd left her. She wanted to give up, to forget the whole project. "But," she thought, "I'm the only person up to the task. I'm the only one willing to listen. And here I am, alone with his notebook, with time on my hands and a willingness to work, and I can't understand any of it." She'd given it her all. The stuff she could understand fascinated, interested, enlightened her, but she knew she didn't have the facts to string them all together. To get at his inner argument. It made her madder than hell.

She shoved away from the desk and grabbed her bag, feeling inside to make sure her wallet was there. She'd make the four-minute walk to the student center, buy some chips and a drink, try to clear her head. She grabbed David's notebook and stuffed it in the bag,

then berated herself for bending one of the corners.
Even if it felt as though David were keeping her from
something vital, even if she wanted to yell at him as she
had when he was alive, the least helpful thing she
could possibly do was to punish the only physical ob-
ject currently tying them together. As she pushed open
the library door, her right hand flattened the new
crease, trying to ease it back into its original smoothness.

She sighed. The day was bright, brisk, easy. Light
was everywhere, reminding her of her attempts to explain to all those lifelong easterners the joys that came
with Oregon sunshine. Because you weren't just getting sun when the Oregon sky was wide and blue; you
were getting opposition to rain. It was a double bene-
fit. As a child, she'd thought everyone lived this way,
that light always came in layers: first you didn't have to
have rain anymore, then you got to have sun.

Myla turned right across the grass and startled a bird
pecking in its depths. Normally she wouldn't have noticed, but the bird hastened up before her and trans-
formed into light itself—the wings and tail glowed
from behind, carrying the sun and the golden disposi-
tion of the day. She gasped, and this startled her, her
own gasping. Because now, standing stock-still, she realized she was gasping from beauty and beauty only.
Yesterday she'd noticed distinct leaves, and now there
was this beautiful bird. She was seeing things.

Myla heard quiet steps behind her and turned just as
a middle-aged man with rolled-up shirtsleeves and
wire-rimmed glasses began to tap her on the shoulder.
He was the reference librarian. He could have been a

colleague. She'd noticed him on her comings and go-
ings past the reference desk, and he'd smiled at her.
Hadn't been suspicious at all of this young woman appearing out of nowhere with a huge research task and
no ID. That, in her experience, was the usual problem
with librarians. They tended to rely heavily on the
usage of identification.

But now he stood close behind her because she'd
stopped dead in her tracks to notice a glowing bird.
They were surprisingly close to each other, but she
didn't shift away from him. He backed up a half-step,
shy. "Hi, uh . . . I'm Tim."

"Myla. Nice to meet you."

"Myla. Okay, good. I thought so. I think someone
left something for you in my mailbox last night." He
shook his head and shrugged, and Myla noticed that
the sun lit up his ears, much like the wings of the bird,
only his ears glowed pink. "Um." He was clutching a
thick, oversize manila envelope under his left arm, and
he pushed it toward her, laid it in her hands. "Is this
you?"

The envelope was heavy and soft. She turned it over
so she could see what was written on it. Penned in unrecognizable handwriting: "Myla Wolfe." It must be
from Marcus Berger.

"Yeah." She waited a long time for the words to
make it out of her mouth. "That's me. Do you mind
telling me—"

"How I knew it was you? Well, there aren't so many
new people coming in and out of the library these
days."

"Wait." She smiled. "I was going to ask how you knew it was delivered last night."

"Oh." That made him smile too. A nervous habit. "I checked my mailbox at about two-thirty yesterday afternoon on my way to work, and when I checked it at ten on my way home, this was in it. So I guess it could have been delivered in the afternoon . . ." Then he cocked his head. "Wait, you weren't expecting this?"

Myla tapped the package with her fingers and laughed. "Tim, I don't even know what it is."

Myla sat on a bench, curled her fingers under the flap of the manila envelope, felt the tug of paper around her hand as she pulled it open to see inside. It was simple, once she saw. It was an answer, almost as good as if David had decided to come sit down on the bench beside her to try and explain everything himself. Because it *was* himself. Himself in 581 pages of words and footnotes and diagrams and images. His book. The Book. Someone had kept it for her. And now it was in her hands.

It smelled like their house. God, it was overwhelming, the smell, and her childhood came back in the smooth, knife-edged paper, ripped diligently from the all-night ding of the typewriter. The smell of it, the sound of it, brought back the smell and sound of him, of the stoop of his shoulders when he ducked into a room, of his whistling in the morning, of the efficiency the length of his hands afforded him when cutting vegetables or holding a fork. How could this weight in her hands do this to her mind? Bring him back out of darkness and light to a place where she imagined she could touch him again?

Was touching him. For here David was. Here in Myla's hands. If this wouldn't help her know him better, she didn't know what would. She would read his words. She would recognize him in his brilliance, make up for all those years she hadn't listened to him speak. Then she'd share his mind with the world. People would finally know he'd been a wonderful father, a genius, and most of all, a good man. People would finally know all that had been lost with his death, all that had been denied the world. Hope swelled.

She lifted the cover page and leaned it, face forward, against her chest. She read the first words of his book.

There are no straight lines in nature. Of course, there are a few naturally occurring linear gestures that suggest "straightness": a shaft of sunlight breaking through a cloud and hitting the ground below; a stiff reed/tree/stem rising single and upright against the light; the smooth horizon stretching on the far side of a plain, a desert, a sea. These things have always been visible. But look at the rocks, the trees, the shrubs, the waters that make up our natural world: not a straight line in sight.

So where did the line first appear? Inside the human imagination. The straight line was an idea in a person's mind before it became a thing in the world. But once this abstract notion became visible, it became obvious, and was easily translated into projects that required straightness.

Think of the pyramids, the temples of the Greeks, the planed marble floors of the Romans, the simple wooden beam. The constructed world became linear, and the linear world became the place that civilization met nature. The straight line entered the natural world so naturally that there was no good reason not to base human experience on its existence. Its eternal existence. The line looked as if it had been there from the

*beginning, providing the correct way of seeing, the correct way
of thinking, the correct way of making the world.*

David. David. His words flowed toward Myla like
liquid truth. He'd always had the gift of saying something that was so obvious, it shocked her with its newness. His words were his ideas and his ideas were him
and he was her father. She missed him achingly. And
the typeface, from his sturdy typewriter, was his handwriting. She swirled with his ideas, with the philosophical possibilities that lay in the architecture of an
argument launched with such simple authority. She
sifted quickly through the manuscript, catching frag-
ments, phrases. His voice, throughout, was familiar, as
if she'd heard the words in a dream now forgotten.

Then reality ripped through her musing. Where had
this manuscript come from? Ruth via Marcus Berger?
And if so, how had Ruth gotten her hands on David's
book? Why hadn't Ruth given it to Myla sooner? The
answer to that question haunted Myla the most, because it was almost as if Ruth had read her mind, had
heard her reaching the end of her hope, and had decided to offer her a real incentive to keep going. Suddenly Ruth flitted onto her path as surely as the golden
bird, and Myla didn't know what to do with such a
thought, mainly because it added to the ached missing
in her heart.

She pushed these thoughts to either side of her
mind, parted them with the knowledge, the weight, of
what she held in her hands. Once she flipped through
and came to page 581, she lined the pages back up,
straightened them out on her lap and read what she
hadn't yet let herself read. The title.

It was typed neatly, centered: *Spectacular Futures: How Art Makes Up Our Minds*. Clever—no surprise—but beyond her amusement, she was also intrigued. Myla didn't quite know what the title meant. "Well," she said to herself, "he always did know how to tell a story."

WE LIE ON THE DOCK AND squeeze lemon juice into our hair to make it shiny and blond. The water from Myla's hair pools out onto the wood and gets warm under us. I use it to draw pictures that dry in the sun, and I use the end of her hair as a paintbrush. We've been at Elk Lake for two days now, with no photographs yet, but the feeling's there, the knowing that today we'll do it. We don't even have to talk about this because we're so ready. We stand up together and go back to the cabin. Myla and I pick up the film coolers and Ruth says, "Let's head back down to the water," so we do.

The eight-by-ten has a small depth of field, and its lens is long, so every picture it takes has a long exposure. These are things that I've known forever, and I know Ruth must have explained them to me sometime. But they're things I know without her speaking them—they're why she always says "hold still" when she's about to take the picture. But now she tells us about the tricks she has to use sometimes to get a sharper focus. She explains depth-of-field theory for the millionth time, and I can tell Myla's bored and wants me to be bored too, but I'm not. I want to hear about the way the wide lens of the camera works, the way the shutter opens, the way Ruth has to figure out how to get all of our bodies in focus, and not just the tips of our noses.

I want to keep Ruth talking, but Myla jumps in the lake, so I wade in after her. I let it wet my knees but nothing more because it's cold from the icy mountains. Myla doesn't mind, though. She sees Ruth's camera is out and is ready for anything. Then Ruth says, "Great. Just there," and Myla stands in the water, her arms spread out like the legs of water bugs, and Ruth starts taking pictures.

At first I help Ruth by handing her the film she keeps in coolers, making sure to touch only the metal edges of each holder and not the soft negative middles, but after a while it gets boring. So I go back to the cabin and make myself a peanut-butter sandwich and watch them out the window. They move their heads the same way, but it's not like they're copying each other or anything. It's that they know each other so well. They share thoughts, and that's easy to see when they're making Ruth's pictures.

Myla moves up to the dock, and Ruth does some pictures of her face. I get tired of waiting for them, and I feel like exploring, so I put some peanut butter on my fingers so I can lick it off while I'm walking. I decide to walk around the lake. I hop over the rocks at the edge of it, wondering if they'll even notice I've gone away. My sneakers get wet but it's fun, and pretty soon I'm far away from them, on the other side. Ruth waves her arms at me and motions me to come closer. So I start coming back around, and when I get into a spot of sun, she puts up her hands for me to stop. She yells, "Take off your shoes and hide them," so I do. And then I turn around and she yells, "Hold still." The sun is bright, so I close my eyes. Then Ruth takes a picture of me, with my eyes closed, in the sun, on the other side of the water.

chapter twelve

from the street, Myla saw Samuel sitting in the porch swing, reading a magazine. Her hand gripped the shoulder strap of her bag, aware of the heavy manuscript inside, nestled with David's notebook. She loved the privacy of her new treasure and was distracted by its presence. She walked up the stairs to the front porch. Samuel looked up when he heard her steps.

"Hey," he said.

"Hey. Good day in the city?"

"Oh yeah. I went up to the Rose Garden. It must be gorgeous when they're in bloom. And Mount Hood—it's so . . . present. Like the moon. I feel as if it's been following me around all day."

"You can see a long way when it's sunny," said Myla, sitting down on the top step.

"Are you okay?" asked Samuel after a minute. She could feel him looking at the back of her head.

"Sure," she said. She couldn't describe the feeling inside her. After the initial euphoria of having held David's manuscript in her hands, she now felt a sorrow so simple it threatened to overwhelm her. The book in her bag would likely be the last unknown piece of David she'd ever get to have. Every time she read one of his words, it would be the last time that word was new.

Samuel rose and walked across the porch to sit beside her. He held a piece of paper in his hand. He cleared his voice. "Mark called." He handed her the paper and she saw Mark's name on it, and the time he'd called. Only an hour before.

Myla studied the paper, hoping it would offer some clue to Mark's emotional temperature. "Was he angry?"

Samuel shook his head. "He didn't sound angry. I can't really imagine Mark angry."

"Exactly," said Myla. "Neither can I. And that's what scares me."

"What makes you think he's angry at you?"

"He hasn't returned any of my phone calls. And you know how much he loves the phone."

"Actually," said Samuel, pointing to the piece of paper, "he *has* returned your phone calls. It just took him some time."

Myla nodded. "How long did you guys talk?"

"I don't know—like twenty minutes?"

"What did you talk about?"

Samuel shifted his weight, and the board underneath him groaned. "I don't know. Mostly you."

Myla rolled her eyes. "I'm not an interesting topic of conversation, let me assure you."

"Au contraire," said Samuel, then laughed. "Or at least that's what Mark would say."

Myla felt tears buzzing into her eyes, stabbed with

missing Mark. Samuel squatted down beside her. "Just call him back, Myla."

Fifteen minutes later, Myla had hidden herself in the bedroom with the clunky rotary phone, after getting up her nerve to dial the number. It rang four times—long enough to convince her Mark wasn't home anymore, long enough to make her nearly lose her nerve—and then he answered.

"Hi, Mark."

"Well, this is one of those situations not covered in the best-friend handbook: how to talk to your estranged partner in crime who's been living under a false identity for the full duration of your friendship, and who now has an entirely different name with entirely new initials and, most important, an entirely new monogram. I mean, how embarrassing for me! Those hand towels I got you last Christmas! I could just die."

Myla smiled. "Hi."

"Hi."

"So my name's Myla now."

"Yeah, I gathered that. Somewhere between waiting for them to find your body and wanting to kill you myself, I picked that up."

"I'm sorry I didn't tell you."

Mark's voice turned serious. "See, I've thought a lot about that. When I got your letter and Samuel explained what it all meant, I was pretty much ready to be done with you."

"So what changed?"

"Oh, so you assume I've changed my mind. You're a presumptuous lady, Miss Myla Rose Wolfe. Okay, okay, yes, I've changed my mind. But I can't quite figure out why. Samuel's faith in you certainly helped."

"Yeah. And now he's here."

"*Yeah*. You wanna dish about that one?"

Myla shook her head, as if Mark was in the room with her. "Frankly, I'm puzzled. I thought I'd made it clear that I never wanted to see him again. And correct me if I'm wrong, but most men tend to take that kind of thing at face value. Most men don't get on an airplane the same day."

"Most men aren't simultaneously brilliant *and* perfect without a shirt on. Then again, most men aren't Samuel or me." She could hear Mark biting into an apple as he casually added, "You guys done it yet this time around?"

"Mark! No comment."

"Oh, please don't tell me the new you doesn't dish on sexy details—"

"It's not like that," she interrupted. "Things just haven't gone that direction."

"Hm," said Mark. "So you're not interested."

"I didn't say that."

"Or, I know, you're miffed at him for invading your privacy by following you all the way across the country just so he could profess his undying and eternal love . . . You know, on second thought, you're right. Poor you. I absolutely *hate* it when that kind of thing happens."

Myla realized she'd tangled her fingers in the cord of the telephone. She pulled her hand free and sighed, ignoring Mark's mocking tone. "I'm not exactly angry. I like having him around. But there's something about him, something he said—"

"Right. The stuff in his lecture. He explained it to me. And by the way, when he was telling me about it, putting two and two together, he got all red in the face and excited, and I realized: no wonder seeing him lecture turned you on."

"Mark!"

"Okay, okay. So do you want to know my opinion or not?"

"Of course I do."

"I say let it go."

Myla felt her voice rising. "It wasn't the kind of thing one can just let go. He believes the photographs I was in as a child were the cause of my sister's death. He essentially accused my father of murdering her with his own hands." Myla shuddered. "I can't kiss a man who believes that about my father. I can't just let something like that go."

"If you can't, you can't," Mark said. "I'm just saying go easy on the guy. He's a good man. He obviously likes you. He probably feels really bad about what he said. And maybe being with you, maybe seeing that *you* don't believe your father murdered your sister, will bring him around to your point of view. I don't know."

"Okay," said Myla. "Thank you. I've got to remember to lighten up."

"Yeah. Don't let Myla Rose Wolfe be a downer. Let her be one of the cool kids. You get a clean slate, after all."

Myla smiled again. "Thank you, Mark." She paused.

Then she asked, "But I have to know, if you'll tell me. Why'd you decide to call?"

"Oh, *that*," he said. "See, I thought about it a lot. And realized that we're all pretty fucked up, which is not a highly profound statement, but go with me on this one. We start out as these tiny bundles and then along the way we get fucked up, and we fuck up in the process. My dad—you asked about my dad—he wants to be a good man. His name's Pedro, since you were so curious. He was raised in a conservative Spain, by very traditional people. He's a devout Catholic, he loves his wife, he loves the children who follow his vision of what life should be. He's tried to love me. I truly believe he has. But that doesn't help me when I know he won't speak to me because I'm gay. That doesn't help me when I'm not invited home, or when one of my sisters—the super-Catholic one—won't even call me anymore. My mom's called me once this year."

Myla had heard only snatches of Mark's family situation in the five years she'd known him. Now, laid out before her like this, the story was excruciating. "Oh God, Mark, that's awful."

He continued, "And this is why I don't talk about it in the first place: because it just turns into this maudlin sob story that depresses everyone. The truth is, I've come to terms with it. I've made myself a pretty great life, and I pity my father for not wanting to know me just because of who I am. It's probably caused him much more pain than it's caused me. But that's not my point."

"What is your point?"

"My point is that you, Miss Myla, are brave. At first

I was very angry at you, and then I came to realize how much I admire what you're doing. Horrible stuff happened in your family. We're talking Greek-tragedy horrible. It obviously screwed you up—when you're orphaned, that's probably it for most people—and I'm guessing it wasn't some luxuriously sneaky plan of yours to simply pretend to be someone else. I'm guessing you felt it was a last resort. So how cool is it that you've decided to finally tell the truth about yourself? Yeah, I'm mad you didn't want to let me in on the secret, but that's mostly my own shit. What I'm talking about is bigger than that: I'm impressed by you. I'm impressed by who Myla Rose Wolfe is. She's the person I'm excited about knowing. Forget Kate Scott. It's a new phase! It's a new you! It means you can buy a whole new wardrobe!"

Myla was laughing hard. She felt giddy, wound around by understanding. They talked and talked, and she explained everything: David's notebook, David's manuscript, Jane and Steve's house, Samuel's arrival, Portland, and the bits of her past she wanted to revisit. With each word, she felt more whole, more confident. It was glorious: one half of herself meeting her other. She felt, at last, that she'd arrived.

WE'RE EATING DINNER IN THE house, and by "we" I mean Myla, me, David, and Helaine. She's made us chicken with broccoli on the side, and rice. Myla loves broccoli, so she's eating it even though she wants to hate this food. She's mad at David for telling Helaine this is her favorite meal.

Then the doorbell rings. I go get it and Ruth's outside. She smiles. "Hey, can I come in?" and I say of course, but when I bring her into the dining room they all make sounds like they're apologizing. Ruth says, "Oh, I didn't realize—" and David stands up so his chair scrapes on the floor and he speaks too loudly. He says, "Don't be ridiculous," while Myla gets up to get Ruth a chair. The only person who doesn't say anything is Helaine. Then there's confusion about whether Ruth will eat with us or not. She says no but David says yes. She settles for a glass of wine. She says she already ate but I can tell she's lying.

When we're all sitting, Helaine says, "So, to what do we owe the pleasure of your company?"

"Glad you asked," says Ruth, even though she's not. "I got a call yesterday, from a gallery in New York City, and they love my portfolio. Not only do they want to represent me, but they want to do a solo show! Of *my* photographs! Can you believe it? The gallerist said they haven't been this excited about someone's work in at least ten years."

Myla's up and jumping and comes around the table to hug Ruth and me. Then David's laughing and everyone's saying congratulations and forgetting all about the meal. It's just that kind of moment. We don't mean anything by it.

Once we're all quiet, Helaine says, "Congratulations, Ruth. What's the time frame for this?"

"Pretty soon, actually. January." Ruth looks at Myla and me. "And I would really like it if you guys could come along. Obviously, we've got to talk to your dad about it, but I'm hoping—"

"What pictures would you be showing?" Helaine says over her wine-sipping.

"Well," says Ruth. "Recent stuff." She smiles. "Stuff of the girls, probably."

Myla giggles and claps her hands. She says, "Oh my *God*, Ruth, I can't believe this is happening! New York City?" But Helaine says something while Myla's speaking, and we can't hear Helaine. David asks her to repeat what she said, and she cuts the chicken slowly with her knife.

"So it's pictures of the girls you'll be showing, then?"

Ruth's voice gets hard and she says, "Yes. Partially. That's what this gallery's really excited about."

"Have you asked the girls?"

"I always ask the girls." Ruth looks at David and then at me. She doesn't know what to say.

"Yeah," I say. "She always asks us." I don't sound as brave as I'd like.

"Good," says Helaine, and smiles so we can see her gums. "Looks like you have it all figured out. I'm so proud of you, Ruth. I know we all are."

Myla gets up and puts her napkin on the table. Her chair doesn't make the sound she'd like it to. She looks at David and says, quietly, "Unbelievable," and picks up her plate and leaves the room. We hear her as she glowers up the stairs, and her door-slamming shakes the house.

Ruth pats my back. "I'm sorry if I came at a bad time. This is obviously something we all need to talk about. So." She gets up. David says he'll walk her out.

And they go to the front door and he walks her out onto the porch.

Helaine's still eating. I watch her while she chews. She has a strong jaw. I tell her about my day. I eat my rice.

MYLA BURST AWAKE TO FIND Samuel shaking her. "You were having another nightmare," he said, letting go of her shoulders as she rose into consciousness.

"Jesus," she said. She'd been dreaming about the dark room again, about the interview with tiny Pru alone onstage. Myla looked at Samuel, and his face pulled her back to reality. He stood up.

"I just wanted to make sure you were okay." He headed toward the door.

"Wait," she said, her voice too loud in the nighttime.

He stopped. His back to her, he looked smaller than usual, like a boy who needed permission. She checked herself before saying: "Come back." As she moved into full waking, she cloudily remembered the reservations she had about this man. She knew, in the daylight, that she had all sorts of reasons not to trust him. But she moved her legs so he could sit down, scooped against her. A breeze came in slowly, swooning the curtains. There were dogs barking in the neighborhood.

He said, "I don't like the way your nightmares sound." It was a perfect thing to say. She was starting to notice small details about Samuel: the timbre of his voice, the way he hesitated before lifting his water glass, his attention to the outside when they were driving, and, most of all, the simple truths behind his speech. It seemed that he did not lie. His honesty struck Myla at that moment as an extraordinary thing.

"I don't like being in them," she said.

"What happens?"

She tried to think of the best way to explain. "They're all about not being enough. Fast enough, strong enough, brave enough. Not catching up in time."

"In time for what?"

"In time to save her." Myla tried to start again, but she'd lost her voice. She looked at Samuel, traced his features with her eyes. She was being pulled under by something stronger than sleep, but familiar in the way that sleep was. She wanted to explain to him, but she couldn't.

Finally he spoke. "Tell me about Ruth."

So here it was: his way of helping her. Asking her questions she wouldn't explore on her own, in search of an answer he believed she needed to find. She leaned closer to him, then tried to locate Ruth in her mind. Ruth was a taste. Ruth was a feeling. "Ruth was tall. She had this amazing long black hair. She spun all sorts of wild tales about traveling through Asia with only a camera and a backpack. She collected legendary boyfriends with names like Luca and Giancarlo. We never knew much about her childhood. We knew she grew up in Kentucky and that she didn't have much family, but that was about it." Only here in the darkness could Myla easily assemble truths about Ruth and speak them out loud. "She loved us as she loved herself. She wanted to make glorious, transcendent art."

She shook her head, listened to her hair rustling the pillow. "Pru loved the photographs."

"You'll think this strange, after what I said in my lecture, but I find the photographs profoundly compelling," he said. "They're riveting."

"I haven't looked at any of them since I left here."

Samuel touched her then, softly, on her hip. "I'll look at them with you, if it helps. We can look at them together."

"I'm not ready."

"Are all the rest of them—what's the estimated figure, ten thousand negatives?—really missing?"

"Yes," said Myla. "Not to mention her prints. She was a great printer. None of us has any idea what Ruth did with them. She probably destroyed them," and the thought of all that lost art brimmed Myla with sorrow.

"Later, then, when you want to." His fingers rubbed a circle on her hip, starting small, moving big.

"How long will you stay?" she asked.

"As long as you want." It was what she wanted him to say. "I don't plan on going back. So here's as good a place as any."

Immediately a question rose in her—why was he refusing to return to his life at the college?—but just as quickly, her hands were on the corners of his shirt, pulling him toward her.

They'd done this before, but this time it was different. This time she was aware of him in a way she hadn't been before, because she knew him so much better. She wanted to know him. It was quiet and soft, this way of lying against someone you might grow to cherish, and afterward, they pulled the covers up around them and slept hip to hip. They awoke to the dawn, creeping blue into the room. They made love again, and then Myla lay on her back, watching Samuel slip into soft sleep.

David's manuscript was still her secret. She waited until Samuel was breathing long and deep, and she then eased her body away from his warmth. Myla's bag, which held David's book, was nestled beside the bed. With her fingers, she found the thick manila envelope and pulled it up onto her lap, relishing what was to come. She slipped out the cover page and read the title again. *Spectacular Futures: How Art Makes Up Our Minds.* Underneath it, David had typed the titles of each subsection:

i. *Gaining Perspective: Sight and the Invention of the Real*
ii. *The Sacred Body and the Nude: Visual Salvation*
iii. *The Momentous Birth of Photography and the Advent of Technological Time*
iv. *Blessed Are the Art Makers, for Theirs Is the Kingdom of Change*

Myla quietly read each chapter heading, her tongue lilting over the vowels. The words reminded her of the titles of the books that had lined the walls of her childhood home; she'd fingered the spines, wondering at the mysterious content of each tome. She closed her eyes and remembered how thick all those books had felt. Thick with pages, and knowledge, and possibility. This was how it felt to hold her father's book.

She sat up in bed and flattened the manuscript on her lap. She began where she'd begun the other day, and when she reached the end of the first three paragraphs of the section she now knew was called *Gaining Perspective*, she continued reading. The thrill of her father's ideas made a patch of hope around her body. Nothing could stop her.

WE GET ON THE AIRPLANE TO New York and I choose the window seat once I convince Myla she'd rather sit by Ruth. David sits in front of us, and every once in a while he turns around and makes sure everything's okay. It's the first time I remember being on an airplane. A whole decade ago, when I was just a baby and my mom was still alive, we went on an airplane down to San Francisco to visit her family. But I don't remember that.

What I remember is maybe the feeling of flying, because when I lift my feet as the plane takes off, the flip in my stomach is familiar. But just when I know how to name it, what to say, we've already shot up past the clouds, and the world below is only patches of green. By then the words leave my mind and I have to turn back to the dim humming inside of the plane, to conversation with my family. The lurch, the pull, is gone.

Myla wants to talk about the pictures. Ruth is happy to have a million conversations about them with her. I don't know why we have to talk about them. The doing seems all that matters; even looking at them feels funny. Myla thinks I don't want to talk about the pictures because I think she's vain. But that's not it. She's not vain. The pictures make her count all the good and bad things about herself. She wants other people to look at her pictures that way, to have them declare who

she is, but I don't. I just want to be me. I just want the
me in the pictures to be left alone. I want to speak for
myself. To be.

Ruth keeps trying to talk to me. She asks me about
New York and whether I'm excited and I say yes,
mostly because I'm supposed to. I'm excited about the
city, and David's saying we can explore some museums
and shop at FAO Schwarz. What I'm not excited about
is the gallery with all sorts of people standing in front
of my picture whispering. What I'm not excited about
is sitting in a corner, waiting for Myla to decide she's
bored and wants to go home, like I have for the last
hour. What I'm not excited about is the moment when
I look up and catch my own eye, across the gallery, on
the wall, and remember the particular day—the sun on
my back, the song in my head—and know I can never
be there again in that perfect bright moment. I'll be
jealous of the me in the picture, warm and alive. It's a
strange thing. Even Myla doesn't understand.

proof

the two girls are together on a trickling streambed. The older one is in front, and she stands with her feet a shoulder's width apart, her hands poised on her hips. She looks as if she's up for a challenge, her chin set in such a way that there's a trace of rebellion on her face. The muscles in her arms are flexed. Her legs are strong. She has breasts and the fierceness of someone who knows the world, who expects a fight.

The younger one is behind, softer, out of focus. She curls on a rock, a dollop of brightness behind her sister's sour stance. At first glance you think she's threatened by the older one's towering presence in the foreground, but then you see that's not the case. You look closer and realize she's content. A smile settles on her face, in the corners of her mouth, and her eyes look lovingly in the older one's direction.

The older girl is a mammal. You see that she's guarding the younger one from something unnamed. Not the camera, for she's obviously comfortable in front of it, knows her way around its edges. Not the viewer. Or at least not you. If you're looking at this picture, and you're able to see the protection in her body, then you're not the person she's guarding against. It means you have an eye for the girls' well-being. It means you're not the one who ends it.

chapter thirteen

Steve cleared the last of the dishes from the breakfast table and kissed Myla on the cheek. "You two be good," he said, chuckling. Apparently he'd noticed Samuel's move upstairs.

The screen door banged shut, and Myla turned her gaze to Samuel. He was engrossed in the *Times* crossword, something that had never particularly interested her. In her mind, puzzles had always seemed a waste of valuable research time. But there Samuel sat, closing and opening his eyes, deep in concentration. She watched him for a time, until he looked up at her. He said, "So I guess we aren't in a fight anymore."

Myla smiled. "We were never in a fight. We were distant. But if you want to call it a fight, then yes, I guess we're no longer in it."

He took a final bite of corn muffin and raised an eyebrow. "I wouldn't mind if that's how we make up from now on."

"I'm sure you wouldn't," she said, blushing. Her body was flushed with life, touched by her father's ideas and Samuel's body. Even the rain outside seemed to convey a brightness she knew other people probably weren't seeing. She felt lifted by language, by wanting to tell Samuel all sorts of things. Words were ready to tumble out.

Samuel set down the crossword. "Do you want to go back upstairs? I've been feeling distant from you for, oh, the last forty-five minutes or so."

"Let's take a walk."

He shrugged. "Not the answer I was hoping for."

"It'll be better after the walk," Myla said, standing up. He groaned in complaint.

"Think of the distance we will have established by then," she teased, smiling at herself as she went to put on her jacket. Pulling her bag onto her shoulder, she giggled at how effortless this flirting was. Samuel followed her and kissed her against the front door. She managed to find the doorknob behind her. "Your methods of persuasion won't work on me. Besides, I have something to tell you. A secret."

Outside, the rain was hard to distinguish from the gray sky. Samuel squinted up at the clouds and said, "Umbrella?"

Myla laughed. "No native Oregonian would ever be caught dead with an umbrella. Especially on a day like today. This? This is nothing." She stepped off the porch. "Unless you're scared of a little water . . ."

"No, I relish being soaked to the bone. But in case it starts raining any harder . . ." He picked up a small umbrella resting by the door and put it in his jacket pocket.

*   *   *

Steve and Jane's house was only a couple of blocks from the lookout point above Oaks Bottom. Standing on the lip of the lookout, one could see the marsh below, and beyond it an old-fashioned, still-intact amusement park where Steve had taken them when they were kids. Beyond that unfurled the ribbon of the Willamette River, then the buildings of downtown Portland. The West Hills rose dark green behind Portland, glowering and brightening with each passing cloud. This place, where they were standing, displayed the wide vistas Myla was craving.

Looking out over the city, she told Samuel about the mysterious manuscript. She told him about its unknown origins, about the bright bird that had seemed to summon Tim the librarian, and the smell of the manuscript, the weight of it, the familiarity of her father on each page. She told him she wasn't ready for Steve or Jane to know about the book's existence. She didn't look at Samuel as she spoke, almost couldn't look at him, because she felt that such sight might break the spell of this conversation. She wanted to trust him, but she trusted her own words more. She needed to do whatever she could to speak.

"And have you read it yet?" Samuel asked when Myla finally came to a resting place.

"This morning. I read a hundred and fifty pages. You were sleeping." She could look at him again as she was brought back around to her memory of him curled up beside her.

"And?"

She took a deep breath. "It's unlike anything I've ever read. He calls it an essay, but it's five hundred and eighty-one pages long. He uses very familiar language, accessible language. He makes it clear that he wants this to be a book anyone can read. And I know my father: he thinks it's a book that everyone *should* read." Myla shook her head and smiled. "It looks as if he's read everything, and not just to agree with someone else's point of view. He's scrutinized every piece of art ever made—I'm exaggerating, of course—but I mean that he leaves no stone unturned if it will help him shape his ideas. Because that's essentially what he's doing: shaping ideas, small arguments, into a huge, sweeping theory."

"What are some of the arguments?"

Myla slipped the pages out of her bag. A few drops of water splotched down on the cover page, and she brought the papers up to her chest, under her jacket.

Samuel gamely pulled the umbrella from his pocket and sheltered her with it. "I hope I'm not going to get you arrested by the rain police," he joked. Then he lifted his head, shouting out to the city: "One Oregonian over here, risking her reputation for a little shelter! Send out the squad cars! Alert the media!" He grinned down at Myla, and she couldn't help but laugh.

Then she looked down at her father's manuscript. "Okay. So the book is called *Spectacular Futures: How Art Makes Up Our Minds*. What he means by that is pure David: he believes that humans think they shape art, but that's not necessarily true. Art shapes them. At the very least, it's a reciprocal relationship."

"I like the title," Samuel said. "I'll be lucky if my first book is called *Samuel Blake Thinks About American*

Culture. But enough about me. How does he launch his theory?"

"Well, his first assertion is pretty direct: he says that straight lines are a human invention. They're not visible in nature; the human mind made them up."

"Is that true?"

"Well, look around." She spread her gaze across the great vista before her. She had to admit that at least from this view, the only visible straight lines were those that edged the downtown buildings, or spined the bridges over the Willamette River, or tightened the telephone lines. Angles and lines were attached to the human. Messiness and unpredictability rose from the natural world.

"So what does he say next?" Samuel asked. "There are a lot of words there."

As the rain let up, they started walking the edge of the lookout, winding their way into the suburban village. Old trees towered up from the backyards of wooden bungalows. Myla was explaining: "He says that the straight line, or linearity, began to colonize architecture. Human space began to be rationalized and regularized, and artists, naturally, depicted human space the way it looked to them. Once you live inside straight lines, you begin to *see* along them. Which heralds the invention of perspective."

"Wait, so he's saying that before the straight line was 'invented' by some prehistoric man, people didn't see the same way we do? They didn't see the world with perspective?"

She shrugged. "It's not just about seeing. It's about a whole way of life. David argues that the invention of the straight line had a huge philosophical impact on Homo sapiens. He cites cave paintings as an example of how art worked before the straight line: early peoples drew the stories of their hunts with no depiction of the ground beneath their feet. They drew one man hundreds of times, moving from moment to moment. And David believes that points not to a lack of sophistication but rather to philosophical differences between their lifestyle and ours. He maintains that much of the philosophical shift owes itself to the invention of the straight line." She paused. "Even today countless aboriginal artists favor a nonlinear perspective."

Samuel was smiling. "So David's seeing the development of art and the development of human consciousness as essentially the same thing. He sees them as inextricably linked."

"Yes," said Myla. "One example: he takes the idea of the single motionless viewer, gazing at a canvas depicting a single moment in time, and shows how Alberti used that concept to invent Renaissance perspective. That's the perspective we know and love—you know, the one with straight lines, lines we *know* are parallel, running from the corners of the painting back to a single point, the vanishing point, right in the center of the picture. And that's where *we* come into it. I mean, essentially he's saying that we've based Western art on the idea of perspective, but that the concept of perspective is not a given. It's as much an invention as the straight line."

Myla watched Samuel as he wrestled with what she'd just said. "So he's talking about our desire for the real. He's trying to look at truth and how we see it. He's

arguing that there can be no objective visual truth, because we're always looking through the filter of culture,
and the filter of human consciousness, and probably a
dozen other filters besides."

Myla wanted to rejoice. "Exactly! Exactly." She
leafed through the pages she'd been clutching to her
chest. "Listen to his ideas at the end of this section:

"'This depiction of ideally organized space was not
inaccurate, but it discarded other versions of what, by
seeming valid, seemed real. To see was to believe; the
eye became the privileged arbiter of truth. The rule of
the line determined what could be known. Reality de-
pended on the line.'"

"It's certainly rich with implications," said Samuel,
and he took Myla's hand. They'd been circling through
the neighborhood and were heading toward the center
of town. "The rule of the line determined what could
be known," he repeated. Myla felt her father's ideas
swirling around her. And Samuel's hand was warm.

DAVID TAKES ME TO THE Metropolitan Museum of Art,
which is on Fifth Avenue. There are twenty-eight steps
you have to climb just to get to the front door, and then
you enter a place like a big marble ballroom. Once
you've bought your tickets and folded the candy-blue
metal button over your collar, you walk up this fancy
staircase with twenty-three steps, and then there's a
place to rest, and then twenty-three more steps. It's like
a palace inside. David tells me there's more art in this
museum than he or I could even look at. And then he

laughs and says, "Imagine that, Pru, imagine how many people for how many years have made all this art. And we're the luckiest people because we get to see it."

He takes me to the Nineteenth-Century European Paintings and Sculpture Galleries—that's what it says on his map. When we first walk in, there's this big painting of a lady, and her eyes watch you when you move. It's like she's in charge of making sure the right people can come in. Then David says, "Ooh, wait until you see this." He takes me to a little room that seems hidden away. Outside the door is a metal ballerina dressed in real clothes and with a real ribbon in her metal hair. She's so still that it makes me think about holding still for Ruth's camera. And then we go inside the little room and it's like being inside a wooden and glass box. The air is cool on my face. Behind the glass are all of these horses, small sculptures, running and jumping and prancing and standing still. It's funny, because I know they're just sculptures, and of course they can't move, but the horses look alive. They look alive and miniature, and I want to have one for my own, but I could never choose which one. I wish Ruth had come to the museum with us, because I know she'd like to see how they're alive in the same way that her photographs of horses are alive.

Also in the room are these miniature dancers. But they aren't holding still like the ballerina outside. They have their legs in the air, and they're bending over, and they're stretching. And if you turn your head, it seems like they've moved when you weren't looking. David says all the sculptures are by Degas, even the ballerina outside, and it's funny to see how one man could make sculptures both so still and so ready to jump and move and play.

David says, "Let's go to my favorite room." He takes my hand and we go through room and room and room. We walk by a painting of a little girl named Marguerite and she has buggy eyes. I'm glad my eyes don't look like that, even though I know it's mean to think that. Then we get to the room David's talking about. He lets go of my hand like he can't hold on to anything while he's looking at these paintings, and that's how I know we've arrived. He makes a sound like a waterfall through his lips.

"It's called *Cypresses*, and it's by—"

"Van Gogh." I saw the sign, but I also knew it had to be by him just from walking toward it.

"Good eye," says David. The painting is thick, like it has hands pulling out to me, asking me to walk closer, to touch it. I know enough about museums to know that isn't allowed, but I also know enough about being David's child to know he's thinking the same thing I am.

"Pru," he says, "there are things you need to know about painting, and then there are things you need to *know*."

"What do you mean?" I ask him.

"You know how you thought those tiny dancers sculpted by Degas looked alive? That's the word: alive. And you're right; they do look as if they could leap and twirl right out of that glass case!"

He beams down at me and squeezes my shoulder. "Well, most art critics and historians use the word 'real' when what they really ought to be saying is 'alive.' I think just about every artist who ever lived is making art for one main reason: to show what it's like to be alive, what it's like to be really here."

He stops talking for a minute, and I think he's going to start saying things about van Gogh, because he's just standing in front of the painting and nodding at it. But instead he asks me a question. "Did you see anything else today that seemed particularly alive, Prudence?"

I nod because I'm thinking of a statue of a man, a big naked statue made out of marble, with a broken-off nose. I tell David, and he nods and laughs. "Good, good. He was Greek, and looked as if he could breathe or toss a ball. We're a lot like the Greeks." Then he asks another question. "What about the medieval church paintings, you know, the ones with Mary and the baby Jesus, the ones in that long gallery we walked through? Did they look real to you? Alive in the same way the dancer did?"

I think back to those funny pictures where the colors were bright and beautiful but everything was all the wrong size, and the tables all sloped the wrong way. "Not so much," I say.

David is excited. "Exactly, exactly. To us, those paintings don't look alive, don't look real. But I'll tell you a secret." He leans down and looks me in the eyes. "That's just because we have a different idea of what it means to be alive than the men who painted those pictures. To them, God was everything. Jesus was everything. Mary, Jesus' mother, was everything. So they're the biggest things in the picture. And the saints and other holy people, like the leader of the Church, are the next biggest. And then comes the man who paid for the painting. And then comes everyone else."

I can see how that makes sense. "But why doesn't the place look real? Why didn't they try harder?"

"Because to those men, no place on earth was ever as important as the reality of heaven. Their paintings are glorious because they show how important it was for them to love God more than the way they loved the look of the world."

"So what about van Gogh?" I ask.

"What about him?"

"How is *he* real? What does he believe in?"

"Why don't you tell me?"

He sweeps his arm in front of him, and the painting moves out to meet my eyes. It moves me. Moves me closer and moves me far away. Because it has thickness. The actual paint sticks out. It's a painting but a sculpture too.

I tell David that and he squeezes my shoulder. "Look, it's so simple. The trees are just there. Two trees in the middle of the canvas. So effortless. We know that one tree is farther away only because part of it is obstructed by the other one, not because van Gogh has forced perspective on the painting, not because there are some artificial rules imposed on the trees themselves."

David smiles. "The painting scatters your eyes—you don't know where to look. The grasses in front make you want to touch them, but also refer back into each other, so you're constantly moving over them like wind over a meadow. And the swirls of blue and pink and white in the sky have the same effect, making your eye move swiftly through the air like wind. There, in that corner, a cloud curls like a wave. And the purple mountain majesties loom in the distance. But there's no distance, really; instead, the trees are in the middle, and the color of the hills spreads out on either side. We only see a distance there because our reality insists that's where the hills must be. But that's our brains, not our eyes, not van Gogh's brushstrokes." I can only catch a few things that jumble out of David's mouth, but I don't stop him. I don't want him to stop. I watch him, watch the painting, and van Gogh's colors and David's words swirl inside me.

"Ultimately, the painting insists that you'll never be allowed to settle on one still, stagnant point. Your eye is required to bounce and cascade about, like a breeze. You're tossed. There's movement everywhere. And what's brilliant about that movement is that just by looking, just by standing here in a museum, we get to feel what it actually felt like for van Gogh to stand in this field, looking at these cypresses. We look at this painting, and we're alive on this hill with van Gogh's eye. It's just breathtaking." David laughs and squeezes my hand.

"So I guess he's trying to tell us what it feels like for him to be alive?"

David is so happy, he can hardly hear me. "Yes, Prudence, yes. And if you lived with this painting, wouldn't you want to touch it?"

He's right. You always would, running your fingers through the grasses and hills and tall sharp pointy trees. Then I'm glad we're alone and Myla isn't with us.

She'd never let us stand still like this for so long without moving. She wouldn't understand.

EMMA BOUNDED UP THE FRONT steps and threw her arms around Myla. "Surprise! I made Mom and Dad promise they'd keep me a secret." Myla had been in the kitchen when Jane called her out onto the front porch. Now, burrowing into Emma's familiar warmth, Myla believed that if she relaxed long enough, possibilities would keep on coming. First there'd been the notebook, then Samuel, then the manuscript, and now Emma—entirely herself but older. Safe.

Emma's head smelled like Emma's head. Her arms were longer, and her eyes met Myla straight on as they stood nose to nose. When Emma kissed Myla's cheeks, Myla realized that were Pru alive, she'd be even older than this woman standing before her.

"You're so short," said Emma, touching the top of Myla's head.

"I'm taller than you are."

"Barely. And anyway, not the way you used to be." Emma laughed. "I imagined you were eight feet tall or something. Like a giant."

Jane played with the ends of Emma's hair. "Well, the last time you saw Myla, you were, what? Ten? And Myla was eighteen? So that makes sense." Jane's words weaned Emma from Myla's arms for a few moments. Jane and Emma hugged briefly, and Myla watched the way they became one, their shoulders meeting each other.

Emma looked at Myla. "Let's get this out of the way. I know Mom told you. I'm in recovery. But that means I'm fine. I've gotten my life together. I'm with this great guy, Jake. I'm working for a nonprofit. And that pretty much brings us up to date, right, Mom?"

Myla could feel herself being pulled by sadness, by the knowledge that Emma's life had obviously been difficult, when Emma stopped her. "No. No one's allowed to feel sad about it. I made my choices, and that's that. I've made big changes in myself. And one of them is total honesty. Full disclosure. Which means we'll get along, because Mom told me you're on a big honesty kick too." Then Emma squeezed her arms around both Jane and Myla. Myla could feel Emma's body gripping toward something, could feel her own body Velcroing back.

They went inside, and Steve came downstairs. Emma unlatched Myla long enough to give him a bear hug. They were both forthright, up front with their bodies and emotions in a way Myla deeply admired. Emma said, "Jake says hi. He was going to come up, but he couldn't get off work."

Jane looked worried. "So you drove up all alone?"

Emma rolled her eyes, and Myla glimpsed the adolescent she'd never known, an impertinence she'd never witnessed. "I was *fine*, Mom. But can someone help me with my bags? I brought laundry."

Now it was Jane's turn to roll her eyes. "You packed the car with laundry again?"

Emma giggled. "It's my birthright."

Samuel came inside from the backyard, and looking at him, Myla realized that in all her excitement about

Emma, she'd practically forgotten about him. Jane introduced Samuel as Myla's friend. Emma was having none of it. After they'd exchanged pleasantries, he headed back outside to help Steve with Emma's laundry. Before he was out of earshot, Emma couldn't resist saying, "He's *hot*, Myla. He's, like, really attractive. He's your *boyfriend*?"

"Something like that," said Myla, trying to shush her.

Jane smiled. "He's a lovely person. How about some tea?"

On their way into the kitchen, Myla asked, "So what're you up for tonight, Emma?"

Emma swiveled with a pained expression on her face. "Oh, that sucks. Mom told me you had plans, so I made plans too. I actually have a dinner party tonight— one of my best friends from high school's getting married." She made a face. "To a creep. But I'm here for the whole weekend. I'm not leaving until Tuesday."

Myla was disappointed. But Jane piped up right away. "Don't give me that look, Emma. Even Myla doesn't know about tonight." Myla noticed Jane's glance land on someone in the doorway, and Myla turned to meet Samuel's gaze.

"I'm taking you on a date," he said, smiling.

"Oh," said Myla.

"Well jeez, Myla, don't sound excited or anything," said Emma.

Myla was standing still in the middle of the room. She couldn't switch gears. Emma's being here changed things. She could feel herself kicking into sister mode and ached with the realization that Samuel was going to serve as a distraction from that, from what she needed to make up to Emma for all those years of being gone. But Emma nudged her into a smile. "Yeah, okay. A date."

"A date," said Samuel.

"You know, dates aren't really a big deal, you guys. Especially when you're already seeing someone," said Emma.

"Of course they aren't," Myla said, trying to look excited. And then Jane made tea.

WHEN WE GET BACK TO PORTLAND, we don't talk about New York that much. We show Steve and Jane the snapshots from our trip, and I give Emma a miniature snow globe with the Empire State Building inside. But then we all have our lives to get back to. I have fifth grade, Myla has high school, and David has his classes, so I think less and less about our time in New York.

Then one day Myla comes into the bathroom looking like she has a secret to tell me. She says, "In *The New York Times*, there was an article about our pictures."

I don't know if this is a good thing or a bad thing. I don't even know what *The New York Times* is. I say, "Really?" and Myla doesn't even have time to act annoyed.

She says, "Yeah, and it didn't say very nice things."

"What did it say?"

"It just said all this . . . all this stuff." She's waving

her hands around in small circles, and she looks upset. "Just stuff about us and Ruth and the pictures."

"Bad stuff?"

"Yeah. Bad stuff." She looks at me suddenly, like she sees me. "Never mind. Forget I said anything."

I shrug. I say, "Okay."

Myla looks like she's going to leave, but then she stays instead. She says, "No, you know what? If they aren't going to tell you, then I am." She's saying this more to herself than to me, and now I'm curious what this bad stuff could be.

"There were protests," she said. "Some people think the pictures are obscene. That they're porn."

I know this word, but I don't know exactly what it means. I just know it makes me feel creepy, makes me want to not think about it. I'm embarrassed to ask what porn is, because if I wasn't such a baby I'd already know, and I'm afraid that hearing what it is will change the way I think about things, will turn what is creepy and shadowy into fact. But I don't have to ask, because Myla tells me. "Porn means sex pictures. Pictures of people doing it."

I giggle a little bit. "But the pictures of us aren't pictures of people doing it."

Myla looks serious, which makes me want to stop giggling but also makes my giggling harder to control. Every time I look at her makes me giggle harder, and thinking about pictures of people doing it makes my stomach flip into more laughing.

Myla rolls her eyes. "Do you want to talk about this or not?"

"Yes," I say, "yes I do." I try to make my face serious. "What are we supposed to do?"

"Nothing," she says. "I was waiting to see if David would say anything, but he didn't. And Ruth didn't either."

"So are you going to ask them?"

"No," says Myla. "Maybe." She looks at me. "Do you want to?"

I can see why she brought this up. "No," I say. I remember that talk David and I had about the picture of the Great Wave, but I don't know how to explain it to Myla.

After that, she leaves. I look in the mirror and try to figure out what exactly a picture of people doing it looks like. I get close to seeing it, but I can't see it all the way. It makes me feel weird, trying to imagine it, and I try not to think about people mixing up pictures of that with pictures of me.

I stay in the bathroom for a while. It feels easier to be in here, where things are white and clean and sorted.

chapter fourteen

they were on an official date now. Chicken and fish had been ordered, and they were sipping expensive wine. It was strange to be here with Samuel across a table, discussing Northwest regional cuisine. Across this table swathed in linen, in the soft light emanating from a candelabra, surrounded by the gentle tones of classical music, sat a man whom Myla barely recognized. He'd held her chair for her when she sat down. He was wearing a tie. This was Oregon; real men didn't wear ties here. They didn't need to. She felt irritated with herself for wanting Samuel to know something he couldn't possibly know.

She was trying to enjoy herself. But what she really wanted was to be at home—at Steve and Jane and Emma's—immersed in the world of her father's thought. She felt guilty about that desire, telling herself she should appreciate Samuel's effort instead of finding him trivial for wearing a herringbone tweed jacket and making small talk. And then she felt guilty about sharing the manuscript with him in the first place. Oh, he'd been great at the time. Very supportive. But wasn't she somehow betraying Steve and Jane and Emma by keeping the book a secret? Why had she wanted to tell Samuel about it and not her family?

His voice came across the table. "We can leave if you want to."

"No," she said. "That's okay."

"This is supposed to be fun. Remember what Emma said? We're supposed to be having a good time here."

"I just wish you'd told me you were planning this."

"It was a surprise."

"I don't like surprises," she said, aware that she sounded like a brat. But that didn't stop her from saying it.

"Okay," he said. Then: "But come on. Are you kidding me? We're on a date. It's not like I took you skydiving or something."

"But the point is, you didn't ask me. You didn't take the time to know whether this—specifically this—was something I'd enjoy."

"Exactly. And that's what being with someone is about. Stretching. Learning by trial and error." He lowered his voice as the waiter delivered their appetizers. Then he said, "I don't get it, Myla. We have these great conversations, and then, just when I think we're having a good time, you shut down. Like you're not allowed to have fun."

She ate her salad in silence, feeling her anger and hurt mounting as she speared baby spinach onto her fork. Finally she glanced up, her eyes nearly spilling with tears. "That wasn't just any old 'great conversation,' Samuel."

"What do you mean?" he asked.

"This morning? My father's book?"

"I didn't mean it like that. I just—" He paused, trading his smile for a look of sincerity, seriousness. "Are you regretting sharing David's book with me? That we talked about it?"

She felt the heat entering her cheeks. She was caught in her own mean emotion. She hesitated.

"Come on." Frustration was creeping into Samuel's voice. "Be honest with me."

"Yeah," she admitted, looking down. "I don't like that I just handed it over to you. I mean, where is this actually going, anyway? And then I think, well, you're being so *nice*, and I wonder why I have to be so cynical all the time." She folded and refolded her napkin. "What kind of person *am* I that I can't just relax and enjoy—"

"Whoa." Samuel had propped both elbows on the table and was leaning forward. "Myla, look at me."

She lifted her head.

"You're a perfectly normal person. That's what kind of person you are. That manuscript is precious to you. If anything, I worry about it being too precious. He seems to have pulled you in so fully. But I'm happy that reading it makes you happy. I want you to trust that you can tell me about it. I understand how much it matters to you."

Myla felt herself flooding with relief as the waiter, a gray-haired man wearing a starched white apron, caught the change in mood at the table and refilled their wineglasses. She took a bite of bread and felt a bit more like herself again.

"I don't know," she said. "Reading this book, as dense and difficult as it is, is exactly like being a child again. Being held inside one of my father's huge stories." She paused. "It becomes everything that matters. In fact, I was thinking about the way David makes me, made me, question everything. Right now, in the section I'm reading . . ." Her voice trailed off.

"Still the first section, right?"

"Samuel, we don't have to talk about my father's book just because I'm obsessed with it. This *is* a date, after all."

"Yeah," he said, brandishing a bread stick, "and we're overly educated intellectuals. What else do we do? What do you think I liked so much about Kate Scott? Your looks? I don't think so." He pointed the bread stick at her. "Hit it."

Myla gathered herself. "Well . . . David was suggesting that linear time—you know, this idea of past, present, future time flowing in one irreversible direction—piggybacked its way into society's mind on the back of the straight line. The straight line is something we can see; time is something we can't. But the idea of time going from start to finish, birth to death, works a lot like the idea of a straight line moving from left to right."

"So we're talking the typical time line here. The kind I made in fifth grade for my report on the Trojan War: first this happened, then this, then this."

"Exactly. David says we've *learned* to think about time that way—and then, and then, and then—because it's so simple, so satisfying. We can link certain events to other events, thereby making time more manageable. What an easy way to digest history. Except David says that for most people, time isn't really experienced like that at all. Instead, it seems to move in cycles, like seasons. Things pass and then come again."

"What do you mean?"

"Well, tell me, does time *feel* like a straight line you just follow through your whole life? I mean, does your life feel like some clear trajectory from past to future?"

Samuel closed his eyes and wrinkled up his mouth as he thought. "I guess not," he said after a moment. "It's just this big jumble of *times*. And then I look up and everything's changed."

"Exactly." She smiled. "But empirical Truth, Reason, Logic—all the stuff that started in the Renaissance and then became the way all Western culture thinks—relies on linear time as the only kind that's really valid. David doesn't say it *isn't* valid; he just claims it wasn't and isn't *real* in the way we've come to believe in it. We don't naturally experience time as a line; we *learn* how to live as *if* it's a line."

"How so?"

"Think of painting. How the artist takes a two-dimensional canvas and creates three-dimensional space. He does it through tricks, through illusion. We all know that the room in a painting isn't a real room, even though it looks like we can enter it. That's because painters have learned how to create the illusion of empty space. We can't see emptiness itself, but we can see objects placed in emptiness. Just look around," she said. Emptiness surrounded their table, and yet it was not visible in itself. Myla nodded and continued.

"In a painting, all these things around us—that table,

the wine bottle, the maître d's podium—would be measured out on lines radiating from a fixed point, the viewpoint outside the painting. Because everything is so neatly done, so accurate, it's possible to measure the exact distance between our wine bottle and that table over there to find out how far apart they are. This is where linear time comes in. As a practical tool. The shortest distance between two points, two objects, is a straight line, right? Well, it takes *time* to walk along that line. Time is the tool we need to make that measurement. The expanse of space, and all the things in it, make this specific kind of time necessary. The farther apart the objects, the longer it takes to move between them. If you want to reproduce the look of material reality, you need to know about this kind of time."

She sat back. "And David goes on to say that the things that appear along the time line begin to be seen as related in specific ways. Cause and effect enters the rational world. Something happens at point C, and its effect appears at point K. We now accept cause and effect as a given, but it's really one more abstraction . . ." She shook her head. Trying to re-create David's argument exhausted her. She was suddenly self-conscious.

"What?" asked Samuel.

"Nothing," she said. A column of silence surrounded them as Myla tried to find her footing again. Her father's mind was like a pulse inside her that she wanted to release into the room, into the world. But she felt the world resisting her excitement. Even Samuel, as sympathetic as he was, couldn't help her reach the limits of her father's mind.

Then Samuel spoke, his gaze never leaving her. The

warmth in his voice surprised her. "Hearing you talk about your dad's book reminds me of when my dad and I built a boat together one summer. I was eleven or twelve. He knew everything. It was amazing to spend every afternoon in the garage with him, using his tools, following his lead. And then we got to sail it together." He smiled. "I think that must be how it feels for you to read David's book."

"Yeah," she said. "I guess it is. It sweeps me up."

"So how can *I* sweep you up?" he asked as the waiter set down their main dishes.

"What?" The question surprised her.

"I want to light you up like that. You're glowing." Samuel's eyes were straight on her. "You're lit from inside."

Myla felt herself flush with color. She didn't know what to say next.

But Samuel did. "To dates," he said, lifting his wineglass. "To making you glow." And then they ate.

RUTH AND I SIT AT HER BIG BLACK table; she's wearing white gloves and is turning pictures from one end of the table over onto the other. The pictures are big. They're black and white. They make me look both real and fake at the same time. The reason is this: to have the picture taken, I have to have been there. But the picture seems fake, because that can't be how I really look. And I don't even mean how my face looks or my body or the way my hands hang. It's more like this: how can you look at a picture and know what's inside me? And because it's my face, because I was actually there, I remember that particular day, and my face is like a book I can read. But I don't know what other people see.

Ruth ends the picture turning and says, "There they are."

"Wow." There's a lot of them. I haven't seen them all together like this, thick in a stack, making willowing sounds when she turns them. I haven't ever seen how much paper I take up.

"Here's a question, Pru. If you could use these pictures to tell a story, what would it be?"

It's a hard question. I guess the story would be me, but I can tell she wants more, wants to know what the story would be that I'd tell about myself. And what is that story? I don't know it yet. So I tell her, "It's about the changes in me. You've been taking pictures of me since I was three. And now I'm ten. And someday I'll be a teenager and then a grown-up with babies. That's the story. Like the first pictures of me are almost when I'm still a baby, when I haven't done anything exciting yet, or brave, when I don't even know you that well, when I don't even have a favorite kind of food. And then later, now, you can see those ways I'm more myself, more grown. And the cool thing is you'll take just as many pictures this year and next year, and every time, the pictures will be one more piece of the puzzle."

Ruth knows the rest. She says, "They're great pictures, Prudence. But not because of me. They're you, all you." And then we look at them again, this time the other way, backward, starting with me now and flipping back to the new, the little, the beginning.

MYLA EXTRACTED HERSELF FROM Samuel's arms and pulled a sweatshirt over her head. It was dawn, and the blue morning slimmed itself under the window shade. She was thirsty. She'd go down quickly for a glass of water, then come back up to read the next installment of David's manuscript.

When she first walked into the kitchen, she didn't notice Jane sitting at the table. But Jane turned around at Myla's footsteps, and then Myla saw the look on her face. "I didn't expect you to be awake," said Jane.

"What's wrong?" Myla pulled out a chair and sat, putting her hand on Jane's arm.

"I don't know what to say."

"What is it? Tell me."

Jane took Myla's hand and put a small notebook into it. The notebook was curved and bent, as if it had been carried in a pants pocket. "I've been trying to convince myself this isn't what it looks like."

Myla opened the notebook and saw her name at the top of the first page, followed by a description of her outfit on the day Samuel had first arrived on the front porch. She turned the page to find a family tree, *her* family tree, with direct lines from Sarah and David to her and Pru, and dotted lines connecting her family to Jane and Steve's. As she flipped through the dozen pages with writing on them, she caught words: *David's Book (they call it The Book); Jane a mother figure?; Logistics of Myla's Disappearance.* Myla kept turning, her hands buzzing from rage. And then she recognized her own words, something she'd said to Samuel the first night he'd stayed in this house: *"I learned a long time ago that no one can be responsible for anyone else's beliefs. You believe what you believe. You know what you know. The best any of us can do is to examine our own prejudices, our own assumptions, and correct ourselves when we're wrong."*

"What the hell is this?" she asked. "Jane? Where—"

"When you guys were out last night, I was doing a load of darks and had some extra room. So I grabbed a pair of jeans off your chair. And when I was cleaning out the pockets, I found this."

"Samuel."

"Yes." Jane rubbed Myla's arm. "But let's not jump to conclusions. Who knows what—"

"He's taking notes on me. I don't need to draw any other conclusions than that." Myla felt herself rising, moving through the kitchen, climbing the stairs, bursting into her bedroom, where Samuel lay sleeping. He'd actually had the gall to tell her to trust him. She towered over him, amazed at how her body was leading her mind. The sheer force of her anger woke him.

"What the fuck is this?" she said, waving the notebook over his head.

Samuel woke up quickly. "What?" he said. "What is that?"

"Doesn't it ring a bell?"

He put his hand up, and halfway toward the notebook, his hand faltered. "Wait a minute," he said. "Where did you get that?"

"Where do you think I got it?"

"That's private," he said. "That's none of your business."

"Excuse me for thinking that it *is* my business, since every single fucking page has my name on it."

"I can explain it," he said. "If that's what you need. An explanation."

"Don't explain it. I want you out."

Samuel sat up in bed. "Myla, be reasonable—"

"You told me I could trust you and I did." Myla's voice was under control, and she spoke slowly. "What was that bullshit last night about making me glow? Are you kidding me? I can't believe I fell for it." She tossed the notebook on the bed. She turned around and strode to the door. "Get out of my sight. I mean it. I want you out by the time I get back."

She got in her car and she drove.

MYLA STARTS TO CHANGE. IT'S like her face changes every time she looks at me. Sometimes I'll see something in her that's untrue or too different, and I can bring her back into something familiar all by myself. But sometimes I don't recognize her at all. She's wrong to pull away that way. Because it makes me notice her more, notice her difference, notice her pulling.

Then one day we're downstairs after school. She's sitting on the counter with a Coke she bought with her own money, and I'm making cereal. She says, "If I show you something, can you keep it a secret?"

"Sure," I say, and she pulls a folded-up piece of paper out of her pocket. "They don't think you're old enough to see this stuff, but I think that's bullshit," she says, and then I'm glad she's my sister, even though I don't know what I'm about to see. When she hands it to me, I realize I'm expecting an article about Ruth's photographs, and it's true, that's what it is. But when I try to read it, it's not half as exciting as I expect it to be. In fact, it's kind of boring. Talking about what kind of film Ruth uses, and what time of day she shoots, and how long she's been taking pictures. It's from a photography magazine. Myla points me to a couple of places she thinks are important.

There's one part in particular that criticizes Ruth in a way I've never thought of before. It says that Ruth calls her pictures important because they explore innocence. The person writing the article says that would be just fine, as long as there were only innocent people looking at the photographs. But, it says, "Ms. Handel's photographs showcase innocence for a fallen adult world, one in which she surely knows such innocence is long gone. Hence, she relinquishes any personal responsibility for her nubile subjects, exhibiting their innocent nakedness for all—innocent and corrupt alike—to see."

I've never thought of myself as innocent at all. Just me. That's it. That's all I can understand about those long and complicated sentences, all I know is true. I try to say this to Myla, because I think she's handed me this article to talk about the ideas in it. I say, "It sounds like this guy just had his own opinions before he even saw the pictures. Like he didn't really look at them."

Myla shrugs.

"You know what I mean?" I ask her.

She shrugs again. "Can I have it back?" she asks, and I fold the article back up so she can put it in her pocket.

She seems upset at me, or like she wants to leave, and I don't know why she showed it to me in the first place. She drinks her Coke while she's looking at me. "Our family's just plain weird," she says.

That makes me kind of mad. "How do you mean, weird?" I've already poured the milk on the cereal. I need a spoon so I can eat it before it gets all sludged, but Myla's legs trap the drawer that holds the utensils. I can tell by her face that now's not the time to nudge her knees aside. So I watch the cereal as it slowly fizzles.

"Like. Okay. Naked pictures all over the place—"

"They aren't all over the place, Myla."

"—and I don't know. All these people who aren't related to us but we owe them stuff."

"I don't know what you mean," I say. Now I want to jerk the drawer out hard and hurt the backs of her legs. Then I realize there are spoons in the dish rack. I grab one of those and jam it into the bowl.

Myla sighs. She says, "Ruth expects us to be in the pictures. Jane expects us to babysit Emma. I'm the one who has to show you the articles written about us in national publications. David's never home."

"David's home as much as any other dad."

"David makes us call him David."

"That was you. You called him David from the beginning, and it stuck. Don't blame me."

"Jesus, Pru, I'm not blaming anyone. I'm trying to have a conversation here. You're ten. You're not too much of a child that you can't talk to me about this shit."

"You're a child too, Myla."

"I'm fifteen."

"Whatever." I roll my eyes back at her.

"Listen." She hops down from the counter and stays where her feet drop. "I just don't think any of it's as important as I used to. I mean, I have a lot of other things going on now, and maybe if I don't agree all the way with articles like this one, I can see they might have a point."

"You're wrong," I tell her. "We're not innocent, and we're not the opposite of it. We're just us. Happy in our family. Happy in Ruth's pictures. Happy with Jane and Emma."

"Maybe."

"So are you just going to, like, not hang out with us anymore?"

Myla rolls her eyes at me and I want to hit her. "You don't get it." Then the thing that makes me really mad comes next. "I guess I shouldn't expect you to. You're still a little girl. You still need them for everything."

I haven't finished eating, but I slam my bowl into the sink and don't let her say one word. I have to get away from her. So I go to my room. A while later I hear the front door closing and know she's gone. That's how we begin to stop talking.

chapter fifteen

as the rain summoned a gray morning, Myla drove around Portland trying to gather herself, trying to avoid the liquor stores and bars she kept noticing. Rage burned in her like a clear white light, purifying her. She wanted to blind herself with alcohol, but she was strong enough to keep herself in the car, even when her body was desperate to slake her thirst. Finally steering her car back in the direction of the house, she hoped—for Samuel's sake—he was gone.

She walked in the front door, and Emma looked up from the couch, where she lay curled under a blanket. Myla checked her watch and realized it was only nine-thirty on a Saturday. "What are you doing up?"

"It was kind of hard to sleep," said Emma. "He's gone, though. He left."

Myla nodded. Looking at Emma caused a wave of simultaneous guilt and pride to surge through Myla: she wasn't drunk. But she wanted to be. "Sorry for waking you."

"Don't feel bad for *me*," said Emma, looking back at

her magazine. Her voice carried a trace of resentment that Myla didn't want to hear. Myla went upstairs.

On her way past Jane and Steve's closed bedroom door, she heard the lilt of conversation lull for just a minute. "Myla, is that you?" came Steve's voice.

"Yup. Sorry for all the drama."

"You okay?"

"Sure." She closed her bedroom door behind her. "Just leave me alone," she said so no one else could hear.

She sat down on the bed, still wrinkled with sheets and blankets, and looked at the wall for a long time. So that was that. There was going to be a before and an after. Before Samuel. And then this. She remembered looking across the table as he'd said, "Trust me." So simple. And she had.

She just had to push him out of her mind. Getting wasted was the way Kate Scott had accomplished such tasks. But now that she was Myla again, she wasn't going to allow herself such easy escape, no matter how tempting. Yes, Samuel Blake had obviously come here with one intention: to research her, to get the "unauthorized story" on Myla Rose Wolfe. Yes, she'd been an idiot to trust him. Yes, he'd trapped her with goodwill. But instead of drinking herself into oblivion, she'd simply have to pretend he'd never existed.

The way to begin that was to read. She pulled David's manuscript out of its manila envelope and flipped to where she'd left off. David would vault her mind out of this place. David would remind her of what was truly important.

Life is so difficult, so challenging, that we desire the Truth.

Not the truth of revelation or confession, but the truth of certainty. Certainty is more comforting if others share our convictions; we are social animals, and so the comforts offered by a commonly held belief are sought after. The faculty of Reason, with all its advocates, gave hope to humankind. It was possible to believe that Truth lay at the end of a line of reasoning.

Think about it. God dwelt in the realm of faith and grace, gifts only God could give. Reason dwelt in the mind of every man and required only the discipline of thought. Reason, and its child, Science, gave man's mind something vastly important to do, something every man could *do. It "takes time" to discover the true nature of reality. But that is ever our goal. And Reason—*

There was a knock on Myla's door. Sharp. Insistent. Then Emma's head poked in. "Just making sure a suicide's not in progress." She laughed. "I get to say things like that." She looked at Myla, who was madly rummaging under the covers to hide the manuscript. "Seriously, Myla." Emma stepped into the room. "Are you okay? What are you hiding? Show me." Emma's voice was forceful, and Myla felt ashamed.

"Okay," Myla said. "Close the door." She pulled the pile of pages out from under the bedspread and held it in both hands. "The Book, Emma. David's book."

Then Emma said the most surprising thing. She didn't ask where it had come from, or why Myla was hiding it. She just asked, "Can I hold it? Can I touch it?" Myla handed the manuscript over, and Emma took the heavy paper in her hands. She shut her eyes, and a smile spread across her face. "I remember your dad was the one who taught me how to write my name. He told me it was like I had four mountain peaks in the middle of it." She laughed softly. "So it wasn't until second grade that I realized my name didn't actually contain four mountains. Kind of an abstract thought for a little kid, I guess. But I remember explaining how confused I was, and Pru not making fun of me. Just explaining how letters mean only one thing—their sound—and how a bunch of sounds together make words. And I remember being horrified by how little possibility that left." She looked down at the book in her hands. She handed it back to Myla tenderly, as if it were a small animal.

Myla felt guilt wave over her. "I didn't tell your parents about David's manuscript. I don't know why. I'm sorry."

"Why are you apologizing?" asked Emma, her clear eyes searching Myla's face.

"I don't know." Myla took Emma's hand. "I feel as if I'm doing everything wrong. I wanted to come back here to reclaim . . . I don't know, to try to correct some of my wrongs. But I don't know how to do that. I don't know how."

Emma nodded. "That's familiar territory. But why are you so mad at Samuel?"

"He kept this notebook—"

"I know *that*. Mom told me. Why really? The real reason."

"He's been lying to me."

"But Myla—no offense, you're the one who's been lying; you've been lying to *everyone*. You're much more irresponsible than he is. You up and left thirteen years ago and didn't say goodbye to any of us. Then you just show up one day and expect everything to be solved? Mom told me how you just showed up at the house. And then you storm out this morning, and Mom and Dad think you're never coming back. They'd never admit it, but I can tell. And you've been keeping the manuscript a secret, and you don't talk about where you've been all this time, and you're not forthright with your feelings, and you pretend the pictures never even existed. That's not lying, exactly, but it's close. It's not being honest. And maybe this is mean to say, but I don't think Pru would know what to do with you. I don't think she'd be very proud."

Myla couldn't meet Emma's eyes. "But I don't know *how* to make her proud."

Emma's voice was full of conviction. "Make her proud by being honest. I know you're pissed off at Samuel. I know he did something that makes you feel uncomfortable. But you didn't even give him a chance to explain why he kept that notebook. And yeah, I'm not inside your head, but just in the nearly twenty-four hours I've been here, I see a big connection between you guys. At the very least, you owe yourself a chance at a true conversation. That's the honest thing to do." She paused. "That and telling my poor dad, *at least*, about this book."

"I'm going to," said Myla weakly. "As for Samuel, maybe it's, you know, just a physical thing."

Emma raised her hand. "Hello? Will you listen to yourself? I *know* you don't believe that."

Faced with Emma's toughness, Myla accepted she was going to have to give Samuel a chance to explain himself. "But he's gone."

"He'll call."

"What if he doesn't?"

"I don't know," said Emma. "But it shouldn't end like this."

Eight hours later, there was still no word from Samuel. The whole family had tried to make the best of it, but Myla knew they were all worried. Even Steve seemed annoyed at Myla for having demanded Samuel's departure. And what she'd initially felt as rage had now ebbed into frustrated curiosity. She wanted Samuel to call her so he could tell her the secrets he'd kept from her.

She called Mark instead.

"I was wondering when I was going to hear from you," he said.

"Have you talked to Samuel?" she asked.

Mark coughed. "Yeah. I have."

"And?"

"I don't know," he said. "I'm in a weird position here. I don't want to be unfair to either of you."

"Oh, come on," she said. "Do you know where he is?"

"I don't know why you care," Mark sniffed. "You're the one who sent him away."

"Yes, I did. Exactly. I sent him away because he was taking notes on me, Mark. Notes. Like in a little notebook. It's creepy and an invasion of my privacy, and we all know that's the worst possible way to impress *me*, of all people. So I got mad and asked him to leave."

"I understand," said Mark. "But then why don't you just let him leave? He's doing what you asked."

"Because I think we should at least have a conversation before he takes off."

"Okay, how's this?" asked Mark. "You give me a compelling, totally honest reason for wanting to see him again, and I tell you where he is. And I'm serious. No bullshit. Tell me why you want to see him."

Myla sighed. She knew there was no reasoning with Mark when he dug in his heels like this. "I want to give him a chance to explain."

"Not good enough. What about *you*? What are *you* going to do?"

"I don't understand, Mark. It's a perfectly reasonable desire: I want to hear why he did this. He broke my trust. I deserve an explanation."

Mark sighed. "I'm only going to say this once. But my God. Listen to yourself. Listen to how typical you sound. If I've learned anything about you in the last week, it's that you're truly an original. I mean, you're someone who's actually changed your identity. Twice. And yet you're whining like every other thirty-something woman who's pissed at her boyfriend. I'm not saying you don't have a right to be pissed, but don't you see what's at stake here? He's leaving on an airplane tomorrow. This is a man who flew across the country to find you. And he's prepared to leave because you asked him to. He actually thinks he doesn't want to talk to you again."

"Well, if he doesn't want to talk to me again—"

"Oh, come on," groaned Mark. "Act like Myla Rose Wolfe. Act like Kate Scott. Be yourself. Rise above this pettiness. You're not someone who's going to let this man go just because of some stupid misunderstanding about a notebook. The only reason you'd let him leave is that you're afraid. Afraid you might truly care about him. But at least clue him in to that, Myla. He thinks you hate him. You've got to cut through the bullshit and tell him, honestly, what's on your mind. Enough already with the dumbass fight about the notebook."

Myla sat down on the bed. She listened to the dead air for a while, as Mark's conviction swirled inside her. He'd said she should be herself. And his words were making her think. "I don't know," she said. "He fed me all this bullshit about wanting to make me glow."

"Maybe it wasn't bullshit," said Mark. "You don't have to take advice from me; I'm Mr. Can't Keep a Man More Than Two Months. But I think I'm right about this one."

"And I just go to him—and what?"

"This from the woman who knew how to disappear off the face of the earth? Yes. You go to him. And you tell him—"

"But what if I can't tell him?" she asked, her heart starting to beat fast. She had an idea, but it wasn't in words. She didn't even know how to explain it to Mark.

"I don't think I know what that means," said Mark.

"What if I need to show him?"

"Then show him," said Mark. "Whatever that means, you go and show him."

"Okay," she said, filling with resolve.

"Okay."

"So you've got to tell me where he is."

"Oh, right." And then he told her.

I MAKE A PLAN. IT'S BEEN something I've been thinking about for a while, something that's finally ready to say out loud. I want all of them to be there. I'm not going to *ask* either. I'm going to be as bossy as Myla.

So I invite them—Jane, Steve, Emma, and Ruth—over for dinner. I don't invite Helaine, because she's too scary to boss around. When I tell Myla I want to make them a big feast, I can tell she thinks it's a little weird, but then she says okay. She even helps me make invitations.

The day of the dinner party, David drives us to the grocery store and helps us get ingredients. He wants to pay for the food, but I tell him I'm using my birthday money. Myla says to me, "Do you have any idea what this is going to cost?" And the thing is, I do. I've planned for it. I've paid attention to how much ground turkey costs and which kind of pasta is the cheapest. But I can't let them know, so I act surprised when I see the total, and let David pay for half so he feels like he's helping.

We make spaghetti and meatballs and garlic bread, and Emma helps us with the salad when she comes over. We set the table with a tablecloth and my mother's silver, which no one has touched in years. And we've even washed cloth napkins, which we nestle under the forks. The table is shining with glass and candles, so when Ruth comes over, she and Jane can both compliment us and don't have to talk to each other.

Everyone is acting like this is a big party, and that's good because I want them to feel that way. Steve is wearing a T-shirt, but he put a bow tie around his neck, and when he comes in the kitchen and sees me, he says, "It's the hostess with the mostest!"

Then we sit and everyone compliments me on the food, and Myla tries to embarrass me by saying, "Pru knew exactly what she wanted and exactly how she wanted Emma and me to help. When we cut the carrots the wrong way, she freaked out."

Then Steve says, "It sounds like we've got another cook in the family," and he smiles at Jane.

They all toast me with cranberry juice and David tells them, "It's the greatest thing, Pru wanting to have this dinner. She felt so strongly about having you all here together."

Then Ruth looks at me, and it's like she can see right through me. "Any special reason, Pru?"

I wasn't expecting to have to answer this question already, but then I realize I might as well tell them. "Actually, yes," I say. All of their eyes look in my direction, even Emma's. I clear my throat. I say, "I've decided I want to give an interview."

David says, "What, sweetheart?"

"I've been thinking about it a lot," I say. "Since you and I had that talk a long time ago about the pictures. I know that people are writing articles and stuff, criticizing the pictures. Talking about pornography—" I look at Emma when I say that word. "Sorry." I wish she didn't have to hear this, but I want her to be here too.

I look at David, and I can see he's trying hard to act like this doesn't matter. I can see it worries him. The part of me that wants to protect him, and everyone else, almost makes me quiet. But I want this so badly I have to say it.

"You guys talk about art all the time. And you talk about how you want me to be an artist, if that's what I want. And I do. I want to be a painter when I grow up. But the thing is, I already am an artist. I'm an artist in Ruth's photographs. And everyone is saying bad things about me, about the art I make, and it's my responsibility to talk about my participation." Then I wait a second. I look at David and I say, "My mother would want me to do this. I know she would." He doesn't say anything.

But Jane does. She says, "Honey, you aren't responsible for anything. You don't have to say anything about the pictures." She's looking at Ruth then, and I can hear blame in her voice.

Steve asks me, "What would you like to say?"

Steve knows it matters to me. He sees that I wouldn't invite them all together like this if it wasn't important. I say, "I'd tell them how much I love the pictures. How much I love being in them, and how important they are for other people to see, because they're about respect and beauty." I turn to Ruth, who hasn't said anything yet. "My whole life, you guys have let me decide about being in the pictures. But now I'm eleven. Now I want to do more than just be in them. I want to tell people how good the pictures are. Why do you think I'm not old enough to do that?"

David clears his throat. "Jane's point is that being in the pictures is all you may need to say. We don't want to burden you—"

"But *this* is a burden," I say. "Sitting here in our family and pretending nobody has any opinions about us."

"Frankly, I don't care what people think," says David.

And I say, "Well, I do. I care. Myla cares." I look at her then, for the first time, because I know she's angry at me for saying this, for planning this and not including her. Sure enough, she's playing with her food and won't look at me.

Steve looks at her too. Then he says, "Myla, what do you think?"

Myla keeps scraping her fork back and forth across her plate. When she looks up, she won't even look at me. Then she says, "Pru can do whatever she wants."

Ruth says, "Don't be rude, Myla. Tell us what you think."

So Myla looks at me, and it freezes me to see how much I've hurt her, leaving her out of this. She says, "Pru should say whatever she wants to say. It's her right. She's the star model."

"No one's saying anything," says Jane. "Nothing has been decided." She says that looking at David.

David sighs and rests his elbows on the table. "I don't know what to say."

"Why is everyone so sad?" I ask. "This is a good thing. Think about it. I'll answer people's questions, and they'll see that I'm really healthy, that I'm smart, that the pictures have made my life better. That will be good. That will help us."

Jane is looking at David like I'm not even here. "You can't give them her voice too. You can't let them into her life like that."

Steve puts his hand on Jane's arm. David sighs. He looks at me. "It's a good idea, Pru."

"It's more than a good idea," I say. I look at Ruth. "Don't you see? It's so much better than you giving interviews. When you give interviews, people think you're just justifying something bad. But if they see that I trust the world, that my family and I are not afraid of the pictures or people's opinions of them, that will make a difference."

Ruth looks up at me and nods. She looks at David, then Jane. "I want to say right now that I knew nothing about this."

"Of course you didn't," says David.

"Of course not," says Myla, and I can hear that she's sarcastic. "It's never *your* idea, Ruth. It's never your plan. It's just what *we* want."

"Myla!" says David.

"Let her say it," says Ruth.

"It's like you just walk in and out of people's lives, deciding what you will and won't give them. You give people something one day and take it away the next. Well, I don't care." Myla stands up. "You want my honest opinion? I think you'd be fools not to take up Pru on her offer. She wants to. She asked for it. Do you listen to what people are saying about us? I read the fucking newspaper. I show the articles to Pru, because I think she deserves to know. Someone has to defend our family." I can see that she's angry, but she's also agreeing with me. She stands back from the table and picks up her plate. "Excuse me," she says, and she leaves the room. We can hear the plate clattering into the sink and then the front door slamming shut.

Everyone's quiet then. No one knows who's going to speak next, and it surprises us all that it's Emma. "I really like the pictures," says Emma, "but even you guys fight about them. If I didn't know Pru, I'd want to understand her point of view." She looks up at Jane. "Sorry, Mom."

Jane looks down at her plate. "Steve?"

Steve shrugs. "I don't think it has to be a big deal. She's already in the public eye. An explanation might help things. Might help people let go."

Jane says, "We need to talk about this. We need to figure this out before anything is decided."

"Yes," says David, and I'm satisfied. At least he'll think about what I've asked.

Then Steve asks, "Pru, is there any dessert?"

"Yes," I tell him, "ice cream."

"Excellent," he says. "How about I help you clear?"

So we clear the dishes and leave the conversation behind. We scoop vanilla ice cream into bowls and stab a spoon into each. When we come back to the dining room, we talk about different things. They know what I want. I have to wait for them to tell me yes.

THE TIRES OF THE CAR crunched over broken glass as Myla edged into the parking lot of the Hillcrest Hotel. She was undeterred. Even four flat tires couldn't stop her now that she was burning with action. Talking to Mark only an hour before, it had seemed impossible to even imagine telling Samuel the wide expanse of her mind. But in the interim, somehow, she'd realized that she needed to let Samuel in on every truth she had. She'd walk barefoot over broken glass if that was what it took. He needed to know, and she needed to show him.

She hadn't actually stopped at the Hillcrest Hotel's front office to ask for his room number; she knew how she'd be treated. Rather, she'd simply picked up the phone at Jane and Steve's before driving over, and demanded the desk clerk give her her husband's room number, as she was sure dozens of wives had done before. It worked. One too many domestic battles fought on Hillcrest Hotel turf, probably, convincing the establishment it wasn't their job to lie to women.

As she pulled into the parking space in front of Unit 18, she chuckled at Samuel's choice. How could he have known what everyone who lived in the neighborhood did: that the Hillcrest Hotel had begun a steady decline twenty-five years ago toward drugs and illicit sex, and had never recovered? She remembered David recounting the tale of a job candidate up from California for the weekend. This man had been put up by the college in the Hillcrest, and on his first night in town was awakened by sirens and flashing lights, only to find that just outside his door, a mere twenty minutes earlier, someone had been stabbed to death. Perhaps it said something about the perilousness of academic life that when this man was ultimately offered the position at the college, he gladly took it.

But Myla wasn't afraid. If anything, the implication of danger emboldened her. She turned off the car and made out the flash of a television through the gauze curtain. Stepping out of the car and locking it, she imagined for a moment that the man working in the front office had given her the wrong room number, and that behind this door, instead of Samuel, there was just the kind of man Jane and Steve and Ruth and David would have described with dread in their voices: greasy, fat, and crude. As she strode to the door, she smiled at such a possibility. She felt it in her: such strength, such surety, such insistence, that she knew she'd bowl over any such man. Perhaps her actions would only alienate Samuel further. But the risk of alienation was her last chance.

She knocked. As she saw the dull light from the television flick off, and heard the rattle of the chain, she could feel her adrenaline pulsing. Evening light warmed her back and glanced onto Samuel's body as he opened the door. He squinted into the red, bright evening.

"May I come in?" asked Myla, her voice full of conviction. She was more Myla than she'd ever been.

Samuel's expression barely changed. He looked at her for a long time, apparently deciding, then stepped aside, directing her in. The hotel room was warm and small. With soft orange light filtering through the curtains, there was a coziness to the room that she was sure existed only for these twenty minutes every day. Her lungs met with ancient smoke, baked into the walls. Brown, rough wallpaper had peeled off in patches, and the furniture consisted of one bed draped in a greasy brown bedspread, a small bedside table, a fraying burgundy armchair, and a television. Samuel's suitcase remained unpacked in the corner.

Myla dropped her purse on the bed. She surveyed the room steadily, turning. She knew this might be mistaken for hesitancy or indecisiveness, but what she was actually feeling was calm. She was readying herself for what she had to do.

"Myla—"

"Please sit down," she said, pointing to the armchair. Samuel shook his head as he walked to the chair and sat, watching her. He leaned forward, resting his elbows on his knees, trying to appear comfortable.

"We should talk," he said.

"I'm sick of talking," she said. "Give me five minutes. Afterward you can do all the talking you want." She knew her voice was steady, and that all he could do in the face of such steadiness was let her say her piece.

"At first I was angry about the notebook." Myla's heart was beating fast as she put her hands to her collar. Her words rolled out of her, clipped and clear. "I thought I was angry because of those stupid notes. But that's not really why I'm so mad. I've been angry at you ever since I heard you lecture. And it's not even because of what you said about my father or Ruth or my sister's death.

"Now I know why." She could see him hanging on her words, but she wanted to get them over with so she could do some real speaking. "I'm angry because you're being so conventional. I'm angry because I see so much more in you; I see the man lit up by my father's ideas, the man who flew across the country after a woman he knew he'd enraged, just so he could tell her he wanted to give her his help. The man who put his jacket over that poster in my bedroom before he made love to me. I know that wasn't just a suave thing you did to impress me. You believed you were doing something important when you hid her that evening.

"And yet you keep a notebook on me, and you don't even hide it well. I see it and I can't trust you anymore. It's so typical, such a dumb thing for us to break up over. And yet how am I supposed to react? The notebook makes me think you've been lying to me, that you have bad motives for having followed me here. But do you know what's so strange? What makes me even angrier is that you truly believe the best way to figure out who I am is to keep a log of my actions. Do you know how unimaginative that is? Think *beyond* that, Samuel. You really want to know me? You really want to know who I am?" She felt the smooth head of the top button of her blouse. She slipped it from its buttonhole and moved her hand down to the next button. The cotton of the blouse was rough against her fingertips. Again she released a button from its restraint. She undid the button at her navel as Samuel shook his head.

"What the hell are you—"

"I let you talk," said Myla. "You showed up on my front steps and insisted you could help me. So I listened. Now you let me do what I have to." She released the bottom button and shrugged the blouse off her shoulders, tossing it on the bed behind her. She felt herself quicken with energy. Her hands found the top button of her jeans, and she released her belly. There were deep red lines on it where it had been cinched and pulled by the heavy denim. She took a deep breath. She unzipped the jeans efficiently, pulling them down as she used her left foot to edge off her right sneaker. She pulled her jeans and her right sock off with her hands, then fiddled the left shoe off with her other set of toes. The thick shag carpeting scratched the sole of her right foot. She wondered how many other women had stood half-dressed in this exact same spot. She removed her pants and the remaining sock, and left them crumpled where they lay.

Samuel held his head in his hands. He was speaking, incredulously, to himself: "I don't know what this is."

Myla expertly reached behind her, finding the clasp of her bra, releasing it. The cups moved off her breasts. She used her right thumb to pull the bra away from her right shoulder, then let the other strap shimmy down her arm. She dropped the bra on the ground and hooked her thumbs in the waistband of her underpants, feeling the tug of the elastic around her hips. She pulled the underwear down her legs and off. She stepped out of it. She was naked.

"Look at me," she said.

Samuel shook his head, his eyes closed tight.

"*Look* at me," she said. "I want you to look at me, Samuel. You look at me, and I'll put my clothes back on. But I won't put them back on until you do." She waited. Her skin bristled with the air on it. Through the window, the light was duller now, less red. It was moving up the wall. She could see in it tiny motes of dust, the only movement in the room. They billowed and bucked as the air moved up her skin. Outside, a car backfired. Still Samuel didn't move. Myla softened her voice. "Just look at me. That's all I'm asking. Then I'll go away."

He shook his head. His eyes were closed as he lifted his face from his hands. His face looked smooth in the dim light. "I don't know why you're doing this," he said, and his voice was young and full of anguish.

"I'll tell you," she said.

Samuel opened his eyes. Guilt tripped across his face, but Myla fixed him in her stare. She could feel his gaze moving up and down her. At first it was harsh and full of judgment. His eyes hovered on her legs and then her torso, skipping over her pubic hair. Then he looked at her arms, first her right, then her left. When she closed her eyes, his gaze was so strong, she could feel it moving over her.

"This is me," said Myla. "This is my body. This is where I've lived. You want to know me? Know *this*. Know this scar, here on my knee, where I fell off my bike when I was ten, racing Pru to the end of the block. Know this mole, here on my hip, that didn't appear until I was nineteen. And here"—she leaned forward— "these freckles on my shoulders? I've had those as long as I can remember." She turned in Samuel's gaze. She bent to touch the back of her left ankle. "I did this to myself the first time I shaved. I was fourteen. I pressed too hard with the razor. And these"—she pressed her thumbs into the two silver-dollar–sized indentations at the base of her back—"are my sacerdotal dimples. Inherited from my mother, who had them too. I remember her kissing them when I got out of the bathtub, as she gathered me on her lap." She turned back around. She stretched her arms into the air, making them as straight as she could. "My elbows don't straighten out. See? This is as flat as my arm gets. Not a hundred and eighty degrees. More like one-sixty. These are my father's arms." She reached down and grabbed her stom-

ach. "And this is my belly. I've always loved its round-
ness. It's the way I'm made."

The light was gone. Now the room was almost completely dark, but Myla could see Samuel's eyes flashing
every time he blinked. He was still watching her. "This
is where I *be*, Samuel. This is what I have. I came into
this world like this, and I'm going to leave it like this.
And by God, I'm alive in it. It's mine. And here's what
matters: when I stand like this, inhabiting my own
skin, I'm not doing *anything* to you. It's not about *you* at
all. You can call that conviction whatever you want: rad-
ical politics, naïveté, but I call it my human right. My
flesh is all the birthright I have. It was all I had of *me*
when I was Kate Scott. And I get to tell you its meaning. No, that's not conventional. But it's what I believe.
Hell, it's one of the few things I *know*."

Her arms were at her sides, and she kept them there.
She wouldn't use her hands to gesture. She wouldn't
modulate her voice. She'd speak to him with all she
had, with the truth of her body. "It comes down to this.
The people who vilify Ruth's photographs, who blame
them, don't understand the fundamental point that in
those photographs, Pru and I got to be *in* our selves. I
know you disagree with Ruth's photographs. But the
self that's in them is the self I want you to know. I just
realized that. The self in those photographs is the honest, real me. It's who I am. I don't know how to know
you if you don't understand that person."

The room was silent and dark. Though her insides
were shimmering, beating, thrumming, whirring,
Myla's outside did not move. Then a shiver slid up her
spine, and still she waited. "I want to know you that

way too," said Samuel finally. "I don't know what else
to say. I want to. But what if I don't know how?"

There was no way to answer that question. It hung
in the space between them, filling the dark room. The
temperature of the room was just right on Myla's body.
She knew she'd promised Samuel she'd put her
clothes back on, but cloth on her skin was the last
thing she wanted to feel. It was dark enough that she
knew he could make out only the outline of her white
flesh. She shifted her weight. She waited for him to
speak. She waited and she waited. Words kept pushing
up to the surface of her mind, but she insisted on
keeping them down. No, it was not her place to talk
anymore. She had said everything she knew.

"I've never seen anything like this before," said
Samuel, breaking through the thick night. His voice
was lower than she expected.

"I've never done anything like this before."

Myla heard Samuel stand. His chair creaked a response to his movement. "I kept the notebook because
I have a friend in publishing. He convinced me I could
help you by shaping your story, with your help, into a
book. The book would be a set of interviews. You'd
speak for yourself. In exchange, I'd get money, and a
ticket out of the academic world, which I've been
wanting out of almost as long as I've been in it. I
thought things would be easy. But I knew, the second I
saw you on the front steps, that I wouldn't know the
right way to put forth such a proposition. So I kept the
book a secret, not because I wanted to lie to you but
because I thought it was a good idea, a real way I could
help you, and I knew you weren't ready to hear it. And

yes, I wrote in the notebook. But don't worry. I'm off that project now. Maybe someday we can talk about the possibility of a book. I still think it would be a good idea, for your sake. But I stopped taking notes—"

"No more talking," she said. She was sick of having to explain everything in words. "Not about this, at least. We both kept big truths from each other. I couldn't tell you why I've been so angry, and you couldn't tell me one of the real reasons you came. If we want a chance at this, we can't lie like that. Not again."

He stepped toward her. His face was growing more distinct with every step, and Myla, now tired, now able to relax, was glad to see his kind eyes, his soft, good lips, his gentle hands. She was hungry for him. She thought he was going to touch her. But no. His hands found the bottom of his T-shirt and pulled it off and over his head. "I want you to know me too," he said, and then he started to undress.

DAVID AND RUTH ARE HANGING out downstairs, and they ask me to come down and talk to them. Their voices are serious, and I know it's about my proposal. When I go down to the living room, they're both sitting, and Ruth has her hands folded in her lap. She seems nervous. I've never seen her like this before.

David starts first. "I want you to know that regardless of what I have to say about this, Ruth and Jane and Steve and I all admire your incredible bravery in bringing this concern of yours to our attention. Each of us thinks it's wonderful that you trust us enough to tell us what you want to do."

"Good," I say. I want him to go on.

"And it's a hard thing for me to know how to handle. As you know, I believe that a parent's responsibility is to help guide his children into learning how to make their own decisions. That's why you and Myla started out in Ruth's pictures in the first place, because you *wanted* to be in them. And that's why I've tried to protect you from people who say harmful things about them. People like Jane have disagreed with me on this point, but it's the kind of parent I've decided to be."

"Okay," I say. I want him to tell me if I can do the interview or not.

"This is a tough decision for me to make. You brought up your mother, and I know you think she'd like for you to speak on behalf of those pictures. To tell you the truth, I've been battling myself about that. Sarah loved you more than she loved herself. She wanted you girls to be strong and brave, and I've tried to carry on that legacy in your upbringing. But she would, and I do, have your safety in mind. And so—I know this is going to be disappointing—I'm going to have to say no."

I open my mouth to say no back, but Ruth starts talking before I can even make a sound. "Pru, please listen to your father. He's right. There are people out there who are very angry about these pictures. Our best way to answer them is to let the pictures speak for themselves."

I shake my head. I want to make them understand. I want to tell them that saying no to me just proves they don't want me to have an opinion, but my head is so full of all sorts of thoughts that I can't come up with something right to say. My eyes start stinging, and I try not to cry, but I can't help it. I feel like they've taken something important away from me, and I know there's nothing I can do about it. I say, "But I need to. It's important."

David comes and sits next to me, and I let him hug me. "We know it is. We know. We love that you want to talk about this. And we want you to. Someday. Just not now, not when some people are so angry. Not when you're still a child."

"But that's the point," I say. "I *am* a child! I am a child in those pictures, and that's who should be talking about them."

"I understand," he says. "Believe it or not, I agree with you. But I'm also your father. And it's my duty to protect you. And this is what I can do to keep you safe."

I shake my head, and I push his arm off my shoulder. I want to stand up and shout at him, tell him and Ruth I hate them, that I'm the one in charge of myself, but Ruth comes and sits in front of me on the floor, and in her hand is a three-ring binder. She opens it, and I can see that every page is a different photocopied article. She puts it on my lap and says, "We thought you weren't old enough to read this stuff. But we were wrong. You want to know why we don't want you to give an interview? Here's why."

The book is heavy on my lap. I flip through the articles, and they start around the time of Ruth's first show, here in Portland. Some are just reviews of her show.

But then when it gets to her New York show, there are some pictures of me, and parts of my body are blocked out with big black boxes. It's really scary to see my body like that. There are headlines about pornography and a description of a protest where some people were arrested for throwing eggs at the gallery owner. There's a picture of a man yelling and his hand is in a fist and he has a sign that says "Protect our children from filth." I can guess that he's talking about our pictures, but only after I think for a minute. It makes me dizzy to see all these words written about us, and all these pictures, and they all seem so angry, my body X'd out, and people shouting.

After a while, I'm done looking. I don't exactly agree with David and Ruth's answer, but I can see more of their side. I want to be mad at them for not showing me these articles before, but they seem so serious and sorry and so interested in hearing my side that I know they were trying their best. I tell them I'm tired, and that's the truth. I want to go to my room and be alone, not because I want to sleep, but because with all the words whirling through my mind, I need to sit still and think. They understand. They tell me I can ask them anything. But for now I don't have any questions. Just thoughts.

An hour later, there's a knock on my door, and I think it's David or Ruth. I don't want to answer it, but they know I'm in here, so I say, "Come in."

It's Myla. She peeks her head around the door, and at first I think she's coming to boss me around or tell me how much smarter she is, but when I see her face, I realize she's going to be nice. "You okay?" she asks.

I nod. She comes in and closes the door behind her.

"They showed you?" she asks.

"Yeah," I say. "You've seen them?"

"I found an article on my own," she says. "A while ago. Remember when I brought up that *New York Times* review?" I nod. "I asked David about it, and he was kind of forced to tell me."

I don't have the energy to be mad at Myla for keeping all this a secret from me. Especially since she's being so nice. Then she smiles and says, "They're in such a tizzy downstairs. Debating our emotional development and wondering if they've scarred us for life or something." She flops down on the floor and lies on her back. I lie down next to her. "*That's* what I mean when I say our family is weird."

That makes me laugh, and Myla says, "The pictures are really important to you right now. I understand that. But look at me. I did those pictures for years, and now I don't anymore. And I know you think it's because I hate Ruth or something, but it's not. I just... you know. I want to move on."

She props herself up on her elbow and uses her other hand to play with my braid. I know what she means about the pictures, but it's always seemed to me that the pictures are so full of us moving, growing up, that they can't hold us back at all.

Myla looks up at the ceiling, so I do too, tracing the cracks across it. After a long time, she says, "You know that story David told us once about Paul Gauguin and

Vincent van Gogh? About how they lived in the country together?"

"No."

"You know, about how they gave each other an assignment to paint the same thing, and then one of them made one kind of picture and the other made another kind. You remember. We used to talk about it all the time. I think we might have even been so lame as to play an actual game called Paul and Vincent in Arles."

I remember, and laughing about it makes me lie back down. "Yeah," I say, "we were lame. Huge huge dorks."

"So anyway. You know how David told us that the story got a little sad at the end—"

"If this is about van Gogh's ear, I already know about that."

"I know you know he cut off his ear. But did you know *when* he did it? Listen, Pru, it's weird. So he wants to have this thing called the Yellow House or something, this place in Arles where he and Paul can start an artists' community. It takes all of this convincing to get Paul to come down there, 'cause he's kind of this jerk who doesn't care about Vincent and doesn't even like his work that much. Did you know Vincent van Gogh only sold one painting in his lifetime?" Myla looks at me. She smiles and says, "You don't have to tell me I sound like David, because I know I do. But just listen.

"So Vincent is desperate to get Paul to come down, and even paints all these paintings to decorate their bedrooms, the house, and so on. Paul finally comes, and he says all these mean things about the paintings, and Vincent listens because he has, like, no self-confidence. Paul agrees to stay. They do all this work together, and Vincent is really the happiest he's ever been. Paul is only there for, like, nine weeks or something, because Vincent starts to drive him crazy. And then one night he tells Vincent he's leaving, and that makes Vincent storm out, and he goes to a local prostitute and cuts off his ear and gives it to her. That night. Then Paul and Vincent's brother, Theo, arrange to have Vincent institutionalized. He shoots himself a year and a half later."

She's serious. Her voice is quiet, like this is the most important thing she's ever said. "The point is, Pru, David didn't always tell us everything that was happening, or that would happen. The end of that story is sad. He told it happy. When I first found out how the story really ended, I was pissed. At David. I felt like he'd lied to us. And then I thought about it. I realized he hadn't lied to us; he'd just left out the bad parts. So that we'd enjoy the story. And maybe that's not such a bad thing. Maybe that's how he loves us."

We watch the ceiling. We watch the ceiling and think.

proof

the younger girl is old now, old enough to have breasts. She's standing in an orchard. The trees are curled like fists up and down the hills behind her. She's standing alone. If you get close, you can see the goose bumps on her body, her hair tossed to the side by a gust. Her nipples are hard. But there's no blanket in sight.

Her body is standing still against the wind. One might think she looks afraid, that she's wild or crazy for standing out alone in an orchard on a day like this.

But you see it. She is brave. You see it. She does this because it matters to her. Making this art is the thing that has made her know, more than anything else, who she is. The cold is worth that. It will be enough to hold this day in her hand. The picture will mean she's been here.

chapter sixteen

they drove in one car, and it was a tight squeeze with their five bodies and the three plants. But it seemed right to come together, now that the rain, falling consistently all morning, had finally stopped. Even Steve had made it clear that though this wasn't his favorite activity, it was the right thing to do. And with everyone together at last, feeling good about one another, Myla wanted to share her excitement at what she was reading in David's book. An outcome of the "Hillcrest Hotel Episode," as she and Samuel were calling it, was that Samuel had begun to read the book. Myla had needed to offer this gesture of trust; Samuel needed to accept it.

Myla had worried Steve would be hurt that she hadn't shared the book with him and Jane immediately, but they were simply thrilled that the manuscript had surfaced. "You've got a great anonymous benefactor working on your side," Steve said. "Do you think we could get them to recover some long-lost treasure belonging to *my* family? Money? Jewelry?" He assured her that he would read David's book in his own good time, relishing every word from his old friend.

Everyone wanted to hear about the book's content, and Myla found herself recounting David's take on the great Italian poet Dante. "You know," she said, "we all regard Dante's *Inferno* as a beautiful poem, and it is. But it also shows the terror everyone in the Middle Ages felt about their two lives: their Life and their *After*life. They believed that if you did good or bad things in your Life, some external force would mete out compensation or punishment in your Afterlife. The oh-so-good earned heaven; most people drew purgatory. And for the worst rule breakers, it was hell.

"That belief in linear time, in cause and effect, kept you honest. It kept you from stealing your neighbor's pig or horse or wife, because if you did those things, you knew you'd be roasting with Satan."

"Basic Sunday-school stuff," said Steve, eager for her to get to the point.

"Sure," said Myla. "But listen to what comes next. Because David believes that with the growth of science and the exalting of human reason, the belief in God faded. Divine law was replaced by human logic. All sorts of things were invented, proving how great the human mind could be. In the eighteenth and nineteenth centuries, all these discoveries and inventions seemed like miracles. God's miracles. The only problem was that things grew ugly. You know the Industrial Revolution? How we always see it as progress? Well, it literally looked like hell. Like depictions of hell from the Middle Ages. Dark furnaces, billowing smoke, starving, misshapen children."

"I never thought of that before," said Steve.

"Like the paintings of Hieronymus Bosch," offered Samuel.

"Exactly," said Myla. "And when hell came to earth, it was as if time had contracted. Now the span of a man's existence didn't just stretch from before his birth to after his death to some grand judgment day. No, what David claims is that man's existence became concentrated into the simple span of his material life on earth. And all that behavior you got punished for? Well, you didn't have to wait until after you died. You began to punish *yourself* while you were still alive."

"Sounds like Freud to me," exclaimed Steve.

"You win the jackpot," said Samuel. "David claims that the medieval Church provided the template for psychoanalysis."

"Imagine that," said Steve. They sat in silence as Jane pulled off the highway. "God, I miss him."

As she opened her car door, Myla realized that the cemetery was in a place she remembered as rural. All that had changed. From up here on the hill, the light-rail tracks were traceable, weaving in and out of strip malls and parking lots, where there'd once been woods and hillsides.

David had picked this cemetery when Sarah died. Myla remembered nothing of the actual burial, only that she'd found out somehow that her mother's body would now lie underground, intact, and this revelation had simultaneously fascinated and repulsed her five-year-old brain. Pru and David's cremated remains had subsequently been buried here as well. Myla was sure that if David had been in his right mind, he would have wanted Pru to be let free and loose somewhere, like in the ocean, but in his grief, he'd done exactly what the funeral director had suggested, and buried her ashes in a wooden box in the ground. It had fueled Myla's anger into hyperdrive.

But Myla pushed away these resentments and looked up, noticing the clouds moving swiftly across the sky. Steve leaned against the car. He'd agreed to come up here, but he wasn't interested in going to the actual graves. "Nothing there for me," he said. "But you go on, Myles." Myla was glad for his reluctance. Emma and Jane and Samuel seemed so well equipped for being here. It was a comfort to know visiting cemeteries wasn't commonplace for Steve either.

David had purchased a double plot for himself and Sarah, counting on his daughters growing to a ripe old age to decide about interment with partners of their own. But when Pru died, there'd been no surrounding plots available, so David had insisted on yielding his place to his daughter.

And so the headstones read, side by side:

WOLFE	WOLFE
Prudence May	Sarah Rose
Beloved Daughter	Beloved Wife
and Sister	and Mother

It all sounded so simple. Two distinct categories for each, and Myla was a participant in the second category for both. She was what made Pru a sister and what made Sarah a mother.

Emma squatted before both graves and placed her hand on Pru's. Myla tried to listen to what she was saying. "And Jake says hi. I wish you could meet him. You have the exact same sense of humor. And I wish you could meet Myla's boyfriend, Samuel. I know you'd approve. I'm really glad she's back." Emma looked over her shoulder at Myla and smiled. "She looks great. I bet you can see her, and I bet you're really proud of her. So, okay. Well. I'm gonna go now. Send another cardinal my way if you want, just so I know you're listening." Emma put a potted flower on each grave and said apologetically to Myla as she stood up, "I never met your mother, so I never say much to her. I just tell her that we want you to come home, and if she can help at all, to send you in our direction. So maybe she listened." Emma pointed toward a tree where Samuel and Jane were standing. "I'll be right over there if you need me."

Myla was left alone with the stones. In her life as Kate Scott, whenever she'd imagined being here, at this cemetery, she'd always thought it would make her profoundly sad. But actually standing here, she was surprised to not feel much of anything. It was as if the place held no meaning. It was strange to hear Emma speaking so matter-of-factly about the reality of the graves. The stones, the actual ground, meant something to her; she relied on them as a place where she might speak to her friend and her friend's mother. They were loci of some kind of faith that the dead were listening, and though Myla knew most of the world believed in something similar, such a concept had always been foreign to her.

She looked at the two names on the headstones, traced them with her eyes. "Hi, Pru," she said. "Hi, Mama. I'm back. I'm finally back." She squatted down and put her hands on the feet of both graves. "I know you're not really here, but I guess I'm supposed to think you are. So I'm just going to try to go with it. I've been reading David's book, and I'm finally getting a glimpse into how much he knew about the way the world is built. I wish you guys could see it." The grass was cool and wet underneath her hands. The odd thing about graves was you could sit there for hours, or you could simply visit for five minutes. It didn't matter all that much.

"I love you," she said. "I'm doing much better than I was. I'll come visit again much sooner." She rose and went toward the living. They joined her and trekked to the opposite end of the lawn, where, years before, Jane and Steve had found a plot after much wrangling with the manager of the cemetery. Myla remembered Steve on the phone demanding to speak to someone's boss. At that point all she'd felt was a need to blame them. But now she could see that they'd been extraordinary in their handling of David's death. Though she'd turned them away, they'd kept their hands open.

David's grave was cut into a slope. Jane and Emma kept their distance, Emma urging the last pot of geraniums into Samuel's hands. Samuel joined Myla at the headstone. The words on the headstone had been chosen by Jane and Steve, after Myla had told them repeatedly that she "didn't care about that bullshit." So David's stone read differently from Sarah's and Pru's:

WOLFE
David Smithson
Extraordinary Father,
Brilliant Scholar,
Remarkable Friend

Myla knew that David would have been embarrassed by such glowing reviews, but she had to admit it had helped with the media. At the time, the photograph of his headstone had appeared on more than one magazine cover, raising the content of conversation in American households to include at least some suggestion that David Smithson Wolfe had been a good father. His death had elevated him to a position of pity in the eyes of the public. But Myla had wanted, and wanted now, as she looked down at his small patch of earth, something more for him. Wanted to award him what he deserved, in his own right.

She leaned down. "I'm reading your book," she said. "Your mind." She shook her head. "God, I wish I'd known your mind when I had the chance to know you. I wish I'd known what you thought about this world." She used her fingernail to clear some moss from the curve of the first S in his middle name. "I'm back. I'm back and I'm getting better."

She stood. She'd said what there was to say. It didn't make her sad to be here, but it didn't make her happy. She wanted to be back in the car, talking about the book with her family. Samuel was weeding the edge of the headstone. He looked up at her, surprised at her quickness.

"I'm ready to go," she said.

And they went.

RUTH AND I RETURN TO THE stream where we used to go to all the time with Myla, the one that has a lagoon if you walk far enough. It's the first time I've been here without Myla, and I miss her, but not just because I have to carry the film coolers all by myself. I asked if she wanted to come along, and she almost said yes, I could see it. But then she remembered she had plans with her friends and told me she hoped I had a good time. So Ruth and I came here alone.

It's sunny in this little patch of water, and I stand in between two big rocks, and Ruth starts taking pictures. It doesn't feel right this way, to be here without Myla, even though it's beautiful and warm and I can't wait to go swimming in the deepest part of the water.

Ruth notices I'm distracted. She asks, "What's wrong?" And I say nothing. I don't want her to feel bad, but I can't lie.

Then she stands up from underneath her dark-cloth and says, "Come here."

"What?" I ask.

"Come here." So I come. And she has me stand next to her to look at the outside world the way she sees it. It's different from over here. When I was little, I used to try to identify everything through the glass; now I want to loosen my seeing. It's all smudges of colors and lines, circles and ripples of light in the water, the curve of branches echoing the curves in the clouds. Color. I squint and notice the light and dark, the shadows from the boulders that hint down on the river, and the shimmer from the water that glimmers on the boulders in turn. I love the way it's almost too much. So much to see. And then she says it. The thing I've been wanting her to say. "Take a picture," she says.

We move under the dark-cloth together. Together we look at the upside-down world, smaller and more manageable in this darkness. She can tell I'm afraid I might do something wrong. She says, "There's no one I'd rather trust with this camera."

"But I'm just a kid," I say.

"You're more mature at eleven than most people ever are. I trust you. Take a picture."

So I act like a photographer. I say, "I need a subject."

Ruth smiles. "Uh-oh. The torturer becomes the victim."

"Get out there," I say, and so she helps me do a light reading and reminds me how to focus the lens and how to cock the button that makes the shutter work. She goes and stands out where I was standing, and I move back and forth between the front of the camera and the back, trying to remember all the different things to do as I've seen her do them all these years. Ruth gives me little hints, but she lets me fix it on my own.

Then I tell her I'm ready. I go to the cooler and get a film holder from the front, with the tab pushed up, so I know it's unexposed. And then I close the lens and slip the holder into the back of the camera, and I pull out the slide. I notice Ruth standing there, and I see she's not comfortable standing there, and it's something I never even imagined. So right before I take the picture, I say, "Say cheese," and that makes her laugh.

Afterward, she comes over to me and says, "William

Henry Fox Talbot, who invented the photograph, called it 'The Pencil of Nature.'" It seems like the perfect thing to say right then, to comfort me, because it sounds like something Myla would know. I need someone to tell me I can see the world and make it look my own way. I look out at the world from this perspective, and it's wide and wild and lovely. I want to see it this way from now on. And then we take more pictures.

THEY WERE IN THE CAR AGAIN. This time just the two of them. Samuel turned on the radio, and they listened to oldie fading into oldie, until the signal faded as they ventured first east and then up the mountain. It was early morning. Myla had fretted about leaving Emma, but Jane assured her that left to her own devices, Emma would sleep until noon. Jane had practically pushed them out the door, unable to hide her relief that Myla and Samuel seemed to be thriving.

Myla slowed down, trying to make out the small unmarked road to turn onto. It had been fifteen years or so since she'd been here, but she thought Samuel would appreciate the gesture. She'd told him she was going to be honest, and that honesty had to include her past, the life she'd left behind. This place was also incredibly beautiful, and she wanted him to see it.

"Is this where those pictures of the lake were taken? You know, the one of you in the water, with your arms spread out on either side of you, and your hands resting on it. And what about the photograph of Pru standing on the other side of the lake?"

"Those were taken at Elk Lake. It's a four-hour drive from here, down by the town of Bend, on Mount Bachelor. No, this is where that picture of us was taken . . . you may have never seen it, actually. I don't know if it was ever published. But it's me in the foreground, looking, I don't know, sullen and fifteen. And Pru on a rock behind me, crouching."

"She's this bright ball of light in the background?"

"Yeah. That's the one. It was taken here. If I can ever find where 'here' is." She steered the car down the gravel road, and eventually into a small dusty parking area.

As they walked down the path, Myla recognized its details. Her conscious mind had forgotten the path's idiosyncrasies, but she walked down it often in her dreams. First she glimpsed the stream, and then it curved into full view, bringing both its glimmer and its gurgle. Here was the boulder on which she and Ruth and Pru had taken their water breaks as they made their way down the path. As Myla walked, her back remembered the excruciating weight of Ruth's gear: the coolers filled with film holders, the backpack filled with reflectors and the lens. Everything they'd needed had to be carried in.

"Just up here," she said, and Samuel stepped aside to let her pass. They walked up the small hill, and then below them opened the lagoon, or the ravine, or whatever it was. Myla felt a small tremor of again being fifteen, when her mind had been looser. She didn't care what it was called. She didn't care how they'd gotten here. She simply longed to slip off her clothes and dip herself in the water, to cool herself after their hike.

She took off her shoes, stepping onto the smooth stones lining the stream bank, and then into the stream itself. The water was a shock, melted snow that ached her arches. And still she stood there, numbing her feet, looking at the rock where Pru had crouched all those years ago. "Why do I keep moving?" she asked, forgetting even Samuel.

But he was there. He'd taken off his shoes too. He was standing beside her.

"All I want to do is drive," she said. "All I want to do is walk. This is the first place I've felt I could stand still. And even here I want to swim."

"Maybe you think that if you move fast enough, or far enough, you'll stumble across the answer. Maybe that's why you're racing through your father's book."

"Yeah," she said, "but I don't want the journey to be over." She couldn't feel her feet anymore, and when she looked down at her toes, layered underwater, she barely knew they belonged to her. "Have you reached the stuff about Rubens and Rembrandt yet? You know, their work with nudes? It's in the second section."

He cleared his throat and looked out across the river.

"What?" she asked after a second.

"I just—" He looked at her. "I don't want you to take this the wrong way. I'm glad you're reading David's book, and I'm glad you love it. But it seems to be consuming you. I mean, I'm as intrigued by his ideas and theories as you are. But after all, that *is* what they are: just theories. I hate seeing you get diverted from your own search for the truth about your past—"

"I don't know what you mean," said Myla, folding her arms around herself. "What do you mean by that?"

He stepped closer to her and tried to put his hand on her shoulder, but she shrugged it off. "Myla," he said. "Please listen to me the way I listened to you at the Hillcrest Hotel the other day. Please?"

She nodded, silent, looking out across the water and not at him.

"I think I need to get at this another way," he said. "So humor me while I try to get my bearings. I've been thinking a lot about what you did and what you said when we were together at the Hillcrest. And I agree with a lot of it. I've read all sorts of stuff about Ruth's photographs. There are some people who look at the pictures of you and Pru and see innocent little girls who've been put in a precarious spot by the adult capturing their image. Then there are others who look at you two and see girls who're worldly, who know a thing or two, who might even have been tempting something bad. The other night you showed me that both of these opinions are irrelevant. They're irrelevant if you believe that every single human being, no matter their age, gets to be in charge of their own body. I have no doubt that was what your father and Ruth and you girls all believed. And I admire that belief, because it's so simple. But it's also something we as a culture seem to have completely disregarded. We don't think of that as a basic human right. We think of it as out of left field."

He cleared his throat. "But I'm a man who wants to protect children. Just as I want to protect that tree over there. I don't want anything to hurt it, and I don't want anything to hurt you."

"We can talk about this if you want to," she said. "We can *really* talk about it."

"I don't want this to be a fight," he replied. "I'm trying to get to the bottom of what we both believe. I think we can agree to disagree."

"But it isn't even about that, Samuel," she said, her voice loud in the cathedral of trees. "You said yourself that you don't think there's anything erotic about the photographs of Pru and me. And yet you want to protect us. Why do you think you have to?"

"Well, because someone else might look at those pictures and misinterpret them. Like the man who—"

Myla put up her hand and silenced Samuel. She wasn't going to let him say what she knew was coming next. "No," she said. "I know you're a good man. I know you want to protect children. But such 'protection,' the kind that labels some art as safe and other art as potentially dangerous, is a subtle, dark form of censorship. The potentially dangerous art gets put into a dark room, and everyone who passes that dark room knows there's something bad inside. Passersby don't get any chance to see the art for themselves, don't get to figure out what they believe on their own. Someone, you, who wants to protect children, has made the decision for them."

Samuel lifted one foot and swooped it back and forth in the water. "That's a good point," he said, raising an eyebrow. He shook his head. "It's just so much to think about. It's hard to find the right words."

This was something they could agree on. "I know what you mean," she said. She let herself smile at the surprise on his face. "I *do*. I don't have the language to talk about this huge cultural controversy surrounding my baby sister's life and death. And it seems to me that to bring speakable words into the conversation about the photographs is to destroy the conversation itself. The pictures have their own language: the language of the visual. That language is undeniable. It doesn't lie. And I can't even describe that, because it's too essential. It's too embedded in me.

"It's like when I began reading about sightings of the Virgin Mary. I knew I couldn't write a book about the sightings if I didn't believe the sincerity of the people who'd experienced them. And so I read account after account, looking for truth. And do you know what convinced me? The blue. Just knowing that when Mary came, everyone saw her blue robes. No one who'd seen her could describe the color of her blue accurately, and that confirmed it for me further. Everyone was seeing a color that didn't exist in our world. It was the color of truth."

She looked down at the clear water rushing over her feet. She breathed in. She looked up at the blue sky above them, tossing clouds toward the mountain. Then she remembered. "But wait a sec. You had a point to make, didn't you? We were headed somewhere before we got diverted by this never-ending debate about the photographs."

"Yeah," said Samuel, smiling. "I did. But I don't want it to offend you."

"I know I get huffy," she said. "I'm sorry I get so defensive. I've just spent a lot of time having to protect my father's decisions."

"Funny. That's what I want to ask you about."

"Okay," she said. "Ask away."

"Tell me why you're so eager to read David's book."

"Because," she said, shrugging. "What else would I do? It's all I have left of him. I need to know what he was thinking. I need to know what mattered to him."

"Exactly." Samuel nodded. "But I don't think you're going to find out what you need to know by reading the book. I think you're asking the wrong question."

"And what, pray tell, is the right question, Professor Blake?" Myla tried to make the teasing in her voice obvious, but for a moment she thought he was offended.

Then he stepped toward her. He put his hand back on her shoulder. He squeezed her there, and his palm was warm through her sweatshirt. "What you need to know is not so much what David was thinking about art, but what he was thinking about the photographs of you and Pru. Your dad loved you, adored you, never would have done anything to hurt you. But what did the pictures mean to him? Why were they so important? It can't just have been only because they were important to you girls and Ruth. There was something about them that mattered to *him*. And I don't think his manuscript is going to tell you why."

Myla searched Samuel's face. "But how am I supposed to answer that question? All I have left of him is his book. He's dead, Samuel."

"I know," he said. "I know. But I think you have more of the answer inside of you than you think." He pulled her to him, and his breath was warm against her. "You've got a *lot* more inside than you think," he said. She closed her eyes and smelled the clean air.

WHEN HELAINE FIRST WALKS into the house, she hasn't seen Myla's hair yet. I can tell when she sees it that David hasn't warned her and she's mad. But she hides it under her smile. "Why, Myla, what a change!" She whisks off her coat and hangs it in the coat closet. She always uses the coat closet, ignoring all the coats that sleep on the floor in the closet's general direction.

Now at dinner, one of Helaine's long-chewed meals, she asks Myla if the dye job's permanent. She asks in a way that isn't really asking anything. She's asking David if he thinks he's a good parent.

Myla rolls her eyes. "It's Manic Panic."

"Oh my, what's that?"

Myla looks at her for a while. "The name of the company that makes the dye. It stays in for a month or something." Then Myla stands up to clear the plates. I help her. I want to get away from Helaine's eyes.

After we're done clearing, we only have the choice to go upstairs. Otherwise we'll have to watch TV all together or something. So we end up in Myla's room. She has Christmas lights up around the ceiling, so it's all glowy in there. I sit on the bed, and she throws stuff off her chair and sits there and looks at me. She turns on music, kind of rocky, but also quiet. "Lord," she says. "That woman." The way she says "that woman" makes me laugh. I look around her room. There are posters on the walls, and ripped-out pages from magazines. But bits of the room are the same as they've always been, especially the wallpaper, which has tiny blue bows on it. The room smells like Myla too. Even under all the new parts, it's familiar with her.

Myla looks at me and suddenly seems excited. "I have an idea," she says. "How about you do my makeup?"

I look at her like she's crazy. I don't know anything about putting on makeup, and I tell her so.

"That's stupid," she says. "Of course you know about makeup, because you know about painting. It doesn't matter what we end up looking like. All my friends ditched me tonight, anyway. Let's just paint our faces. For fun." She goes to her desk and opens it up and pulls out handfuls of eyeshadows and blushes and powders and lipsticks.

"Where'd you get these?" I ask.

"Around," she said. "When Ruth gets bored with a color, she gives me her leftovers. And if you buy something at the beauty counter at Nordstrom, sometimes they give you freebies." I want to ask her when was the last time she bought something at a beauty counter, but I don't want her to get grumpy. So I tell her to sit back down, and we take the makeup over to the bed and spread it out.

It *is* kind of like painting. At first her face is blank, plain. I think it's beautiful, but I know that's not what makeup is about. Myla can tell I don't know what to do, so she grabs an eyeshadow and says, "Dip your finger in it and rub it around. And then put some on my eyelid."

It's a blue, and I start with that, and then I layer a green over it and above it. Pretty soon I like the feel of smoothing the colors over her skin. I add some red to her cheeks, and then she gives me eyeliner and I draw Egyptian eyes for her. She puts a mustache on me, and lipstick, and mascara. We talk about all sorts of things, like my painting, and where she thinks she wants to go to college, and whether we think David and Helaine will get married. We both hope they won't. After a while, we get tired and move over to the bed. We lie on our sides, and the glowing lights make us drowsy.

Myla puts her arm around my stomach and holds me to her. It's warm. I wake up sometime later and she's gone. But the lights are out, and her pillow smells like her hair. When I wake up the next morning, she's there again, her face a smudge of colors that I painted. Like we never stopped being here together.

chapter seventeen

emma asked, "Are you sure you want to do this? We don't have to."

"I know," said Myla. "But I think it's a good idea."

Jane was fixing Emma a snack-pack for her drive back down to California, and Myla could tell she was eavesdropping and pleased. Jane turned and said, "Emma, your laundry's in a basket by the front door. Give Jake a big hug. And you're going to leave right after this errand, right? I don't want you to get caught in traffic." She looked back and forth between their faces, and Myla could tell she was about to cry. "It's so good to have you both in this house," she said.

Emma put her arms around her mother. "I love you, Mom. Have a great day at work. I'll see you soon." Myla recognized Emma's desire to comfort her mother, but a bit of Steve also came through, the unindulgent part of him. It seemed Emma had little patience with Jane's sentimental streak.

After Jane left, Samuel descended from his shower, smelling fresh. Myla felt herself drawn to him, and she blushed when Emma rolled her eyes and said, "Get a room, people."

"Let's go," said Myla. "We've been waiting."

Samuel put his hands on Myla's shoulders. "I'm going to let you two do this one on your own," he said.

And then she and Emma were alone in the car heading toward Myla's childhood home. Myla remembered hearing kids from college talk about growing up in suburbia, but their depictions of overwhelming blandness had been far from her experience. For one thing, her neighborhood was one of the first of its kind, designed in the 1930s, before contractors got greedy. The streets curved and swayed, wide like avenues, and the houses—sweet wooden bungalows—were positioned on large lots. There were trees, broad and arching over the lanes, making each road lush.

When they drove up the intersecting street, Myla knew what the air should smell like. They passed under the wide branches of the old oak perched on the corner. It was ancient, had done all its growing even before she was a child, which was an odd comfort. No change there. Perhaps not as much time had passed as she believed. Then she clicked on the blinker and they turned left.

The house was two lots in, on the right. It nestled on the top of the hill, so she had to strain through the trees to see it, but there it was, all right. Something in her chest let go. She could breathe again, slowly. She pulled up in front and turned off the engine. She opened her door and stood up to see.

The house was the wrong color. The new people had

painted it gray. Green shutters. Green trim. Myla envisioned what the house had looked like when she and Pru and David had lived here: a buttercream yellow, with white trim. She'd been afraid that just one touch of memory while standing here in front of this house would be enough to send her over the edge. Afraid the past might consume her.

She held her breath, but no wave of sorrow loomed. She looked at her old home and still held on to the present. What she felt, surprisingly, was no more than nostalgia. She looked at the house and thought: "Living in this house happened ages ago." She'd left this house long before she'd really left it. Looking up at her childhood home, she remembered that it had always felt like David's, his own place where he opened doors and typed papers and turned lamps off and on. When she was a young child, that life had tantalized her; she'd sneak downstairs in the night just to make sure he'd turned off the lights she'd left on for him. But something had changed in her now, something simple: she'd grown up. She would have abandoned this house anyway. And that was the natural thing to do; it was what Emma and Samuel and everyone else who'd grown up had done. They'd left home.

Myla felt her limbs buzzing in relief; they'd braced themselves for sorrow, but it hadn't come. Emma pointed out places they remembered: the rhododendron bush where she and Pru, and later, Emma and Pru, had built their forts. The swings, on which she and Pru had draped themselves for hours. The roses in the side yard that David had tended methodically. Myla counted the steps that ran up through the middle of the driveway, and realized for the first time how strange it was to have grown up thinking that a driveway with steps in the middle was normal.

Emma was behind her. "I think it's good for you. Just to see it's still standing."

Myla nodded. Emma's gesture asked if Myla wanted to knock on the door, and Myla shook her head. "I'm fine," she said. "I've seen what I need. We lived here, is all. And now we don't. I'm fine."

Emma kicked at a stone. She said, "I thought if you saw the house, you'd get it."

"Get what?"

"That you can't ever leave anything behind. No matter how hard you try." Emma turned her face to Myla's. "It was a horrible thing, the way you walked out on Mom and Dad. Forget me, I was just a kid. But they lost people too, you know? It wasn't just you. And then you left them."

Myla nodded. "I'm sorry," she said.

"I know. I know you are. But how about instead of apologizing, you promise me, right here, that you will never ever disappear again. You don't have to be friends with my family—"

"Of course I want to be friends with you guys—"

"Wait," said Emma, putting up her hands, betraying a maturity Myla hadn't given her credit for. "Let me finish. This isn't about hanging out with friends. This is me telling you: you're not allowed to walk out on my family again. You're not allowed to do that to anyone. But especially not my parents."

"Of course, I promise. Of course." Myla pulled Emma in to hug her. "I was messed up. You're right, I was only thinking about myself. But I'm not going to do that again. I promise."

"Good," said Emma, resisting Myla's pull. "I'm only telling you once. You nearly destroyed my parents. And *I* couldn't help them. They needed *you*." Myla's world became blurry from her tears. And then Emma hugged Myla back, softly at first, and then holding hard to her. Myla could feel Emma begin to cry and soothed her gently, rocking her back and forth.

"I want to know how you are, Emma. I want to know what happened with you."

"Good," said Emma. "Someday. Someday I'll tell you. But for now you promise you'll never disappear again. You tell us if you're going."

"I'll never disappear again," said Myla, and it was a promise, for the first time, she truly felt she could keep.

WE'RE AT AN OLD SHED ON the edge of someone's property by the coast. There are apple trees. It's afternoon, and the wind will turn soon and whip us where we stand, but for now I'm fine, protected by the shed. Ruth's hair is red in the light and whips behind her like a scarf. And the camera is here, set and ready. I'm curving my body, my arms steady and solid. I can see what I look like—this is how good I've gotten at knowing what will click Ruth's mind into wanting to get me down on paper.

She never wants to talk about her work unless we're looking at it. It's like the pictures aren't real for her until she sees them on paper. It's the opposite for me. When I see them on paper, they get less real. It's like the moment has faded by the time it gets to where you can hold it in your hand.

But this is one shoot we talk about before we do it. I can quote Ruth about subject and ground. Subject: well, I'm the subject. Ground: "There are three kinds of possible photographic ground: those that harm and distract, those that are just there, and those that present the subject like a jewel in a setting." The orchard is the first type, but could become the third, if Ruth can pull it off. She tells me this. She says the only reason she's trying is because I'm willing to get bored trying. The orchard is tricky because of all the "bright, distant ground elements in the sky and the busy-ness of orchard trees set apart." This is how Ruth talks to me. Black and white is already contrasty and busy. I know that. Ruth wants to know if I'm up to the challenge.

So this time I give her a challenge too. This time I stop her right before she starts making the pictures that I know she'll love. I want something else from her, something bigger. I just say, "Can we try something different?"

That brings her out of her quiet head. She says, "Sure, okay. What do you mean?"

"Like. I don't know." I walk forward. I realize for a second how silly I look, naked in an orchard with a shed behind me and this big eye focused in my direction. "Try to take a picture that isn't pretty."

She laughs. "But how can I possibly do that, when your beauty is beyond measure?"

"Ha ha. You know what I mean. Just try it for a second. Take a picture of me that feels ugly. Or plain. Take a picture of the part of me you aren't interested in."

Ruth looks worried. "Honey, what do you mean? What part of you could I possibly not be interested in?"

"C'mon, Ruth. You've taken pictures of me since I was three years old. So that's what? Nine years? And you always take pictures of me where I look beautiful or happy or easy to get along with. But there's got to be something about me that you choose not to take pictures of. So try to take a picture of that."

Later, she shows me the proof sheets from that day. I can see we never achieved my goal. But I can also see something else: that my idea worked. There are moments in some pictures that aren't just beautiful. And those are the ones that are interesting, at least to me. They show us working together, they show my ideas helping her pictures.

There's one picture I make her print even though she doesn't want to. She says it just doesn't make any sense. But she prints it as a favor to me. My body looks the way it always looks in her pictures, like a statue. But my eyes are different. They are wild at the corners, though only if you glance at the picture from one angle really, really fast. If you didn't know me, you'd think maybe I was just sneezing or something.

I like that picture because I look afraid.

THAT NIGHT MYLA LAY IN bed, Samuel curled deep in sleep beside her, and watched the light from the street-lamp patterning the wall. She was happy, alive. She'd been waiting for this moment for years. A sensation of peace and excitement all at once. When she was a little girl, she'd often fallen asleep this way, watching over Pru's dreaming body and thinking about the big stories and ideas David had left behind him in the room, after he'd kissed them both good night and closed the door.

Reading his words was so much like hearing his voice that at times it took her breath away. And today was the day he'd started to tell the story of photography. She'd had to restrain herself from flipping ahead to this section—*The Momentous Birth of Photography and the Advent of Technological Time*—while she'd been reading the earlier parts of the book. But today's reading had been wonderful. She'd felt the old familiar joy of following her father's train of thought. It was a physical sensation, full of rising and lifting, resting and lying low. And what he'd said made such sense that it made her want to laugh.

Photographs had been central to her life for so long that she'd never before even tried to imagine what the world must have looked like, and seemed like, before their invention. All day long she'd noticed pictures everywhere she looked. And now, as she watched the light playing on the wall, she could imagine the longing that had made inventors want to capture that light and write with it on paper. It must have been so discouraging for the first photographic inventors to realize they could capture a picture but had no way to fix it on the page. Then came Niépce and Daguerre, who figured out how to coat a copper plate with chemicals to secure the picture exactly. But the real miracle, the world-altering miracle, was William Henry Fox Talbot's invention of the paper negative. Then pictures could be reproduced again and again, multiplying the same vision.

The reason all this mattered so much was simple: photographs weren't just pictures, they were moments. For what the invention of photography in the 1820s and 30s provided was visual proof that there was such a thing as the historical moment. For centuries, artists had been painting such moments, but none of the resulting pictures had been made in a moment's time. Photography captured the moment *in* a moment. And technology made it possible.

Myla lay in bed and thought about Ruth's camera, how foreign and strange and machinelike it had always seemed to her. Wood, metal, cloth, glass. It was both extremely fragile and very tough. It *worked*. And then there was the chemistry of the darkroom. Myla had never been interested, but Pru had agitated to be allowed downstairs to help Ruth print pictures. Both Ruth and David had vetoed that idea. Too toxic, they'd told her. Way too toxic for a little girl.

Myla could hardly lie still; David's thoughts filled her with energy. She slipped out from under the covers, slid her feet into a pair of Jane's down slippers, and pulled a wool afghan around her shoulders. Quietly she made her way downstairs in the dark and let herself out the front door. The spring air was fresh, not too cold, damp. A fuzzy halo shimmered around the streetlight. She sat down in a wicker chair and tucked her feet under her. Above her in the house, Samuel, Steve, and Jane all slept. Myla understood that this was a moment, a distinct moment. And if she had a camera, the right lenses, the correct film, she could photograph it. All of them asleep in their beds, this wicker chair, the cold light. Every single moment could, theoretically, be depicted; every picture would allow that moment to endure.

What her father had claimed was that through the act of making the moment visible, photography not only affirmed the existence of such moments but also provided a way for the human mind to think about reality, about the experience of living in time. If linear time was evident everywhere, then photography allowed human beings to think of their lives as actual moments strung like beads along the time line of their lives. Every moment, whether photographed or not, was always visible in theory. And with multiple prints of a single moment traveling through time and space, the moments of an individual's life gained a force never before experienced anywhere at any time.

Myla felt the sweep of her father's mind carrying her along and was surprised to look up and see Jane standing in the doorway, her arms wrapped around her. "You okay, Myla?"

"I'm fine. No, better than fine." Myla smiled. She felt the coldness in the air and stood up, shivering. "I think I'm happy, Jane. Right here. Right now. In this moment."

The older woman stepped forward and set the screen door back in place as quietly as she could. She enveloped Myla in her arms. "That's what we want, sweetheart. But we don't want you to freeze to death."

Together they entered the house, and Jane said, "For what it's worth, if you ever want to talk . . ." She left off. "About anything. You know. Samuel. What you're going through now. The past." Jane sounded awkward. "I don't want to interfere in anything now, but I wish I'd been more present for you in the past." She paused. "I just feel awful about that, Myla. You needed me, you know. And I wasn't there."

Myla was shocked. "Jane! You of all people. You couldn't have been more there." She hugged the older woman. "Please don't worry. I know I told you that all the adults let me down. And maybe I believed that then. But now, well, now I'm a grown-up. I know better." Jane hugged her, then pulled away as Myla went on. "But I'm ready for a mom now, so I guess you'll be stuck with lots of conversations."

The two women made their way back upstairs, and soon Myla found herself stretched out beside Samuel. She'd lost none of her contentment, but Jane's words had awakened a memory, a moment, and she realized that only in her present happiness could she afford to feel this moment and let it expand into the scene it was, the scene it had been.

She remembered waking up and hearing the two adults arguing below. Usually Helaine had gone straight home after dinner, but Myla remembered that on this night she and Pru had been angry about something and had retreated upstairs. They'd put on makeup for hours, then ended up curled against each other on the bed, until she'd woken up. Pru stayed asleep as Myla had slowly eased her arm out from under her sister's hot head. The house was quiet but not asleep. No David in the next room. Too many lights on, that was the first sign.

Myla had crept down the stairs, missing creaky number five and sitting on seven to see if she could hear anything. She knew she could go downstairs if she wanted to, but it felt right to hide somehow. She listened, knowing that their voices would come. And they did, still from the kitchen. She thought they would have moved out of there a long time ago.

"The point I'm trying to make here, if you'd just give me a chance to make it, is that this stuff is potent." Helaine's voice, shrill.

"And you don't think I know that? You think I haven't deliberated long and hard about the consequences? These are my daughters—"

"Well, I may not know what it's like to be a parent, but I know what it is to love Myla and Prudence. They're terribly important to me."

"If they were terribly important to you, then you'd understand."

"You asked my advice, David, and I'm trying to give it to you. Now just calm down and listen."

It was quiet for a long time, and Myla could see in her mind's eye the way that David's face was trying to cool itself, the way his hands would be pulling at the knees of his pants. She'd never heard him angry like this before. At last he said, "Go on."

"You've been having problems with Myla."

"Not problems. She's a teenager. It's normal. She's pulling away."

Helaine's voice again. "And she's not in Ruth's pictures anymore."

"Yes," said David. "Myla's decision."

Helaine sighed. "I just think . . . I think it's more than that. I think this is more about Ruth's work than you or Ruth or even Myla would be willing to admit. Whether or not one agrees with the pictures being considered pornography or what have you, your daughters are going to be lying on their therapists' couches talking about those pictures for the rest of their lives. Don't you get that?"

"No. I don't. I don't choose that for them."

"But you don't get to choose, don't you see?"

"Fine, Helaine. You're right. I don't get to choose their futures. All I can do is offer them possibilities, open up their childhoods so they know they have freedom of self and expression. That gives them the tools to choose what they want for themselves. That people look at those photographs and think they depict something they simply don't—well, that has nothing to do with my girls. That's a cultural problem. And the only way to fight against that problem is to encourage art that stretches the boundaries of what is conventional, of what is mainstream."

"Your girls aren't experiments. Your girls aren't here to expand the imagination of millions. They're just girls."

"I know that, Helaine. I know my girls. No one pressures them. Myla's chosen not to be in the photographs anymore. When she made that decision, everyone supported it. Besides, Ruth consults us on each photograph she prints, making sure we want it out there in the world. There's a whole slew of photographs she took of Myla that she chose not to print because she felt they were too charged. Not because Myla was doing anything overtly sexual in them, but because Myla's grown up. She has a woman's body now. And her stubbornness, her self-knowledge, can be easily perceived as sultry. Ruth made that call. That's her job as a responsible artist. That's my job as a responsible father."

Myla hadn't known that. She heard one of them scraping a glass across the table and then clapping it back down again. Then Helaine said, "David, I know you've had the best of intentions since day one. And I honestly believe that if Sarah were still alive, the girls would have been in pictures just the same. But—and I know I'm wading into treacherous waters here, but I've got to say my piece—if Sarah were alive, those pictures would be different for the girls. Ruth and those images wouldn't be all they imagine about what it is to be a woman in this world. Don't you see? As a man, you've made things too simple for them, you've required them to believe they live in a world where women can do or be or think anything, where bodies aren't used as weapons, where a smart woman isn't threatening. I think Sarah would have given them a dose of reality that you haven't been able to, a reality that Ruth's artistic vision just won't include."

Helaine's voice sounded clear, not angry, as she went on. "Those girls love you. They love Ruth. I know they don't love me because I'm not fun. But also because I won't play along and pretend that what you've all chosen isn't dangerous—" It sounded as if Helaine were going to say something else, but she didn't.

"And?"

"And nothing, David. I can help you if you'll let me, but I can't sit by and watch you expect so much of them. They're children. They can't be theories and research and proofs. They're your daughters, and they would be anything for you. So let them see the pictures in all their complexities, talk openly with them about the things people are saying about them, as brutal as those things might sound to you. They've both asked you about them. Pru even wanted that interview. Just showing them articles isn't enough. They need to hear from you—"

David's chair pushed across the floor as he stood up. "They won't ever hear anything like that from me. And before they hear it from you, I'm going to have to ask you to leave."

"Now, David, really, be reasonable."

His voice was painfully quiet. "Please go."

When Helaine's steps clipped across the floor, Myla sprang up the stairs. She slipped back into her room and closed the door as David and Helaine walked into the front hall. She listened and listened, but she never heard a slam or even a click from the front door.

Curling up again behind Pru, Myla had been drawn to the swirl of her sister's hair on her pillow. Hair the color of their mother's hair. Something she hadn't realized before. It struck Myla as odd that she hadn't noticed the resemblance in the past, and she felt far away from herself. How did any of them know who they were with Sarah so fully gone from them? She'd been gone almost thirteen years. Too long to understand. Too long even to imagine what life might have been with her there.

I'T'S MY THIRTEENTH BIRTHDAY, but it's hard to feel very excited about it. Myla is packing up so she can fly to college, and she and David are frustrated at each other about everything. They celebrate my birthday, of course, but there's no time for it. I'm old enough to understand. Jane has promised she'll make a cake, but that won't be until Friday.

So I'm up in my room reading, when someone knocks on my bedroom door. I say, "Come in," and it's Ruth. She's holding a wrapped box, and she says she hopes she's not disturbing me.

I tell her to come sit down next to me. Ruth can tell I'm curious about my gift, so she places it in my lap and says, "Happy birthday to the artist."

Usually I take my time with wrapping paper, slitting the tape with my fingernail so the paper can go back into the wrapping-paper drawer. But I don't care this time. I rip the package apart, pulling off the ribbon and letting it fall on the floor.

And it's exactly what I wanted. A set of oil paints. Not acrylics, or watercolor, or any other paint that isn't real. Oil paints are what real artists use. I can't believe it. I read the names to myself, memorizing them: Green-Blue Shade, Prussian Blue, Hansa Yellow, Cadmium Red, Midnight Black, and Flake White.

Ruth says, "I hope you like them," and I hug her hard and fast around the neck.

"These are amazing," I say. "Thank you thank you thank you." I can't sit still because I'm so excited. So I get up and hop around.

Ruth says, "There are some canvases downstairs in my car to get you started. And we can always buy you more."

I hug her again. She laughs and says, "I haven't seen you this excited in a long time."

I say, "That's because this is real. I get to paint now. I can paint from the time Myla leaves until school starts."

Ruth says, "I know it's hard with Myla going to college."

I don't want to think about it, but I know what she means. I sit down again and look at the paints.

Ruth says, "Myla's nearly an adult. But these paints are for you. You're a teenager." I look at her. I can tell she's trying to tell me something.

She goes on. "You're growing up." She pauses for a few seconds, then says, "Let's talk about the pictures sometime."

I don't understand. I tell her.

"Well," she says, "you're older now. You'll be starting high school next fall. There might be some pictures you don't want . . . out there anymore."

"What do you mean?" I ask. I never expected to hear anything like this from her.

"I mean we just need to think. We need to have a conversation. Not now, not on your birthday"—she smiles—"but someday soon. After Myla goes."

"Okay," I say. "If you want." If Ruth doesn't believe in the pictures, I don't know what to believe. But I steer myself to a better part of my mind, the part that wants to use my new oils.

After Ruth leaves, I look at the paints one by one and imagine myself inside the colors. They're rich, and a part of me wishes I could eat them. I look at them until Myla comes to get me for dinner. A week later, she's gone.

chapter eighteen

myla came downstairs to the smell of sautéing onions. "Smells delicious!" she called from the living room, but there was no response. She set down her magazine and walked into the kitchen. Samuel was there, but he was standing at the sink, gazing out the window. The onions were burning. Myla turned off the heat and moved the pan off the burner, scraping wildly at the brown glue stuck to the bottom of the pan. It wasn't until the smoke alarm started its high-pitched squeal that Samuel startled out of his reverie.

"Now, that's what I call lost in thought," Myla said after climbing on a chair and pulling apart the smoke alarm. "Where exactly were you?"

Samuel smiled, a kind of laziness on his face. "Thinking about your father's book."

"Ah," said Myla, a feeling of satisfaction creeping into her.

"I've been thinking about what he says about moments and how they argue against linear time." He shrugged his hands into his pockets and turned back to look out the window. "Take the moment when I decided to come here. To follow you. I was standing in Mark's apartment, in the middle of his living room. He was talking a mile a minute, piecing everything together, and I looked down at my feet. It was something about the way my right tennis shoe looked. I saw it and I knew. I was going to buy a plane ticket and come here. There was no element of reason in my decision. I knew that no matter what happened between us, there'd always be a before and an after. I would be changed forever. I *am* changed forever."

He turned his smile to her. "And it's funny, because people talk about moments: the moment they fell in love with someone, the moment they looked at their baby and knew they'd never be the same. Those moments are about change. My dad always tells this story about my stepmother—about how when he saw her, he just knew he'd spend the rest of his life with her. I always thought it was bullshit. I didn't think something like that could happen in a moment. But now I see. It doesn't matter if it actually happened in a moment's time. What matters is that my father has that moment to look back at, to point to. It's his. He can live it a million times, can't he?"

Myla nodded. She put her hand on Samuel's arm and pulled him to her. He continued speaking. "And it makes me wonder. Everyone who looks at Ruth's photographs has noticed that at a certain point you simply stopped appearing in them. Was that your choice? And if it was, at what moment did you decide you wouldn't be in them anymore?"

Myla let go of him. She was stunned by the accuracy

of his question. She moved backward and found a chair to catch her. She knew exactly the moment she'd describe. At first she could hardly speak, because the feelings were so immediate. Then she began to tell Samuel about the trip to New York when she was fifteen and Pru was ten. She described the cold whip of air on her face, the thrill of women running down sidewalks in high heels as the sky spilled snow, the unfamiliarity of tiny white dogs trotting by in winter coats. She described the soaring feeling of belonging to this sophistication, knowing photographs of her would be hanging in a New York gallery on West Fifty-seventh Street.

And then, on the appointed night, they sped down Park Avenue in a limousine, swirling white air eddying around them. It seemed that everyone in the city was going to the gallery too, and she imagined people recognizing them through the window, remembering that she was now Rose, that Pru was now May, that people would hand them glasses of punch, curious about their lives, then tell them how extraordinarily beautiful they were. It was an easy thing to do this. It swelled Myla's heart, like she was helping people who needed hope.

They got to the gallery. Tumbling out of the limo, Myla noticed someone passing out gallery announcements. The picture was of Pru on the far side of Elk Lake. People were collecting the announcement in their hands, but as soon as she saw which picture had been chosen, Myla's brain could catch only glimpses of other people's words. She was suddenly too cold and wanted to push her way inside, where she wouldn't hear their talking. She looked back over her shoulder. Pru was smiling shyly, quietly. Pru wouldn't say anything. Pru wouldn't point out, "That's me!" And Myla was angry. At Pru. Pru didn't know how to do this. *She* did.

Myla shuddered now, remembering her plan to get inside before Pru did. She'd plant herself beside an image and try to look the same as it. That night she'd counted her pictures and counted Pru's pictures and compared.

Myla continued talking to Samuel. "I thought I stopped taking pictures with Ruth for one reason, but I know now that it was really another. The reason I told myself was that Ruth didn't seem interested in taking pictures of me anymore. I mean, actually, that was probably true. I was in high school by this point, and Pru was still a kid, and she was probably in a much better mood most of the time. I told myself that I could see how much more Ruth loved Pru than me, simply by looking at the photographs she took of her, and how many more of them there were. And I hated the jealousy I felt for Pru. I knew she was only a little girl, and I wanted to protect her from my feelings of envy."

Samuel was sitting in another chair, across from her. The aroma of burned onions still hung in the air. Myla went on, "But what was really going on was both harder and easier: I grew up. I was a teenager. I wanted to go to the mall and hang out with boys and gossip and go to dances. I wanted to *live*. By the time I was sixteen, seventeen, eighteen, the last thing I wanted to do was make high art with my baby sister and a middle-aged woman, to live my life by someone else's moments, by someone else's vision of what my life was like, even if that someone was wonderful Ruth."

And so she told him about the last shoot she ever did with Ruth. She was fifteen. They'd gone to the stream, attracted by the eddy of light and cool and water. Pru had leaned down, looking at something in the water, and that had galvanized Ruth, compelling her to take out the camera and start shooting. Myla had felt the dread begin, had felt the pull to make Ruth want to see her. She didn't know whether she should cooperate or sulk. She'd chosen the former. There was always the possibility Ruth would want to shoot her.

And she did. They'd taken some good pictures that day; Myla could feel it from the tingle of the work. Ruth had said so. But then Ruth hadn't printed any of the photographs with only Myla in them. There'd been that one photograph that Ruth had printed of the two of them on the riverbed, but Myla had resented being relegated to photographs with Pru in them too. Ruth had printed pictures from that day of Pru alone, but none of Myla standing by herself.

Looking back on it now, Myla told Samuel, there'd been something she hadn't known, something she'd overheard David tell Helaine the night they'd broken up. Myla had believed Ruth didn't think she was pretty enough anymore, but that hadn't been it. Ruth had looked at the negatives, at Myla's new body, at the look on her face, and felt the photographs were too sultry to print. It had been her call to make. She'd risked Myla's hating her. And all Myla had known was that to feel invisible was to be rejected, and to be visible was to be accepted.

So Myla had made a decision, mainly to show Ruth what she was missing. No more photographs. She'd just say no. And she wanted the first "no" to be dramatic. She wanted to see Ruth's face dissolve, then rework, to stammer out an "Oh, that's fine." Because Myla knew it wasn't fine. Myla knew that Ruth needed her.

But then Ruth called a few days later and said something like "Let's take pictures this weekend," and it wasn't even a question, that's what prompted Myla to do it. She responded, "No, thanks." Just as easy as that.

Ruth said, "Okay. Are you feeling all right, kiddo?"

"Don't call me kiddo."

"Well, someone's grumpy."

"I'm not grumpy, I just don't want to do it, okay?"

"Great. What're your plans?"

"None of your business."

"Charming, Myla. Can you put your sister on?"

Myla held the phone against her heart and yelled Pru's name. Pru took it upstairs, and Myla wished she could sneak up there without Pru's hearing. But the outcome was obvious. The next morning Pru was sitting on the stairs with her backpack on by the time Myla ambled down into the world.

"We're going to a pond," said Pru.

Suddenly Myla wanted to be going too, and she considered running upstairs and grabbing a bag. She knew she had time, that they'd wait. But then the familiar three honks came from the road, and Pru stood up, walked to the door, and jerked it closed behind her. She didn't say goodbye.

By the time Myla finished talking, she was nearly crying. She sat quietly for a long while. And then she said, "You know, that's one reason I got so mad about the photographs after Pru's death. Not because the pictures aren't great, but because they're the only way the world remembers my baby sister. And they're just pictures. Just moments. Pru was in those moments, but she was so much bigger than they are." Myla stood up. "Come with me," she said, and walked into the living room.

Samuel followed.

"You want to see my sweet little Pru? Emma showed me this the other day. She told me I can make a copy of it." Myla and Samuel sat down on the couch. She opened a leather album and turned the pages until she reached the right one. She held the album out to him. He looked. There stood a little girl, about five years old, playing a recorder in front of the very couch on which he was now sitting. On the couch was a row of stuffed animals with books propped open in front of them. A hand-painted sign said "SCHOOL." The little girl's hair was frazzled, her eyes wide open, her cheeks puffed out. She looked silly and fun—like any other five-year-old.

"Jane took this," Myla said. "I'm showing you this because I want you to know that Pru had more moments than the ones she's famous for." Myla took the book back. "And maybe she too would have grown to love the mall and hanging out with friends. Maybe she would have decided that taking pictures with Ruth didn't interest her anymore. Maybe she would have taken some pictures of her own. She just didn't get the chance to find any of that out."

I START WALKING HOME FROM school right at three so I can get home in time to still have light in my studio. It's not really a studio, it's Myla's room, but the light in there is nice in the afternoon, and David has set up one of his old easels for me. Every night since Myla left in September, I've worked in there until dark. I'm working on my fifth painting. The funny thing is, I don't have a hard time thinking about what to paint, I have a hard time narrowing down my ideas.

But an even better thing has happened in my studio than just the paintings. An even better present than the oil paints. I have to keep this present a secret. I know I should give it back, that it isn't really mine.

I was moving some of Myla's things into her closet when I noticed there was an old box way back in the corner that I'd never seen before. I pulled its flaps open, but the box was heavy and wouldn't move, so I had to take out Myla's shoes and pull and push the box to get it out into the room. It was dusty and full of books. Old books. Books that looked like all the other ones downstairs, all the other ones filling up the bookshelves.

I was about to call out David's name so he could come take the box away when I noticed a blue book at the top of the pile. I pulled it out and looked at it and read the title. It was amazing. It was like the book was written for me. It was called *The Craftsman's Handbook*, but that isn't even its real name. It's called *Il libro dell'arte*, and it was written by a man who lived in the fifteenth century in Florence. It's a how-to book for medieval artists. For painters. It teaches all sorts of things, like how to make a drapery in fresco, how to paint wounds, how to make a mordant out of garlic, and how to distemper inside walls with green. I don't even know what half the words mean, but I knew immediately that I liked it.

And then I opened to the inside front cover and saw my mother's name written there. In dark blue handwriting. So this was *her* book. It was almost as if she'd left it for me, as if the book had been waiting for my studio to be set up. I knew why my mother had it. She was a poet, and she needed to play with words. And so she had this book, with all these words that feel amazing when you say them. And now I'm learning how to paint from it. And there was a piece of paper in there that she'd written on too, and her handwriting was so neat and so beautiful that I knew immediately I wouldn't tell anyone what I'd found, not even Emma, not even Myla when she calls.

I'm almost done reading the book. You'd think it would be hard to understand, but it isn't hard at all. It's about making paint come alive. It's about me. I've decided I'm going to make a blue velvet case for it, and I'll keep it hidden in my drawer. I don't want anyone to know about it. I want it to be a secret between my mother and me.

So I don't even notice the man. I'm thinking about getting home—I'm almost there—I'm thinking about finishing the book tonight, when all of a sudden I look up and there's a man standing in front of me. He's just there on the corner where no one usually is in our neighborhood at this time of day. I walk past him and then I hear his voice. He's asking me a question and part of me wants to keep walking but I don't. I listen to the other part that wants to pay attention, to be polite. So I say, "Excuse me?"

He says, "Can you tell me where I can find— Hey, wait a minute, aren't you one of the Wolfe girls? From Ruth Handel's pictures?"

I don't know what to say. I realize I don't know him. He's too old to be a student. Not dressed right to be a professor. He's just a man. But I nod. I forget that it's strange he knows my last name.

He says, "Poor child."

"What did you say?"

He smiles and says, "Don't worry."

"I'm not worried. I'm going home." But already it's too late. I turn to walk away, and then there's something over my mouth that makes my legs wobble and my hands loosen from the straps of my backpack.

Right before I go to sleep, I hear his mouth against my ear saying, "Sorry sorry sorry." I feel like I want to tell him something, but I can't remember what it is. That must be when he carries me to the car.

IT WAS MIDNIGHT, AND MYLA couldn't sleep. She couldn't even lie down. Light from the streetlamp whitened the far wall and fell in a stripe across Samuel's still body. He'd drifted off easily, peacefully, and now lay serenely on his back, his face the image of rest. Myla stood with her back to the window and gazed down at him.

She'd counted on reading David's book, on being lulled by the rhythms of his voice, carried by the sweep of his logic. Everything about him felt familiar and safe. And now here she stood, David's unfinished manuscript a series of stacks strewn across the dresser top. She had no desire to pick it up. She knew she didn't want the reading to be over; that was part of the reluctance. The thrill of hearing her father's voice, fresh with authority, would be over too soon.

But that was only part of it. Another part was strange, almost uncanny. As she'd begun to feel more and more like her old self, relaxing into this comforting life, into her known body, David's words and arguments had come to seem more and more familiar, predictable. Not because they'd lost their originality. No, not that at all. It was stranger than that. It was as if she already knew what her father was going to say even before he said it. Like hearing a familiar music, a music that had been humming in her bones silently for years and was audible once again.

She knew, for instance, what David would conclude about art, its role, its moral power. He would say that art isn't just something made by artists; it has a life of its own, independent of the people who make it and the people who see it. Kind of like a cultural agent that exists to contribute to the evolution of society. Artists don't just represent what's already there; they make what's coming look so familiar that when it arrives, it looks natural. Art is like some sort of oracle.

And tampering with that oracular force, by silencing it or condemning it or banning it, will never work. It's no more possible than trying to stop a hurricane or volcano. Art is a force of nature, of *human* nature. Art is what we make and what makes us. Art is what makes us human.

As Myla gazed across Samuel's features, she felt a tremendous tenderness. He'd asked her the right question: why were the pictures so important to her father? Samuel had realized that the answer didn't lie inside David's pages; it lay inside Myla herself. And here, in the darkened room spilling with light, she knew that she'd always known the reason, but until now had been too young, too sad, too small to *let* herself know.

Love. Love was the reason. Once, when she was little, she'd come upon her father sitting on the floor of the study, with what looked like all the proofs Ruth had ever printed of her and Pru spread around him. She couldn't even enter the room, what with all the pictures on the floor. What had surprised her at the time wasn't that her tidy father had made such a big mess, but rather what he'd said when he'd seen her standing in the doorway. He'd smiled a broad, silly grin and said, "I was just thinking of your mom."

That was it. "I was just thinking of your mom." Sarah. Sarah was the answer. The photographs had been a way to seize moments as they raced by in the flood of time, and by seizing them and stopping them, a way to expand them into broad planes of light and dark and shadow in which Sarah's two little naked babies could be seen growing into beautiful strong girls and young women. And in that place of stillness, of time out of time, Sarah could enter too. They could all come together once again, in the act of art, defying the relentless passage of time.

Myla looked at Samuel's strong jaw, lax in sleep, his

delicate long lashes dark against his cheeks. She felt such tenderness, witnessing this offering of vulnerability. She left her cold stance by the window and, slipping her body between the covers, curled next to him. In the morning, after a good sleep, she knew what she'd do. It was time now. She would take him there.

WE'RE DRIVING IN A CAR AND I ask him where we're going and he won't tell me. He doesn't like me or he likes me too much, I don't know which. He has my hands tied. He calls me Poor Sweet Lamb and says he won't hurt me the way my father does. He listens to the radio, turning it up to hear it over the coarse and grumbling road. He keeps his window down so the evening comes blasting in. Pretty soon the air smells clean, and I make out the shadows of pine trees above us. We're in the country.

My head hurts, making me sleepy, but I also know the smart thing is to look around, to memorize where we're going, to leave marks anywhere I can. Fear doesn't enter me. I think of Myla, think of her strong face, think of what she'd do.

Then we get out of the car. We get out of the car and it's dusk. He pushes me forward, and I walk, but I ignore him too. It's darker here in the forest. It's like there's a clear blue wash over everything, like looking at the evening through dark glasses. But I can still see the trees. Their trunks are tall and I can see the leaves above, green like verdigris and terre verte and malachite. We start to walk and the pine needles crunch beneath our feet. The needles are yellow, and I say the words for "yellow" to myself, the words from my mother's book: ochre and giallorino and orpiment and realgar and saffron and arzica.

And I let myself think about the sheet of paper my mother wrote on. The sheet of paper in *Il libro dell'arte*. The one that fell out when I opened the book, the one that feathered down to the floor.

I picked it up and read it and I knew it was written for me. Now, more than anything, I want to tell Myla what it said. At first I thought it was a list of paint colors. But as I read down, I realized it was a message about who I was, and who I was supposed to be.

I see the words before me as I walk. A list. I do not listen to what the man is telling me. I will not hear him as he tells me I'm a good person. I hear only this: "Carmina.

"Jonquil.

"Lilac.

"Lila.

"Violet.

"Azure.

"Azura."

They're names. Names for me. Because under that list, my mother wrote: "Myla Rose and Azura May," and I knew then, and know now, that my name is really Azura. Even if they didn't name me that. Azura was my mother's secret name for me, the beautiful name she chose.

I want to ask David why they called me Prudence. I want to make Myla call me Azura. I will be Azura when I'm an artist. That will be my name.

Then we stop walking. The man is crying. He wants to touch me but he won't, I know he won't, because he can't even look in my eyes. It's cold in the forest and I'm frightened. But I do not close my eyes. He asks for my forgiveness. There's metal in my mouth and it tastes cold and empty. The tall trees point up from us into the evening, spreading their branches over us like hands. The smell of pine comes strong up from the ground. He prays. And then he kills me.

proof

the person in this photograph is a woman. You don't recognize her. She's standing, her body facing forward, leaning hard on one leg; she looks to her left, and she's almost in profile. It's clear she isn't standing comfortably. She's not used to being in pictures.

This woman's hair is dark and long and very straight. There's no wind, and her hair falls like a mane down her back. Her hands hang long at her sides, and two of the fingers on her right hand grip the bottom of her T-shirt.

The photograph is slightly out of focus. But it doesn't matter. The woman is smiling, and that's what you notice. Although you can tell she's unused to this, unaccustomed to being seen, you can also tell that the photographer has said something wonderful to make this woman happy. She's on the verge of laughing. For a brief moment, though her legs don't know exactly how to stand, though her arms only know to hang limply at her sides, though she's held her breath, waiting, for the click of the camera, the woman is comfortable.

chapter nineteen

they drove out of the city into farmland, heading west, straight for the coast. Myla was like a lit fuse, moving fast. She was going to go and get it over with once and for all. Samuel didn't ask where they were going. She told him what she could.

"I was at college when Pru was abducted. I was finishing up the fall of my freshman year. I had a boyfriend, someone I thought I might love. It was the first time. It was bigger than anything I'd ever felt." The afternoon had been soaked in light. They'd come back to the boy's room after eating lunch in the dining hall. It was the first time they'd done this, the first time his roommate was out of town. When the boy clicked the door closed, locking it behind them, she'd felt the first shudder of embarrassment. She'd walked briskly to the window, looked out over the quad, contemplated yelling hello to two of the girls from her French class who were passing underneath. That would have ended things. Maybe it would keep her from wanting this. Then she heard him ease himself onto the bed.

"I was happy." Myla looked at Samuel now, saw that instead of looking at the speeding-past world, he was looking at her. "Truly happy. I'd found a simplicity that I thought would last forever."

She'd turned to face the boy, slowly, aware that the sun was streaming itself around her. She'd felt her limbs bathed in gold, her hair like a wildfire of red and yellow, her white cotton shirt folding itself around her breasts. She'd seen herself through the boy's eyes. She was irresistible.

The boy had sat down and put on a tape, Chet Baker. That had done it. It had turned something in her, and at that moment a voice inside her had told her she'd never go back to the place she'd been before. It had pushed her over the threshold. She'd fiddled with the buttons of her shirt.

"I can't describe it, but I felt . . . in control. In control of me and what I wanted and, hell, who I was. I wanted this and I was going to have it."

She'd closed her eyes. It wasn't dark inside her own head; it was golden. She'd felt the cotton slip down her arms and onto the floor, felt her nipples sear with the boy's looking. The sun warmed her back. Her fingers found the buttons of her skirt and deftly released them. Then she slipped her fingers into the waistband, slid her hands under the elastic of her underwear, and pushed both skirt and underwear down until they let loose around her ankles. The boy had said nothing, could only watch.

"I'd been nude a million times but never naked. This was the first time. The first time I was naked, the first time I let someone love me. And it was the same day my father called and told me my sister was missing. I came back to my room after having sex for the very first time, and when I walked in the door, my roommate said, 'I've been looking for you. Your dad called. I think something's wrong.' And then the world shattered.

"I flew home, even though Jane and Steve and David assured me Pru would be back any day. I think a part of me knew she was already gone. I felt cut inside, unbound.

"Anyway. I'm sure you know this part. It was three days of waiting. We didn't sleep. Jane made us elaborate meals and we didn't eat them. We were holed up in our house. I saw my father pray for the first time."

She remembered David's back, out in the early-morning sun, on the porch, hunched. His voice saying, "Dear God, protect her." The surge of rage in her when she heard those words. Everyone was giving up. People were showing weakness. One couldn't show weakness. That would let Pru die.

"And then someone found her." Myla ignored the grit in her voice. "My sister's body, in a pine forest near the coast. She hadn't been raped, but it doesn't make much difference, does it? The two hikers who made the 'discovery'—as the media so charmingly termed it—found the man who'd killed her lying by her side. He'd had the decency to blow his own brains out.

"I tried to be a dutiful daughter. My life was over, but Jane sat me down and told me I had to go on. David and I had only silence between us. I didn't have any words for him, and he kept his to himself. I stayed home for Christmas vacation, mainly in my bedroom, and then everyone insisted I go back to college. Something normal, something regular, they said."

She remembered her father at the airport, the last time they'd seen each other. His shy touch on her shoulder, her insistence that he hug her instead. Jane wrapping her in a scratchy brown scarf she'd knit, urging Myla to come home soon. Myla had dumped the scarf as she'd transferred planes in Chicago.

"So I go back to school, and everyone knows what happened. Everyone stares at me. The campus police has to ban the media, who wait outside the school gates every time I step beyond them. I'm invited to join dozens of counseling groups: for abused children, for people dealing with grief, for those *not* dealing with grief.

"And then. Two months go by. And I get a second call. From Jane. My father has died of a heart attack, and they want me to come home. No one even apologizes anymore. People don't want to look at me. I'm a reminder of what's sad in the world, and college is for people who are happy."

She remembered her roommate's words: "I think maybe you're depressed." As simple an assessment as that.

"So I go home. I go to the funeral. Two nights later, I get into an excellently huge argument with Steve and Jane and leave their house for good. I go to a local bar and get wasted. I decide I'm going to leave Portland and never come back. But before I do that, I drive out here."

Myla swept her arm against the outside, which had turned from a country highway, thick on either side with wheat fields and old farmhouses, to a forest road winding its way through the dark and light of leaf shadows. She remembered this drive from the only other time she'd taken it, in the darkness, driving fast, drunk. It hadn't been dark enough for her, the moon nearly full and punching too much light into the open air. She'd listened to music, loud, angry music, and had swerved in and out around cars. She'd decided this was a night when she deserved to be out of control. She'd wanted to see where it had happened.

"We're going to where she died, aren't we?" asked Samuel.

"Yes."

Pru had been killed up an old logging road, and Myla knew the way reflexively. As they turned, she saw the road was barricaded with a couple of old logs, but she wasn't going to let that stop her.

She remembered that first night, when the turnoff was fresh from two months of police activity, easy to spot even under the cover of forest. Then there'd been no need to get out to move anything. She'd driven full throttle into the forest.

Now she stepped from the car and was hit with the smell of pine, strong, sharp, with a tang in it that made the back of her throat rise. Samuel was already helping her move the logs before she needed to ask.

The car moved from the blacktop to the slickness of the pine needles with relative ease. The tires crunched against the layers and layers of woven ground, basketed over time.

In the darkness of that night years before, she'd

revved up the turns, oblivious to speed. She'd stopped when forced to stop and, spilling herself into the night, had been hit with the strong smell. She hadn't expected that, the way a potent smell could solidify a moment. She'd vomited then, sick with the world. Then she'd stood and walked.

Myla turned to Samuel as if this were a perfectly normal moment. "It's just a mile or two up here." He nodded, silent.

The road climbed steadily, and the trees above them ached with green, some branches brushing against the top of the car. Then the road turned, and she knew they'd reached the end. The pine smell insinuated itself through the car vents, and she believed that at last she was prepared for its full-on power. There was only one way to find out.

The slam of the car door in the old-growth forest was tinny. She was overwhelmed by the smell that had met her in her nightmares, the smell of these trees, but she wasn't dreaming now. She looked up and watched the trunks, huge, old, proud, swaying slowly, moaning with wind. She'd had no time to notice them the last time she'd been here. Now she knew those trees were the source of the smell she hated. Looking up, she realized they'd towered over Pru at the moment she'd died, and Myla suddenly felt grateful to them for their grace. Grateful in a way her teenage self hadn't understood. It comforted her that things of beauty had filled Pru's last sight. She memorized this new idea—that she *liked* these trees—to keep herself from vomiting.

Myla walked alone up the hill to her left, climbing over fallen trunks and moss and small caterpillars hol-

ing the wood. She stepped over ants on their produc-
tive expeditions and the warm nests of baby voles. She
stepped over new ferns unfurling their wands of green,
over worms drilling through the damp and fertile earth,
over mushrooms pushing their way into sunlight. She
stepped over and over until she stopped. Samuel
stopped behind her.

Years before, this had been as far as she could go.
She'd walked to this spot, and something in her had
broken. The next thing she'd known, she was driving
away, leaving everything she'd once known behind her.
She couldn't remember what had happened to her
when she'd seen the spot where Pru had died, and now
she was seeing it again. She was back. She wanted to
diminish its power to nothing.

Myla looked at the spot on the ground. Here was the
place she'd dreamed about, dreaded all this time. She
wanted to understand it, wanted to dissect it until it
yielded nothing. As she examined the ground, examined the last spot where Pru had claimed breath, Myla
watched and waited. For something to make this place
crushable. For something to make this very spot something she could destroy.

The problem was basic: there was nothing special
about this place. Just a patch of forest floor. People
walking in these woods would have no idea this was
where her beloved sister, her light, her breath, her bud
of a companion, had fallen. There was nothing to set it
apart. There was nothing to destroy. There was no answer.

Samuel stood apart from her and watched. And then
he came to her and touched her. A small touch, on the

back, a small tap of understanding, what understanding he could give.

Samuel's touch, his push against her back, was enough to fill Myla with all the thoughts she'd avoided for so long. All the things she wanted to believe in: David's faith in what he'd known to be true, Pru's bravery, Ruth's vision, Sarah's silence, and now this man's, Samuel's, love for her. It pushed these thoughts out of her mouth, into a cry she didn't know she'd held inside herself, a release of all burden. It was weeping, it involved tears, but it was more than that. It was more basic than anything she had ever felt. It was raw, without thought, or words, or a need to understand. It simply was.

It lasted.

MYLA AND SAMUEL CAME back many hours later, as afternoon light skimmed over the city. What Myla felt now was a combination of giddiness and deep exhaustion that she knew would not be worn off in sleep.

But as they got out of the car, she jolted with knowing this was a perfectly normal moment, without weight or meaning. They were just a couple returning from a day spent together. She knew that her life would be filled with more and more moments like these. Moments without significance or portent. Moments just like everyone else had. How would she order her life without a dark center? What could she orbit around? How would she recognize herself freed from the grip of anger, of terror, of the deep rawness of death? It was uncharted, this next step.

"I'm going to call Mark," she said as she walked up the front steps.

"Good," said Samuel as she opened the screen door. And then she saw the envelope.

It was leaning against the front door, hidden for only her to find. Myla knew Steve and Jane were at work; she picked up the envelope, felt the outline of a key through the paper, felt it weigh heavy in her hand. Her name was not on the envelope, but she knew, by instinct, that it was hers.

She opened it. Inside was the key she'd felt, a dull brass that had lost its shine; the number 24 was etched on its head. Then a card, typed: *Fairview Storage Units. Now.*

Myla whirled, turned to Samuel. "I have to go."

"Where?" His hand on her arm asked her to invite him.

"I'll be back soon," she said.

The light sweeping over the Portland afternoon was crisp, broad. Myla saw with such clarity that she didn't want to put on her sunglasses even though the world glared. She knew where she was going. This was the third test, the third trial, the third envelope. She knew it would be the last.

She let herself imagine what was waiting. She wanted to laugh, knowing there was something locked away for her, waiting for her discovery. Something of David's, perhaps. Something saved by Ruth. For with every turn she made, Myla was more and more certain

this was Ruth's doing. She wasn't even going to specu-
late how Ruth had made it back to Portland without
people noticing, how Ruth had read Myla's mind after
all these years of distance, how she'd known exactly
which pushes and pulls Myla needed. It was Ruth's
way, and Myla realized that she was seeing the world
differently. It didn't feel so divided. Things felt possible.

There'd been a last time she'd seen Ruth. They'd
both known it would be the last time, though neither
spoke a word about it.

Pru was dead. David was dead. Myla had left Steve
and Jane's house after railing against them. And then
she'd taken her first trip, in the middle of the night, to
the spot where Pru had been murdered. The moon rose
and set. It was two in the morning, and winter. Myla,
driving back into Portland, knowing she was never
coming back, had steered her car over to Ruth's. The
house was dark, but Ruth's car was parked out front.
Myla had marched across the dark lawn and knocked
on the door. There was no answer. She huddled on the
cold sagging steps and waited for something to happen.

Something did. She caught Ruth's shadow emerging
from the basement with a box in her arms. Ruth walked
down the driveway, moving awkwardly with the weight
of the box. Myla heard Ruth opening the trunk of her
car, saw her outline as it struggled to place the heavy
box inside, and heard the whisper of the latch in the
dark cool night. Ruth came back up the driveway, and
Myla stood. Ruth stopped. They faced each other. A
cold wind whipped up around them.

There was nothing that could be said. Myla knew

that now. It was impossible to say any of the millions of things each had to say. There was simply too much tangled up.

But they knew each other. Myla knew Ruth was leaving. Ruth knew Myla was leaving. Myla didn't blame Ruth. But how could one say that? How did one say, "You didn't murder my sister"? How did one speak of being an orphan? How did one mourn for the newly dead? There was nothing to be done. There was nothing she could have said to Ruth that would have freed her. There was nothing Ruth could have said that would have made any difference. So they just stood in the cold dark, an arm's length between them, and watched their breath plume out into the night. Myla remembered closing her eyes and opening them again, waiting for day to come. But it seemed it never would. And then, in a split second, she knew she was ready. To leave this life she loved. To leave this life that had already left her. She walked away. She left Ruth's house, and then she left Portland. She'd never seen Ruth again. They were gone from each other.

Myla parked in front of storage unit 24. She took the key out of her pocket. She straightened herself and walked to the storage door, but the padlock was already unlocked, the garage-type door halfway up. She slipped under the open door and stood in the harsh rectangle of light on the floor.

"Hello?" she said. It was quiet. When her eyes adjusted, she could make out countless boxes piled in the middle of a large room. A mountain of boxes. She said it again. "Hello?"

There was a cough. A man. A voice she knew. "It's me, Myla." Steve. She made him out, standing in the back of the unit, leaning against the wall.

"Steve," she said. "Where's Ruth?"

Steve was walking toward her, apologetic, his head down. "I don't know. Not here."

Myla felt her heart drop. "She sent me—" She gestured in the air, and Steve shook his head.

"Honey, that was me. Just old me trying to help you out."

Myla backed up. "Don't mess with me, Steve. What's going on?"

He moved slowly toward her, through the dark. "I'm it." He paused. "I'm the man behind the curtain." He waited for her to respond, and she realized he expected her to be angry. Then he spoke again. "Myles, a million times I've tried to figure out where to begin. And I realize I want to tell you a story. That's where I want to start." She nodded, letting him begin, even as tears stung her eyes. She wanted Ruth, but she had Steve. What else could she do but listen?

"Once, ages ago, there lived four young friends, two men, two women. They were artists and thinkers, people who had plans for the world. They had faith in art's value. In its importance."

Steve's face was shadowed, but she could hear a smile in his voice as he spoke. "One of the men and one of the women fell in love, that once-in-a-lifetime kind of love. This couple stayed awake until all hours of the night talking philosophy and theory and sharing their thoughts. The ideas that spouted from these conversations only made their love stronger."

He cleared his throat. "Well, once the first man and woman had gotten together, the other two decided to become a couple themselves. Only this couple didn't really know how to make it work. They spent most of their time arguing, breaking up, getting back together, and arguing again. They were too restless for the caliber of love the first couple shared.

"Meanwhile, the first couple had a baby. One and then another. And then the woman—the mother and wife—was killed in a car accident. Sarah. She died and left you and Pru and David all alone."

Steve leaned his weight back and forth between his legs, swaying slightly in the darkness. "Even though we'd broken up, Ruth and I were still in our brutal cycle: fighting, all mixed up about how we really felt."

Myla was stunned. She said, "You and Ruth . . . ?"

"A thousand years ago, Ruth and I were that other couple."

Myla said, "Wait. I always assumed David and Ruth had been lovers at some point."

"Seemed that way at times, didn't it? But they weren't. Just old friends." He put his finger up to show he had more to say. "But in any case, long before Sarah died, Ruth and I knew things were over. I'd already met Jane; when Sarah died, Jane moved into my house, so we could take care of you girls. So your father could grieve.

"Ruth and I had ended our affair once and for all, but we swore we'd stay in your lives, for David. I loved Jane, and Jane wanted, well, she wanted simpler things than Ruth did. Jane wanted me to be who I was. She didn't need me to prove anything. So I married her."

The whites of Steve's eyes were bright against the darkness as he looked at Myla. "I'm telling you this so you'll understand the first reason I'm here, so you understand what I'm sure you've understood for a while, now that you're an adult and have a love of your own. Things were complicated. When you were kids, we weren't any older than you are today. Imagine yourself with small children of your own." He shook his head. "We were idiots. We put on a good show, but we had no idea how to do anything."

Myla was reeling. She'd never known this. Now it all fit together so perfectly: Jane's jealousy and disapproval of Ruth, Steve's silent defense of Ruth's art, the constant division of their childhood between Jane's world and Ruth's world. She'd thought Jane and Ruth hadn't liked each other for political reasons.

Steve continued. "The thing was, Jane had a very hard time with my insistence that Ruth stay in our lives. For a long time Jane didn't understand that I loved *her*, that I'd chosen *her*, and I'm afraid that's all my fault. Ruth was an artist, and Jane was a teacher. Jane saw herself as a consolation prize. Which is neither here nor there, except to say there were many, many things going on of which you girls were entirely unaware."

The sun was pricking the back of Myla's legs, keeping her tied to the outside. "Where is Ruth?" she asked again.

Steve stayed where he was. "No one knows, honey."

"I thought I was going to see her. I thought she was here," she said, aware that she sounded like a child.

"Ah, yes," he said. "I knew that would break your

heart. I knew it would." He choked back tears. "I'm so sorry, Myla. I'm so sorry."

Myla was shaking her head no.

Steve stepped toward her. "Let me continue with my story," he said. "Let the story do its work, and then we'll be done." He waited for a response from Myla, but she gave him none. Didn't move a muscle in her face. Exhaustion was overwhelming her.

"Jane and I started our family, and David was blessed with you girls, and Ruth, as she saw it, had no one. It wasn't that she wanted me, she made that clear. But she wanted something to tether her the way our families tethered all of us.

"One day—this is how it was told to me—David was talking to her, and she was describing the disappointment of her life, how she'd never have a great love, never do great things. And David objected. He told her she possessed a talent unlike any he'd seen. Which was true, if you want my opinion. He told her he'd pay for a portrait of you girls. When she scoffed, he said—and I'll never forget the way he repeated it—'You wouldn't deny a widower such a simple request.' She told him that photography wasn't even real art; she called all those horse pictures she'd been taking hackwork. But David insisted that photography was even a greater art than painting, because a painter can always lie. A painter chooses a subject and can set that subject against the perfect background. She can paint over that first background and make a better one. But a photographer has to think fast and instinctively, has to accept what the world offers.

"And then David told her: 'This is what Sarah would

have wanted.' He told her that he and Sarah shared the belief that one should live one's life as a work of art, and wouldn't she like to be a part of that in the lives of you girls. So that's how the photographs got started."

"I remember," said Myla. "We wanted to be in them. They were our decision."

"Of course," said Steve. "We know they were. If you get the impression that Jane and I didn't approve of them, or didn't like them, well, it was more complicated than that. Jane says her greatest regret is not having a portrait of the three of you girls. She, well, she was jealous, and at first she didn't know exactly how to feel about the photographs. I wanted her happiness, so I backed off. Oh yes, she wanted to protect you girls, and as a schoolteacher, she knew more about the so-called real world than the rest of us, but her reservation was more fundamental than that: she didn't want Ruth to get a part of you she couldn't have.

"So." Steve sighed. "The proverbial house was divided. David and I were busy at school, and you girls spent some days at Ruth's, taking pictures, and some days at our house, playing with Emma. 'Being regular' was how Pru put it—remember that?"

Myla smiled, nodded. "Yes."

Steve walked the last steps to the doorway, to her. It was a relief to see him in the brighter light. "Do you want me to go on?"

"Yes," she said. "I need to hear it all, once and for all."

"Good," he said. "I think so, too." He continued. "So. Once and for all.

"That's when the pictures started attracting attention. They were hailed as masterpieces and as filth. Simultaneously. Simple as that. Jane urged David to talk to you girls about the range of opinions, but he saw it as his duty to protect you. He didn't want to make you feel self-conscious about your choice to be photographed. He knew you loved the images. He didn't want to take away what you loved. At about that time he started dating Helaine. As I'm sure you remember, this changed things in everybody's life—"

"I remember," said Myla.

"Yes, and the significant change for us was that Helaine and Jane, though not close friends, realized they had similar feelings about the photographs, feelings of concern. But David wanted none of it, and I, well, I'm afraid I was too much of a coward to express an opinion one way or the other.

"Then Pru, bless her heart, came up with the idea for the interview. You girls were smarter than we thought, knew more about the world than we guessed. You knew there were people who disagreed with the pictures. Pru believed that all she needed to do was explain why she loved those photographs, why they weren't dirty or exploitative, and people would understand. Ruth was the one who said no before David even had a chance to sort through his feelings on the matter. Pru, as you may remember, was terribly disappointed about not being able to do it."

They let their conversation rest again. Myla was winding and unwinding all of these facts, all of these stories. Then it hit her. "So you're Marcus Berger's mysterious client?"

Steve nodded. "I'm afraid so."

"Why? Why now? Why not be straight with me?"

He sighed. "I've been getting up my nerve to contact you for two years now, since I knew where you were. It was all very detective-movie. Once we knew your new name, we knew you were still alive, which was a comfort to us both. But I had some things for you. And I knew you needed them. So I thought of a plan, and then set it in motion."

"But why didn't you just contact me yourself? Why did you want me to think Ruth was behind this?"

Steve ran his fingers through his hair and whistled. "That's the toughie, isn't it? And it's not even the part I feel the worst about. Let's put it this way: I knew Ruth would be the only reason you'd come home. But I didn't want to lie to you. So I kept things open. If you'd never come to our house on your own, I wouldn't be standing here. All these things—your inheritance—would have been handed to you, one by one, by our friend Marcus Berger. The final thing you'd said to us was that you never wanted to see us again. And I wanted to respect that."

"I never should have said those things that night," Myla said. "I don't even know how to apologize for them."

"Water under the bridge, sweetheart. And really, the way you've apologized is by coming home. By granting us the pleasure of your company." Steve smiled as a tear gleamed down his cheek. "Seeing you—it's like seeing Emma get her life back together. It's a miracle."

"Oh, Steve—"

"Enough," he said, and his voice put him in charge. "Let me answer your question about Ruth. Here's how

I justified it to myself: I was acting in her name. Wherever she is, I know she wants you to have these things. I know she wants you to take them so you can move on."

Myla stepped away from the doorway into the room. "What are the things?" She could make out the boxes more clearly now, stacked floor to ceiling in the storage unit that surrounded them.

Steve went on. "This is where I make my confession. This is where I tell you something that risks all the goodwill we've restored." He cleared his throat. "The day you came home, the day after your father died, I was in your house. I found your father's manuscript in the bottom drawer of his desk. And I took it. I ran across your father's notebook, and I took it too. Just put them in my bag and brought them to my house. I didn't tell Jane. I hid them in a box of my own notebooks from college. Two years ago, Jane was cleaning out the attic, and she found your father's things. Needless to say, she was quite angry at me. She told me I had to find you."

"Why would you do that, Steve? Why would you hide David's things from me?"

"You were so angry," he said. "The second you stepped off that plane, I knew you were in no place to read your father's book. You would have ripped it apart, no matter what it said. And I wanted to protect him from that. But I also wanted to protect you from the pain and anger you were going through. Of course, I thought I'd only be holding his things for a couple of months. I didn't know you were going to leave forever."

Myla was stunned, and angry, but also relieved to know the truth. She was thirsty for it. She needed to know. "Did you read his manuscript?"

"No," he said. "No way. Even thinking about having taken it filled me with guilt. That's why I hid it. I hid it from myself. Once it was clear you were gone for good, I pushed what I'd done down deep inside me." He smiled. "Maybe that's why I'm so fat. You can hate me for doing what I did. But you didn't have parents anymore. I was doing my best."

Myla nodded. Her fingers were folding around the golden key that Steve had left her at the door. "But I don't understand," she said. "What does that have to do with this room? What about all these boxes? What do they have to do with anything?"

Steve nodded. "And this is where Ruth comes into the picture. After your father's funeral, after our argument on the front porch, after you'd left town—though we, of course, didn't know you'd left yet—Ruth came to my house. She was sweet and solemn in a way I'd never seen her before. She handed me the storage key that's right there in your hand. She told me she was leaving.

"I begged her not to leave. I told her no one blamed her. I told her you needed as much family as you could get. And I would have grabbed her around the ankles, tied her to my house, locked her in the attic, if she hadn't said to me what she said.

"She said, 'Steven, I can't be here anymore.' She looked me in the eye, and I saw her heart was breaking. She told me, 'All I'm worth in this world can be found behind the door that this key opens. I love you all, but

I'm not your family. I've never done family. I've done my pictures. David was right: they're the best of me.' She made me promise I'd look in on this storage unit every once in a while. She pressed the key into my hand and handed me this. And then she was gone. I've kept this room a secret ever since."

He gave Myla a faded manila envelope. It had her name written on it in Ruth's hand. Myla turned the envelope over and wedged it open with her finger. Out slipped a heavy packet of paper. A small, opened letter, loose from the packet, fluttered to the ground. She stooped to pick it up, and her fingernail scratched the concrete floor, bringing her back to herself. She stood, glancing at the small brown envelope with David's name on it and an unrecognizable return address. Then she looked back to the flat piece of paper lying atop the thick stack she'd pulled from the manila envelope. It had Ruth's handwriting on it. Myla read what it said.

Myla,

You'll read this and I'll be gone. Perhaps by the time you see this, you'll have forgiven us all for disappearing one by one. I hope, above all, that you'll remember the art we made. I hope that art will bring you happiness, that someday you'll look at it and be able to know how beautiful you are.

I leave you what we've made together. They're yours, Myla. All the photographs we ever took. They're the best things I've ever done. And I'm giving them to you.

Myla looked up, into the room, and saw the boxes for what they were. They held every single picture that Ruth had ever taken of May and Rose, of Myla and Pru, of the camera girls. All the negatives, all the prints, all the proofs, all the photographs they'd made together. Myla touched her chest, full of relief. "They said they were destroyed."

Steve was an outline in the brightness. "They said wrong."

Myla walked to the first stack of boxes and traced her fingers down their dusty height. "What am I going to do with them?"

"That's up to you," Steve said. "They've been in the dark all this time. Maybe they need sun."

"What if I don't know how?"

"You have time," he said. "They've been waiting for you. And Ruth took care of the legal end. A trust fund makes them yours. She wanted you to have them. What matters is they're in your hands."

Knowing the pictures still existed filled Myla with amazement. Then Steve pointed to the corner of the room, where Myla could just make out the fragile shadow of the tripod, and this sight made her gasp. She walked to the corner where it rested and found the familiar backpack set down beside it. She could feel the heavy weight of the lens in its pocket.

"But this is *hers*," Myla said. "This is Ruth's camera. I don't know how to use it."

Steve was next to her, squatting at her side. "I know," he said, sighing. "This is the hardest part of the whole deal for me. Because it means she gave up her art. And for Ruth, that'd be like giving up her legs. But

I tell myself it means she's out there somewhere, making other art. Ruth is an art maker. That's what she does. That's what she's doing."

Myla nodded. The tripod was cold to the touch. She longed for a slice of sun. Then she looked back at the piece of paper in her hands and read the first postscript.

P.S. Enclosed you'll find two things. The first your father gave me, the small brown envelope. He didn't know what to do with it when it came to him in the mail. But I think it's best you read it yourself.

Myla fingered the small envelope with David's name and address. She edged it open at the neatly sliced top, where her father had already opened it. She pulled out the slim, small letter and read it.

Dear Mr. Wolfe,

My brother was the one who murdered your little girl. He'd always been off. I guess I never knew how off he was.

Three months ago, he came over for dinner. He told my family he wanted to save the innocents. We'd never been too religious so I didn't understand.

A couple weeks later I brought him leftovers. He'd been listening to the radio and he told me about these little girls out in Oregon whose father made them be in dirty pictures. I mean no disrespect but that's what the radio had said. The guy on the radio said someone had to save those girls.

I asked my brother if he'd ever seen the pictures. I said maybe they just showed your girls in the bathtub or something. I'd heard about people getting in trouble for taking pictures like that.

My brother said these were different. I asked him again how he knew. I asked him if he'd seen them himself. He said no, he didn't have to see them, he knew they were dirty.

That was the last I saw of my brother. I'm sorry he killed your little girl. I wish I could undo what he did. I thought it might help you if you knew my brother never saw those pictures. This morning I opened up my paper and saw some of them. They're beautiful.

Sincerely,

Lacey Johnson

Myla sat down. The world was spinning outside of this small spot of truth, this small knowledge, that Steve and Ruth and David had handed her. And here it had come: some kind of answer, an answer she never thought she'd have, that she'd longed for for so long. The knowledge that the man who'd killed her sister had simply listened to what others had told him, that he hadn't been thinking for himself. She smiled, surprising herself. David, in the midst of all his sorrow, all his desperation, must have felt something like satisfaction. For wasn't this exactly what his book was about? Wasn't he full of the knowledge that people were afraid to see, afraid to think for themselves?

Even as she smiled, Myla knew she was crying. But she was wiping away her tears with her sleeve. She read the other postscript, the last words she had from Ruth.

P.P.S. I also enclose in this packet the seven best photographs my camera ever took. *Look* at them, Myla. They'll tell you what to believe.

Myla stood and walked to the light. Her heart was pounding. She was afraid, but she was braver than she'd been. She withdrew from the packet a piece of cardboard and leaned it and Ruth's letter against her chest. She turned over the top print. And she looked.

Contact prints. Printed on eight-by-ten paper, directly from the negatives. Printed beautifully with aching detail, they were stunningly real. Every single dot of light, every single goose bump, every single shiver was lit up for her to see. Seven photographs. Rose and May on the floor. Rose and May standing side by side. Rose in the water. May by the water. Rose and May on the riverbed. May alone in the orchard. Ruth standing at the stream. They were them at their most *them*.

For thirteen years, Myla had been afraid to look at Ruth's photographs. And now that she looked, she saw what she'd been afraid of. It wasn't that arguments clanged through her head or justification rang in her ears. It wasn't that she envied her youth or felt critical of her flaws. No, what she saw was simple: she *loved* these pictures. They were her life and she loved them, full of their shadows and darknesses, of curves in the river and the hot, dappling sun, of the sweep of her sister's small hands curled into air. This was what Myla's life had looked like. The gilded light of that past was now manifest in her hands. It was so beautiful that the ache from missing it was unbearable.

Steve said to her, "I'm leaving now. I'll be at home, with Jane and Samuel. We'll be waiting for you there."

He touched her shoulder then, before ducking out under the garage door. She heard his car start some moments later, and realized he must have hidden it behind the units, just so she wouldn't drive away. She was crying, gathering herself. She turned to the room and peered into the darkness.

There were boxes and boxes to look at. Boxes and boxes of hope and beauty. Beauty Ruth had given her, a chance to see her life, to hold it in her hands. Myla knew then, just knew. There was work. And she was going to do it. She wanted this work. She was choosing it. She wanted it more than anything in the world.

MYLA AND SAMUEL ARE ON A bench. They are sitting across the river from the city, perched on the hill that pitches down to Oaks Bottom. The sun is sinking behind the West Hills, behind Portland, and it catches the wet shine in each cloud skipping overhead. The breeze in the sky is softer, calmer, down here on this hill, where Myla lies with her head on Samuel's lap, letting him care.

She is bone-tired. She is sick of thinking about it all and afraid to stop thinking about it all, but where once she feared that would mean Pru and David and Ruth and Sarah were gone from her, she now feels that somehow they're here.

Samuel says, "Just rest now. Relax."

She can barely move her head from where it rests on

his thighs. She can barely find her voice. She has no tears. It's comforting to have as much of the truth as she'll ever know.

Samuel lets her be quiet. He says to her then, as the sun is only a bright sliver slicing behind the dark hills, "I've been thinking a lot about you. About your family. Like a nineteenth-century novel, your family, and mine's like a seventies sitcom." She can hear laughter in his voice, and it makes her wish she had the energy to smile. "I've been thinking about your minds. You're all so smart. Close your eyes," he says. So she does.

"I've been thinking about your father, Myla. About what he believed about time and the way it doesn't work in a straight line. I think he's right, that there are bigger planes of experience than the ones we can see from the vantage of our limited time lines. Think about it: dreams, memories, connections between people." His fingers trace the outline of her upper arm. "That's what moves us into a bigger realm. That's what expands our visions. That's how Pru and Sarah and David live on, through your stories of them, and their images, and your love for them. There's truth to that."

"But what does it mean, finally?" she asks, summoning all her strength to make language.

"It changes lives," he says without a second's hesitation. "It's changed my life. You want to know why I'm leaving academia? Imagine that you'd come to that second lecture about Ruth Handel. Imagine you'd had the chance to hear my class, the one I taught two days after you walked out of my lecture.

"I started by letting the students talk. You'd be amazed how vocal they got about the story. Everyone had an opinion. That kid you called the Dream Student started us off with a definition of censorship, and that led to fifteen minutes of wrangling over the definition of pornography. Someone mentioned that she'd almost been abducted out of a grocery cart when she was four, and I steered the conversation back to the topic, encouraging them to focus. I asked them to tell me what fascinated them so much about the story of your family's tragedy.

"And inevitably, someone raised his hand and said, 'The dad was an idiot to let anyone take those pictures of his kids.' Someone else said, 'He must have been a pervert.' Someone disagreed and asked, 'What about Ruth Handel? It's her fault.' And so the blaming began. People blamed the media, the galleries, the newspapers, the endemic spread of pornography in our country. They blamed your family. Someone blamed art, claiming our constitution allows too much freedom of expression."

Myla feels Samuel's hand tense on her shoulder as he speaks, and she opens her eyes to see his face gazing out across the water, toward the darkening city. He continues, "And I said nothing. I let them blame art. I didn't know how not to. It seemed that something or someone should be blamed. So I ignored the obvious. I was so caught up in my academic, theoretical appraisal of the events that I didn't have any grip on who else to blame."

His voice breaks, and for the first time since he started speaking, he looks down at her. "But I know now." He stops. "There *is* someone to blame. There is someone to blame, but it's a simple truth. People don't want that. This debate about whether the pictures are or aren't 'decent' isn't supposed to be eclipsed by such hideous, horrible reality."

His voice washes over her. "A man murdered your sister. A man. Not art. That's the truth, and there's no way around it." Samuel's warm hand presses into Myla's, and his voice grows low and full of sorrow. "Let go of every other truth you know. *Someone* murdered Pru. Your growing up didn't kill her, and neither did Ruth's photographs. Some will say the photographs set into motion a series of events. But I think that's a dumb way to see our lives. A dumb way to see time. That way embraces fear, and I want to be like the artist your father talks about, the one who stretches our culture for us, who makes room for a glorious, expansive future. Art is a force that cannot be stopped."

He takes into his hands the seven artist's prints Ruth has left for Myla. He brings them out into the dimming light and pores over them slowly, one by one. "They're so beautiful," he says. "You're both so beautiful."

He's crying, and the evening descends, cooling them both. Myla lets Samuel's words cradle her thoughts, and feels herself tucking into him, slipping into a sleep she can't resist. At the end of it, she's dreaming, and her dream is a memory, and the memory is this.

They were in a bathtub, an unfamiliar bathtub. It was summertime, and they were staying in a rented cottage on the coast. Over the swish of the water, Myla could hear the deeper pull of the tide, the thick resonance of the ocean. She could see darkness out the window and was frustrated at David for being in the other room, doing work when it was vacation and they should be making dinner together, or walking on the beach. In the bathtub, there was barely room for her and Pru, especially because Pru's slippery four-year-old legs kept trying to walk back and forth across Myla. Pru's hair was plastered on her back, and her body was hot like steam itself.

And then the bathroom door swung open, and there was David with a smile on his face and two towels in his hands. He swept Pru up and scooped her into a towel and said, "It's amazing out there! Just wait until you see!" Myla stood up, incredulous that he'd been out in the night without them. He told her to hurry up, and she grabbed the other towel from him and wrapped it around her shoulders. She followed him out of the bathroom, out of the house, letting the screen door slam behind her.

The night air was warm, which was a surprise; most evenings like this on the Oregon coast, you needed at least a sweater, and here she was with only a towel wrapped around her. She made out the shapes of David and Pru as they broke over the dune, and she ran to catch up with them. The sand was cool and silky underneath her feet, and the reeds scratched her ankles and shins as she raced forward.

When Myla reached the top of the dune, she looked down and saw David and Pru already running toward the water. Myla's heart was pounding from running, and she wondered what the big deal was. The sound of the ocean made it too loud to ask, so she hurtled herself down the hill, loosening her knees so it was a smooth way down. When she hit the sand of the beach, she felt the towel slipping from her shoulders, and the warm night air shocked her body. She left the towel behind her, felt the delight of the ocean breeze all over her. She started running to where David and Pru were stopped, stomping the ground, laughing.

And then she saw. She looked down at her feet as she entered the cooler sand, the part that had been licked recently by the ocean, and as she drew closer and closer to the water, she saw light bursting around her every step. At first she thought she'd made it up, that her vision was just sparkling from all that hard running, but then the tiny bursts of green became more and more obvious each time she pounded the sand. Soon every step was an explosion of light, setting off a chain reaction around her feet—a series of moving constellations.

"What is it?" she asked David when she reached him.

He was jumping up and down as if the light might make him fly, and he was laughing. "Plankton, I think. I've heard it called phosphorescence. That, or it's magic."

"I choose magic!" yelled Pru, who was running around them, leaving wide arcs of brightness behind her. Myla watched her run, traced the sprint of her sister across the sand, the way Pru's arms clapped toward the sky, the way her legs tensed and released as she made footprints of light. Myla admired her father's long bright stride along the water, into the distance, as if he were jumping onto luminescent lily pads. She lifted her right foot and sank it down into the sand, felt the squish of the cold between her toes, watched the bright flash of impact. She lifted her left foot slowly, then sank it into the beach; another burst, and then another.

She looked up and saw her father and sister hurtling back and forth around her, leaving comet trails behind them in the sand. She wanted to be able to run like them, but it was as though the light bursting from the sand had turned reality so far on its head that she'd forgotten how. And then Pru came rushing toward her in the night. She ran to Myla, grabbed her hand, and pulled her along. It was only then that Myla's lungs quickened, that her ankles lifted into the night, that her hair flew from her shoulders. Each time she stepped, she admired her own bright wake.

acknowledgments

Although David Smithson Wolfe is a literary creation, many of his ideas derive from the essential conversation I've been carrying on with my mother, Elizabeth Beverly, for as long as I can remember. Words cannot express the gratitude I feel for the love she has showered on this book of mine: without her, it would not, could not, be.

Research into David's theories on art, history, and time has led me to some fascinating thinkers and their books: Rudolf Arnheim's *Art and Visual Perception: A Psychology of the Creative Eye*; William V. Dunning's *Changing Images of Pictorial Space: A History of Spatial Illusion in Painting*; Mary D. Garrard's *Artemisia Gentileschi: The Image of the Female Hero in Italian Baroque Art*; David Freedberg's *The Power of Images: Studies in the History and Theory of Response*; David Hockney's *Secret Knowledge: Rediscovering the Lost Techniques of the Old Masters*; Martin Kemp's *The Science of Art: Optical Themes in Western Art from Brunelleschi to Seurat*; Simon Schama's *Rembrandt's Eyes* (Myla reads this on her first

acknowledgments

day of notebook research); Leonard Shlain's *Art & Physics: Parallel Visions in Space, Time & Light* (which asserts, "There are no straight lines in nature"); Debora Silverman's *Van Gogh and Gauguin: The Search for Sacred Art;* Rebecca Solnit's *River of Shadows: Eadweard Muybridge and the Technological Wild West;* and Philip Steadman's *Vermeer's Camera: Uncovering the Truth Behind the Masterpieces.*

Thanks to Margaret and Geoff Lobenstine, and to Amy March for having such faith in my project that they literally invested in my future; to Maia Davis and Jock Sturges, and to Mona Kuhn for explaining the mechanics of large-format camera work as well as for offering me seven years of gorgeous insight into the many-faceted relationships that may exist between photographers and their subjects; to Adam Blau, Daniel J. Blau, Jennifer Cayer, Annie Dawid, Amber Hall, Rosanna Marshall, and Wendy Salinger for reading this book in its many incarnations and readily offering the perfect blend of unquestioning encouragement and incisive criticism; and to Hannah, Sandy, and Steve Engel for gleefully letting me borrow their home, their cat, and pieces of their family.

The intellectual and artistic life zinging through the Wolfe household borrows in no small way from the discussions that occurred around my own childhood dinner table, from the encouragement pouring forth from my parents each time I pursued another creative project, and from the steadfast love I have never lived without. Profound thanks to my mother and also my father, Dr. Robert Dunster Whittemore II, for teaching me, through the example of his fieldwork, that obser-

acknowledgments

vation is the best way to learn the workings of a people; my sister, Kai Beverly-Whittemore, for the kind sharing of her elegant mind, unwavering trust, and sweet heart; and my husband, David M. Lobenstine, for continuing to show me that there is much in this life that lies far beyond the bounds of language.

Finally, thanks to my agent, Anne Hawkins, for writing the best rejection letter I could have imagined, and to my editor, Rick Horgan, for understanding this book from the moment it was cast in his direction.